Two Nights in Lisbon

TWO NIGHTS IN LISBON

CHRIS PAVONE

THORNDIKE PRESS
A part of Gale, a Cengage Company

GALE
A Cengage Company

Copyright © 2022 by Chris Pavone.
Thorndike Press, a part of Gale, a Cengage Company.

LIBRARY OF CONGRESS CIP DATA ON FILE.
CATALOGUING IN PUBLICATION FOR THIS BOOK
IS AVAILABLE FROM THE LIBRARY OF CONGRESS.

ISBN-13: 979-8-8857-8086-5 (hardcover alk. paper)

Published in 2022 by arrangement with Farrar, Straus and Giroux.

Printed in Mexico
Print Number : 1   Print Year : 2023

Justice is truth in action.

— BENJAMIN DISRAELI

■ ■ ■ ■

PART I
THE DISAPPEARANCE

■ ■ ■ ■

CHAPTER 1

Lisbon, Portugal
Day 1. 7:28 a.m.
Ariel awakens, alone.

Sunlight is streaming through the gap between the shutters, casting a stark column of brightness on the wall, nearly painful to look at.

She's hot. She flings aside the sheet, toward the other side of the bed, where her new husband should be, but isn't. Her eyes jump around the room, as if hopping on stones across a stream, looking for evidence of John, but find none, plummeting her into the fast frigid water of a familiar panic: What if she's wrong about him? About this whole thing?

The bedside clock displays 7:28 in emergency red. Much later than she normally awakes, especially this time of year, the busiest months on the farm, when the birds begin chirping around four A.M., the fieldwork starts at dawn, dogs barking, men yelling above the noise of sputtering engines. It's hard to sleep through all that racket even if she wanted to.

Ariel has been an early riser ever since George was born, a matter of necessity when he was an infant, but even when the kid started sleeping later, she didn't. Waking early became a matter of policy, of character. This was how she wanted to be known, if only to herself: early to rise, early to bed, hardworking between, a serious responsible person, after a misspent youth. Worse than misspent.

Despite her quickening pulse, Ariel is still groggy, her mind muddy. Last night must have really walloped her, the dehydration and generalized exhaustion of international travel, the jet lag, the food and wine and sex, the sleeping pill that John ultimately foisted upon her.

He'd risen from bed, both of them slicked with sweat, spent. He turned to stare down at Ariel, to admire her, naked, sprawled, a pink bloom spreading across her heaving chest and up her neck and into her cheeks, like a rapidly advancing infection. He leaned down toward her, but stopped just before his mouth met hers, stared into her eyes, making her ache until she could no longer wait for him, and she craned her neck upward for a kiss that was long and deep and almost too much, setting off a fresh wave of tingles to accompany those that hadn't yet completely subsided.

10

Her skin felt so alive, all prickling nerve endings, pure arousal.

Ariel watched him move slowly through the dark room, taking care not to trip, not to stub his toe. He stood naked at the window, working the old shutter's apparatus until he found the groove, the satisfying click as the whole thing came unlocked. He grasped one shutter in each hand, and gently pushed the large panels apart until fully spread, wide open. A familiar physical phrasing, the softest touch of fingertips, as if asking permission.

Exactly what Ariel has always wanted most. Exactly what she had gotten least. Until now.

Ariel hears something out there, beyond the morning-disarrayed bedroom.

"John?"

No answer.

She walks tentatively toward the ghost of the sound, then stops short at the suite's door, aware that she's wearing nothing but a T-shirt. She glances down to see how much it covers. Not quite enough. She hears the same noise again, it's definitely from out there, just on the far side of the door.

"John?"

"Desculpe." It's a woman's voice, muffled by the door. *"Serviço de limpeza."*

Ariel peers through the peephole: a chambermaid, organizing her cart.

"Desculpe," she repeats.

Ariel turns away from the door. She looks around the sitting room, whose walls are painted a shade of pale gray that's so luminescent it's like being inside an oyster shell. Her eyes fall upon last night's nightcap glasses, the sofa pillows strewn on the floor, the kicked-off shoes. The couch is where they'd started up, still clothed but unzipped, unbuttoned, pushed aside, caressed and fondled, licked and sucked, knees bumped and rugburned until John said, "Let's move to the bed," his voice quavering with excitement. Ariel couldn't even speak.

She checks her phone: nothing. No notification, no alert, just the locked-home-screen photo of a little boy hugging two big dogs, a picture that's four years old but so perfect that Ariel can't bear to replace it with something newer but not as ideal.

It's still two-thirty in the morning on the East Coast, where nearly everyone she knows lives. Ariel hasn't even received any fresh spam. She launches the app that tracks her family's devices — her son's cell, her husband's, her own. The data takes a long time to load, to locate the disparate geo-positions. The first bubble that appears is her own, AP, right here in the center of Lisbon. Then her son's, GP, exactly where he belongs in the middle of the night, four thousand miles away, asleep, no doubt with at least one of the dogs — Scotch — in his bed, probably

12

Mallomar too. The dogs are very loyal to George, and vice versa. The narrow bed can get awfully crowded, a pile of smelly mammals, all of them pressed up against one another, dreaming.

The app still hasn't found John, his JW icon "Locating . . ." but then surrenders, admits failure, "Location not available" in the passive voice, as if she should blame it on the device, or the person, or the vagaries of the ether, anything except the app itself. Even apps don't want to accept blame.

Ariel has been awake for three minutes.

When she left her first husband nearly fifteen years ago, Ariel left behind everything else too. She emptied her life completely and started from scratch, filling her new existence one piece at a time — a new old house in a quiet new place, a new baby, a new crazy dog and then a crazier second dog, a new hairstyle and wardrobe, a new career in a new field, new friends and hobbies, a new way of holding herself, of interacting with the world and inviting the world to interact with her. She no longer wanted to move through life first and foremost and always and only as an attractive woman.

It was just recently that she realized she was ready to add the final new piece, to complete her full new life, which wasn't so new anymore, and maybe not quite full enough. She can't help but wonder if she conjured John from her desire, or if it was the other way around.

He had remained standing at the window for a long time last night, up-lit from the street-lamps that cast a distended shadow across the ceiling, a creepy Munch-like shape in the eerie bluish light of city night, causing Ariel a quick spasm of fear, an unwelcome old feeling that sneaks up on her now and then, surprise attacks that are surprising only in their timing. She knows they're coming, just not exactly when.

Ariel had closed her eyes tight, and inhaled deeply, trying to focus on the immediate physical sensations — the warm breeze blowing up from the Tagus, the distant scream of a seagull, a whiff of seaside air, salty and maybe a little fishy, the needles and pins of her hot prickled skin. She exhaled through her mouth, slow and long and completely in control. It was all about control.

She opened her eyes, ending the little drama that had existed purely in her mind, a private world of panic.

Ariel had been fearless when she was young, which is when people tend to be bold. She'd been an actor, after all. What's bolder? But then life conspired against her audacity, sapped her courage, shattered her confidence that she could move safely through the world.

14

She couldn't. She didn't.

John was still at the open window, his nude form at once very familiar — she felt like she'd explored every inch of his body, with her eyes, with the tips of her fingers, the tip of her tongue — but still so foreign, as any other body is, any other person. She could know what he looked like, what he tasted like; she did. But not how he felt, not what he thought.

Years ago, Ariel had lost all faith in her ability to see other people clearly. She'd been so sure about her first husband, yet ultimately so wrong, the sort of wrong that's shockingly obvious in hindsight. Ariel had seen only what Bucky had wanted her to see, what he'd put in front of her to see. She'd been an unwitting accessory to his self-misrepresentation until it was too late. Not just too late for that relationship, but for all of her relationships. She'd lost confidence in her own judgment, in her ability to see anyone's true self. For a long time, she'd barely tried.

Did she learn anything? Of course. But all lessons fade if you don't keep up your studies. Calculus, French, colonial history, Greek myths, Ariel doesn't remember any of this. She can't remember what calculus even *is*. A couple of years ago, she looked up the word in the dictionary, but that didn't clarify a damn thing.

"What are you thinking?" she asked.

John shifted position, turned toward her, angled his face away from the streetlight. Now she could see even less of his expression. Nothing, really.

"You know," he said. "Just about tomorrow."

Tomorrow was here. Tomorrow was now.

She'll shower, that's what she'll do. She'll shower and she'll dress herself in today's outfit, which she chose a week ago, deliberating through her closet with a little chart of what clothes she'd need, for what purposes, on what days of this short trip. Today it will be a mid-length skirt and a peasant blouse, simple, unfussy, yet sexy. Ariel's normal outfit is jeans and a T-shirt and no makeup whatsoever. But this Lisbon trip is not normal, so she'll put on makeup, and a low-hanging pendant necklace, accentuating parts of her body that she usually doesn't.

Then she'll open the door and find the American newspaper on the doormat, with the stories about the memorial service for the vice president, and about the man who has been nominated to succeed him, news that's been dominating American media for months.

Ariel will scoop up this newspaper, and walk carefully down the hotel's wide staircase, taking her time on the slick marble, her hand trailing the wooden banister that has been buffed smooth and shiny from two centuries of friction, the long-term degradations at the hand of man. She'll stride into the large sunny breakfast room that's perched above the bustling square ringed by elegant buildings and those lethal old trams clanging and screeching on their tracks, disgorging early-bird tourists and bleary-eyed commuters munching on their breakfast *pastéis,* their eyes drawn up to the hotel's elegant façade, where curtains are billowing through the first floor's middle set of French doors just in front of the low table where Ariel and John have eaten their breakfast two days in a row already, it's their table, and that's where her new husband will be, sitting there with his coffee and his newspapers, waiting for her, looking up with that grin —

He isn't.

CHAPTER 2

Day 1. 7:49 a.m.
WHERE R U?

Her finger hovers above SEND, but she doesn't press the button. Ariel is not a hysterical person, and she doesn't want to be seen as one. She'd been accused of hysteria before. Of overreaction. She'd been disbelieved about serious matters more than once. She'd become reluctant to assert any claims that couldn't be absolutely proven with incontrovertible evidence; nothing he-said-she-said. She'd already said. It hadn't sufficed.

Only one other table is occupied in the breakfast room, the retiree-looking Australian couple who were here yesterday too; she can only imagine what sort of jet lag they're battling. Behind the bar, a small television plays cable news with an unfamiliar logo in the corner of the familiar story, footage of the memorial service in Washington — senators, ex-presidents, a couple of Supreme Court justices, the president of course.

Ariel turns away from the big screen, back to her little one. She hits SEND and waits for the swoosh to confirm that her message was dispatched successfully, staring back at her from its little bubble, the pathos of an unanswered missive to a loved one.

Joao the waiter is wiping down glasses while a busboy unloads a tray of pastries onto a platter. Breakfast is self-serve. It doesn't make sense for Ariel to sit alone here like this, at a table with neither food nor drink. She should have coffee. She should sit here and sip coffee and read the newspaper and wait for her husband.

This is the hard thing about an intense relationship, isn't it? One of the hard things. The waiting. Maybe it was easier back when the only way to communicate was by handwritten letter transported by hand, by pony express, by three-mast schooner. It would take months to exchange a few lines, no possibility that any lover of any level of ardor of any sort — real or potential or purely imaginary — could respond instantaneously. No reason to sit around wringing your hands, eyes cutting over and over to this little lifeline, waiting, hoping for the thing to light up, the little window to pop up — *Here I am, yes I still love you!*

Ariel sits at the table with her coffee and her American newspaper, and forces herself to stare at the front page, the lead story, the only story these days. She has long been comfortable sitting by herself in coffee shops and restaurants, usually with one of the mystery novels that she never stops consuming, projecting herself into the role of the investigating detective or the scheming culprit, losing herself in crime-scene science and legal arcana.

But not today. Today she stares at the newsprint but can't bring herself to actually read. Today she is not at all comfortable.

"Can I get you anything?" It's Joao, very solicitous, as usual.

"No," she says, *"obrigada,"* which is one of only a dozen Portuguese words she knows. She studied the little vocabulary primer in the back of the guidebook, but didn't get very far.

"You are sure?"

Ariel doesn't want to be a woman who's wondering where her husband is, such an archetype of insecurity. But where is he? She has no choice.

"Have you seen my husband this morning?"

For a second Joao doesn't know what to say, then decides on "I am sorry" with an indulgent smile, the sort that anyone would give in this pitiable situation, to this pitiable creature. "Not today, senhora."

"Oh he must have left for work already," Ariel sputters quietly, nearly a mumble, as if

20

to minimize her commitment to this patent falsehood.

"I can ask my colleagues?" Joao seems genuinely concerned, which adds to the humiliation. At this moment, she'd prefer the American style of ersatz caring, the sort that's more customer service than personal interaction. The sort that's completely insincere.

"In the mornings we have two — how do you say? — *quarto* maids —"

"Oh no, that's nice of you, but please . . ."

"— and Duarte at reception, and —"

"Oh God no, please don't bother." Ariel shakes her head vigorously. "Really."

"It is no bother —"

"My husband needed to work early today." She's digging a deeper hole in this conversation. "And I overslept." Shoveling nonsense over her shoulder, convincing no one of anything.

"You are sure?"

"Quite." She wants to crawl under the table. "You're very nice to offer."

"If you change your mind?"

"I will let you know immediately." She will do no such thing. "Thank you so much."

It has been only twenty-four minutes since Ariel awoke.

"What was that about?" Rodrigo asks.

Joao doesn't want to spread rumors; he doesn't gossip about hotel guests, nor about

21

anything else. But there's something worrying about the American woman, the way she keeps cutting her eyes to her phone, her barely contained distress. She looked so happy, just yesterday.

"Do you know that woman's husband?"

"Yes of course."

The hotel is only half-occupied. It's easy to keep track of the guests, especially those who linger over long breakfasts, making eyes at each other.

"Have you seen him this morning?" Joao asks.

"No. Why?"

"Neither has she."

Ariel looks around the suite more thoroughly. John's phone charger is here, but not his phone. She opens his work-issued laptop, and is immediately prompted for a password; she doesn't bother guessing. John has brought no papers on this trip, no files, no binder filled with charts and graphs. Nothing except his clothes, his phone, this inaccessible computer, and . . . what else . . . ?

She returns to the bedroom, the armoire, the safe inside it, a keypad that she unlocks —

Yes, there's his passport, hers too. Along with their house and car keys and American currency, all the important but unnecessary things.

■ ■ ■ ■

How long has it been? Fourteen minutes since Ariel sent that text. Time enough for him to respond, if he could. John makes it a rule to return calls and messages as quickly as possible. This is one of the things she knows about him. She knows that his favorite wines are hearty reds from the South of France, she knows his birthdate and shoe size, lots of little things. He knows the same sorts of things about her. Mostly meaningless crap.

She has waited long enough. It's time to escalate to a phone call, which goes straight through to voicemail without a single ring. It's not that her husband is declining to answer; it's that he can't. He doesn't even know she's calling.

"Bom dia," Ariel says, looking around the well-appointed reception room, the antiques and artwork, the leather and silk, all the signifiers of luxury.

"Good morning," the desk clerk answers in English.

"I'm staying with my husband John Wright in the Ambassador's Suite."

"Yes Senhora Wright. My name is Duarte. How can I help you?"

Ariel thinks about correcting him about her

last name, but why bother. "When I awoke this morning, my husband was not in our room, and I cannot reach him on the telephone."

Duarte looks uneasy, probably wondering what he's going to be asked to do. This is the type of hotel where guests can complain about anything. Some people practically make a sport of this — the water is too hot, the electricity is too loud, the towels too plush, there's no Splenda. Duarte is prepared for any insanity.

"Joao mentioned there might be other employees we could ask. So maybe you could?"

"Could what, please?"

"Ask them. If they saw my husband."

"Yes, it is possible. I am taking care of it." Duarte, not understanding the urgency, expects Ariel to leave now. She crosses her legs, making it clear that she's settling in to wait.

"Ah," the young man says. "I see." He picks up his handset, has a quick conversation, turns back to Ariel. "Maria and Leonor are coming. One minute, please."

Ariel nods.

"Is everything good with your room, Senhora Wright?"

"My name —" she begins, but cuts herself off.

By the time she married John, Ariel had already changed her name twice in her life.

There was no way she'd ever relinquish her new, meticulously constructed identity. John hadn't disagreed; it wasn't even a question.

"Yes," she says, "thank you. The room is fine."

Maria and Leonor enter together; Maria is the one Ariel saw in the hallway a few minutes ago. The three colleagues speak quickly in Portuguese, which sounds to Ariel like Russian crossed with Spanish. She doesn't grasp a single word. The only thing Ariel can detect in this language is tone — good or bad, yes or no. This must be what it's like to be a dog. What she's sensing is no. Bad. If she had a tail, it would be down between her legs.

"Maria, she knows who your husband is, but she did not see him this morning. And Leonor, she does not know who your husband is."

Ariel scrolls through her phone's photos — castle, cathedral, cobblestones, and yes here: a couples selfie with a scenic backdrop, the sort of image that Ariel would post on social media if that were a thing she did.

"Here, this is my husband."

The chambermaid looks at the image, then at Ariel, then back at the screen, as if confirming that the woman in front of her really is the same woman as in the photo. Ariel wants to scream *But that's not the point!* but restrains herself, listens to more unintelligible Portuguese.

25

"I am sorry," Duarte says, "Leonor did not see this man today."

Now three generations of Portuguese hotel workers are staring at Ariel, all wondering if they can move on with their day, away from this American woman.

"Obrigada," Ariel says, and they all give restrained smiles of relief, released from the discomfort of a stranger's marital problem.

The absence of clues is, itself, a clue.

CHAPTER 3

Day 1. 8:58 a.m.

Before Ariel steps out into the street, she adjusts her posture, and hardens her face, armor to dissuade the male gaze, or discourage uninvited interactions, or at least minimize them. For a brief while she had been quick with the middle finger, the muttered profanity, the hostile retort, biting her tongue only when she had no obvious escape route, or no witnesses. But she knew that the combative responses never made the situation better, and sometimes made it much worse. And in a small town like hers, any of those men, even complete strangers in passing cars, might become enemies she'd have to confront again someday in a dark parking lot, on a deserted beach, in her own home.

So Ariel swallows her pride and suppresses her militant instincts, aiming instead for evasion, for de-escalation, for appeasement, an indignity to be sure, but preferable to aggravated assault, or worse. Because the men who aggressively proposition women on the sidewalk are the same men who hit women, who rape them, who beat them to death with tire irons.

The strong morning sun is bouncing off the hotel's bright white façade. Ariel glances down the hill, toward where John would be if he were at his client's offices, which are somewhere near the massive Praça do Comércio, with its imposing arch dominating one side and the miles-wide estuary spreading away from the other. This main square was once the beating heart of Portugal, one of the most important commercial centers in Europe, of the entire world. Not anymore. These days business is done in glass-clad towers in farther-flung neighborhoods.

The *praça* is to the south. Ariel heads north, up the steep slope of Bairro Alto, through the narrow streets strung with party lights and laundry lines, dish towels and soccer jerseys flapping above clusters of tables in front of *cervejarias* and *tabernas,* hole-in-the-wall convenience stores, boutiques selling sneakers, sardines, a mind-boggling array of items made from cork.

It's Monday morning. The city is coming to life quicker than it had over the weekend, with stores opening and cafés filling, with people strolling to work on sidewalks made of mosaics, leafy trees everywhere, walls graf-

28

fitied with names and initials and peace signs and big toothy smiles and cartoon dogs. No guns, no RIP notices, no gangster signifiers. Lisbon's graffiti is a reflection of exuberance, not despair.

Ariel walks with her phone in her palm, hitting the home button again and again, swiping across the screen, receiving nothing and nothing and yet more nothing.

The bakeries are all open, emitting different aromas, the butter-and-sugar richness of pastry from one and the flour and yeast from another, these European smells, which like sidewalk seafood markets and fresh-juice vendors are not part of life back home. America has other food smells; most involve animal flesh or deep-fry.

Ariel continues to climb the steep hill, her legs growing tired. She feels a twinge in her left ankle, the one she sprained last fall when she was knocked over by someone's Labrador on the village green. That injury was just the latest insult: the thumb jammed by a heavy carton of books, the rotator cuff torn while changing a light bulb, the plantar fasciitis in both feet just because, the compressed disk in her neck for the same unfair nothing of a reason.

"What can I tell you?" the chiropractor said. "Welcome to middle age."

For a while Ariel kidded herself that someday she'd be rid of all these nuisances: the tendon will heal, the new orthotics will work, regular yoga will mitigate the back pain, this or that will get better, then all will be fine. But it has now been years of uninterrupted overlapping complaints, and Ariel is coming around to accepting that she'll never again be completely pain-free. It'll be one minor injury after another, augmented by occasional major ones, plus increasingly severe illnesses, an unrelenting deterioration leading to an ultimate demise. Like climate change, a trend that goes in only one direction and culminates in inevitable catastrophe, with no alternative endings.

She realized that whatever she was going to do, ever, she needed to start doing it.

Lisbon's steep hills offer vistas everywhere — the medieval castle over there, the warren of the old town beneath, the big bend in the wide river, the Golden Gate–esque bridge spanning the narrows. From up here Lisbon looks massive, so many neighborhoods, spread so far.

Ariel has grown unaccustomed to cities. When things fell apart for her in New York it was wholesale, it was everything, and she no longer wanted any part of the city — all the people, all the men, the constant oppressive press of it all. She left behind the loudness, the crowds and smells and generalized sensory assault, the bigness of everything. She

30

barely visits cities anymore, just a business trip or two per year for a couple of nights apiece, when she enlists her mom to come up from South Carolina to take care of George and the dogs, as she's doing now.

Ariel tries calling John again, gets the same nonresponse again: straight to voicemail.

She gazes across the street at her destination. She doesn't want to do the thing she needs to do now, doesn't want to start the unpleasantness. This reminds her of a moment last winter, she'd just about fallen asleep when her chest was suddenly hurting, and her whole body felt cold. She groped for her phone, hit her best friend's number with fingers that were alarmingly numb.

"Ariel?" Sarah's voice was croaky with sleep. "What's wrong?"

"I think." Ariel could barely gather the breath to speak. "Need. ER."

She didn't want an ambulance, she'd heard horror stories about unreimbursed costs.

"Oh my God I'll be right over."

George reclined in the back of Sarah's Subaru wearing a parka over pajamas, clutching Teddy, while Ariel shivered in the passenger seat, increasingly terrified as they approached the hospital where her life might be forever changed: She could be having a heart attack, an aneurysm, who knew. She was a young woman — relatively — and the symptoms of life-threatening illness were familiar

31

to her only from TV and movies. Ariel had no idea what her body was really trying to tell her. She needed an interpreter, and body interpreters worked at hospitals.

Within seconds of arriving at the ER she was wheeled down a bright corridor on a gurney, people asking her name and birthdate over and over, tests and more tests, a dye pumped through her circulatory system, hours passing, George dozing in a waiting room next to a vending machine, the repetition of the horrifying phrase "pulmonary embolism," until finally at two-thirty in the morning a doctor strode to her bedside with a sense of purpose and a grin; Ariel was unclear if it was of reassurance or relief.

"Ms. Pryce, you have pneumonia."

After two days of rest and antibiotics, she was fine, easy-peasy. But if she hadn't gone to the ER, she might have died that very night. Sometimes you can put it off. But sometimes you really can't.

She climbs the steep stairs, and steps inside.

"Bom dia," she says to the sergeant at the front counter. "My husband is missing."

Ariel is trying to absorb the uniformed policewoman's long string of rapid-fire Portuguese, which sounds at turns like statements, accusations, maybe a couple of questions.

"Desculpe," Ariel says, using the word she learned from listening to other people apolo-

32

gize. "I don't know Portuguese. Is there anyone here who speaks English?"

The policewoman glares.

"Desculpe," Ariel repeats, trying to look sorry, pathetic, worthy of sympathy.

More glaring. How can she fix this?

"Ah!" Ariel pokes up a finger, the universal signal for *one moment, please.* Although Ariel didn't learn much Portuguese before this trip, she did purchase an app. The typical American approach to any problem: buy something. This was one of the things she hated the most about the people she hated the most: the reflex to throw money at everything, as a matter of routine.

But here she is, typing into her phone too quickly, making too many errors, and just one is too many. There's no way for a translation app to guess at misspelled intentions. She holds up a finger again, mutters another apology, then hits TRANSLATE, and hands over her phone.

The policewoman looks down at the screen, takes a couple of seconds to read. Then she looks up at Ariel, reassesses this jabbering woman who strode into the police station first thing on a Monday morning. Her face softens, and she says, *"Um momento."*

"My husband." Ariel looks back and forth between the two detectives.

"He is missing, you say?" the male detective asks. António Moniz has a warm, open face, but Ariel can already see the skepticism in his eyebrows, in the slight narrowing of his eyes.

"Well, I don't know about *missing*. But I can't find him."

Moniz nods. "When did you last see him?"

"About midnight."

Ariel's final memory of the night was John standing at the open window again, gazing off at the night, at his tomorrow. She doesn't know precisely what time it was when she finally slipped out of consciousness, but midnight seems reasonable.

"Midnight?" Moniz looks surprised. "Midnight of *last* night?"

"Yes."

"That is" — Moniz checks his watch — "ten hours?"

"Correct."

The policeman inhales deeply. He obviously doesn't know what to say next, what to tell this woman. He exchanges a glance with his partner, an attractive but severe-looking woman named Carolina Santos who thus far has said nothing.

"I understand," Ariel says, "that this hasn't been much time."

"No," Moniz agrees, perhaps too quickly, too heartily. "It is not."

"But this is really not like him."

"Of course," Moniz says. "Of course," he

34

repeats, but it doesn't seem like a reiteration, more like a contradiction, or perhaps sarcasm.

This conversation is not yet about John. This is still about Ariel, and her credibility.

"I'm worried." Ariel looks back and forth between the two cops, looking for support, finding none. Not only has Detective Santos not spoken, she hasn't even picked up her pen. Her role here seems to be to stare at their visitor. Ariel is a little scared of Santos.

"Does your husband run?" Moniz asks. "For exercise? Is it possible that he has gone running?"

"No." Ariel shakes her head. "His running shoes are in our room."

"Does he have the — how do you say it, when you are having trouble with the sleep?"

"Insomnia? No."

"I am sorry, that is not what I mean. Because of travel? Time changes?"

"Jet lag?"

Moniz snaps his fingers. "Yes. The jet lag. Perhaps because of the jet lag he is awake too early, and he goes for a walk? Is this possible?"

"Maybe, but why wouldn't he leave me a note? Or call? Or answer my calls?"

"I do not know, senhora. Can you think of a reason?"

She shakes her head. "Anyway, John took a sleeping pill last night. Me too. To help us adjust. So that he'd be well-rested for work today."

"Work? You are in Lisboa for business?"

"My husband is a consultant, visiting a client."

"Have you contacted the client? Maybe he is already at the offices."

"I can't. I don't know who the client is. John told me, but I can't remember it. I should've written it down, I know. But I didn't."

"And you?" he asks. "Are you also here for business?"

"No. I'm here just to come along."

Ariel notices that Moniz has a spot of something on his tie, grease or sauce, something oily.

"Do you have an idea, Senhora Pryce? About where your husband is?"

"No. I'm just worried."

"What is it you are worried about?"

It could be so many bad things, couldn't it? John could be the victim of some crime or accident, in a hospital, struck by one of those trams, or a car, a truck, anything. Or facedown in an alley, mugged, bleeding, unconscious. He could be dead in some abandoned fish market on the far side of the Tagus, chained to a rusty pipe, his blood sluicing into industrial drains, washed out to mingle with the brackish river.

Maybe he has been falsely accused of

something, under arrest at another police station, interrogated at an embassy. Or down in Tangier, detained by security forces, accused of being a spy, a smuggler, a fugitive from justice.

And maybe the accusation isn't false. Ariel doesn't know every dark corner of John's history. Maybe he has a questionable past that has finally caught up to him, or a questionable present that he's adept at hiding. He could be engaged in money laundering, fraud, tax evasion, hiding behind the disguise of consultant; who the hell knows what a consultant even does.

Or of course he could be fine. Ariel will end up looking overprotective, insecure, silly. Exactly what she'd been accused of before: unbelievable.

"I don't know," she admits.

Moniz taps his pen on his paper, which Ariel notices is almost entirely blank. She hasn't said much worth writing down.

"Senhora, I hope you understand that it is not possible for the police to search for every man whose wife cannot find him in the morning. We would never do anything else!" His attempt at a joke falls flat, he sees that immediately, and pushes past. "I am sure it is nothing. Your husband is at work, and he will return to your hotel at the end of the day."

This is the kind of bland baseless optimism that Ariel abhors. Like an athletic coach. Ariel can't stomach pep talks.

"He will have an explanation, and it will be an explanation that is okay to you, or an explanation that is not okay to you, but either way it will not be a criminal explanation. Not a serious one. And in any case, he will return."

Moniz extends his hands, drawing a conclusion to the story.

"But what if he doesn't?"

"If your husband continues to be missing tomorrow morning, please return to us. Or telephone to me." Moniz takes a business card from a brass box, extends it to Ariel.

"Listen, I know it's been only a few hours. I know I don't have any evidence. I know I don't have as much information as I should. I know all that. But I'm really worried. He's not answering my calls or texts, he didn't leave me any note, and he's not that type of guy. So can't we start looking for him *now*?"

Moniz nods, understanding her lack of understanding.

"Senhora, these informations that you are giving us, these are not evidence of wrongdoing, if they are evidence of anything. And this amount of time that you have not seen your husband, this is not enough time. Right now there are hundreds of people in Lisboa, perhaps thousands, who have not seen a family or friend since last night. Whose wife or husband does not answer the phone or return a text. These days, we expect everyone to be always available, to be in contact with us during all the hours of all the days and nights, merely because it is possible. But just because it is possible does not make it desirable. Not all of the time, not for all of the people."

Moniz is definitely right about that.

"So that's it?"

There's no point in arguing with him, is there? Not with a man who has made up his mind.

"I am sorry that we cannot take any action at this moment." He stands, proffers his hand for a shake. "I hope you understand."

Ariel very well may need the police's help in the future, so she doesn't want to fight an unwinnable battle now.

António Moniz watches the American woman walk away. "What do you think?"

His partner takes a few seconds before answering. "I think that this woman does not know her husband as well as she believes."

In Moniz's experience every cop is cynical, but Carolina Santos takes it to a whole different level.

"This is of course true for almost all women," Santos continues. "We are all lied to. All the time."

Moniz does not argue with Santos. Her fuse can be awfully short on this subject. Plus he does not disagree.

"Hey, Erico," she calls out. A few desks

away, a younger detective looks up from the football pages. "Did you see that American woman who just left?"

"Yes."

"Follow her."

CHAPTER 4

Day 1. 10:44 a.m.

"Good morning, my name is Saxby Barnes." He extends his hand for a shake that lasts a fraction of a second too long. "Please, if you'd be so kind as to follow me."

Barnes is a doughy man wearing both the flag-pinned lapel and the plastered-on smile of a politician. A smile that everyone knows is bullshit, but we all agree to pretend otherwise, the smilers and the smilees, a vast covenant of feigned ignorance.

He swipes a magnetic card, then leads Ariel through a large open-plan room, glancing over his shoulder a couple of times, probably to make sure that she hasn't separated herself to run amok. There's a lot of security here at the US embassy, forms and formalities and filtering, an emphasis on preventing something negative from happening to this facility, instead of providing a positive anything to visitors.

From across the room Ariel feels an insistent gaze. She glances over just long enough to absorb a middle-aged man in a short beard and a rumpled oxford shirt and something that might be a press badge.

"So I understand that you can't locate your husband," Barnes says as they turn a corner.

"That's right."

"And I guess we know that he hasn't simply *left* you."

Barnes turns back with a smile, and Ariel gives him a quizzical look.

"How could *any* man leave a woman like you?" Now he's beaming, proud of himself, of finding a way to hit on a worried married woman within a minute of meeting her.

"Certainly no *sane* man," he adds, looking at her expectantly. He wants her to be grateful for the compliment.

Ariel makes a conscious effort to see the humanity in everyone she meets. She tries to start every new relationship by granting the benefit of the doubt. But this guy is going to make it hard.

She swallows her pride, and obliges Barnes with a smile.

"In here," he says, holding open the door to a small, tidy office. As Ariel passes him, she catches a whiff of booze on his breath. Today's? Or still last night's? She knows this type of guy, who never passes up the opportunity to have a drink, and never has just one.

42

"So, Mrs., um . . ."

"Ariel Pryce. Ms."

"Right. *Ms.* Pryce," with a smirk. "May I offer you something to drink? Some water?"

"No thank you," as gentle as possible. No in the tone of yes.

"You look a little, um . . ."

It had taken a while to find a taxi in the beating sun, and the car's air-conditioning was unconvincing, then she'd needed to wait outside the embassy, and then in a close crowded room filled with frustrated people. What Ariel probably looks like is a sweaty mess.

"It's awfully hot out there," she says.

"Portugal in July! To be expected. But this heat is quite familiar to me; I'm from Georgia."

Of course he is, pink-faced Saxby Barnes, ogling Southern gentleman in his tight blue seersucker suit and regimental tie and white bucks. The whole costume.

"You're sure? No water?"

Barnes clearly doesn't understand how a woman could reject this everyday politeness that he's trying to inflict, unsolicited and undesired. Ariel has learned that it's the excessively polite ones whom you should trust the least, the ones who try to convince you of their gentlemanly manners, their generosity, their chivalry.

"Fine," Ariel concedes. "I appreciate it."

Barnes grins at this tiny victory of aggressive solicitousness, this conversational cudgel: foisting a favor upon her, with the expectation of extracting something later.

"Don't take no for an answer," his mother had no doubt told him, teaching her son the proper manners of a polite host. "Don't take no for an answer," his father had told him, teaching his boy how to succeed in business, in politics, in any profession. "Don't take no for an answer," his frat brothers had told him, teaching him to trust his own judgment of what a girl wants, despite what she may say. So now here he is, trying to do all at once, just like he's been told all his life, by everyone.

Chivalry can be just another form of hostility. Chivalry can be the weapon itself.

"Sparkling all right? I'm afraid I'm out of still."

Of course: give something, take something away.

"Sparkling is perfect."

It looks as if Barnes is practically caressing the door handle. Ariel realizes that it must be a recent acquisition, this refrigerator. Something Barnes had to earn, or wheedle. He's proud of this little unit of his.

"Thanks again," she says. "You're very kind."

"You're quite welcome." He takes a seat. "All right then, we need some, um . . . details . . ."

44

Barnes opens a desk drawer, removes a couple of pieces of padded nylon. "Carpal tunnel," he explains, wrapping his left wrist into one of these contraptions.

Her eye is drawn to the American newspaper that she failed to read this morning, blanket coverage of the events back home. The front page is dominated by a photo of a man who has been thrust into national prominence, first as a special adviser to his old pal the president, then an unexpected but largely unobjectionable appointment to the Cabinet. But now, after the VP's cerebral hemorrhage, this political novice is suddenly poised to step onto the world stage. With the POTUS term limit looming, this man would become the presumptive nominee for president of the United States.

Barnes tightens his Velcro, then rips it open and refastens, makes sure the fit is optimal. He repeats the process for his right wrist, then turns back to Ariel and nods, fully protected against the twin ravages of tendinitis and gravity. Ariel can't help but feel a little sorry for this guy. But just a little.

"Could you describe your husband, please? Height, weight."

"He's about five-ten. I don't know what he weighs; I don't watch him weigh himself."

"But generally?"

"He's thin, narrow." She doesn't know how to describe John's body. It's perfectly propor-

45

tioned, beautiful. "Muscular, though not big muscles."

"Okay." Barnes clearly doesn't want to hear about any other man's pleasing physique. Insecurity and homophobia are so highly correlated that Ariel suspects they're the same thing.

"What else? Let's see, hair?"

"Dark brown, full and wavy. Green eyes."

"Any identifying marks? Scars? Earrings? Tattoos? Facial hair?"

Ariel shakes her head. John is one of the few completely unadorned men she knows, with a wardrobe utterly devoid of logos or labels or identifiable branding, no sports-team or college merchandise, no jewelry or baseball cap. Even his car is generic, a statement of nothing so much as being a statement explicitly of nothing.

"Age?"

"Thirty-six."

Barnes looks up quickly, then back down at his keyboard. She can see his calculation in that quick glance: Ariel is older by a decade, a difference that's more than incidental when it goes in this male-female direction.

"Would people call him attractive?"

"Definitely."

She knows what thread Barnes is tugging, what assumptions he'd made when she'd first arrived, what additional narrative he's now constructing: It's not that Ariel married a

46

younger man, it's that John married an older woman. Barnes is around John's age. Maybe Barnes is wondering what might compel him to marry an older woman. This older woman.

Ariel examines him, while he examines her. His suit fabric is straining, wrinkles in all the wrong places; his shirt's top button can't close. This is a man who has put on some weight recently, more than just a pound or two, and his wardrobe hasn't caught up. Maybe he's in denial, telling himself that this extra weight will slide off easily once he stops eating dessert. Next week, maybe. Or the week after.

"Okay, so, this morning: no communication at all?"

"No. He hasn't responded to my texts or emails. When I try calling, his phone goes straight to voicemail. I left a couple of messages."

Barnes glances at Ariel's hard-copy paperwork, which had been like filling out medical-insurance paperwork, something you do on a plastic clipboard with a click-trigger ballpoint emblazoned with the brand name of a new diabetes medication.

"So what have you two been doing in Lisbon?"

"Normal tourist stuff."

"Such as?"

They'd taken an early-morning Segway tour, zipping along a waterfront dedicated to leisure pursuits — restaurants and discos separated from marinas by a ribbon of trail for runners and cyclists, like a twenty-first-century dream of urban revitalization. They'd ridden one of the old creaky trams, the famous number 28, lurching around sharp corners, up and down steep hills, like a vintage roller coaster, crowded and uncomfortable and more than a little scary.

Barnes is not a very good typist, using just a few of the fingers that are peeking out from his orthosis, toggling his eyes between keyboard and screen with occasional side glances at Ariel, at her breasts. She glances down herself, to make sure she's sufficiently covered.

"Any contact with anyone?"

"Of course, plenty of people. At the hotel, restaurants, a couple of museums."

They'd visited the Gulbenkian, a brutalist hulk with one of the world's great private art collections, the spoils of a nation-state level of wealth. Also a convent that had been converted into a museum of tiles, which are everywhere in Lisbon — building façades in mesmerizing geometric patterns, the interior walls of shops and cafés, lobby floors. You feel cooler just looking at the blue-and-white smoothness.

"Anyone you knew? Or anyone your husband knew?"

"No." Ariel is not going to tell Barnes about

48

the woman in the café. "We have a formal dinner scheduled for tomorrow night, with the partners from John's client company and their wives. That's why John asked me to come on this trip; these sorts of businessmen apparently like to meet the wives."

"What sorts of businessmen?"

"European ones."

Barnes grins knowingly, which he probably thinks is charming. It's not. Every aspect of this man's Southern smarm has grated on Ariel from the start.

"Does your husband travel for business a lot?"

"A few trips per month, usually for two or three nights, mostly in Europe."

"Do you accompany him often?"

"This is the first time. We lead busy lives, and it's not easy to find time when we can both travel. Our only other trip together was our honeymoon."

"And when was that?"

"Three months ago."

Ariel can see in Barnes's raised eyebrow that his theory is taking on a more definite shape — you're newlyweds, maybe bickering, you don't really know this man, perhaps he simply left you. Who'd blame him? The poor guy has been gone for only a few hours and you're already at the embassy? Take a chill pill, lady.

"So why this time?" he asks. "Other people's business trips are not normally anyone's idea of fun."

"True," Ariel says. "But I've never been to Portugal before. And all I needed to do for this trip was buy a new dress."

"Not a *terrible* imposition, was it?"

Ariel had not in fact wanted to buy the dress. She was as a rule very careful with money, also averse to fashion in general. When she was young, she'd of course read all the magazines that tell you what to buy, and how to sexualize yourself — the makeup, the clothes, the shoes, the waxing — but she no longer even glances at these headlines, SUMMER'S HOTTEST F☆☆☆-ME SHOES, TEN STEPS TO A TIGHTER TUSH, GIVE HIM THE BEST B☆☆☆JOB OF HIS LIFE. Not anymore.

"Have you checked your bank balance today?"

Ariel is surprised by this pivot, but on the other hand she's not. "No."

"Don't you think you should?"

She doesn't. And there wouldn't be all that much to withdraw, even if what Barnes is insinuating were true. But it's impossible.

"Why don't we just get this out of the way?" Barnes suggests. "Cross it off our list."

Ariel knows that the only reason not to do this would be if she's scared of what she might find. She definitely is not.

"Would you like to use my computer?"

"No thanks." She takes out her phone.

50

"What's the wifi?"

Barnes scribbles something, slides the paper toward her. She types the digits into her phone, and launches the banking app, waits for the log-in to load, then the next screen —

Ariel can feel her pulse speeding up. Is she actually getting nervous? She should know better. She *does* know better.

The wifi signal seems to be strong, but her phone's response is slow. Ariel suspects that this is the opposite of a secure connection, it's probably a network designed expressly to capture the browsing history and screens and keystrokes and passwords of any guest who uses it. She's not really worried about the State Department stealing the four thousand dollars in her checking account, but she is getting antsy waiting for the page to load, waiting, waiting —

The screen loads, displaying a balance exactly what it should be. "It's all fine."

"Great," Barnes says. "That's great news." But he's clearly disappointed to have to discard his theory: attractive younger man marries older woman, empties her bank account, and disappears in a foreign country, out of reach of American law enforcement. Maybe that's what she'd assume too, if she were sitting on his side of the desk, confronting a woman like her, showing up in a situation like this.

Ariel is keenly aware of being observed here, by cameras, by people who might be watching. She couldn't help but notice all the lenses as she walked through the offices; she can't help but imagine there's one somewhere in this room too.

Cameras are not new to her. Ariel had been an actor in her youth, always hyperconscious of her appearance, of what she was communicating not only through spoken words and inflections but also by facial expressions, by body language, by finger fidgets or bouncing knees or shifty eyes, by the many signals we're constantly emitting, not just when we're on a stage or in front of a camera, but always, because we're all being observed through some lens or another. Sometimes you can forget it, or ignore it, or pretend to. But sometimes there's an actual camera right there to remind you, mounted in the corner of a room like this one. You're being watched. You're being recorded.

After a few more perfunctory lines of inquiry, Barnes has made it clear that he's disinclined to lean on the local police, or to involve other embassy staff in looking for John.

"Isn't there *anything* you can do?" Ariel gives her most pleading doe-eyed look. This used to be something she was good at, leveraging her looks to charm men, especially the ones not shrewd enough or self-aware

52

enough to recognize that they're being manipulated. Some men are instinctually suspicious of good-looking women who are overly nice; Saxby Barnes isn't one of them.

Ariel leans forward; she can see his eyes flicker down to the opening of her blouse. "Please?"

This is a skill that she'd allowed to atrophy, one she wished she'd never possessed in the first place, never needed. A skill she'd wished didn't even exist. But she grudgingly admits that there can be a utility in making bargains with the patriarchy.

"Look, Ms. Pryce, I'm not a policeman. We're not . . ."

She drops her head in dismay, and she can practically feel him taking the opportunity to look down her blouse.

"That's not what we do here," he continues, "track down people who have left their, um, companions for a few hours. That's a job for the local police, if it's a job for anyone, which I sincerely hope does not turn out to be the case. But merely because your husband left your hotel this morning without telling you? That doesn't make him missing. That just makes him a man in a rush. Or an inconsiderate man. Or a distracted man. All of which are far more likely than a man who has come to harm, and none of which are crimes. So at this stage, we can't . . ."

Barnes trails off, hoping that Ariel will jump

in and agree, yes I understand. But she won't. He stands, extends his hand and another grin. "I wish I could be of more assistance."

"Do you?"

He nods, trying to look extra-sincere in his patent insincerity. "I do."

She's disappointed. Not just that he won't help her, but also that she was unable to sway him, that her charms have been resistible by a man who seems like he'd surrender so easily.

Saxby Barnes is not going to be her ally. Ariel will be better off with the Lisbon cop, who at least has a sympathetic face, and a female partner. Not much, but more than nothing, which is what this American functionary is offering. Nothing, plus a bottle of water. Sparkling.

Ariel is more than disappointed. She's suddenly angry — at this man, at herself, at the world. It sneaks up on her, this fury. Like a volcano erupting after years of pressure buildup.

"What kind of name is Saxby, anyway?"

"A family name. Goes back ten generations."

As if the mere fact that something is traditional makes it admirable, or defensible. The same exact justification has been used for pretty much all the injustice in the history of the world.

"So it's, what, your proud Southern heri-

54

tage? From the good old days?"

The fake grin fades. "That's right."

Ariel calls bullshit. She has plenty of first-hand experience with the insidious, corrosive effects of fetishizing tradition.

"Like sweet tea?"

Barnes drops his unshaken hand.

"Or slavery?"

He puffs his chest out, puts his chin up, wanting to defend his honor, frustrated that he can't argue with this woman. He's chivalrous! Plus it's his job to be accommodating.

Ariel turns away, steps toward the door.

"Oh, Ms. Pryce?"

Something about his tone worries her. She looks back over her shoulder.

"Do you, by chance, go by any other name? Or does your husband?"

CHAPTER 5

Day 1. 11:27 a.m.

She stands in front of the embassy, waiting for her pulse to slow to a regular rhythm, for her mind to regain dominion over her body. On the sidewalk, a woman in backpacking gear is holding her phone aloft, taking a picture of the embassy, with Ariel in the foreground.

Ariel unlocks her own phone, and opens the various communication apps, one after another. She's old enough to have clear memories of life pre–cell phones, without apps, without computered cars and smart TVs and remote thermostats. She doesn't believe in tech's infallibility, always harbors the suspicion that the alarm clock will fail, the weather report is wrong, the voicemail never arrived.

But no, there's nothing from John. Nothing from anyone, anywhere.

"Excuse me?"

A man is suddenly by her side, and Ariel

flinches away.

"Excuse me," he repeats. "I'm sorry to bother you." It's the bearded man she saw when she walked through the embassy. "My name is Pete Wagstaff. I'm a reporter. Maybe I can help?"

Ariel squints at him in the blinding sunlight. She can already feel sweat beads surfacing on the back of her neck.

"The embassy, you know, their hands are often tied." He reaches into his pocket, extends a business card. Ariel recognizes the logo of a news organization, LISBON CORRESPONDENT, phone numbers, email, an office address.

"Thanks," she says. "I don't want to seem ungrateful, but I can't talk to you. I'm sorry."

This man is not as old as he seemed from across the room. Better looking too, with a reassuring softness to his eyes.

"Did someone tell you not to?"

Ariel shakes her head. "I just . . . can't. Don't take it personally."

He smiles. "Okay. But if you think of a way I can help, whatever the problem is, please do be in touch. I know my way around this town, and I'm always available."

"You're sweet," she says, bestowing in turn her sweetest smile. Ariel knows she can't reach out to talk to a reporter; that's out of the question. But that doesn't mean that a reporter won't be useful somehow, at some point. "I'll keep that in mind."

Ariel checks the time: yes, now is good. Or if not good, at least an acceptable time to send this text: YOU DOING OKAY TODAY? She can't help herself when they're apart, even when she knows she should.

Her phone dings almost immediately, and her heart flutters as she grabs the device.

YEAH MOM, ALL GOOD.

Well at least there's that. But that's not enough, she realizes. She places the international call.

"Hi," her son answers. "How's Lisbon?"

"Hot." She doesn't want to tell her kid what's happening. All she really wants is to hear his voice. "How are things there?"

"Fine."

These days that's how George answers almost every question: *fine*. Or sometimes: *good*. Tweenaged-boy taciturnity, to go with his tweenaged-boy beanpole shape. But every few weeks he says something that reminds her that he's still a kid, despite the body. "Are dogs citizens?" This was just last week, they were driving, the radio tuned to a news story about undocumented immigrants.

"No, Sweetheart," she said, careful not to laugh at him. It was hard. "Dogs are not citizens."

Ariel couldn't imagine what rights and

privileges and responsibilities George's imaginary dog citizens might have. Would they vote? Pay taxes?

"How are the dogs?" she asks now, knowing that this is the only subject he's reliably willing to discuss.

"Well. They're eating brebberties," which means breakfast in the private language that they pretend the dogs speak. Dinner is dibberties. Teeth are tibberties. There's a theme. "Mallomar is taking one kibble and running out of the room to chew it. Scotch is ignoring him."

"Mallomar is crazy."

"Very. But listen, Mom, I have to go? The camp bus is about to arrive. Love you."

That's it, she realizes: That's all she wanted from this call. He's still willing to say "love you," albeit only in private, and maybe just to end a call. She takes what she can get.

Chief of Station Nicole Griffiths senses a presence in her doorway. She places the tip of her pen on the page so she doesn't lose her place, then looks up to see Saxby Barnes standing there, a piece of paper in his left hand, his right raised.

"Knock knock," he says, while knocking on air. He thinks this is clever. "May I come in?"

Barnes regularly shows up here thinking that he has just unearthed intelligence, which always turns out to be not. Nicole hopes this

59

is because he's seduced by the idea of the CIA, not by her.

"If you must."

Barnes shuts the door behind him. "An American tourist just reported that her businessman husband has disappeared. She woke up this morning and he was gone, not answering his phone."

"Interesting," Nicole says, in a tone of voice that suggests it's not. There are people in consular whom Nicole trusts, but Barnes is not among them. He is intelligence-adjacent, in more ways than one. "You sent her to the police?"

"She'd already been. Said the police wouldn't do anything, it's too soon."

This is normal. Nicole doesn't respond.

"She seems like an upstanding citizen," Barnes continues. "On paper, the husband too. Except for one little thing: They both changed their names, separately, years before they ever met."

Nicole's nib is still aimed at the page in front of her, a ludicrously dense report about a surge in illegal crossings from Tangier via the Strait of Gibraltar, a mere nine miles of rough water that separates Africa from Europe. The author of this report must think he's being paid by the word. Like Dickens, with whom Nicole never had any patience. Get to the point already.

"Him, just a few years ago; her, more than

a decade. I ran a quick check on both of them while she was waiting." Barnes looks proud of this routine inquiry. "And get this," he continues. "The wife doesn't know about the husband's name change."

For once, Barnes is possibly here on legitimate intelligence business. This is one of the reasons that the chief of station's office is in the embassy, along with a staff of Agency operatives. Also why the COS's identity is not secret.

"So, Mr. Barnes, what can the Agency do for you?"

He places the sheet of paper in front of Nicole, already signed by his boss in consular. "Can you please find this gentleman's phone?"

"Sure thing."

"And could I ask that you please keep me in the loop?"

"Of course," Nicole says, although she has no intention whatsoever of doing this. Barnes is neither clever nor discreet, which in her world is a dangerous combination.

Ariel walks through the Alfama neighborhood, which looks like a completely different city, a labyrinth of narrow cobbled lanes and steep staircases and ancient whitewashed buildings with red-tile roofs, the only section of Lisbon left unscathed by the 1755 earthquake and tsunami-and-fire aftermath that destroyed eighty-five percent of the city's buildings and killed perhaps a fifth of the population. There's a small-town feel here, neighbors chatting on narrow streets, kids kicking balls against walls, the smell of fish stews and steamed clams and roast pork, cats slinking along windowsills and dogs trotting with impunity on the pedestrian-only streets.

This looks like a happy sort of place, a safe place where nothing bad happens. But Ariel knows there's no such thing.

There are three hospitals in downtown Lisbon, and these are the ones she calls first. None has a record of John Wright, nor of any unidentified American. She tries a few farther afield, up the river, down the river, inland. No, no, no. He's not in a hospital.

"Come on, old man," Kayla Jefferson says. "Orders from the boss: We need to go find a phone."

"A phone?"

"Well, we're looking for the person whose phone it is."

Guido Antonucci grabs his aviators, hangs them from the neck of his blue polo, and rises gingerly. His feet have really been killing him; probably needs new prescription insoles. Antonucci has been working here in Lisbon for more than two years, but he hasn't yet faced the challenge of finding a local orthopedist.

Fucking pain in the ass.

"The device apparently hasn't moved in like six hours," Kayla says. "So chances are we're not going to find the actual person. Unless he's dead."

Kayla is a young athletic woman, just a few years past varsity track at Howard. She makes fun of Antonucci with old-man jokes, bald-spot jokes, orthopedic-footwear jokes. She's at a point in life when her best friends are still her sorority sisters, but she'll learn, soon enough. Life in the CIA's Directorate of Operations takes a physical toll quicker than you'd think, no matter where you start on the physical-fitness continuum. Antonucci was once a college athlete himself, but that was too long ago to mention anymore. He can't remember the last time he spoke to a fraternity brother.

"This is where we're going." Kayla extends her phone, a map of the city, a red dot that's about five miles from the embassy. "There's nothing there, far as I can tell. The nearest address is an unoccupied warehouse."

Antonucci unlocks his bottom drawer, pulls out his gun, tucks it into his ankle holster. Empty warehouses are practically custom-tailored for illegal activities, and he's always happy to bring along his weapon.

"Dead seems not impossible," he says, heaving himself out of his chair.

"Nice grunt," Kayla says.

63

Antonucci knows he's old-school, and Jefferson is decidedly not, and that's why they're often assigned to work as a team. He likes the young woman, and doesn't mind her old-man jokes, not usually. When Antonucci joined the CIA, there were practically no women; there were barely any Italian-Americans. But these days his partner is a woman, his boss is a woman too, and sometimes he misses the easier camaraderie of working with men. Now he needs to be so careful all the time. Another type of exhausting.

Even his name is a relic of the past. Will there ever be another American kid named Guido? Doubtful, and good riddance. He hates his name, such a caricature, so easy to ridicule. Then again, these things have a way of recycling, freshened up with a sheen of irony.

"Whose phone is it?" he asks.

"American businessman."

"He lost his phone?" They head for the garage. "So what are we now, the Genius Bar?"

"No, his wife lost *him*. But don't worry, Guido. If we hustle, we can be back in time for your afternoon nap."

CHAPTER 6

Day 1. 12:48 p.m.
Ariel looks around the swarming square at the banks, the shops, the cafés, the flashing green neon of a pharmacy. This square is a busy place all day long and late into the night, it's a spot that seems like it could be both incredibly safe but also sometimes dangerous, it's a location that would —

Of course.

Yes, she identifies one over there. And another there, and — yes — one right in front of her own hotel, which she's now rushing toward, and into, taking the smooth stairs two at a time, bursting into reception where Duarte looks up in alarm at the American wife, sweaty and panting and more than a little crazed-looking —

"Can I see your security footage?"

Detective Carolina Santos hangs up the phone, finishes writing her notes, then turns to her junior partner. António Moniz is a few years older, but he joined the force much later, after spending his twenties doing things he does not talk about. Over the years, Santos has come to suspect that Moniz spent this decade on drugs and travel, maybe the hippie tour of Southeast Asia and Latin America, or maybe just cruising around Europe, Berlin or Prague or Bucharest, the places where people fritter away their youth, before they realize that youth is not something to fritter away. Now Moniz is just another middle-aged man with a picture of a kid on the desk at his respectable government job. Everybody becomes respectable, sooner or later. Unless they go to jail. Or die.

"That was Erico?" Moniz asks.

Visitors assume, of course, that the kid is Moniz's daughter. That is why the photo is there.

"Yes. He has been following the American woman since she left us. She spent more than an hour at the US embassy. When she emerged, she was accosted by that American reporter who is always hanging around. Erico cannot remember his name, me either. You?"

Moniz shakes his head.

"She had a brief conversation with the reporter, accepted his business card, walked around for a while, then took a taxi back to her hotel. Before she entered, she spent a minute standing on the sidewalk, looking around, spinning slowly, examining the whole square. Looking for clues, maybe."

That would certainly be the obvious explanation. Moniz is not so sure, but he holds his tongue. Santos is going to develop her own theories, based on her experiences and attitude. Moniz will develop his. Hopefully their theories will match; those are the easy cases. But Moniz has the suspicion that this will not be one of those.

How should you feel when you realize you're on the cusp of a mortal crisis? When it becomes clear that any second the wildfire is going to engulf your car, the hurricane is going to rip the roof off your house, the bar fight is going to evolve into manslaughter? Something that looks at first like nothing much, just a hiccup, but then you're choking to death, and you have only seconds to save yourself.

Is this how Ariel should be behaving, right now?

Last winter, if she hadn't called Sarah and gone to the ER in the middle of the night, she might have died from the pneumonia. Sometimes what looks like panic is really rational self-preservation.

"Jesus," Guido Antonucci says. "What the fuck are we doing?"

"We're looking for a phone, Guido. Did you forget already? Is it the Alzheimer's?"

67

Antonucci continues sifting through the garbage. "I know what we're *literally* doing."

"So you're asking, what, figuratively?"

"Is this why you joined the Agency, Jefferson? To root around through Portuguese garbage, looking for cell phones? Like a rookie beat cop?"

"Specifically? No, I'll admit that this was not precisely what I had in mind."

"We should have brought gloves."

"Here. Look."

"Don't touch it."

"You think I'm a dimwit, don't you? Maybe you wonder who ties my shoes in the morning?"

Antonucci steps aside, takes out his phone, uses a secure app to call his boss.

"We found the device in a garbage can in front of an abandoned warehouse."

"No sign of the owner?" Nicole Griffiths asks.

"No sign of anything. We're near the river, other side of the tracks."

"What does the warehouse look like?"

"Looks unused. There's a locked gate to the loading zone, and no vehicles are visible. We can see through one of the street-facing windows, and inside appears to be completely empty. Though it's possible that there's stuff or people in there. To be definitive, we'd have to, um . . ." Antonucci trails off. Secure app

68

or not, he doesn't want to discuss breaking the law.

"No," Griffiths says. "A dumped phone wouldn't be right next to the reason for dumping it."

Antonucci glances at the trash can, oddly full considering how out-of-the-way this spot is. People must use this can to illegally dispose of household trash.

"This bin is pretty packed," he says. He has worked in cities with underfunded, deprioritized sanitation services, garbage everywhere. Lisbon isn't one of these. Trash cans here aren't allowed to overflow. "I'd imagine pickup must be soon. Should we take the device?"

"Definitely," Griffiths says. "Let's have ourselves a look."

The time stamp identifies that it was 6:51 A.M. when John strode through the small lobby, which is not really a lobby — no furniture, no desk, it's just a roomy foyer, a cool, airy, tile-floored space, one end of which is the hotel's front doors, the other is the elevator and the staircase that winds around the center of the building. Reception is upstairs, on what everyone in Europe calls the first floor; like the word *entrée,* this means something completely different than it does in America. From up there in reception, the downstairs foyer is monitored via a

69

security camera that's mounted in one corner, next to the elevator, facing the front door.

By the time John exited the building, a few hotel employees had already entered: a kitchen worker at five-thirty, then, just before six, Duarte, followed minutes later by the two chambermaids.

A second camera hangs on the building's exterior, facing the front door obliquely, providing a semi-profile of anyone who enters, and a decent view to a small swath of sidewalk. There's no way for this vantage to do a good job of identifying any faces; this camera's main benefit must be to identify the activity, or merely to deter it. This is a camera that would be noticed by anyone with a mindset to look for one, which you'd do if you were up to no good.

It was still 6:51 when this camera captured John pushing open the door and glancing around. He took a single step out to the sidewalk, and raised the angle of his head incrementally, as if noticing something, or someone. He froze for a moment, perhaps surprised, or perhaps debating, not sure how to proceed. Then he made his decision and took a couple of strides in that direction. Then he disappeared from the frame.

This footage shows mostly John's back, with a glimpse of side. Ariel can see that he's wearing suit pants and a white shirt but neither jacket nor tie, and he isn't carrying

70

anything — no briefcase, no newspaper, nothing. He doesn't look like a businessman on his way to work.

"Let's watch that again."

Duarte glances at Ariel. They've already watched this footage twice, and there's nothing to see. But the clerk isn't going to argue. You don't argue with guests about anything, and certainly not a guest in this type of predicament. With this type of personality.

They rewatched the whole thing, saw John exit the frame again, seemingly the end of the evidence. But Ariel keeps her eyes glued to the screen, looking for something more, anything, any movement, any change, any —

"There," she says to Duarte. "What's that?"

"Excuse me? What, please?"

"That. Look: Go back a few seconds."

The young man slides the cursor.

"*There.* Do you see? That big shadow? It moves, just a couple of seconds after John leaves the frame in that exact direction. What do you think that is?"

"That direction is the street, so that shadow is an auto, maybe. What else can it be?"

"I don't know. A streetcar?"

"No, a streetcar is much bigger, and with a different shape."

The young man leans away from the screen with the satisfied look of someone who just solved a puzzle. "I believe that is a car, sen-

71

hora. And it drives away. After your husband gets into it."

Ariel stands in the spot where the phantom car would have been. The hotel is on one side of this street, the park on the other. She scans in every direction, taking in everything, the trees, the streetlights, the front doors and first floors of buildings, the entrances to businesses and residences. She identifies at least a dozen security cameras, but can't see any of their lenses; none of the cameras are facing this precise spot. And if she can't see the lens from this spot, then the lens can't see this spot. Isn't that the way it works? Ocular physics? Logic?

A large part of being an actor was being hyper-observant. When Ariel gave up professional acting, she didn't become any less observant; she simply trained her observations on new objects. And in the decades since, her steady diet of mystery novels has reoriented her toward exactly this: looking for clues.

There are too many trees here, blocking the view. Trees are abundant in Lisbon, not just in parks and squares but growing out of circular cutouts of sidewalks, planted in pots in front of shops, providing refuge from the relentless sun.

Ariel knows that none of the other cameras around this square can provide any useful evidence.

Another dead end. They're mounting up quickly.

CHAPTER 7

Day 1. 1:49 p.m.

Lunchtime has arrived. The downtown sidewalks are crowded, but people here don't seem to be rushing around, they're not staring obliviously at handheld screens, jockeying for position at street corners, challenging cars, trucks, one another. Instead it seems to be a leisurely break that people are taking, moving slowly in the heat, jackets off, sleeves rolled, sticking to the shady sides of streets lined in pastel-painted buildings, pale peaches and plums, faded lavender and mint and every conceivable shade of yellow, with thin black lines of suspended lamps and window frames and balcony railings, ornamentation that looks like India ink over watercolor washes.

Ariel should eat. She never got around to breakfast — too anxious — and she hasn't grown any calmer since. It's hard to imagine sitting at a table, behaving like a calm civilized person, waiting for the waiter, for the menu, for the check. These are tediums that she can barely endure even on the best of days.

"Senhora Pryce, how nice to see you again. So soon."

It sounds like disappointment that's coming from Moniz. But what should she expect?

"I have evidence." Ariel puts the thumb drive on the detective's desk.

"Oh?" He squints at the little device. "Excuse me," he says, and pats his jacket, removes a pair of glasses. "It is inconvenient, losing your vision. Unpleasant. Has this happened to you?"

She shakes her head.

"Not yet? You are fortunate."

Fortunate is not what she'd call herself, but now is not the time to argue. Not about that.

Moniz turns over the thumb drive. "What is this, please?"

"It's a memory stick. A flash drive. It contains footage from the hotel's security camera that shows my husband on the sidewalk this morning."

"This device — this video — these are supplied by the hotel?"

"Yes."

Ariel can see that Moniz is not enthusiastic about connecting his computer and the police network to this piece of hardware delivered by this possibly unhinged American. He puts the thing down, pushes it away, as if it's dangerous, or smells. He picks up his land-

75

line, has a quick conversation.

"One moment." He indicates a chair. "Please."

They hold each other's gazes for a second, then both look away, Moniz down at his notepad, Ariel across the large room, taking in the usual assortment of things you'd expect to find in any police station. Ariel hasn't been in one in a long time, but she can remember her last visit vividly.

She returns her gaze to Moniz, who's also what she'd expect to find in a police station, the standard off-the-rack model of cop — mid-forties, thinning hair compensated for with bushy mustache, a bulky frame with twenty extra pounds that sit in the front of his belly, distended in a bulge at the beltline, the way some men carry their middle age and their beer, as if six months pregnant. When she was here earlier, Moniz had a spot of something on his tie. Now he has added a splash of what seems to be tomato sauce on his pale blue shirt.

Next to his desktop monitor, a silver frame holds a photograph of a plain-looking young girl of five or six; no mother in the shot. Ariel looks to his ring finger, finds none.

A uniformed colleague arrives, delivers a laptop to Moniz, who inserts the thumb drive into the port, plays the brief clip. Then he leans closer to the screen, and replays it.

"Look," Ariel says, "after John disappears

from the frame? See that shadow?"

"Yes."

"Do you see it move? I think that's a car driving away. With my husband in it."

Moniz doesn't dignify these bits of conjecture. He continues watching the screen closely, a completely static scene, for another ten seconds, twenty. Ariel wonders what he's looking for. Maybe nothing, maybe he's just buying time, figuring out what to say, how to get this woman out of his guest chair, this problem out of his hair. Ariel can't imagine doing a job like his, spending all day every day confronting other people's problems.

His partner walks over. Santos nods at Ariel, then has a quick conversation in Portuguese with Moniz. He points at the laptop, and Santos leans over, and both detectives watch the video, concentrating intently. Moniz removes his reading glasses, places them deliberately on his desk, adjusts their angle.

"I am sorry," he says. "I understand that you are worried about your husband. But this video does not appear, to me" — he jabs his own chest with his forefinger — "to be evidence of anything illegal."

"But do you see the shadow?"

"Yes, I see it."

"Maybe the video can be enhanced? Then we'd be able to identify details about that car?"

77

"You mean, about that shadow?"

"Isn't there some software you could use, to — I don't know — figure out the make of the car? From the shape of the shadow?"

Moniz bites his lower lip, as if chewing on the idea. He turns to his partner.

"It is possible," Santos says. She speaks!

"Okay," Ariel says to the woman. "Then let's do that."

Both cops are struggling with the idea. Maybe whether to accept Ariel's suggestion. Or maybe how exactly to reject it, and which one of them is going to do it.

"If this shadow is a car, is it not possible that your husband gets in because this car is taking him to the office of his client, where he is at this very moment working?"

Ariel almost rolls her eyes.

"Is this not a possible explanation? Is this not the *most* possible?"

"Yes, of course, that's *possible.* But look: He's not wearing a jacket or tie. He packed *four* neckties for three days of business. Why would he bring all those ties to Lisbon if he wasn't going to wear any of them to the office, on a day that will be full of business meetings?"

The cops don't have a rejoinder to that.

"He's *missing,*" Ariel says.

"Perhaps. But being missing, while wearing no jacket or tie, is not a crime."

"But . . ." What can Ariel say? "I'm worried

that something bad has happened to him."

"Something bad," Moniz says. "Which something bad?"

Ariel inclines her chin at the frame on his desk. "Is that your daughter?"

Moniz doesn't answer.

"What if you woke up this morning," Ariel continues, "and she wasn't in bed where she was supposed to be, and she hadn't left a note, and you couldn't reach her? What would you do?"

Moniz doesn't respond, so Ariel turns to the woman, who has remained standing, not committing to participating in this conversation.

"Please," Ariel says. "Can't you do *something*?" Ariel doesn't like this, appealing to the woman, it feels so feeble, so reductionist. But it works. It almost always works. Santos nods.

"Okay," Moniz says, "please, let us start at the beginning: Why is your husband in Portugal?"

Leonor shuts off the bathroom lights, and turns her attention to the bedroom. The linens are a messy tangle, pillows everywhere, sheets on the floor. A wild night, she thinks. And then apparently the husband disappeared. Leonor is half-expecting to find blood, or drugs, something. She does not trust Americans.

79

Before she pulls on the fitted sheet, she drops to her knees — the most painful part of her job — to check under the bed. That is when she sees it.

"I should know the name of the client," Ariel admits again. "I realize that. I should know the business name, the address, the name of my husband's contact. I should know all this info, or at least some."

It sounds bad, the many things that Ariel should know but doesn't, itemized this way.

"But when John told me these details, I didn't write them down, and I just don't remember any of it. I'm sorry."

"But he did tell you these informations?" Moniz asks. "You are sure?"

"Of course."

"Do you know what type of business it is? Perhaps we can reduce the choices."

"Manufacturing."

"Good, good, that is something." Moniz writes down a word. "Manufacturing of what?"

"Maybe involving natural resources?"

"Good. Good! Mining is very important here. Iron, zinc, cop—"

"I don't think it's mining, no."

"Fishing? Winemaking?"

"I think I'd probably remember those things as mining, or fishing, or winemaking. Not just as natural resources."

"We have a very large timber industry. Especially cork. Did you know that Portugal is the primary cork producer in the world?"

"I've noticed."

"So, cork?"

Ariel pauses for a respectable interval before shrugging her shoulders. She doesn't want to seem too dismissive of cork, of the cops' efforts. They're trying. That's all she can ask.

"I think," Ariel says, "that the relevant executive is named Jorge."

"Jorge, okay. And his family name?"

Ariel shakes her head.

"Okay, that too is more than nothing. Anything else?"

"Jorge — I'm pretty sure that's his name — is a low-handicap golfer."

Moniz jots this down.

"When did your husband tell you these things?" Santos asks.

"About a month ago. When he was inviting me to come on the trip."

"One month, that is not so long. Why can you not remember?"

"When John told me these details, I'd had a little too much to drink. I'm usually very careful."

She glances at Santos, a cop who's a woman, a person who doesn't need any further explanation. Ariel can't help but glance down at this cop's hand too, looking

81

for a wedding ring, finding none.

"But we'd had a big meal with other people in a restaurant, the whole thing was a long evening, my glass kept getting refilled . . ." Ariel shrugs. "Anyway, it was on the drive home, I remember sitting in the car, thinking I was glad I wasn't the one driving. That's when John bombarded me with details that I didn't absorb. I assumed he'd tell me the relevant bits again some other time, so it didn't seem that important to pay attention. But he never did."

Santos maintains eye contact. Ariel can feel her assessing this story. These cops have been assessing Ariel all along, every bit of herself. That's always the case in a situation like this, a possible crime being reported by a woman, involving a man with whom she's been intimate. It's all about credibility.

"Do you have a photograph of your husband?" Moniz asks. It's clear that this interview too is about to come to an inconclusive end. "We can share it with our colleagues, and the hospitals."

Ariel retrieves her phone, finds the same couples selfie that she showed to the chambermaids. Moniz squints at the screen, sighs dramatically, then finds his glasses again. The reading-glasses situation is really hitting him hard.

"Maybe a different photo?" The one she offered is really about the backdrop, the panorama of the city from high above, a spectacular view. "Perhaps closer of his face?"

"I don't think so." Ariel scrolls through her library, pointlessly. She knows there aren't any others. "I don't really take photos of John."

"Oh no? Why is that?"

"My husband doesn't like it, all this documenting that people do. I don't either."

Nothing, and nothing, and more nothing; the hotel staff, and the police, and the embassy. No one is taking Ariel seriously, they are all seeing an emotional woman, an irrational woman, a confused woman, a mistaken woman, a disbelieved woman. Again, and again, and again.

The summer sun is blinding, bouncing off all the light-colored walls, the stone sidewalks, every surface seems to be hard and reflective, every structure designed to repel the sunlight, to keep the buildings' interiors cool. This turns the sidewalks into open-air ovens.

Ariel is trudging toward her hotel, hugging the shady sides of the streets. Sweat is trickling down her temples, her scalp is tingling, she feels her skin flush all over, her cheeks, her chest.

It's only tourists and desperate people who are out in this heat. Ariel feels like both, a desperate tourist, weaving between the iron bollards that separate the narrow roadways from the narrower sidewalks. She turns a corner onto a block with no shade whatsoever, now facing directly into the overwhelming sun beating down on both sides of the street, no refuge anywhere. It must be a hundred degrees plus humid plus so goddamn bright that even with sunglasses she's squinting. The heat is like a physical assault.

Ariel considers turning around, ducking inside somewhere. Her head is throbbing — the sun, the fatigue, the tension, the worry — and she realizes that she's parched, she has barely had a sip of anything to drink all day except coffee, she's dehydrated, light-headed, dizzy —

She has to stop walking, if only for a minute. She's on the verge of collapse. She steadies herself with a palm on the hot stone wall. She notices a small market back around the corner, a cool place where she can guzzle a bottle of water, wait for a taxi to the hotel, take a cool shower, lie down and guzzle more water.

Yes, that's what she'll do.

She turns her back to the sun, and starts walking whence she came, slowly, deliberately, possibly looking like a careful drunk, someone who doesn't want to be seen stumbling at least as much as she doesn't want to actually stumble. Heat exhaustion and dehydration are so often ignored, and she —

■ ■ ■ ■

Wait.

That man across the street, walking in her direction? Ariel has seen him before.

Behind the privacy of her sunglasses, she examines him closely, his aviator shades, a plain blue polo draping a pear-shaped middle-aged torso, squarish rubber-soled leather shoes beneath the creased khakis. It's been a long time since Ariel cared about fashion, and she has never paid much attention to what men wear. But she forces herself to focus on the lower half of this guy's outfit, to memorize it. The top half would be easy to change.

She turns the corner, out of the guy's sight, then searches for a window that might provide a reflection, and yes there, a gift shop's big expanse of glass, and — yes! — she can see that he too stops in his tracks, turns back in her direction.

It's hard to make out his features in the reflection of the window display — lots of items, lots of cork — and the angle isn't great, nor the light. He seems to be leaning against the wall, head down, looking at . . . what? . . . must be at his phone, or pretending to look at his phone, just another guy attending to his device. But circumstances betray him: He's standing in a nonsensical

85

spot — hot, bright, uncomfortable — that's explicable only if what he's really doing is something else. Like waiting for Ariel's next move.

She watches for thirty seconds, and he doesn't move. That's all the confirmation she needs.

Ariel steps into the small market's aggressive air-conditioning, stands in the chill to drink a bottle of water while looking out the window. She hands her empty plastic to the cashier, buys a second bottle, steps back outside, stands amid the trays of produce that beckon passersby with the bright promise of oranges and peaches, cherries and lemons.

She peers again at the cluttered window's reflections: Ariel can't see him anywhere. She searches the real-life street in one direction, then another. He's gone. At least for the moment.

What should she do? She could turn the same corner, try to see if she can locate him, to prove to herself that she's being followed. But that would run the risk of making herself easier to follow.

Or? Or she could take advantage of her momentary freedom, and elude him.

Or she could confront him.

The answer depends, doesn't it, on who's following her.

Ariel holds the door handle for dear life. The

taxi driver has floored the gas pedal again, and swerves violently left, into the lane of oncoming traffic, trying to accelerate past the slowing streetcar, but he sees another car coming straight at them and slams on the brakes and yanks the wheel to the right —

"That was close!" he yells in English, with what seems like glee, and pulls back behind the tram. As the oncoming car zooms past, its driver makes an obscene gesture. The taxi driver shrugs, as if this is just part of the job, to have other drivers furious at you.

The yellow streetcar comes to a full stop to disgorge passengers while others push aboard. Ariel looks past these people to a building's whitewashed wall, a broad stuccoed expanse to which posters are pasted, advertisements that all seem to be for American brands: a spectacular woman wearing preposterous clothing; screenshots of snark for a social-media app; an influencer hawking cosmetics. American culture, American commerce, American lies, everywhere.

Ariel asks to be let off on the far side of the square, where she can surveil her hotel before climbing out of the taxi. She pays particular attention to the lone men, taking careful inventory while crossing the square, then escaping the heat into the quiet of the hotel, dimly lit, cool tiles. She rides the small elevator, its gears audible, machinery that's hidden but not secret, not mysterious.

In her daily life at home, the only elevators she rides are at the hospital, with which she has an excess of unwelcome familiarity. Some people have never even been to the hospital, barely know where it is. Ariel wishes she were one of them, blissfully ignorant.

George had been born premature, and had spent five terrifying weeks in the NICU. It then took the boy years to catch up developmentally, his whole childhood defined by tests and treatments, doctors and hospitals, specialists and therapists — occupational, physical, speech. Her child was ten years old before Ariel could imagine him sleeping under someone else's roof, even his best friend's house down the road seemed too far, a one-minute drive, Ariel could run it in five minutes if she needed.

Her son was one of the reasons that Ariel felt like she'd been living on high alert, waiting for some bad thing to happen. Something else.

CHAPTER 8

Day 1. 4:27 p.m.

"Hello?" Ariel sees that the call is coming from the landline of her bookshop. She assumes it's a problem.

"Hey! It's Persephone."

"Hi P. What's wrong?"

"Wrong? Nothing. I'm calling to give you the weekend numbers, like you asked."

Ariel had dumped a flurry of last-minute instructions before she left the shop in the care of her employees, a ragtag bunch of part-time high-school kids and a couple of college girls home for the summer, plus full-time Persephone, whose real name is Ember.

"I *loathe* the name Ember." This is the name that's on the young woman's paychecks, her paperwork, her driver's license; she hasn't yet mustered the conviction to make the legal change. "It's not even a, like, *name*. My parents are idiots."

Persephone was probably right, at least about her mother. Just a couple of months ago, Ariel had seen her standing in front of a flabbergasted judge trying to justify her moving violation while wearing a WINE O'CLOCK T-shirt. This was a woman who'd gotten dressed knowing that she'd be a defendant in court.

"It's like they tried to name me Amber — which to begin with is a kinda stupid, semi-trashy stripper name — but, like, failed. They *misspelled* Amber."

"But it's a nice idea, isn't it?" Ariel asked. "An ember? It's a spark."

"No, actually. It's a hot sooty hunk that's left over after a fire has gone out. An ember is a dangerous piece of garbage."

Ariel didn't disagree, but it would be impolite to pile on, especially during the job interview, when Ariel and Persephone didn't yet know each other. She also didn't want to engage in a discussion about the young woman's chosen alternative.

"Per-se-pho-nee," she's constantly repeating slowly, clearly exasperated and perhaps surprised that more people aren't widely conversant in Greek mythology. "You know: queen of the underworld?"

"Per-what?" People ask this all the time, and Persephone inevitably rolls her eyes.

"Per-se-pho-*nee.*" She manages to suffuse that last syllable with her many disappointments, her frustrations. It's going to be a long hard life.

90

But who was Ariel to question someone else's fantasies of herself? Someone else's reinvention? Ariel doesn't begrudge anyone changing her name, trying to become someone other than what her parents chose. Ariel had done the same exact thing.

Her last half-day at the shop before heading to the airport was semi-frantic, spent mainly in the office-storeroom-breakroom in the basement, a low-ceilinged, windowless, claustrophobia-inducing space that had taken Ariel years to get comfortable in, with houseplants under grow lights, and book-promotion posters hammered into the walls.

She finally came upstairs after lunchtime, carrying a stack of heavy cookbooks to replenish the shelves. Persephone was behind the register, engrossed in a postapocalyptic fantasy novel, a genre that was somehow related to her oft-mentioned studies in grad school, that golden moment when everything was still possible, when her future looked so bright. But Persephone was beginning to suspect that it had been a false glow on the horizon, not the rising sun of a bright new day, just the remnants of a dying bonfire of oversold, overpriced, undervalued educational achievements that turn out to be almost meaningless on the job market, after twenty straight years of full-time schooling interspersed with hourly jobs in retail, fold-

91

ing shirts, punching buttons on cash registers.

This is why Ariel had hired the young woman. Not because of her encyclopedic knowledge of nearly everything, especially genre literature, which turned out to be a tremendous asset for bookselling, but because Ariel recognized the terrible weight of world-shattering disillusionment. She wanted to help ease it.

The bell on the back of the door tinkled. Persephone said "Welcome" automatically but cheerfully as a pair of women breezed in, leaving the door wide open despite the carefully hand-painted sign that pleaded, A/C IS ON! — PLEASE CLOSE DOOR — THANKS!

"Assholes," Ariel muttered, pushing the door closed with her hip.

The women seemed to be debating the merits of different safari destinations — "Well yes, *gorillas,* but, on the other hand, y'know, U*gan*da?" — and one of them said something Ariel didn't catch about flying commercial to Africa, and then suddenly there was silence. The women had stopped talking. The unnatural break made Ariel look over.

"Oh. My. *God.*" One of these women was staring at Ariel. "Laurel?"

When Ariel left the city, she didn't secede quietly, she rejected all of it loudly, and she burned the bridge — she blew it the fuck up — on her way out of town. For a while she kept in touch with a tiny handful of people; within months that dwindled to no one. Now a decade and a half later, one of the last of those friends was advancing on Ariel, mouth wide in amazement, arms wide in affection, adorned with a twenty-thousand-dollar handbag, and a massive engagement diamond stacked with diamond-encrusted wedding band, and a perfect manicure; you could see this woman's whole life in her hand décor.

This sort of encounter had nearly happened to Ariel a few times before. At the farmstand where a master-of-the-universe type climbed out of his tank of an SUV to peel a fifty from a money clip to buy corn; he accused Ariel of being her old self, but she denied it, and fled in her beat-up pickup. At the oyster bar where people can arrive by boat from pricier enclaves, an adventure in rusticating, and Ariel spotted that couple first — she's always on the lookout for such people, and they're not remotely thinking of her — and dodged any interaction completely.

Her town is not a place where rich people live, nor own weekend houses. There's some typical small-town prosperity — business owners, professionals, retired whatevers, you could tell by their S-Classes, their Rolexes, by the gaps between the thighs of the PTA wives, same as everywhere. But no celebrities, no mega-yachts, no private jets, no billionaires. No people like this woman here.

"It's been. *So.* Long. My *God!*"

Air-kisses on both cheeks. Ariel was still holding an armful of heavy books, couldn't really hug, tried to indicate so with a shrug. She glanced over to see if Persephone had witnessed this customer using her old name. Oh yes she had.

No one in this town kisses on both cheeks. Absolutely no one. Ariel had once done this as a matter of course, back when she was someone else, double-air-kissing her way through life. There are worse things.

"How *are* you?"

"I'm great, Tory. How are *you*?"

"Awesome!"

For a while Ariel used to see Tory Wasserman all the time, during those few years when Ariel Pryce had been named Laurel Turner. The two women were on the same circuits in the same neighborhood, the same private-club luncheons and black-tie benefits, the same exercise fads, trading in kickboxing for spinning for Pilates for yoga, swapping outfits and accessories and instructors, the rhythms of their days tapped out in beats of self-care, packs of women roving their neighborhood in taxis and town cars — this was before everyone was using Uber as a verb — between gym and studio and salon and school and the very occasional grocery store. In their households, most of the food was carried in through the service entrance by housekeepers.

Tory had once worked in fashion publicity, but quit when planning her wedding became a full-time occupation. That was also when Tory started employing a stylist to come over regularly to prepare her hair for the evening.

"I pay for three appointments per week, though sometimes I use only two, when I just need to, like, chill at home. To re-center. But I always pay for all three as a, like, retainer."

This was explained while nibbling at a thirty-four-dollar salad in a café attached to a museum. The other full-time homemakers around the table all nodded, agreeing that this was a terrific idea, jealous that they hadn't thought of it themselves, this point scored in the competitive sport of spending money, who can play more cleverly, more originally, more impressively — Bentley golf carts, Antarctic expeditions, Old Master oils, radiant floor heating. Trying to come ever closer to the perfect life, amazed and disappointed that it apparently can't be bought.

Tory was now looking around the bookshop, as if searching for evidence of Ariel's role here. Tory's phone was already open to a social-media app, she had obviously become a woman who's always ready to post, always performing, arching her eyebrows and fluffing her hair, exclaiming loudly and laughing louder, the never-ending ad campaign of herself, posing, scrolling, editing, posting, revising posts to comment and adore and wallow in validations — OMG U R SO PRETTY, I CAN'T EVEN — then reciprocating, all the while listening to Taylor Swift or Lizzo or maybe Adele, they're all advising the same thing: Love yourself, that's what really matters. But you knew that already, didn't you? Tory certainly did.

There was a time when Ariel had admired Tory's sort of impudence, this shameless self-affirmation, self-promotion. She'd been in awe of Tory, of her friend's willingness to be unattractive in her quest to be attractive. Ariel had never been able to do this, to be this. It was one of the things that had held her back from being a successful actor; it was something she hadn't liked about herself, before it became something she was proud of.

"Omigod, do you, like, *work* here?" Tory asked in a low, conspiratorial voice.

Ariel felt the urge to answer *I'm the owner,* but reconsidered. "Yes, I do work here."

Tory's face was filled with the unmistakable glee of someone else's misfortune. A *job.*

"That's so, um, *awesome.*" Tory spent thirty thousand dollars per year *on her hair.* "You remember my cousin Madison? We're both in East."

This meant that both Tory and Madison spent their summers in East Hampton.

"Do you live around here?" Tory asked. "Is this where you came when you left the city?"

Ariel answered with nothing more than a

smile. She didn't want to confirm or deny, she didn't want to explain, she didn't want to start apologizing for not returning Tory's calls, for dropping off the face of the earth. There had definitely been a time when Tory might have been the one person she'd have confided in, but Ariel had never explained the whole of her situation to any of her old friends, and she couldn't start here and now.

The door tinkled again to admit a square-jawed man wearing a golf shirt under a fleece vest breast-emblazoned with EXCALIBUR CAPITAL, a crimson HBS baseball cap, and a big gleaming wristwatch, making sure everyone could see in one glance who he was — mega-successful finance bro. It was ninety degrees out; the guy was really dedicated to that vest.

"Laurel, you remember my husband Slade?"

Of course Ariel did, Slade Wasserman was impossible to not remember, a platinum-level jackass who sprayed venom like a lawn sprinkler, drenching everything in his toxic masculinity.

"Hi Slade," Ariel said. Fifteen years ago, Ariel's first husband Bucky had been one of the early adopters of the zip-front-vest-over-dress-shirt look. Now it's practically a uniform for men across every sect of the capitalist religion.

"Oh, hey," he said, managing with his

intonation and body language to communicate his complete lack of interest in Ariel.
There was almost a beauty in it.

"Where are my babies?" Tory asked.

"They went to get ice cream."

"Ice cream." Tory looked at her watch,
which like Slade's was a gold monstrosity.
His and hers. "At four in the afternoon."

"What? There a problem, Babe?"

"It's *an hour* before their, like, dinnertime."

Slade shrugged, what does he give a shit.
Slade's core competency was the deployment
of financial assets, not the eating schedules of
children.

Ariel was now supposed to inquire after
Tory's kids, that would be the polite thing to
do. But she just couldn't bear it. She couldn't
ask what her old friend was up to, how she
happened to find herself here, so far from her
nexus of high-end summering. Ariel was
afraid that if she started asking questions,
she'd be obliged to answer some in return.

Madison hadn't even pretended to browse
for books before summoning Persephone to
the café counter.

"I'll do a decaf almond latte." Madison
ordered while using her phone's camera as a
mirror, angling her face this way and that.
Ariel remembered this woman, she never
stopped finding excuses to look at herself,
touching up lipstick, mascara, pouting into
mirrors, teasing her hair, this was a person

who would just bust out a hairbrush and start grooming not only whenever the opportunity presented itself, but inventing opportunities where none whatsoever existed, whenever she had a spare thirty seconds — in a car, or waiting to be seated at a restaurant, or at a cash register.

"I'm so sorry," Persephone said, "we don't have almond milk."

"Seriously?" Madison looked up from admiring herself. Ariel felt herself cringe; she used to order the same exact thing, and she'd have been the same exact disappointed.

Tory rushed over. "Oh my God, how cute is this?" It was a hand-tinted greeting card, a predictably nautical scene.

"*So* cute!"

The shop did a brisk business in banal.

"Would you prefer whole or skim milk?"

"*Cow?*" Madison was appalled. This was a woman with an alligator-skin handbag dangling in the crook of her arm.

Ariel felt as if she were observing a different species, in some simulacrum of its natural habitat — like the zoo, or the dioramas at the Museum of Natural History. The little brass plaque would read HOMO OBSCENICUS, NORTH AMERICA, C. 21ST CENTURY. And yet there was no denying it: Ariel had been one of these beasts.

She responded to Tory's "Let's do lunch!" with "Absolutely," even though she had no intention whatsoever. Ariel was no longer a member of the tribe, and everyone knew it, but this was still what you said.

"It's so good to see you," Tory said. "*So* good."

"You too," Ariel agreed, and she was surprised to find that she was telling the truth. It was good to see an old friend; she felt the impulse to actually follow up; she knew she wouldn't.

The Wassermans and their Madison side-kick exited in a flurry of more air-kisses and high-pitched laughter, leaving behind a lingering miasma of Hermès and Botox and impending gentrification. There had been other signs of change in the village, including the tattooed Brooklynite who'd inquired about buying the bookshop, which at first seemed ludicrous to Ariel, then intriguing. Things were changing, and Ariel was not sure that she wanted to be a part of what's next. First it had been the homesteaders who were fed up with the rat race, talking about composting and mulch, then the hipsters, and next thing you know it'll be the black–Range Rover crowd. She used to be one of those too.

"I know a lot of people are showing up here, buying land, talking about organic this, heirloom whatever." This is what Ariel had said a dozen years ago, in her first conversation with Pedro. He'd farmed these same fields for the previous landowner, potatoes plus some corn and tomatoes and Brussels sprouts.

Pedro had nodded, straw hat in hand. "Yes Miss." His rent covered the taxes but not much more. Nobody was getting rich farming eighty acres here.

At that point in her life Ariel had given up on a great many of her ideals. They hadn't done her any damn good. She had plenty of battles to fight, and organic farming wasn't the hill she'd die on.

"Not me," she'd said. "Do whatever you need to do."

Ariel looks out the hotel room's window, surveying the street and the square for the guy who was following her. She doesn't see him.

"Persephone, was anyone strange in the shop this weekend?"

"Strange? How do you mean?"

"Anyone looking for me? Or asking after me?"

"No, I don't think so. Why?"

"If anyone does, please make a note of it, and let me know."

"What do you mean, make a note?"

"Write down the day and time, and what the person looks like and says."

"Does this have something to do with those women who came into the shop on Friday?"

"What? No."

"Then are you going to tell me what this *is* about?"

"P., I'm sorry, but can you just do this for me, please? I don't have time to explain now."

Persephone is tremendously curious, constantly asking questions, thinking that she's entitled to answers. Ariel doesn't really blame her. Persephone had been raised in a post-privacy era when there were no longer any boundaries, even when it came to other people's skeletons; perhaps especially then. Ariel regularly catches the young woman looking at documents that don't concern her, asking questions that aren't her business. At first this bothered Ariel, but she can't do anything about anyone's fundamental character. So instead Ariel accepts that Persephone will pry, and controls the things that can be found.

For nearly everything else, Ariel keeps a safe under the desk. She doesn't make any attempt to hide the safe. If anyone ever breaks into the shop looking for valuables, she doesn't want them ransacking the whole goddamned place. And if the thieves are able to actually crack a safe, hiding it isn't going to help. Anyone who can crack a safe won't be looking for the day's cash receipts.

Ariel is prepared for that too.

In the midst of the final Friday-afternoon

flurry of instructions and questions and small-scale panics about the long holiday weekend ahead, Ariel's eye was drawn to the shop window, beyond which a giant pickup was suffering through the final throes of parallel parking. In the past few years, this steroidal type of truck had become the most popular vehicle in town. It seems like every aggressive tailgater, every obnoxious cut-offer, every impatient red-light jumper is now behind the wheel of one of these monsters, looming up behind her, headlights in her eyes, menacing everyone on the road with their suspension lifts and oversize wheels and aftermarket mufflers, their POWER STROKE stenciling on the side. What stroke was being suggested, to whom, and why?

Everything about this vehicle looked like a schoolyard bully, even the bumper stickers — the glowering visage of the New England Patriots, the implicit challenge of BLUE LIVES MATTER, the bizarre armed eagle of the NRA, the crossed sticks of the travel-club lacrosse team for which the driver, Ariel knew, was a coach. He was also a volunteer fireman, and the treasurer of a rod and gun club. This man was, as people say, active in the community. He gave back. He was a so-called patriot, you knew it because he said so, it was even his favorite football team.

You can see the culture war right there, bumpers versus bumpers, on any road in

America.

He lumbered out of the driver's seat, a human embodiment of his oversize truck, wearing a tremendous tent of a T-shirt and basketball shorts that draped below his knees and plastic slides, dressed head-to-toe for a locker room despite being a person who obviously didn't engage in rigorous physical activity. Athletic gear was the wrong label for this category of attire; unathletic gear. He had a long scar across his cheek, and an unkempt beard he'd grown to try to hide it. Ariel knew that he'd refused to go to the ER, unwilling to explain the source of the gash. He'd rather have a scar. Like any scar, a perpetual reminder of something that had gone wrong.

Ariel's bumpers are unadorned.

His eyes met Ariel's across the divide of the shop window, of the street; across so many divides. Ariel would not acknowledge him — no smile, no nod, nothing other than an intense glare of ill will.

He walked away, into what summer people call the wine shop but locals call the liquor store. He had never, not once, stepped into the bookshop.

"You need anything before I go?" Ariel asked Persephone.

"Nope. Have an awesome vacay."

The girl sounded genuine, though it was always hard to tell. Her generation's default was irony, with equivocation not far behind;

nearly every sentiment was mitigated by *kinda* or *sorta,* a constant hedging against any perceived excess of earnestness.

"Thanks," Ariel said. "I'll try." It had been a long time since she'd traveled for vacation. In those first few years after George was born, she'd been terrified of traveling. With an infant, with a baby, a toddler — with any version of preschool-aged child — the meltdowns, the unpredictable sleep, the anxiety, there were so many potential downsides. Plus with George's health problems, Ariel never wanted him to be too far from his doctors, from the well-trod path of admitting or ER to specialist in the small-town hospital where everyone knew her, knew her son. It was a strange sort of comfort level she had with the hospital: one she wished she didn't have.

And the dog — which later became plural — those big eyes staring up at her: What do you mean, you're leaving? Why would you do that?

Plus the eternal concerns of living in an old house on a desolate country road, you never know when the furnace is going to fail, the roof is going to leak, a pipe burst, and no one will notice until the house is wrecked. Hurricanes, snowstorms, vole infestations, downed power lines, the place is never safe. Plus the bookstore-café, which confronts not only all the same potential physical disasters but also the smorgasbord of small-business issues — the absent or disgruntled or untrust-worthy employees, the health-code inspections, permit renewals, delivery delays, payroll and accounting chores, customer-service disagreements, tax bills and sales calls and inventory-management-software webinars.

It takes no small effort to leave behind this whole life, if only for a couple of days, her kid and her house and her shop and her farm and even her crappy old truck baking in the hot sun of long-term airport parking, her borderline-incompetent mother housesitting. Dozens of different negative consequences for Ariel to worry about.

But in all those years of all that worry, never until now has she confronted this particular nightmare: Her husband has gone missing in a foreign country.

CHAPTER 9

Day 1. 5:58 p.m.

Knock knock.

Ariel feels her body seize. What now?

"Who is it?"

"Senhora Wright? It is Duarte from reception."

Ariel opens the door.

"Yes?"

"My apologies for intruding. But I think you are wanting to know."

"Yes? What?"

"We are finding something."

Do hearts actually skip a beat? Ariel's feels like it does.

"We are calling and again calling, but it is only your husband's telephone number that we are knowing, not yours. And your husband, he is not —"

"What is it? What did you find?"

"Here." The young man fishes in his pocket, removes a piece of paper. "Leonor, she is cleaning your room, and she is finding this under the bed —"

Nicole Griffiths has just begun packing up for the day when she notices Saxby Barnes in her doorway again, waiting to be noticed.

"Hey Barnes." She's not going to ask why he's here. Whatever he wants, he's going to need to do the asking.

"So did you find that gentleman's phone?"

"Yes."

Griffiths is quitting out of her applications one by one, careful as always to make sure that every program closes. These days you never know what's going to turn out to be an opening for a backdoor attack. Hackers have gotten awfully clever about sneaking their way into other people's privacy.

"Anything to share with me?"

"Not yet." She locks her desk, stands.

"Where was the phone?"

Griffiths glances at her watch. "Listen, Barnes, I gotta run."

She needs to get home, shower, change, and drive downtown for her date with Pietro, and she doesn't want to be late.

"But you'll let me know what you find?" Barnes asks.

Griffiths doesn't want to actively lie to her half-colleague, which would be bad form. But whatever the problem is with the missing businessman, Saxby Barnes is probably not going to be part of the solution. Especially if this turns out to be in any way related to national security. Which is highly doubtful, but not impossible. It's never impossible. That's why Griffiths is willing to be involved in what at first blush looks like a matter of a common crime, or an accident, or a marital misunderstanding. Barnes will be more than welcome to untangle any of those messes.

Griffiths smiles. It's her tightest, coldest, most insincere smile, but it's more than nothing. She'll leave it up to Barnes to try to figure out what it means, confident that he'll get it wrong.

"Look."

Ariel is standing over the table where the detectives are seated in front of bowls of stew. Ariel has barely eaten a bite in — what? — twenty hours. She's starving.

"Please," the woman Santos says, indicating an empty chair.

When Ariel rang Detective Moniz a few minutes ago, he told her where to find them, after a lengthy pause. "It is no trouble," he said, sounding like he meant the opposite.

Now he reads the note. "This is your husband's handwriting?"

"Yes."

Santos snatches the paper from Moniz's hand, and he throws her a hostile glance, then turns back to Ariel. "You are sure?"

She's not. Ariel and John don't exchange a lot of handwriting.

"Actually, no, I'm not sure. But I think so. A chambermaid found the note under our bed when she was making up the room. I think John must have placed it next to me while I was sleeping, but then maybe I flung aside the sheets."

Moniz notices Ariel glance at his food, and pushes the bread basket toward her. "Can we offer you something, senhora? Have you eaten?"

Ariel shakes her head, though it's not entirely clear to her which question she's declining. Moniz decides it was the latter. He looks over his shoulder, finds the waiter's eyes, then points down at the stew, makes a circular motion, points at Ariel. The waiter nods, says something through the pass to a spectacularly mustachioed cook.

Six o'clock is not really dinnertime in Lisbon; there are just a couple of other customers in this homey restaurant, and one waiter. Ariel can feel all these eyes on her, this woman who strode directly to the detectives' table.

"So you can see now, can't you? John left our room, and meant to return, but didn't."

"Yes," Moniz agrees, "that seems to be true." He glances back down at the note, just a couple of lines: GONE FOR WALK. BACK 7:30 FOR B'FAST. LOVE YOU.

"This is evidence, isn't it?" Ariel leans forward. "This, plus the security footage."

"Well, I do not —"

"Together these are proof that something bad has happened to John."

The waiter deposits a steaming bowl in front of Ariel, clams and greens and potatoes and chunks of some meat or another. Ariel immediately burns her tongue.

"If this was truly written by your husband? Then yes, it is evidence of something. But it is evidence that he left your hotel of his own will."

"And he meant to return. At seven-thirty. Which he *did not do.*"

The three of them eat for a minute. Ariel watches Moniz's arm piston up and down to shovel in fresh bites even while he's still chewing the previous, his mouth never closing completely. He licks his lips and absentmindedly scratches his beard.

Ariel pushes her bowl aside. "But *when* would you check? How long does my husband need to be missing before you'll believe me?"

"If you prefer," Moniz says, "we can keep this paper, and if it does turn out that your husband is truly missing, we can examine for fingerprints. Is that what you prefer?"

He makes an uncommitted napkin swipe at his beard, which he doesn't quite rid of bread crumbs. He meets Ariel's eye, not shying away from her, from her misery.

Ariel has sympathy for these cops; she doesn't enjoy antagonizing them, and she can't afford to alienate any allies; she comes across precious few.

Moniz retrieves his notepad and pen, stares at the blank paper. Perhaps he's formulating his questions, or maybe translating them into English, scouring his memory for vocabulary, verb conjugations. It can't be easy to do this job in a language that's not your first. Just figuring out the correct forms of politeness, the apologies, it must be exhausting.

"Are you ever before visiting Lisboa, senhora?"

"No."

"But your husband is, yes? He has friends here?"

"Friends? Not that I know of. Acquaintances, maybe. Through work."

"Do you know any of their names?"

"I'm sorry," she says for the umpteenth time. She has spent so much time apologizing to dubious men for their doubts.

"He is not speaking to anyone while you are here? Anyone at all?"

"Well, just one woman."

It was late that Saturday afternoon, a time of day when all of Lisbon was gathering under umbrellas in cafés. Ariel ordered what everyone seemed to be having, an unlikely concoction made with white port, a spirit that

Ariel hadn't even known existed, and now the port spritz was her absolute favorite drink, sweet and delicious and barely alcoholic, it went down like a soda, and she was trying to decide whether it would be reckless to order a second —

"Luigi!"

A young woman was suddenly beside their table, smiling down with perfect white teeth between full, red-painted lips, deep dimples, a glorious Afro, flawless glowing skin. Ariel has been surprised by the broad prevalence of Brazilian people, and the influence of Brazilian culture, here in Lisbon, exhibiting a sort of reverse colonialism that she found heartwarming, and hopeful.

"*Olá!*" this spectacular-looking woman said to Ariel's stunned-looking husband.

"Luigi?" John pointed at himself. "Me? I am sorry, but no."

The woman cocked her head, furrowed her brow. This was not a woman whom men denied knowing; being rebuffed was not familiar to her.

"My name is John," he said. "Not Luigi. This is my wife, Ariel."

This woman opened her mouth to argue, then reconsidered, and reconstructed her dazzling smile. God, she was an amazing-looking human, clad in a loose little nothing of a dress.

"Ah," she said, with an adorable shrug.

113

"Desculpe."

She sauntered back to her table, where it looked as if she explained the interaction to her companion, another beautiful young woman wearing another slip of a dress. She too glanced at John, then at Ariel, and met her eye before turning back to the animated storyteller, and there was some acknowledgment in that look, an understanding — I know that you know what we know.

Both women threw back their heads in carefree laughter, they were young and beautiful, the center of attention, of attraction, it was a sunny day, nothing could be better. They took sips of their spritzes to prove it, how fun their lives were, how little they cared about John. Ariel knew that it's not always as fun as it looks. There's such a thing as being problematically good-looking.

Ariel was struck with a certainty: This woman and John had shared a one-night stand, but he'd lied to her about his name. Now he was back in Lisbon with Ariel, running into this old fling, and on the spur of the moment he rashly decided to pretend he'd never met her.

"She's amazing," Ariel said.

"Is she?" John stared down at the menu, avoiding Ariel's gaze, avoiding this conversation.

"Oh please. Even I wouldn't kick her out of bed."

114

John laughed, but didn't say anything.

"It's okay if you know her," Ariel said. "If something happened. You know that, right?"

"Honestly," he said, "I've never met her."

Ariel's head was buzzing from the alcohol, from the heat and the jet lag, from the proximity to such a ludicrously sexy person. Ariel knew that it didn't make sense, but there was no doubt about it: She was a little bit jealous. Also a little bit aroused. Maybe more than a little.

What a bitch, Barnes thinks. What a stuck-up, ungrateful, condescending *bitch.* As soon as he returns to his little office, he makes another call, which is answered promptly with "Hello Barnes."

"Mr. Wagstaff! How is life treating you to-day?"

"Just fine," the reporter says. "What can I do for you?"

Saxby Barnes looks at the world in starkly transactional terms: He does things for other people so that they will do things for him. Every bit of information he comes across, every minute of work he does, is of value to someone else, and he's intent on getting something in return. Not immediately, but eventually.

"Mr. Wagstaff, I find myself in possession of some information you might want to look into."

■ ■ ■ ■

"Yesterday afternoon, at a café. There was a woman."

"Oh?" Moniz's pen finds the next blank line on his paper.

"She thought she knew my husband, but she was mistaken."

"Which café was this, please? Do you remember?"

"Not the name, but it was near that church that has no roof? Not far from here."

"O Convento do Carmo?"

"Yes, that's it. There's a square with a café, maybe two."

"Yes, I know the place. And there was nothing else, with this woman?"

"No, just that: She thought she knew John, he said sorry but no, she walked away."

Ariel notices that Moniz has splashed some dinner sauce on the lapel of his jacket, to supplement the earlier breakfast stain on his tie, and some lunch on his shirt. His sparse hair, neatly combed earlier, is now flying off in untamed directions. She can detect a whiff of body odor. The day has progressively uncivilized him. Maybe he devolves the same way every day, starts afresh each morning. Ariel wonders how much of his schlubbiness is a put-on, how much genuine. Or if there's any meaningful difference.

"When is the last time he is visiting Lisboa?"

"A couple of months ago."

"Before that, how many times is he here?"

"Just one other that I'm aware of, but I've known him only a year."

"One year?" It's not quite suspicion in Moniz's eyes, but it's something. Ariel knows how all this must look to him. Hell, she knows how it looks to her: a short, rash courtship; a couple who don't really know each other; a disappearance that could be almost anything, or nothing.

Moniz is wavering about whether to pursue his next line of inquiry. Ariel can see when he makes the choice. Here it comes, she thinks.

"How well do you know your husband?"

CHAPTER 10

Day 1. 6:33 p.m.
Ariel makes a helpless face, what do you want from me? She turns to Santos, who remains unmoved.

"I admit," Ariel says, "that I haven't known my husband a very long time. But long enough."

Moniz leaves his pen just above the surface of the paper for a long pause. Then he looks up at Ariel and smiles indulgently, not a smile of humor, not of joy, but of pity. He doesn't want to say what he must say next.

"Senhora, I am sorry, I must ask a question that is perhaps uncomfortable."

Ariel knows that a cop might imagine a lot of explanations for John's disappearance, and many of them would be at least vaguely accusatory — accusatory of John, of Ariel, accusatory of both of them. These theories would not be very palatable for this policeman to say aloud, to her. It's a bitter taste, but Moniz has no choice. Ariel can see this

118

whole debate as it crosses his face.

"Does your husband use drugs?"

"No," Ariel answers too quickly, aware that she's protesting too much. "No," she repeats, softer and more rational sounding, as if she'd given the question a second, more serious consideration, then came to the same fully reasoned conclusion.

"Here in Portugal, all recreational drugs are, how do you say, de-, ah, illegalized . . . ?"

"Decriminalized."

"Yes. This law, it is changing a number of years ago. Marijuana, *cocaína, heroína* . . . their use is not against the law anymore. This is a choice we are making to fight the problems of addiction. Problems of disease, of crime, of poverty, I am sure you are familiar, in America."

"Okay."

"One of the side effects of this change is that Lisboa is being a destination for people who are wanting to enjoy drugs. As with Amsterdam, you understand? People are coming here for that reason."

"No." Ariel shakes her head. "Not John."

"It is true that using the drugs is no longer a criminal act, but they still can be dangerous. Unhealthy. And the people who are selling the drugs, these people are not the most nice of people. And some of the people who are using the drugs, they too are not nice. The drug lifestyle, it is not criminal anymore,

119

but it is still not nice. Still not safe. Do you understand?"

"That has nothing to do with John. He doesn't use drugs."

"Is it possible that he did, in his past?"

Ariel doesn't have a quick answer. She doesn't, in truth, have any answer. She knows only what John has chosen to share with her. By the time they'd met, he'd already lived half a lifetime, decades when he could've been doing anything, anywhere.

But that's true of everyone, isn't it? Pasts can be reinvented.

After their first meeting, Ariel had investigated John cursorily, the way you do these days, scouring the web, searching social media, clicking around. She hadn't found much. Then when he became a more interesting proposition, she made a more rigorous attempt — anonymous calls, email queries using aliases. Ariel was prone to moments of paranoia, mostly when she was alone, lying in bed late at night. Especially when she'd been reading one of her crime novels; so many are about psychopathic men, pretending to be normal, who turn out to be doing unspeakable things to women.

In the mornings, Ariel recognized that most of her suspicions about John were preposterous. But not all.

She eventually admitted that her heart

120

wasn't really in it: She didn't want to find anything wrong with John, didn't want to find any lies, any deceptions, misrepresentations. This lack of impartiality was compromising the whole effort. So she hired a PI to do the parts of an investigation that she couldn't, as well as those that she simply wouldn't.

The investigator found out where John grew up, where he went to high school and college, his ROTC and military service, his jobs and his homes, his dead parents and his older sister who lived on another continent. All the basic information that can be found in databases, verifiable matters of fact, references checked with HR departments and registrars and landlords.

But that may not have been everything. It's hard to search for sex-tourism jaunts to Thailand, or coke-and-callgirl weekend binges, or a Ritalin-fueled adolescence or meth habit or online gambling addiction, an on-and-off relationship with crack, freebasing, child pornography, domestic violence, sexual assault. Not unless these activities make their way into the legal system, and almost none do. These things are almost impossible to find unless you know precisely what you're looking for, and where to look, and when.

The PI did find a few things that concerned Ariel, but not many, and they didn't concern her that much.

■ ■ ■ ■

She used to believe it was possible to know everything about another person, at least everything important. She'd said yes to a previous marriage proposal from a man she'd known for a couple of years, ended up living with him for a couple more — plenty of time — before she discovered that she'd never really known him at all, not the important parts. Maybe she doesn't know this new man either.

We tell ourselves stories about each other, about ourselves too, our pasts. We construct our narratives, we start with the big picture and then add details one by one, like building a house, the foundation and the framing and the roof and eventually you're installing doorknobs and light fixtures and banister newels, an entire home where there used to be nothing at all, something that looks like it's been there forever, even though it's a brand-new fabrication.

We can do the same thing for ourselves. Ariel had. Who's to say John hadn't? Maybe this cop is right: Maybe she doesn't know her husband at all.

"Because sometimes," Moniz continues, "this is what can happen with an old habit that perhaps a man is stopping for health reasons, or legal reasons, or financial reasons. Later in his life, he comes to a place such as Lisboa, where the health and law and finances of the drugs are different, and here he thinks, oh, this is so much safer, so much cheaper, I can try just a little. And then . . ."

Moniz sweeps open his hand, there it is: a bender.

"I understand what you're saying." Ariel is trying to not be offended by this suggestion, she knows she shouldn't be, but somehow she is. Taking offense is not a rational choice. "But that's not what's going on here."

The cop nods; it's not his job to convince her. "Is it possible — this also is not a very pleasant question, I am sorry, but I must ask, I hope you are understanding . . ."

"Yes, go ahead."

"Is it possible that your husband is right now with someone else?"

Ariel cocks her head.

"Another woman?" Moniz clarifies.

She's growing frustrated with this line of questioning, even though it's expected, maybe inevitable. Just as it's inevitable that she'll object this way — John wouldn't do that, he's not a cheater, not an addict, not a sociopath. How much of this does she need to actually say aloud?

"Listen," she says, looking from Moniz to Santos and back again. "John practically *begged* me to come on this trip with him. If

123

he was going to come here to be with another woman, or to do drugs, why would he beg his wife to come along with him? *Why?*"

"That is a very good question. Do you have any ideas?"

"Because *that's not what's happening.*"

Santos chimes in: "Is it possible that he is not coming to Lisboa with bad intentions but these things are happening anyway? Life is not always as we intend."

That's for damn sure.

"Listen," Ariel says again, trying to sound levelheaded. "I understand your suspicions: He's with another woman, he's doing drugs, he's scamming me. I can see why those might look like possibilities; I can understand why you'd need to pursue those theories. But I'm telling you, they're all *wrong.* So what I'm asking is: What's it going to take before you start believing me?"

Moniz glances around, looking uneasy. Ariel realizes that she has become loud. What some people might call shrill.

"Please, senhora, contain your voice."

"But *goddamn it,* why don't you believe me?"

"Have we said that we do not believe you? No, we have not."

"Well then why don't you *do* something?"

Ariel is hotheaded, always has been, even as a little kid. Her parents loved telling stories about young Ariel's hair-trigger disproportionate responses to missing toys, canceled parties, bad food. But short-tempered is very different from hysterical. Men often try to reframe temper as hysteria, to recast righteousness as overreaction, as hypersensitivity, as irrationality.

So this is the response Ariel has seen before, the response she expects, this indulgent look, dismissive, saying something like this: "What is it that you want for us to do, senhora?"

It's the tone that a man uses when he thinks he's being the reasonable one. A tone that transcends generations, cultures, languages. The universal tone of condescension.

Moniz leans forward. "Please, I am asking: What is it that you think the police can do for you, now? When your husband left your hotel safely this very morning, when there is no evidence of anything wrong at all? The evidence that you bring" — Moniz points at the note — "is, if anything, evidence that your husband is unharmed, not in any danger, not connected to any crime."

"You can trace the location of his phone."

Moniz leans back quickly, away from this suggestion.

"You can demand it from the mobile provider." Ariel glances between Moniz and Santos.

Santos is the one who answers. "Only with a warrant. A judge is not issuing a warrant because of these evidences that you are bringing."

"Your intelligence service, then. Portugal has an intelligence service, right?"

"Of course," Moniz answers. "This was once the center of the espionage world, did you know that? During the Second World War. More spies here in Portugal than anywhere else."

Who gives a damn?

"So they can do this," Ariel says. "They can — whatever it's called, *triangulate* the location of John's phone."

"Yes, they can. But they are not unless there is evidence that this is a matter of international intelligence. Is there any such evidence?"

Ariel knows she doesn't have a compelling answer, and that's when it all falls apart, her lower lip quivering, her chin too, then the whole bottom of her face.

"I don't know," she blubbers through sobs. She can feel the few other customers watching this scene, and the staff pitying the cops — what are they going to do with this woman? Awfully glad it's not their responsibility. If there's one thing Ariel is sure of, it's that no one wants to deal with a hysterical woman.

CHAPTER 11

Day 1. 6:47 p.m.

Ariel storms out of the restaurant onto the busy street, teeming with life, loud with the music that's everywhere in Lisbon, Brazilian sertanejo and Puerto Rican reggaeton, Euro pop and American rock and the traditional fado, music is spilling out of shops and cafés, pubs and clubs, street performers in every little plaza in front of every little church. She can't imagine what would happen if a rock band set up on the lawn of her Main Street's Episcopalian Church on a Monday afternoon.

Directly in front of the restaurant, the sidewalk is packed with a dense mass of what seems like business colleagues, a dozen people who'd already begun their evening with cocktails elsewhere, spirits high, back-slapping and joke telling and loud laughing, on their way to a big —

Of course.

"Excuse me," she says, turning on her heel. "Excuse me," elbowing past this group, back

127

to the door, inside to the cops who are still at their table along the far wall, relaxing with cake and espresso and dubious looks at the American woman who simply will not quit.

"There must be a dinner reservation," Ariel announces. "For tomorrow night."

Both cops are chewing.

"I don't know the name of the restaurant," she continues. "But I do know that it's walking distance from the hotel, and that it's a place requiring me to wear a fancy dress, and that it's for six or eight people, and that it's at nine o'clock. That's a lot of information."

Moniz swallows.

"So you can call around to all the fancy restaurants near my hotel. Ask for the reservation names for large parties tomorrow at nine. Then call those customers. How many can there be?"

The cops still don't say anything.

"One of them will be my husband's client."

Santos nods; Ariel is right, there's no denying it.

"Yes," Santos says. "We are doing this."

"Oh God thank you. *Thank you.* When?"

"Right now."

Men had called her touchy. They'd called her prickly, combative, hypersensitive. A stuck-up bitch, a cocktease, a cunt. They'd raised their hands as if to hit her, and she'd stared right back: Go ahead, asshole.

128

Surely it wasn't that bad, people said. Even some women said it, and not just her mother that one horrid time, that relationship-wrecking moment.

Part of it, Ariel knew, was that she'd led a life that looked privileged, you could tell by her hair, by her skin, her elocution, her diplomas, by the stamps in her old passports. Her whole life had looked enviable, safe, as if it were always broad daylight in a big crowd with plenty of witnesses, even when it was late night, all alone. Bad things did not happen to someone like Ariel, not in America; everyone believed that, even people who knew the contrary. America was nothing if not cognitively dissonant. That's the real hysteria, the national pretense that we're not what we empirically are.

Ariel's father, her mother, her husband, her friends, the police years ago, and these police now: her whole life. She has been silenced by operant conditioning, by receiving the same response again and again, like an electro-shocked lab rat, or a beaten dog. A disbelieved woman.

The first time: She was thirteen years old, an eighth-grader, and that tenth-grade Mackenzie kid groped her in the pantry when she was looking for marshmallows for backyard s'mores.

"*Brett* Mackenzie?" Ariel's mom had asked,

129

incredulous, shaking her head. "Are you sure, Honey? I've known that boy his whole life. He's a good boy."

Ariel marched away.

The second time: She was sixteen, watching a horror flick in Brittany's basement rec room, everyone blitzed on convenience-store beer. This was the summer between junior and senior years, that season of studying for the SAT, writing college-application essays, working internships, last-ditch efforts to look like serious citizens while getting plastered on Saturday nights to relieve the stress.

Liz was passed out in one of those big leather chairs, and Jared slunk out of the room to call Francesca, and all of a sudden Don was on top of her, smothering her.

"No," Ariel said, but he ignored her. She tried to push him off, but failed.

"Stop," she said. She clamped her legs together. He pushed them apart.

"I'll scream," she warned.

"No you won't," Don said. She could feel his fingers trying to open her pants. "You don't want to wake Liz, do you?" Then an idea dawned on him. "Or do you?"

That's when she gathered her strength, and squirmed to the side just enough to free her leg just enough to slam her knee just hard enough into his groin to make him shift just enough for her to just wriggle out from under

130

him. Just enough, just enough, just enough —

Ariel jumped out of the chair. She thought about fleeing, or shaking Liz awake, or smacking Don in the face. But he was face-planted on the chair, unmoving. Unconscious? No, there was a sound coming out of him, maybe sobbing. Had she really hurt him that bad? She hadn't thought she'd hurt him at all.

But no, Don was not crying. He was laughing. He rolled over, sporting a big drunken grin. "That was funny."

That was funny? "Are you serious?" she asked.

He didn't seem to understand what she was asking. He was concentrating on trying to re-button his jeans, and failing almost entirely. "You want something-a drink?" he asked, without looking at her.

She was stunned, and too drunk herself to trust her brain completely. She was already losing confidence in her understanding of the past minute.

"No?" He gave up on his pants, just one button closed, in the wrong spot. Button flies are a bad choice for drunk people. "I'm-a get a beer."

The next day, Ariel told her mother. Elaine was at the kitchen island, having a lunch of hot water with lemon, reading the Styles section. Though maybe reading wasn't really

131

what Elaine was doing; she was scrutinizing photos of parties and weddings.

"You're telling me that Don tried to rape you." She didn't even bother to close the newspaper, peering over her reading glasses at Ariel, taking her in, the unmistakable look of a hungover teenager who'd emerged from bed at the crack of noon, having made at least one bad choice last night. They come in clusters. "Don Williamson."

"Well, he didn't get that far. But that was definitely the direction he was heading, yes."

"How did that happen?"

"How? I just told you. Which part is confusing?"

"I mean, how did it get that far?"

Ariel was at first too stunned to respond.

"Did you lead him on?"

"What the fuck do you mean, *lead him on*?"

"Don't curse at me, young lady, I won't stand for it."

As a teenager Ariel had been lavish with profanities, largely because neither of her parents cursed, ever. Years later, she realized that women can either curse freely or live on Park Avenue, but not both. Now in her life's second act, swearing freely is one of the things she appreciates about being away from the strict rules of New York society. Which were not that different from the rules where she grew up, her parents' rules. They were just enforced more stringently.

132

"But why don't you believe me?"

"It's not that I don't *believe* you, Sweetheart. But are you *sure* that's what happened? Or is it possible that this is a misunderstanding?"

Ariel's mouth was hanging open. She and
her mom were each in disbelief about the
other. Ariel turned and took a step away.

"Where do you think you're going?"

"Daddy."

Her mom sighed heavily. "Oh Honey."

Ariel turned back. "What does that mean?"

"Your father is not going to want to hear
something like this."

"Well I fucking hope not."

This time Elaine ignored the profanity. She
walked away from her newspaper, from the
shallow entertainment of envying other
people's parties, and put her arms around
her daughter.

"That's not what I mean. Your father, he's
not a . . . modern man. And Eric Williamson
is one of his closest friends. You know this,
right?"

"And?"

"And so I don't think you're going to get
the response you're looking for."

In hindsight, Ariel is amazed at how naïve
she'd been. Now that she herself is a parent,
she tries to remind herself: Kids can begin to
look mature, and act mature, years before
they know a damn thing about how the

133

grown-up world works.

Her dad's study was filled with books and journals and big sheafs of serious-looking reports, which she'd once thought signified that he was a scholar, some sort of intellectual. Eventually she realized that it was all just about making money.

He put down his heavy glass carefully in the middle of the coaster. He took his whiskey on the rocks, one big ice cube. He had a special tray to make these big square cubes.

"I'm very sorry to hear this," he finally said, continuing to stare down into his amber liquid, away from his daughter. She wondered if this was his first drink or second, before lunch on a summer Sunday. "What is it you want to do?"

"I don't know. What do you think?"

"I guess you could confront the boy."

The import of this phrasing hit her like a freight train. Not just the dubiousness of *I guess*, but more important the second-person singular: *you*. Not *we*.

"But what would that accomplish?" he asked. "In the end?"

Ariel realized that no matter how long they discussed this — five minutes, ten, two hours — the conclusion was foregone.

"Do you believe me, Daddy?"

"Of course *I* believe you, Darling. But I'm your father. Other people?" He pushed his lips together, shook his head. "Try to imagine

134

how — *exactly* how — this would play out, conversation by conversation."

Ariel could barely listen to it, his litany of reasons, his excuses, his relationship with Don's dad, the town, the cousins, the gossip . . .

Now she fully understood her mom's warning. Elaine knew her husband, and accepted the whole of him, even the worst parts, even the parts she must have loathed. Much later, this turned out to be exactly what Ariel refused to do, exactly the type of wife she refused to be. Eventually.

"Of course it's entirely up to you, Darling, and I'll support whatever decision you make. But my advice?"

He set his empty glass down on the coaster — theirs was a coaster-laden household, matching sets in every room, even bedrooms — and finally looked her in the eye.

"Forget that the whole thing ever happened."

Nobody wants to acknowledge that their dad is an asshole. So despite compelling evidence for years, Ariel had refused, until she had no choice, until it was undeniable, until this moment. She was sixteen years old.

"Just move on."

The third time: She was a struggling actor, trying to make it in New York, auditions and workshops and waitressing and babysitting, hand-to-mouth month-to-month. She'd been doing this for six years; she was running out of time.

It was during business hours, in a business office in TriBeCa, and she was there for a business meeting. There was no alcohol, no drugs. No history, no prior relationship, no particular reason. She'd done everything right, but still he was saying, "You understand" — unbuckling his belt — "that I can make a lot of things happen for you."

That's when she realized that there was no such thing as doing everything right. That was also the moment she gave up on her acting career. She'd wanted it for such a long time, but she didn't want it this bad; she was not willing to do whatever it took, not if this was what it took. She got the hell out of that room, got the hell out of that life.

She'd wanted to be an actor because she'd thought it would be about art, and creativity. But in her experience it was about only beauty, except when it was about sex.

"What are you going to do now?" her roommate asked.

Ariel didn't want a career that revolved around beauty and sex. Surely there were other options?

"I don't know," she said. "I guess I'll get a real job."

She'd learned that she wouldn't be believed,

136

not even by her own parents. She'd learned that she should never be drunk, not even with her close friends. She'd learned that she should never again believe that any boy — any man — was completely trustworthy. She'd learned that there was nothing she could do, no lifetime of lessons she could learn: It was going to happen any goddamned way.

And it did.

"What do you think?" António Moniz removes a few bills from his wallet. It's his turn to pay for dinner.

Santos takes her final sip of espresso, returns the cup carefully to its little saucer. "I think that the husband is involved in something, and the wife knows nothing about it."

Of course, Moniz thinks. This is Santos's Achilles' heel: quick to believe a woman, quick to blame a man. And she's often right: Men are more frequently criminals than women are. Far more frequently. But every case is a fresh roll of the dice, and with each roll the probability exists that maybe this time it is the woman who is lying, scheming, a criminal. Or maybe just a hysterical wife.

"Another woman?" Moniz asks.

"I doubt it. First thing in the morning is not any time to sneak away for a tryst, is it?"

"Please." Moniz smiles. "What would I know about that?"

"No," Santos says, ignoring him. "I think Senhora Pryce is correct: Her husband got into a car. But I do not yet have a specific theory of why. And you, António? What do you think?"

Moniz hesitates before answering. Just because many truthful women have been disbelieved in the past does not mean that this specific woman, now, is telling the truth. But Moniz knows from experience that this is not something Santos is willing to hear.

"Was it maybe too early that she came to us this morning? Her husband was missing for only two or three hours, and already she is running to the police, in a foreign city, where she does not speak the language?"

"Oh, it seems perfectly rational. If those two or three hours were at the end of the day, then, okay, there are many explanations that are relatively harmless. Maybe he is in a bar, or maybe he is buying drugs, or maybe he has found another woman, or maybe he is lost, or maybe his phone died, or maybe he is in a car accident. And maybe none of these is great news, but also not a reason to be terrified. But for him to disappear first thing in the morning?" Santos shakes her head. "If I were this woman, I too would be worried."

"Okay, but would you be *so* worried that you would come to the police? And to the embassy? Was that not perhaps too panicked? Too soon?"

"What else can she do? What else *should* she do? Nothing?"

Moniz is not convinced, but he knows that it is important to honor — or at least humor — other people's convictions. Especially your partner's.

"So what do you think is happening?"

"I would be surprised if it did not have something to do with sex."

Ariel is in the middle of another pastel-painted Lisbon block when she senses something, a shiver seizes her spine, making her slow her pace, and then she notices a noise, indistinct but nevertheless alarming, growing louder, growing nearer, it's happening fast, and she spins around when the motorcycle is twenty yards behind her, engine whirring through a downshift, the wheels screeching to a halt, and she jumps aside, she can feel both feet actually leave the ground, instinct taking over —

The biker is wearing black jeans and a black jacket and a black helmet with a reflective visor, nothing exposed.

This biker's gloved hand reaches into a pocket of the leather jacket, and Ariel takes another hop away, and crashes into a wall, banging her elbow into the stone, it hurts like hell, and she lets out a yelp, and her eyes dart around for escape while the biker's arm extends, and Ariel yells "No!" before she notices that the thing being extended isn't a gun, isn't a knife, isn't a weapon at all, at least not a traditional sort.

Ariel stares at this leather glove holding this thing out to her: It's a cell phone, just inches from her own hand. These days, the most common weapon of all.

She glances again toward where the biker's face should be, but all she can see in the broad expanse of visor is a reflection of herself, wide-eyed terrified, forehead crinkled and mouth open and shoulders hunched forward. A cornered animal.

The biker's hand extends farther, shoving the phone at her, and as Ariel wraps her fingers around it the bike pulls away from the curb with tires screeching and engine roaring, and Ariel forces herself to watch, to identify any distinguishing details before the bike disappears, but there's no license plate, no markings she can see in the gathering dark, nothing she'll be able to describe to the cops other than a generic midsize black-clad person on a generic midsize black motorcycle, which after just seconds tears around the corner, and Ariel can hear the gears shift and the bike accelerate after the sharp turn, then the noise begins to recede, and that's when she notices:

The phone is ringing.

Part II
The Kidnapping

PART II
THE KIDNAPPING

CHAPTER 12

Day 1. 6:55 p.m.

"Listen carefully."

"Yes," Ariel says. She's trying to wrest some control over her emotions, over her voice, her racing heart, but is failing on all counts. "Go ahead."

"We have your husband." The voice on the phone has been doctored; it doesn't sound human.

"Oh my God. Is he okay?"

"If you want to see him alive again, you will deliver three million euros in cash —"

"Are you crazy, I —"

"— within forty-eight hours."

"But I —"

"No negotiations. No extensions. No police. No embassy. Keep this device with you at all times."

"Who *are* you?"

The caller lets out a burst of mirthless laughter.

"How do I know that John is still alive?"

143

Ariel hears a scraping sort of noise, then, "Ariel, it's me —"

"John! My God! Are you okay?"

And then the scraping noise again. "There: he is alive."

"What do you want from him?"

"I said: three million euros."

"I don't *have* three million euros. Neither does my husband."

"But you know people who do."

"What do you *mean*?"

"You have two days."

And the line goes dead.

CHAPTER 13

Day 1. 6:56 p.m.
Now there are no longer any benign possibilities, no far-fetched explanations or devil's advocacy, no reasonable doubt. Now it's a fact in evidence: John is not merely missing; he has been taken. Now everything is different.

"Jesus Christ," Guido Antonucci says. "There's been some crazy shit out here in Chiado."

Nicole Griffiths has been sitting at her desk, running her eye down an RSVP list, looking for questionable names. Sometimes she wishes she were still a low-level operations officer, out there in the world every day, recruiting agents, slinking around foreign streets, approaching assets in bars and brothels and the hushed hallways of professional conferences, clandestine conversations hidden in plain sight. Management sucks. When you're young, people tell you this, but it's

145

hard to accept on faith.

"Tell me."

"This Pryce woman is walking down the street when all of a sudden a motorcyclist roars up, gives her a phone, then tears away at speed. Pryce immediately gets a call on this phone, which lasts a minute or so. Then she stands there frozen, mouth hanging open, like she just heard her dog died."

"Or her husband?"

"No, I don't think so. She's not wailing, not collapsing, not falling apart. If this woman's husband just died, she's one stone-cold killer."

Griffiths wonders if that too is a possibility, but keeps it to herself. "Then?"

"She snaps to, and I had to get out of there before she made me. I turned the corner, and called you. Jefferson has now picked her up on foot."

"Okay. Keep me posted."

Griffiths checks the time. She's getting the feeling that this is going to ruin her date with Pietro. Their relationship is strictly transactional, and the transaction is strictly sexual. So neither of them will be especially bothered by the cancellation, but still. It's not going to cheer anyone up.

"Yes." Ariel sighs heavily. "I do understand that it's an unusual request. *Please.*"

"It's very disruptive to the other children,

Ms. Pryce. Also to your son."

A handful of boisterous young people are walking by, laughing loudly, life going on, oblivious to a crisis in their midst.

"Yes, and I'm sorry, but it's important." It's the most important thing, always. Surely this man understands? He runs a day camp, after all. This is where George has spent all his summers, it's what he knows of the season, the farm animals, the water sports, the poison ivy, the sunburn, the dead-to-the-world sleep of the just. The camp is just a few towns away, a fifteen-minute drive, but it can seem like they're separated by a continent. By an ocean. And now they are.

"This is a hectic time, Ms. Pryce, we're finishing lunch, the children —"

"*Please,* I'm begging you. And I really don't think I should have to."

Silence. Ariel has met this sort of reluctance before; she checks on George all the time, too frequently for camp directors, school principals, sports coaches. Maybe they'd frown at her less if she explained why, but she refuses.

"I'm sorry, I'm not going to put your son on the phone just so you can confirm he's okay. I've walked outside, and now I'm on the back porch, and I can see George clearly, he's sitting on the grass with four other boys. He's *fine.* And I'm sorry, but that's going to have to be good enough."

It isn't.

"Hi Mom," Ariel says. She phoned Elaine immediately after hanging up with the camp director.

"Honey?"

"Mom, are you at my house?"

"Where else would I be?"

"Is everything all right there?"

"All right? What do you mean?"

"Listen, I need you to do something, and it's going to sound strange: I need you to pack a bag with a couple of days' clothes for you and George, and all his meds, and take the dogs and some food for them, and go get George at camp, and —"

"Oh my God is he okay?"

"Yes. But I need you to take him someplace where no one would look for him. Or for you."

Elaine doesn't respond for a few seconds. "Honey, you're scaring me. What's going on?"

"John has been kidnapped."

Elaine gasps.

"It's not clear to me exactly what's going on," Ariel continues. "If this is about John, and ransom money, or if it has something to do with . . ."

It wouldn't surprise Ariel if her phone is being monitored, now that she has shared her concern with the embassy, which is probably not different from alerting the CIA. Every communication is vulnerable to interception or manipulation, recorded and archived, stolen and leaked, broadcast to the whole world. Any phone call, any email, any end-to-end-encrypted messaging app, any dick pic or booty call or inside-trading intel or ransom note. There's no longer any privacy, certainly not on any cell phone. Ariel has to assume that someone, somewhere, is listening.

"Or if it has to do with something else," Ariel says. "Someone else."

"What are you *talking* about?"

She's talking about the long-buried secrets of powerful men.

"Please don't go to a hotel, Mom. Don't go anywhere you'll need to pay by credit card. Don't use my landline to make the arrangements. Don't use your cell either."

"Then how am —"

"Ask Pedro." Ariel has a quick unpleasant vision of Elaine wandering around the field, asking random Latino men if they're the one named Pedro. "You know who Pedro is, Mom? He always wears a pale straw hat, he's about five-five —"

"Yes, Dear, I know who Pedro is."

"Okay good. Ask to borrow his cell, and use it to call a friend."

"Who am I going —"

"Just figure it out!" Ariel yells. Then, softer:

149

"Please just find a place, Mom, but don't tell me where you're going. Don't tell anyone except the person you're going to visit, and even then not using your own phone. Do you understand what I'm saying?"

"Yes."

Ariel can hear a dog barking, sounds like Mallomar. When Ariel talks on the phone, the brown dog listens attentively, head cocked, and occasionally he tries to talk back. That's what he's doing now.

"What should I tell George?"

"It's July Fourth tomorrow," Ariel says. "There's no camp, so you two are going on a fun adventure. Maybe to visit someone with a swimming pool?" Where Ariel lives is not the kind of place where Elaine would know anyone. But an hour away is a different story.

"I guess I can figure out something . . . But why am I springing this on him?"

"Turn off the water in the house. It's a good enough reason."

This will be understandable to George. It happened a few years ago, their well ran dry, and it took Ariel a few days to get everything sorted, to get that guy — that bastard — to come out in the winter and dig a new well, farther from the house as per new code, and then another few days for the plumber to install the hookups, and in the meantime it was hard living without running water, so eventually Ariel and George and the dogs decamped to a vacant room at a friend's house, where George slept in a sleeping bag on the floor, like camping indoors. A memorable experience.

"Go to the cellar, find the main valve."

"Main valve? I don't know what that means."

Elaine lives in a golf-course condo with a resident manager, and porters, a place where she can pick up the phone and say the toilet is clogged, the radiator is cold, and a man will show up wearing a uniform with his name embroidered on the chest, lugging a toolbox, and maybe he'll need to go to the hardware store for a part, and ultimately Elaine will fork over a folded twenty and he'll reply, "Thank *you,* Mrs. Winston," carting away whatever mess accompanied the repair, wrapped up in someone else's discarded newspaper.

This was how Ariel used to think the world worked: not that you yourself knew how to do household things, but that you called people who did, and when they were finished, they thanked you. This was how her childhood had worked, and her college dorm, and her apartments in New York, living with other young women, then by herself, then with her first husband.

"Oh Honey, what have you gotten yourself into?" Once again, the same old assumption: that it's Ariel's fault.

"I can't explain now, Mom. Can you just, please, do this for me? I'll tell you all about it later."

Ariel can hear her mom breathing heavily, maybe sniffling.

"Mom? Are you okay?"

"No, I am definitely not okay. I'm scared out of my wits."

"I'm sorry." Ariel wishes she could reassure her mother that there's nothing to worry about, but that would be counterproductive. And maybe not true.

"Okay, I'm in the cellar."

"The main valve is a red knob coming off a pipe, near the pump on the cellar floor; it has a piece of red yarn tied around it, plus a hangtag that says MAIN VALVE. Do you see it?"

"Yes."

"Now close the valve —"

"Which way?"

Ariel raises her right hand to remember. "Turn to the right, clockwise." As with car pedals, her body just knows it, but not necessarily her mind. "After the main valve is closed, there will still be a small amount of water flow in the pipes, and a single flush in the tank of each toilet, but after that the tanks won't refill, you won't be able to flush anymore. Show the empty faucets to George."

"You want me to *lie* to the boy?"

"*Want?* No, Mom. I don't *want* my mother

to lie to my child. I also don't *want* my husband to be kidnapped in Portugal. What I *want* is for you and George to be safe, for my kid to not be terrified, and this is the plan I've come up with, and if you have a better idea, please, by all means: I'm all ears."

Buying a two-hundred-year-old farmhouse was not the most rational of the many life-defining decisions that Ariel made during that momentous year. In fact it was irresponsible, like purchasing a vintage car when you don't know what a transmission is. If you have neither patience nor money nor knowledge, complicated old things are not sensible choices.

Ariel didn't know how the house worked. Nor for that matter did she know how her brand-new baby worked; neither came with an operating manual. But her electric toothbrush? That came with a thirty-two-page instruction booklet.

Those first years in the farmhouse were an exercise in nearly nonstop frustration, one thing after another breaking, leaking, failing, and every problem was compounded by Ariel's humiliation at never being able to answer practical questions about her own house — was the heating hot water or steam, where was the septic tank located and when had it last been emptied, what level of electrical power, where does the water come from.

She didn't know a damn thing.

She began to worry that the tap water tasted funny. Did it? Sometimes the things you experience every day are hard to judge. Ariel asked anyone who came over; she received differing opinions. She called a testing service that sent a guy to take a sample and send it to a lab, then emailed her an analysis that she couldn't even begin to understand; it was like a completely different language.

The water was alkaline, the man explained on the phone. A filter would fix it, easy.

A few weeks later Jeb Payne arrived, climbed down through the Bilco doors to her partially excavated cellar — dirt floor, rough-hewn masonry walls, a creepy room filled with cobwebs and mechanical things she didn't understand, lit by a bare bulb hanging from the low ceiling, and surrounded on all sides by crawl spaces populated by mice and rats and raccoons and possums, fighting and fucking and nesting and dying, the stench of dead rodent a wintertime constant.

"Huh," Payne said, approaching the large bullet-shaped thing that looked like a futuristic barbecue grill. "Seems you already have a filtration system." He put his beefy hand on the thing, fingers like sausages, and turned back to her. "Right here."

Ariel absolutely loathed the condescension on his face, like he was exercising admirable restraint by not laughing at her.

"Seems it's disconnected." He leaned over, examined a hose, a pipe. "You don't happen to know why?" He glanced back up at her, over his shoulder, with an obnoxious bit of side-eye. "No, I don't suppose you would."

Ariel could feel the shame surge into her cheeks, and she knew he could see it too.

In that moment Ariel hated herself for being this type of person, with this timeworn type of incompetence, a woman at the mercy of a man like this, his arrogance the natural consequence of her own choices, of her mother's choices, of society's choices about what men know how to do, and what women know how to do, and don't.

He was the final straw.

Ariel called the plumber and the electrician. "Nope," she admitted, "not an emergency. Nothing wrong in fact." She paid each tradesman for an hour of his time to walk through and explain things while she took notes and asked questions — what's this for, how does this work, why is this here. It was embarrassing, but a worthwhile investment in avoiding future humiliations, putting her ignorance on display to conquer it.

And it was more than the tradesmen. It was everything: Ariel decided to bring her whole life under her own dominion, to figure out how to do the things she'd been paying other people to do for her. Most things aren't so complicated. You just need to be willing to try.

Ariel had never wanted to be a woman who looked at everything through the lens of fear, of worst-case scenarios, of escape contingencies, of self-defense, of distrust and antagonism, of risk avoidance. She wanted to be a person who went out into the world without fear, even when she didn't go out at all; she wanted to be undaunted just lying in bed.

Life presents so many choices. Superficial ones of how you look and dress and wear your hair, but everything else too — how you raise your child, how you earn your money and spend it, what sorts of friends you have, what you do with free time, cats or dogs, wine or beer, vegetarian or omnivore, sedans or pickups. Innumerable choices. We don't even realize we're making many of them; don't recognize we're free to.

But we are. Ariel forced herself to look long and hard at her options. To choose deliberately.

What she chose to be was a person who knows how her house's plumbing works in a general way. A person who understands the fundamental mechanics of the truck she drives, the farm she owns. She chose to be a person who will research how to do almost anything, then do it — draft a sublease agreement, change a flat tire, repair a leaky faucet, balance books and file taxes, build a tree house and a campfire, reignite a pilot light, tape and spackle and sand and paint a patch of drywall.

Also a woman who knows how to defend herself. Even how to kill someone, using nothing but her bare hands.

CHAPTER 14

Day 1. 7:21 p.m.

Ariel arrives at the next intersection, and realizes that she's not certain where she is, where her hotel is. She turns left, walks a few steps, then catches a glimpse of the river down the hill —

"Crap." She has been heading in the wrong direction, a long block out of the way, which means another five minutes that she'll need to remain out in the world, walking around, exposed, vulnerable. She spins, backtracks a few steps to the corner, turns —

Ariel feels her breath catch, but forces herself not to react visibly.

He's on the other side of the street, walking in her direction slowly, as if he's just out for a stroll.

She has almost no time to make the next decision. Once again, she can spin and flee. Or she can pretend she doesn't notice him, doesn't recognize him, walk right past. Or she can confront him.

He has changed the top of his outfit, he's now wearing a gray crewneck instead of the blue polo. But the khakis are the same, with creases down the front, albeit less sharp. And it's the orthopedic-looking shoes that are the real giveaway.

Or she can attack. For much of Ariel's life, attack would never have crossed her mind; it would have seemed outlandish, impossible. Not anymore.

She steps off the curb, starts to cross the street. She could do this. She has done it before.

It was two years ago. George was playing at a friend's house, and the farming crew had knocked off at four-thirty, as always. So Ariel was all alone when she heard a truck pull into her driveway.

Her first assumption was that it was the irrigation company, which she'd called a few days earlier, and they'd been noncommittal about when a team would be available for a service call.

Ariel craned her neck to look out the window, and that's when she saw who it was. Unannounced, uninvited, unwelcome.

One of the things that Ariel misses about living in the city is the abundance of choice. In restaurants and bars, bookstores and boutiques, housewares and hardware and lampshades and everything: If you don't like one business, the people who work there, you can go to another, or another, or another. Not here. In this small town she doesn't have options, not about the businesses she frequents, nor the people she interacts with. There's just one orthopedist, one toy store, one pharmacist. And for water problems, just one guy who's exactly the sort of creep Ariel would choose to not deal with, if she had any choice. She doesn't.

She stepped out onto her porch, looked up the street one way, then the other.

"Hello?" She tried to imbue those two syllables with doubt and reluctance and frostiness, but not overt hostility. She didn't want to pick a fight, not unless she had to, not in a situation like this. No escape route. No witnesses.

Jeb Payne climbed down out of his supersized truck, hitched his pants. He wasn't yet as overweight as he'd end up, but he'd made a lot of progress since he'd first visited to repair the filter.

"Hey." He lumbered toward her with a big toolbox.

"I didn't call, did I?" Ariel knew for certain that she didn't. But she hoped that framing this as a question would be less confrontational.

"Nah. I'm here for the three-year follow-up. Just part of our service deal. For, um, *valued* customers."

160

"Not necessary." Ariel crossed her arms, stood in front of the door. "Everything's all right."

"Good to hear." A smirk. "But I gotta check it out anyway. Part of our deal." As if she hadn't understood the first time.

"Really, you don't need to."

"Really," he said, "I do." He was now on her porch. "It'll take just a minute."

He was standing at her screen door, but didn't reach for the knob, as if drawing a distinction between his uninvited arrival and the undeniable crime of entering without explicit permission. Ariel got the feeling that Payne had learned all the finer points of criminal trespass from his cousin the cop.

"Do you mind?" he asked.

She did. But was she really going to say it, *As a matter of fact I do mind, please leave*? Ariel waited a second, to convey her reluctance, but Payne didn't retreat. She didn't want to turn this into an overtly antagonistic situation, but that seemed to be the only alternative to letting him in.

Ariel stepped aside, let him pass. But she stayed out on her porch, debating. She looked at Payne's truck, blocking hers in the driveway. She looked again at the empty isolated road, where very few cars passed at any time of day. She looked toward her nearest neighbor's house, a few hundred yards away, no Buick in the driveway; Cyrus was probably down at the VFW, where he had a beer or two almost every afternoon.

She was getting a bad vibe. Maybe it wasn't a coincidence that she was all alone.

"Could I trouble you for a glass?"

"The cupboard on your right," Ariel said, still outside.

Payne ran water into a glass, took a sip. He left the tap open.

"Is this the way it always tastes?" He was still standing at the sink, holding the glass out in her direction, trying to lure her inside.

She wondered if she was overreacting; she'd been accused of that before. It did seem unlikely that this man had come here, in broad daylight, with the express premeditated intention of attacking her. But it was definitely not impossible.

Ariel walked inside. She ignored the glass in Payne's outstretched hand, and instead pulled a fresh one off the shelf, filled it, took a sip. But she didn't pay any attention to how the water tasted.

"Seems fine to me."

"Hmm." He made a face of disagreement. "I gotta go to the cellar, check out your, um, apparatus. Please keep the water running, so we can get a pure sample. I'll be back up in a few."

He exited, and Ariel breathed a sigh of relief. She returned to dinner prep, dipping eggplant slices in flour, then beaten eggs, then

162

bread crumbs, her hands coated in glutinous goop.

Then Payne was back on her porch, with the dogs behind him. They felt obliged to supervise visitors.

"Hey," he said.

She washed her hands in the still-running water, then turned to the screen door, but didn't approach it.

"Everything okay?"

"Can I come in? Need to get another sample."

Again she hesitated before saying, "I guess." She wanted to register her reluctance clearly.

Payne filled a couple of vials, then closed the tap. "It'll be a week or so for the results."

"Okay," she said. "Thanks for coming."

He made no move to leave. He glanced at the counter, the bowls of ingredients, then his eyes moved back to her, beginning with her legs, moving up slowly.

"It's quittin' time," he said, affecting the extra-thick accent that men around here sometimes use to prove that they're country, to distance themselves from city transplants.

"Well," she said, "thanks again for checking in."

"I'm in no rush." He grinned. "How 'bout a beer?"

During Payne's entire visit, Ariel had felt something bad niggling at her, like a little tickle in the back of your throat that you can choose to ignore. Until you cough, and it hurts.

"Oh I don't think so. I have to get dinner made; my son will be home any minute."

Ariel glanced at the counter, noticed that there was no knife within easy reach.

"In fact some people are coming over," she lied. "They'll be here soon."

None of this was true, and Payne's smirk told her that he knew it. "Havin' a party, huh?"

Ariel had learned lessons; of course she had. She knew what she needed to do here, and when she needed to do it. But this is a hard thing, to say no, to do it loudly, to make sure there's no alternative interpretation, no possible misunderstanding, no hint of ambiguity.

"No, not a party."

He took a step toward her. "I like to party."

To bite the bullet and say: Please leave.

"How 'bout you? You like to party, dont-cha?"

To say: I insist.

"Listen," Ariel began. He was standing too close already. He was a big human, with seventy or eighty pounds on her, a half-foot of height; she didn't want this to turn into a physical fight.

To say: Leave right now, or I'm calling the police.

"You're making me uncomfortable." Ariel

164

glanced down at his footwear, steel-toed boots.

"Uncomfortable?" As if this were utterly ridiculous. "Naw, don't be like that."

"But I am." Ariel met his eye, trying to look firm. To be firm.

"C'mon." Payne took another step, within grasping distance. He gave another lopsided sneer, as if they were playing a game that was slightly funny.

"Please, I'm afraid I have to ask you to leave."

He reached toward her, and she swatted his hand away. His crooked smile collapsed into a frown; his whole face went dark.

"What? You a fuckin' dyke? Like people say?"

There was no reason to add either antagonism or appeasement. Neither would help.

"I tell people, naw, that can't be."

Ariel felt her pulse pounding, her jaw twitching, her whole body gearing up. She was now sure this was going to end badly, just a question of which type of badly, and whether someone was going to end up in the hospital, or dead. And which person that was going to be.

"That chick" — Payne grinned — "she likes dick. I can tell."

This time his hand shot out quickly, taking Ariel by surprise, grabbing her around the neck. He was a big man with big beefy hands.

He wasn't fit, but he was definitely strong. Ariel felt the gag response kick in.

The dogs were barking up a storm out on the porch, on the wrong side of a closed door.

She was ready for this, wasn't she? She had trained, she had practiced. Not just generally, not just in the abstract. She had prepared for this specifically.

There'd be no point in stomping down on the hardened toe of his boot, which wouldn't injure anyone but herself. So she skipped that step, and raised her leg swiftly and carefully, aiming her knee directly at his crotch with maximal force, for maximal pain upon impact, and he howled and released her neck, but she didn't allow him to retreat before she thrust her right arm outward, not any type of roundhouse or hook but just a fast straight jab — accuracy and angle were much more important than power here — leading with the heel of her hand instead of knuckles, aiming at the bottom of his nose from below, driving upward, wrist firm, full arm extension, getting her lower body into it too, marshaling all the momentum of her 130 pounds into violent collision with the small delicate bones of this big man's little up-turned nose, blood gushing as he doubled over, and she took a sideways step and grabbed a cast-iron skillet and swung it at Payne's head, which was now situated directly in her wheelhouse at hip level, and the pan made impact with a resounding clang, and he pitched over and hit the kitchen floor with a thud that shook the whole floor.

Ariel scuttled to the counter, yanked a carving knife from the block. "I should *kill* you."

She was standing off to his side, not giving Payne any opportunity to kick up at her. He was writhing from the pain in his crotch, his nose, his cheek with a large gash, possibly broken cheekbone, broken nose.

"In fact maybe I will."

"No!" He released one of his hands from his face, held it up, bloody palm facing her, warding off the long blade.

"*Beg,* motherfucker. *Beg* me to not kill you."

"Please," he begged, crawling toward the door.

Ariel stood her ground, holding the kitchen knife in one hand and the pan in the other, panting, glaring, like some deranged action-movie character, Revenge Mom.

"Please," he repeated.

She thought of calling the police. But she didn't want to divert her attention, to give him time or space to make a move. At that moment it may have seemed like she'd won this fight, but it was also possible that he was gathering strength to get up and charge her.

It was also possible that he had a gun in the truck. With that crossed-rifles bumper sticker, it was guaranteed, wasn't it? There was definitely a firearm in that vehicle, and he would come rushing back up these porch steps with both bloody hands clutching a semiautomatic, squeezing off shots indiscriminately, killing the dogs first, then turning the muzzle toward her —

Ariel could see this outcome so clearly it seemed inevitable.

She bounded down the steps while checking the position of the trucks, confirming that there was no way she could maneuver her own pickup past his, trees in the way, the garage too. And if she fled on foot he'd chase her down easily in his truck before she could reach any safety. He'd shoot her through his window, like the unsportsmanlike sportsman he definitely was.

Ariel yanked open his truck's door, reached under the seat, found nothing there but trash; she thrust her hand into the door pocket, found more trash.

She glanced back to see that Payne had stood, was crossing the porch gingerly. Like an injured animal fighting for its life, hurt and humiliated and angry and irrational. More dangerous than ever.

There was no gun in the center console.

He was stumbling down the stairs. The dogs were flanking him, barking at him, but they wouldn't actually attack.

No gun under the passenger seat.

He was staggering toward her on the flag-stone path. Just twenty yards away.

She fully extended her body across the driver's seat, reaching across to hit the glove box's release, but nothing happened — *damn* — so she hit it again and still nothing —

He was ten yards away.

— so she banged the heel of her hand against the small door and — *finally* — it popped open, ejecting a tire-pressure gauge and an amber bottle of painkillers and a Twix, this detritus falling to the filthy floor mat, leaving the compartment empty except for the biggest heaviest item in there, a semiautomatic handgun, anchored in place by its own weight.

She grabbed the weapon, then propelled herself backward blindly, sliding rear-first on her stomach, flying off the driver's seat and out the door, one of her feet finding purchase on the truck's rubber-treaded step but the other missing, and she lost her balance and tumbled backward and landed on her ass, a powerful jolt, and then the back of her skull collided with the pebbled driveway, and everything went dark for an instant but the darkness quickly resolved itself into bursting stars and then she could see him standing directly above her, just beyond the end of the gun barrel she was aiming at his face.

She released the safety.

"Step the fuck back," she said.

Ariel scrambled backward, pushing herself away with one hand while the other kept a steady hold of the gun. She shifted her aim away from Payne's head toward the larger, easier target of the center of his mass. Ariel had very little experience firing a handgun, but she didn't think she'd miss from five feet away, or seven, or ten, which was the distance when she stood up.

Her mind raced in debate, one she'd had before, but only in her imagination, in the abstract, about another man. Now it was concrete, it was now, it was this man. She knew that either way, she was probably going to spend the rest of her life second-guessing her decision.

"Get the fuck out of here," she said.

And he did.

CHAPTER 15

Day 1. 7:22 p.m.
Ariel is crossing the street diagonally to the khaki guy's side, closing the space between them quickly. He's trying hard to pretend to ignore her.

She'd learned this lesson more than once: If a man seems like he's going to attack you, he's going to attack you. Don't just hope for an alternative explanation to present itself; don't just wait until he actually attacks before taking defensive action. Most of the time, that's simply flight. Sometimes, though, running is impossible, or inadvisable, or counterproductive. Like now.

Ariel pulls a water bottle out of her bag, opens the cap, balances it on the mouth. She's getting close, just a few seconds. The bottle is in her left hand; the man is on her left side.

Just another few steps, another few seconds . . . Now —

■ ■ ■ ■

Ariel's town is small, especially in winter, with no summer people around. You see everyone. At the gas station, the supermarket, the coffee shop, the movie theater and drugstore and town hall. You see people you know walking on Main Street, across the shopping plaza's lot, into the Chinese takeout, out of the pizzeria. You see their cars and trucks passing you on the road, you know what everyone drives, you recognize your friends' cars from a quarter-mile away. Your enemies' too.

She saw Jeb Payne's wife all the time, a miserable-looking woman herding three kids in and out of a beige Sienna at soccer practice and school drop-off. Ariel also saw Payne's cousin Brooks, the cop. The two had grown up together, thick as thieves their whole lives. This was the reason that Ariel didn't go to the police. One of the reasons.

A couple of months after the attack, Ariel found herself standing behind Beverly Payne at the supermarket checkout with two of her children; the older one was outside, slouching, staring at a screen.

Ariel felt the impulse to say something to this woman. But what? To accomplish what? Ariel definitely wanted to hurt Payne, of course she did. But did she want to hurt

Beverly?

Do you know how your husband got his face busted up? This is what Ariel could ask. Beverly would stare back, insulted, defensive. No matter what bill of goods Payne had tried to sell, this woman probably suspected the truth. It may have happened before, maybe even to Beverly herself. At least one in ten married women has been raped by their husbands. Beverly would not be unfamiliar with her husband's violence.

I don't know what you're talking about is how Beverly would answer, quick and angry, then she'd turn away, hoping the interaction would just end there.

I'm the one who did that to his face, Ariel would say to the back of Beverly's head. *Do you know why?*

Beverly's kids would be staring up at Ariel, mouths wide, implicitly understanding that this supermarket interaction was something important. Something life-defining. And the lives being defined would be the kids'.

Because he was trying to rape me.

One of the boys dropped his sippy cup, which rolled Ariel's way. Beverly heard the sound, and turned while Ariel knelt to retrieve the cup. She stayed in a crouch to extend it back to the boy.

"What do you say, Cole?"

"Thank you, ma'am."

Ariel turned her eyes to Beverly, who also

173

said, "Thank you."

No, this woman was not Ariel's enemy. She was a fellow combatant.

The general idea of Main Street was one of the things that had appealed to Ariel about moving to a little town, the promise of something pure, something innocent that she wanted to believe in, the quirky characters behind the plate-glass windows of the idiosyncratic businesses, friendly small talk and the small superficial niceties of small-town living. She'd hoped that this would be the antidote to everything wrong about her life in the city, and she held on to that hope for a long time, too long, the way you hang on to your last hope: desperately.

It made Ariel feel less safe that she was the one who'd beaten the crap out of Payne; it made her worry about revenge. He knew where she lived, where she worked, where she shopped and ate and filled up her gas tank, where her child went to school and baseball and swimming. He knew when she was alone, he knew how she was vulnerable. And his best friend was a cop.

She considered keeping his semiautomatic for self-defense, but she knew the statistics. Possessing a gun would only increase the likelihood that she herself would get shot. So instead she cleaned off her fingerprints with mineral oil, then used twine to lash the weapon to a cinder block she'd found on the beach, which she dropped off a bridge into a deeply dredged channel. But Ariel had no doubt that Payne owned others; the average gun-owning household has eight of them.

She continued to take self-defense classes, to practice confronting different types of physical peril, using different tactics. She grew stronger, quicker, more confident. She learned a lot of ways to defend herself.

"Okay," she said to her martial-arts instructor, just a few months ago. "Now I want to learn how to attack."

Ariel couldn't stop wondering if she should have shot Payne. Was death a fair punishment for sexual assault? That was debatable. But as long as that asshole was alive, walking around freely, she would never feel safe. And what punishment was commensurate for that?

She had no faith in the police to investigate. No faith in the judicial system to provide a remedy. Ariel didn't want to kill anyone, but she did want to sleep easy. She did want justice. Who could provide that?

No one.

She's just a few steps away from this man who has been following her. Three steps, two, now —

Ariel pitches forward, as if she has lost her balance and is on her way to falling, losing a grip on the water bottle, which tumbles at the man's feet, and the bottle's loosened cap flies off, and a glug of water splashes onto the orthopedic-looking shoe, and he instinctively leans over to retrieve the bottle, or brush off the water, and so his arm is down, his torso bent, his face much closer to waist-height than he'd want if he had any idea what was coming —

Ariel brings her knee up into the man's face, and she hears the sound of teeth cracking upon one another, a groan as he tumbles, and while he's down she swiftly kicks his abdomen without much in the way of aim because it'll hurt him no matter where the blow lands, and she takes a hop backward away from his possible reach, and rebalances herself —

"Please stop," he says in unexpected English, but she doesn't dwell on that surprise as she prepares another kick, this one more careful and powerful, this'll be the knock-out —

"I'm trying to help," he says, then something unintelligible.

She puts her kicking foot down on the pavement. "What?"

"I'm American." He spits some blood onto the sidewalk. "I'm trying to help." He runs his tongue around in his mouth, assessing what level of dental damage has occurred in there.

"Who are you?"

"I'm trying to help," he says again, pushing himself to a sitting position.

"Help with what?"

"With your husband. I'm from the embassy."

From a half-block away, Pete Wagstaff watches in amazement as Ariel now has what appears to be a civil conversation with the CIA man she just beat the shit out of. Then an SUV with diplomat plates screeches up, and Pryce climbs into the backseat with the guy she was just pummeling. And all this just minutes after that motorcycle raced up out of nowhere, whatever the hell that was.

Until an hour ago, Wagstaff thought that Ariel Pryce was probably a waste of his time. Not anymore.

CHAPTER 16

Day 1. 7:43 p.m.

Ariel is again led through the embassy's corridors, but this time the people leading the way are very different from Saxby Barnes, gentleman-douchebag. One is the badly dressed middle-aged guy whom just a few minutes ago Ariel was kicking with all her might out on the Lisbon sidewalk. The other is the young Black woman who showed up at the wheel of an SUV, which she handled like a race-car driver back to the embassy, whose halls are now empty and pin-drop quiet.

"In here, please," the young woman says, leading Ariel into a conference room where another woman rises from the table and walks toward Ariel, hand extended.

"Hi, my name is Nicole Griffiths."

"Ariel Pryce."

"Thanks guys," Griffiths says to her colleagues, and they recede, shutting the door behind them. Ariel takes a seat at the conference table, which is already set with a pitcher

and a couple of glasses of water. Ariel helps
herself. She's parched.

"So I'll get right to it, Ms. Pryce: Has your
husband been kidnapped?"

Ariel doesn't answer.

"Did they tell you not to talk to anyone?"

Ariel just looks at the woman.

"Of course they did. Kidnappers *always* say
that. Why wouldn't they? But if you do talk,
what are they going to do?"

"Oh I don't know, maybe *kill my husband*?"

"But then what? Then their hostage is dead.
Then there's no motivation for anyone to pay
any ransom. Then they have nothing to
bargain with. Then they've committed mur-
der, they've killed an American citizen —"
The woman stops herself. "Your husband *is*
American?"

Ariel nods.

"Then they've killed an American, so they
have the wrath of the United States to con-
tend with. All with no upside. Who wants
that?"

"Maybe they're psychos."

"That's not really the way this works."

"How do you know the way this works?"

The woman just smiles.

"They told me, *specifically*, no police and
no embassy."

"How did they get in touch?" Griffiths is
just going to ignore Ariel's objections. "Did
they call on your cell?"

179

How much should Ariel share with this woman? What's the downside? Sooner or later, someone has to take her seriously. Maybe that someone is Nicole Griffiths.

"A guy on a motorcycle delivered a phone to me."

"Interesting. How much are they asking?"

"Three million euros."

Griffiths takes this in stride. "Do you *have* three million euros?"

Ariel snorts.

"Is there any reason for anyone to think you do?"

Is there? She did fly business class, the type of indulgence that most people would never even contemplate, a cost that's equivalent to a new top-of-the-line boiler for her house, fully installed — twenty winters' worth of warmth — or vet bills for a dog's lifetime, or even a serviceable used car. But it also seemed like the logical choice. Was she going to sit in steerage while John slept fully reclined at the front of the plane? And Ariel's ticket, though exorbitant, would be their only out-of-pocket expense for this trip; everything else is on John's corporate account.

"No," Ariel says. "We're not . . ." She doesn't know how to explain how obvious it is that she and John are not rich. "My pickup has nearly two hundred thousand miles on it."

Griffiths smiles. "But what about here in

180

Lisbon? Do you look different here?"

"Sure," Ariel admits. "We're staying in a nice hotel. We're eating in nice restaurants. It's a business trip. So we're not driving around in my rusty pickup. On the other hand, we're not riding in chauffeured limousines."

Status signifiers: We're processing them all the time, the high end and the low, the frequencies on which we broadcast our strata, those we receive, the way we're perceived. The season's It handbag, the safari vacation, the open button on the sleeve of a man's dinner jacket. Calling it a dinner jacket.

Their driver from the Lisbon airport had been polite and eager for future business — "Please," he said, handing John a business card, "any time, to go anywhere" — but he wasn't wearing a suit, he was just a guy with a clean Mercedes. Relatively clean.

"We're not hopping from one exorbitant experience to another, private tours and exclusive access, superluxury everything. We're not going shopping in those stores" — Ariel flicks her wrist dismissively at all the overpriced boutiques of the world, where people kill time buying shoes and neckties when they can't think of anything better to do with their time and their money.

"Is your husband successful in his career?"

Ariel shrugs. "It's a good job."

"If you don't mind me asking, what does

181

that mean, income-wise?"

"It fluctuates with bonuses, but the average is a few hundred thousand a year."

Griffiths nods: not nothing, but also not three-million-euros-in-cash money. "And your life back in America, does that give any appearance of wealth? Besides your rusty pickup?"

"No, I can't see how. I live with my son on a small farm a couple hours outside of New York City. John's job is in the city, so he sleeps there most weeknights in a modest apartment. He comes out to the country for weekends."

"You said your son? Not John's?"

"George is thirteen. I met John a year ago."

"I see. And what about how John looks online? Is there anything to suggest that he might be important? Or well-connected? Or wealthy?"

There are a lot of people who go to extraordinary measures to look rich on social media, especially those who are not. Taking selfies on fake private jets, for the love of God.

"No, John doesn't look like anything. He doesn't participate in social media. We're both anti."

"Why's that?"

"Because I think social media is ruining the world. John agrees."

"That's pretty cynical."

"Cynical," Ariel says, "is a naïve person's

word for clear-eyed."

Griffiths lets a smile creep up her lips. "Maybe we've gotten a little sidetracked."

"Anyway, my husband and I are both virtually nonexistent, virtually."

"Is it possible that he was kidnapped because of some business reason?"

"I have no idea. Believe it or not, this is my first experience of kidnapping."

"What size of deals does your husband work on?"

"Ten million? Twenty? Somewhere like that."

"Twenty million dollars is a lot of money."

"Yes, in a pile of cash. But not necessarily as an investment from a VC firm."

"Fair enough. Is there any chance that your husband is involved in a criminal enterprise?"

"I can't imagine what that would be. He's a consultant."

"What about you?" Griffiths asks. "Would anyone think you'd have three million euros squirreled away somewhere?"

There's only one person who could possibly think that, and he's definitely not the kidnapper.

"No."

"Do you know anyone with that sort of money? Friends, relatives . . ."

Ariel hesitates before she lies: "No."

"So what are you planning to do?"

"I guess I'm going to try to get as much

money as I can. What else can I do?"

Griffiths continues to look at Ariel in a way that feels vaguely like suspicion. Though maybe this look is not specific to Ariel; maybe it's just a general professional disposition.

"How is it that you're going to try?"

"I'm not entirely sure. But I'm going to start with my ex-husband. He's got some money. Probably not this much, but maybe a start. In fact I should probably call him immediately. May I do that here? In private?"

"Sure, I'll give you the room." Griffiths stands. "While you're doing that, could we do a quick exam of the kidnappers' phone?"

Ariel is confident that the device won't have fingerprints other than her own, nor is it likely to be traceable to a person, a credit card, other phone numbers. No kidnapper would make that type of stupid mistake. But the phone was purchased somewhere, at some point, and these are facts that can be ascertained, and might lead to surveillance records, to clues, leads, locations.

"Please make it quick," Ariel says. "They told me to keep it with me at all times."

"Of course," Griffiths says. "Can I ask: Do you have a good relationship? With your ex-husband?"

"No, not really," Ariel says. "I haven't spoken a word to him in fourteen years."

"Christ, Guido, you really look like shit."

184

"Thanks Boss."

"Why don't you go home."

He shakes his head. "I'm good."

Griffiths turns to Kayla Jefferson, hands her the cell phone. "See what you can find on this. Make it fast. She wants it back in her hands asap, and I don't blame her. Also, let's get taps on all her phones, immediately. Record everything."

The young woman hustles away. Jefferson is not an analyst-level computer geek, but for an operations officer out in the field, she is shockingly tech-literate, which seems to be a competency of her entire generation. Unlike Antonucci here, and unlike Griffiths herself, who are both in the generation that struggles to master their TV remote controls. This is a stark divide in the intelligence community: The older generation continues to prioritize human intelligence above all, the type of intel that's gathered in face-to-face interactions, interrogations, manipulations, betrayals. For the younger, though, it's all about the digital world. If they can find everything virtually, why do anything else?

There's nothing virtual about the condition of Antonucci's face. The whole left side is swollen, as if he had half his teeth pulled, with pliers. "At least put some ice on that," Griffiths says.

"Seriously, I'm fine."

Antonucci knows that it's coming, sooner

or later. It's going to be brutal, the teasing. Maybe he thinks that if he's stoic now, he can mitigate some of that later mockery. He's wrong.

But Griffiths isn't going to start now. Neither is Jefferson. Antonucci will be granted a grace period while they're active in this operation. Even after the op is over, they might still continue to let out the false-security line an inch at a time. Antonucci will have to wait, and wait, and wait, with the torment of knowing that humiliation is just over the horizon somewhere. The waiting might even be worse than the humiliation itself.

"I'm sorry," Griffiths says now. He really does look bad. "Especially if this turns out to be nothing."

He shrugs. Antonucci has been around the block more than a few times. He knows that the CIA investigates plenty that turns out to be nothing, and this may be just another of those: another kidnapping of another citizen for another ransom. Not related to national security, not an Agency matter. They can always decide that later, toss the investigation back to consular to coordinate with the local police, Interpol, the FBI, whichever arms of law enforcement are appropriate.

But if it turns out to somehow involve national security, or espionage, or terrorism? Then it is never too soon to get on top of it. Griffiths would bet a hundred to one that this won't turn out to be a CIA matter. But she wouldn't bet her career on it, not with any odds.

Like nearly everyone else, Ariel has been buying a new phone every few years for two decades, whenever a battery dies, or the GPS fails, or the thing takes a dunk in a soapy sink, or any of the planned obsolescences that are built into these devices. With each new purchase, she transfers all the old data to the new phone, all the old photos and videos and apps and passwords and contacts. Which is why she still has Bucky Turner's numbers programmed into her address book, even though she hasn't contacted him in fourteen years.

She hits CALL, and waits for the international line, and waits, and waits, and —

CALL FAILED

Ariel tries again, fails again. She glances around, sees a landline on an end table.

Griffiths is waiting in the hall, just in front of the door.

"I don't have any cell service in here," Ariel says to her. "Can I use that landline?"

"Sure. Hit star-zero for an outside line, then the plus symbol, then one, then the area code."

"Thanks. There's a labeled number on the handset. Can I get a direct callback on that line?"

"Yes."

Ariel shuts the door, takes a seat, stares at the handset. She has no expectation of privacy on this line, does she? Absolutely not. She punches in Bucky's cell, and this time the ringing starts.

Two rings.

Three.

He isn't going to pick up.

Four.

This isn't a surprise: Bucky doesn't recognize this number, and he won't take a call from an unfamiliar number in Portugal. That has spam written all over it.

"Bucky," Ariel says to voicemail, "it's, um, Laurel. I really need to talk to you, it's an emergency. Please call me asap. It's a matter of life or death." She rattles off the landline number, then repeats it, then right before she hangs up, she remembers to say, "Thanks."

Ariel has no doubt that Bucky will call her back. What ended their marriage wasn't his dislike of her; the other way around. Bucky did eventually become hostile, but not because he hated Ariel. It was because Bucky hated himself, and she was the one who made him aware that he should.

Griffiths leans over the wall of Jefferson's cubicle. "So?"

"There's practically nothing on this phone. Only one connection was ever made, presum-

188

ably the ransom call, which was placed from another burner. Both phones were purchased at the same time and place two weeks ago. A convenience store in Málaga."

"Málaga? That's odd."

"I've left a message at the store, and I'm waiting to hear back about their surveillance footage. But my guess is that there won't be any, which is why that location was chosen. I'd also guess that the transaction was in cash."

"Okay," Griffiths says, "so this phone is probably going to be a dead end. What about John Wright's?"

"Still working on that. America, you know: not completely open for business on the day before the Fourth."

"How'd you meet him? Your ex?"

Griffiths is back in the conference room with Ariel, waiting for Bucky to call back.

"Bucky? God, it was so long ago. I went to a fundraiser with an old friend, we'd come to New York at the same time, fresh out of college, trying to break into the theater. She ended up making it, I didn't, but we stayed friends. She bought this table at a luncheon, and invited me as her plus-one, and Bucky was at our table. Because of this way we met — fundraiser at a fancy club on the Upper East Side, introduced by a well-known actor — he assumed that I came from that world."

"What world? Money?"

"Money is part of it, but it's more. It's fancy colleges, European vacations, Aspen and Palm Beach, luxury hotels, Michelin restaurants, running into friends and family wherever you go, the whole world one big club populated by — in Bucky's phrase — people like us."

"Huh."

"As it turned out, though, I'm not people like us."

"Is that why the marriage ended?"

Was it? "Yeah," Ariel says. "It was complicated."

"Isn't it always?"

Ariel knows that Nicole Griffiths must be a spy. The CIA would probably need to be involved in a kidnapping sooner or later, and Barnes was obviously the sooner, Griffiths the later. This CIA officer might already know plenty about Ariel, about Bucky, about everything. Griffiths might be fishing for contradictions, trying to draw lies out of Ariel. She needs to be careful.

"In the end, Bucky wasn't the man I thought he was. Hoped he was."

Griffiths waits for Ariel to elaborate, but then accepts that she won't. "You miss that lifestyle?"

"Yeah, sometimes."

Especially when things are broken, when life isn't functioning properly, Ariel misses

190

the way sharp edges could be smoothed, when assistance was never more than a phone call away, there was always someone who knew someone, the best orthopedic surgeon, the tailor with twenty-four-hour turnarounds, the driver who'd take you anywhere at two in the morning, sure, I'll be there in ten, no questions asked.

Except of course for the biggest problems. There was no one who could be paid to solve those, for which the opposite was closer to the truth: Those most serious problems were created by the wealth itself, by the entitlement, by the immunity from consequences. By the very idea that any problem could be solved with money.

"But you pay a price for everything, don't you?" Ariel stares down at the table. "In shops and restaurants and hotels, the price is on the tag, on the menu, the rate card, right there for anyone to see."

She still has a few physical remnants of that life, almost talismans: the burled-wood umbrella from the shop in Bloomsbury, the paisley scarf from the rue Saint-Honoré, the Tank watch, the bone-handled hairbrush. Almost no one ever sees these things, and those who do don't recognize their provenance. No one in her new life was ever in that old club.

"But some prices are hidden, invisible. Sometimes the price doesn't become apparent for a very long time. Sometimes you never even recognize it, never understand that you already paid it."

Ariel turns her gaze back up to this CIA officer. "Sometimes," she says, "you yourself are the price."

The landline rings, and Ariel and Griffiths both turn to look at it, then at each other.

"I'll wait outside," Griffiths says, getting up. "Just open the door when you're finished." She leaves, and Ariel picks up the handset.

"Hello? Bucky?"

"Hi. What's wrong?"

She'd been married to this man; she'd loved him more than she'd ever loved anyone. And this is the first time she's heard his voice in fourteen years. She doesn't know what to expect from him; she doesn't know how he feels about her, all these years later.

"Oh Bucky, it's horrible." Ariel takes a deep breath. "I'm in Portugal, and my husband has been kidnapped, and they're demanding three million euros, in cash, within forty-eight hours."

"Oh my God. I'm so sorry."

"Less now, forty-seven hours, whatever. And there's no way I can get that type of money, Bucky. Nowhere near."

Bucky doesn't respond immediately. He has always been someone who weighs all the options carefully before committing to anything. That's why he didn't get married until he was forty.

"I wouldn't be calling you if I had any other choice, but I don't. Can you help?"

"*Help?* How can I help?"

"How do you think? I need the money, Bucky."

"Oh Christ, all of it? I don't have that type of cash lying around, not even close. Plus it's the Fourth tomorrow, US banks aren't open . . ."

Ariel is surprised to find herself crying. She wipes a tear from her cheek.

"Are you okay?" Bucky asks. "Are you in danger?"

"I don't think so. But I'm really worried about my husband, and I just don't see how I'm going to . . ." She trails off with a sob. "This is so bad, Bucky. So bad. I really need help. Do you maybe have money somewhere else?"

Bucky is silent for a second before he asks, "What do you mean?"

Now it's Ariel's turn to take a careful pause. "You should know that we're speaking on a landline at the US embassy in Lisbon."

He at first doesn't appear to understand this non sequitur, then does. "Oh," he says.

Ariel doesn't want to ask him explicitly about assets he might be hiding in tax shelters over a phone that could be — that *is* — being monitored by federal agents.

"No," he says. "I don't."

"I could pay you back, Bucky. Eventually. I'm sure this is covered by John's insurance."

"You're sure? I'm not. But that doesn't even matter. There's just no way I could come anywhere near that amount, not in any time frame that would do you any good."

"They're going to *kill* him," Ariel pleads.

"Oh, Laurel, you don't know that. There's no way to know that."

Ariel waits a few seconds. "Bucky," she says. "Do you know anyone else who could help?"

"*Any*one?" She can hear him take a deep breath. "You know I do. But I'm pretty sure you don't want to go to him."

Neither of them is going to utter the man's name on a nonsecure phone.

"Of course I don't, Bucky. But can you think of any other option?"

"After this call," Griffiths says, "we'll be finished. I'll take Pryce back to her hotel."

Jefferson raises her eyebrows. CIA station chiefs don't tend to serve as personal drivers for American civilians in distress.

This is Nicole's problem with the gender imbalance within the Agency. It's not always a political one; not always an issue of feminism, or equity. It's a practical consideration. Situations often call for women, and there simply aren't enough of them around.

194

"Have you worked a lot of kidnappings?" Jefferson asks.

"Not here. This is the first in my four years in Lisbon. And kidnapping is usually not an Agency thing. Probably won't be this time either. Though that depends on who these people are."

"These people? You mean the kidnapped guy and . . . ? Who?"

"And the wife, Jefferson. Married couples are always a team. Except when they're enemies."

Ariel's mobile is still not getting a signal. She suspects that the CIA is jamming service in this room, forcing Ariel to use their landline, ensuring their access to her conversations. Ariel knows that neither her own cell nor the burner will be safe enough for the next call she needs to make, not nearly. And it would be patently irresponsible to make that call from the embassy's line; it might even be illegal. No matter the extenuating circumstances, Ariel can't relax her vigilance now. Especially not now.

CHAPTER 17

Day 1. 8:48 p.m.
Ariel gazes out the car window. The sun hasn't yet fully set, and golden light is washing the façades of the buildings at the very tops of hills. But down here in the central valley, without direct sunlight, everything has fallen into dimness, muting the colors. Streetlights have come on, casting their sharp-edged cones. Ariel can feel darkness descending quickly, the way it does in cities, with buildings that block the sun's last low rays. In the country, night comes on slower.

"Thanks," she says to Griffiths, "you can drop me here. I want to get something at the snack kiosk." This is not true.

"You sure? I can wait."

"No thanks," Ariel says. "But I appreciate the offer."

"Wait." Griffiths thrusts a business card at Ariel. "Please let me know if you hear anything?"

Ariel takes the card, climbs out of the car.

She surveys the square, packed with people, eating and drinking and strolling and sitting, there must be a hundred people, no way to scrutinize all of them. She walks slowly, her head moving left to right and back, trying to identify the men who are loitering alone. She can see six of them, but two are too old, one is too young, and one is too ridiculous looking, wearing a garish outfit that demands more attention than any tail would choose. That leaves two men who might be watching her; she memorizes their outfits.

For appearance's sake, she buys a juice at the kiosk, then resumes crossing the twilit square, continuing to look around but losing energy fast, her concentration flagging. Ariel feels like her nerves have been flayed, her emotions rubbed raw, her spirit exposed and beaten by the futility of all those meetings today, the phone calls, the failure of every single interaction.

Night is falling. She's about to be all alone, in the dark, in a foreign city, very far from home, a place whose language she doesn't speak, where her husband is missing, where she doesn't know anyone. She feels the weight of all this pressing down on her shoulders, on her psyche, on her everything, it's an overwhelming weight, one she may not be able to bear. What will it look like, getting crushed by this weight?

It will look like this: standing on a sidewalk,

sobbing.

Ariel lets it happen, she doesn't try to stop the flow that's streaming down her face, her shoulders convulsing. She allows herself to feel the fullness of it, her whole body racked by intense sobs. Let it come. What does she care if all of Lisbon sees her crying? She welcomes it.

She cries until she is all cried out, for now. She takes a deep quavering breath, pushes her shoulders back, chest out, head up. Then she resumes walking through the last of Lisbon's light, as dusk gives way to night.

Griffiths listens to the recording of Ariel Pryce talking to her ex-husband, Bucky Turner, via a phone that's connected to the car speakers. Their voices surround Griffiths; the final click that ends the conversation sounds like a needle being removed from vinyl.

"My God," she says to Jefferson, who emailed the playback from her computer at the embassy. Every once in a while, Griffiths is amazed at all the technology, the everyday ordinariness of these extraordinary things that were unthinkable when she'd started at the Agency.

"What the fuck was that?"

"I know, right?"

"Let's hear that bit again about the other man."

"— anyone else who could help?"

"Anyone? You know I do. But I'm pretty sure you don't want to go to him."

"Of course I don't, Bucky. But can you think of any other option?"

There's a long pause before the ex-husband asks, "What makes you believe he'd have this type of cash lying around?"

"Please. You don't think he has numbered accounts somewhere like Luxembourg? Or maybe uncut diamonds in a safe-deposit box in Zurich?"

"I don't know anything about any of that, Laurel. And neither do you."

"Oh you know that he's every type of tax dodger. Not to mention a criminal in other ways."

"You shouldn't be making accusations like this, especially not if you're going to ask for his help."

Griffiths turns this exchange over in her mind.

"What are you thinking?" Jefferson asks.

"They're both definitely scared of the man they're discussing. My first thought was organized crime, but that phrase *a criminal in other ways* makes it sound like he's not a criminal professionally. Just a — I don't know — occasional lawbreaker. An amateur."

"Maybe he's a business associate of the ex-husband?"

"It's possible. Whoever this man is, Pryce

hates him. Are we up on her phones yet?"

"Yeah. Her mobile, and the burner, and the landline in her hotel room. Everything."

"Good. Now let's take a look at the kidnapped husband too."

"What about him?"

"Everything."

"I need to make a call," Ariel says to the night clerk, Alexandra, according to her name tag. "And I don't want to use the phone in my room."

"I'm sorry?" Alexandra is a lean, muscular young woman who looks like she runs ten miles every day plus on Saturday nights goes kickboxing.

"My husband has been kidnapped."

"Meu Deus."

"And I'm worried that my phone" — Ariel holds up her cell — "might be bugged. People might be listening. And if they bugged my mobile, then maybe they bugged my room phone too. Do you understand?"

The young woman has clearly understood all the words that just tumbled out of Ariel's mouth — language isn't the barrier — but not what the hell is wrong with this crazy American.

"So I want to use yours" — pointing at the landline console — "to make a very important call. To try to save my husband's *life.*"

Ariel knows that the clerk is going to accede. She doesn't really have a choice, working in a place like this. "Of course," she says, smiling placidly. "My pleasure."

It takes just a couple of seconds to find the main number, a simple web search, then click the first link and hit CONTACT, no need to scroll, right there at the top of the page. The magic of the internet. It's easy to forget this, looking at the toxic effects of social media, at the economic devastation wrought by online retail and the tech-driven gig economy and the decline of Main Street, at the mis- and disinformation that threatens the integrity of democracy, in fact the integrity of everything. It's a long list of negatives. But they're easy to ignore when you want a late-night ride home from a bar, or a pizza delivered, or an anonymous hookup. Or a phone number for anyone in America.

It's not news to Ariel that this main number is easy to find; she'd conducted this exact search before. She'd even punched in these very same digits, attempted to reach this man in this office, in this fashion. She'd failed before. She's prepared to fail again. She knows what the failure will sound like. And she knows what she'll do afterward.

"Will he know what this is about?"
"Yes he will."
"One moment please."

201

Ariel is now on her third iteration of the same conversation in as many minutes, presumably making progress, each person who answers in closer physical proximity to her destination. All these gatekeepers have been hesitant — they've never heard of anyone named Laurel Turner — but none is willing to be overtly incredulous, or dismissive, or hostile. You never know who's going to be on the phone; you don't want to piss off the wrong caller.

Although American offices are largely closed today, Ariel is sure that the man she's trying to reach has been working. He probably works every day, no holidays, not even Independence Day.

Ariel has been on hold for a long time. She imagines that this must be the final gatekeeper, the person who has walked into the boss's office, waited for a break in the conversation, then leaned over to whisper, "There's a Laurel Turner calling, she says you'll know what it's about?"

He wouldn't immediately respond. He'd sit stone-still for a second or two, his mind racing to game out the scenarios, considering the downsides to taking the call versus refusing it, speculating about what could happen next, how this threat would escalate, why, and to what end.

The conclusion he'll inevitably come to is yes, he does need to talk to this caller. But no, he does not need to take this call at this moment, not in this office, not among these witnesses. "I'll get back to her," he'd mutter, trying to sound dismissive, not meeting the assistant's eye, hoping that his nonchalance will bury this interaction in a haystack, and thus that she won't be able to recall the caller's name, later. Even though he hired this woman precisely because she remembers absolutely everything and keeps immaculate, comprehensive records. Plus, Ariel has no doubt, she's good-looking.

He'd debate this with himself: Should he ask this assistant — who let's face it is not just good-looking, but drop-dead gorgeous — to *not* log this call? Or would that only draw more attention? Should he instead redact the record himself, after the fact? Both choices would seem bad. And this recognition would maybe lead him to worry about the endgame that would eventually follow from this call's opening gambit. The situation is bad, and he has no doubt that the badness has just begun.

He knows that his security is buttressed by ironclad agreements, by incontestable law, by the threat of financial ruin, of jail even. But it's also possible that none of this matters anymore. The world has changed since those agreements were signed; the law has lost some of its bite, some of its relevance. Facts too. Mere accusations can be just as bad —

or worse — in the current climate, when innuendo and rumor and falsehoods can travel farther, faster, than the truth ever hoped to. This shift has benefited him, to be sure. But he's fully aware that it can harm him too. It can destroy him.

Maybe he'd beckon the assistant back, and speak softly so the half-dozen other middle-aged men wouldn't hear him say, "This is personal, please don't put it in the log."

She wouldn't miss a beat, she'd nod, "Of course," while panic rushed through her because it was too late for that, and she'd be trying to figure out how to doctor her records, how traceable that would be, and by whom, and when, and what sort of trouble she'd end up in for that, versus what trouble she'd be in for not doing it, for not even trying — this is the debate that would consume her as she crossed the large room away from all those men, a couple of them probably watching her ass. She wears tight skirts because she knows it's expected. And she really, really wants this job.

"I'm sorry," she'll say, back at her desk, "may I take a number? He'll have to call you back."

Ariel needs to exhaust all possibilities. The cops need to do it, the embassy, the CIA: There's a protocol for everyone, for everything, a set of escalating responses to increasingly urgent indicators, one check after another, marked in one box after another.

She calls John's office, even though she suspects that she won't get through to any live person there. But she needs to make this effort, and hope for something in response, anything. First his direct line, where voicemail picks up immediately: "Hi, this is John Wright, I'm out of the country on business, and our offices are closed for the holiday. We'll reopen on Wednesday the fifth. Please leave a message, and I'll return your call as soon as possible."

Ariel leaves a message relating the bare bones of the predicament, in case someone other than John picks up his voicemail. She repeats the exercise with the company's general line, gets the same response — closed for the holiday, we'll get back to you on Wednesday.

She's doing what she can do. What else is there?

"Bucky? He's refusing to take my call."

"Well I guess I'm not surprised."

"But you can get through to him, right? You're still friends."

Bucky doesn't answer.

"Please, Bucky. I need you to convince him. *Please.*"

"*Convince* him? How?"

Ariel is reluctant to say this aloud; she feels

the severity of it, the crime of it. "I have a recording of our final conversation."

"Whose?"

"Me and him."

"Sweet Jesus. I don't want to hear this, do I?"

"I was wearing a wire. Tell him."

"Oh God Laurel. That sounds pretty illegal."

What it sounds like is a surreptitious recording made without consent. It sounds like blackmail. It is, indeed, both.

"Do you really want to do this?"

Ariel snorts. "No, I don't *want* to have anything to do with that bastard ever again; you of all people know that. What I *want* — sincerely — is for him to be in jail, or better yet dead. But I *need* —" She cuts herself off before she loses her composure. "I don't have a choice, Bucky. So right now I need to make sure that neither does he."

"What if he still refuses?"

"Then I'll make my recording public. And whatever ends up happening with my predicament, and with John, and — I don't know — *jail,* or *death,* for him that'll be beside the point, because his life will be completely ruined."

"I can't do this. I can't threaten —"

"You won't need to."

"This is extortion. You understand that, right? When people talk about the crime of

206

extortion, this is exactly what they're talking about. This is what you're asking me to do."

"You're just a messenger."

"Do you think the police will agree?"

"You know it's never going to come to that. He'll never risk the public disclosure. You know why, and I know why, and he knows why, and unless he wants everyone to know it too — which he cannot afford — then he'll take my call."

Ariel is not surprised at Bucky's resistance. No one would exactly jump at this opportunity. But she's confident that Bucky will give in, eventually. Ariel can extort him too, if she needs to.

"I'm really not comfortable with this."

Of course not. If Bucky were comfortable confronting this man, their lives would be very different.

"Neither am I, Bucky. Comfort is not a luxury I have."

There's nothing to do now except wait. But Ariel can no longer bear to just sit here in her hotel room, staring at nothing, so she turns on the television, navigates through the cable system to the American news network.

"— hearings are due to begin in just five days. The administration is hoping to conclude these hearings, and to confirm the nominee, before the start of the August recess, just weeks away."

Ariel goes to the kitchenette, pours a glass of ice water, returns to the TV.

"— into the nominee's business dealings, of course, but also into his personal life —"

Does she really want to watch this?

"— accusations in the past, although never any indictments."

"So what are we likely to learn about these accusations during the confirmation hearings?"

"In all likelihood? Nothing."

She changes the channel.

CHAPTER 18

Day 1. 10:03 p.m.
Ariel checks her cell, and the burner: still nothing. She confirms that her door is locked, an instinctive gesture in the vague direction of self-preservation. She should check on her son, her mom. She wonders which friend Elaine would've called, and realizes —

Damn.

She opens the device-tracking app, which locates George's phone at an unfamiliar spot, halfway between Ariel's house and the city, in an exurb that Ariel doesn't recognize for anything.

"Mom? Where are you?"

"At my cousin Rhoda's house."

"Rhoda?" Ariel thought Rhoda had died years ago.

"Well, Rhoda passed. But you remember her husband, Bud?"

Bud? "Um . . ."

"That's where we are. Any developments?"

"No, not really. But listen, Mom, I have to

ask you to deactivate your cell. George's too."

Elaine sighs, but doesn't say anything.

"With GPS locators, and cellular signals, triangulating the towers . . . honestly I don't understand the technology. But looking at my phone, I could see exactly where you are. I could even see the kidney-shaped pool in Rhoda's backyard. Bud's."

"Well isn't that good? Don't you want that?"

"But Mom, the problem is that if I can locate you, then someone else could too."

"Who? What is it you're worried about?"

"And I mean not just putting the phones to sleep. Power them all the way off, and leave them that way, all the time. Give me Bud's phone number, I'll call when I can."

"You have to tell me *what's going on.*"

"Mom. Please."

"Don't treat me like a child. I'm your *mother.*"

Ariel takes a deep breath. "How's George? Is he okay?"

Elaine too takes a second before answering. "He said his stomach felt *knotty.*"

Damn. "Did he take his pill this morning?"

"Yes."

"Are you sure?"

"*Yes.* My Lord."

"Okay, can you please put him on? And then after we hang up, *please* remember about the phones. Do you know my number by heart?"

"Are you kidding me? I barely know my own."

"Well, write it down on a piece of paper before you power down. Then if you need to call me, do it from someone else's phone. Or from a pay phone."

"Seriously? When's the last time you saw a pay phone?"

Ariel doesn't say anything.

"Are you really not going to tell me what's going on?"

"I told you, Mom."

"But what does John being kidnapped in Portugal have to do with anyone triangulating my cell phone location on Long Island? What are you afraid of? *Who?*"

"I can't tell you."

"What does that even *mean?*"

"Can't you just *believe* me, Mom?" They're yelling at each other. Escalation happens quickly with them. "Can't you just *trust* me? Why do I have to *prove* every goddamn thing to you, as if we're in court and you're the judge?"

They fall into the relative silence of heavy breathing, like boxers sitting in their corners between rounds, nursing wounds, gathering strength. The round that just ended was not the first.

"I don't see how you can live like this." Elaine

211

said this within five minutes of arriving at Ariel's house on Friday afternoon, barely a half-hour before Ariel needed to leave for the airport. "I really don't."

Ariel's mom expresses some variation of this sentiment every time she visits, looking around the yard, the house, there's always something being torn up, something replaced or rebuilt — the downstairs washroom with an open patch of floor to access a burst pipe, the side porch with a half-built banister, the old maple pulled down next to the driveway and chain-sawed into large chunks but not yet into manageable firewood. There's always a large category of noncritical projects that can persist for long periods in the nonspecific future, awaiting attention. Ariel accepts this permanent state of demi-disrepair, but her mother adheres to the opposite operating principle: everything must be perfect, all the time. Or at least appear that way. Which is really the only sort of perfection: the apparent sort.

"It looks like a hurricane just tore through." Elaine watched Fletcher trot across the yard, as if the goat suddenly realized he was late for an important meeting. Fletcher is supposed to live in the barn with the other farm animals, but often manages to make his way across the lawn and up to the back porch, sometimes walking right through the kitchen door to devour whatever's accessible. The goat can eat a dozen apples in a minute, unabashed, staring at you as he chews, almost as if he's smiling, jaw moving side to side.

"It *always* looks that way," Elaine said, dripping with disappointment and disapproval.

At first glance, yes, Ariel's existence might look like something cobbled together — the different sorts of animals, of income, of cast-off furniture and furnishings and fittings, a life that looks haphazard. But it's on her own terms, under her own control. This doesn't make her life neat, but it's a chaos that's understood, a disorder that's expected.

"It's a farm, Mom. This is what it's like."

Even the chickens have a certain charm. Ariel likes how they wander around, oblivious, minding their own business, not asking anything of anyone, unobtrusive.

"But you're not a farmer, Dear."

"Well, Mom, I sort of am. I live on a farm, I earn farm income, I pay farm taxes."

"But you don't *farm,* do you?"

Ariel took a deep breath. She knew what was coming next:

"You don't *need* to live like this . . ." Elaine swept her hand across the room, across the everything — the mismatched chairs, chipped-paint floorboards, dog-hairy rug, slopped-over water bowls, the lingering memory of a housepettish goat.

"*Like this.* What does that mean, Mom?"

213

"Don't be coy. You know what I mean."

Elaine was convinced that the ultimate luxury was having other people do everything for you; Ariel thought it was having the freedom to do things for yourself. Elaine was like Bucky, who believed that the more people doing the more for him, the better.

It had taken Ariel a long time to realize many things that now seem abundantly self-evident. That's life, isn't it? Realizing again and again how wrong you used to be.

"You have other choices."

"Like what, Mom? Tell me, how should I *choose* to live instead of this? And who exactly should *pay* for those choices? And what in return would I need to sacrifice?"

Elaine made a dismissive noise.

"I mean, what *else*?"

This final jab — thrust in, twisted — was a sore point between them; the sorest. It wasn't merely that Ariel disapproved of her mother's overall lifestyle; that was Elaine's own damn business. Ariel held her mother responsible, at least partially, for her own misfortunes. All throughout Ariel's life, she'd watched Elaine acquiesce to so much, so consistently, with such feeble objections, as if her mom had internalized her dad's opinions, his preferences, his demands. Elaine pre-acquiesced, is what she did. To everything. This was how Ariel was raised, to think that this was what it meant to be a woman, to be a wife. So that's how Ariel had stumbled into her own marriage, without any idea of how to remain herself. She'd been taught not to.

This wasn't totally fair, Ariel knew. But feelings don't need to be fair to be genuine.

Ariel also knew that now was not the time to fight about this, nor about anything else, not when Elaine had just traveled a thousand miles to do her daughter this immense favor.

"Look Mom, I appreciate that you made a long trip."

Elaine's second husband had insisted on a move to South Carolina — year-round golf — and she'd been unable, or unwilling, to talk him out of it. Elaine had given in, as always. Of everything that Ariel resented about her mom — there was plenty — this was perhaps the ultimate: that Ariel might have internalized something malignant from her mother's spinelessness, her unwillingness to tell men anything that they did not want to hear.

Ariel has a hard time overlooking the dislikable parts of people, which is most challenging with her mother. Yes, Elaine can be relied upon to send a Christmas present, to babysit without major incident. But Elaine is also the person who had let Ariel down the earliest, the most surprisingly, the most unforgivably. This was why Ariel had felt so alone in the world, for so long: She couldn't expect

215

unconditional support even from her own mother.

Then when Bucky too failed her in such an awful way, Ariel stopped letting anyone off the hook. And this had become the one thing she most wished she could change about herself: her intolerance of imperfection. She'd tried. She'd failed.

Instead she was trying to convince herself that it was possible to love people while also hating important things about them. This too was hard. But the alternative had been harder.

Ariel took a deep breath. "I don't want to fight with you about how I live my life," she said. "Can we just not?"

The dogs were watching the scene warily, tails at half-mast. They'd been on heightened alert as soon as Ariel retrieved her suitcase from the basement. The dogs know there's nothing worse than Ariel's luggage, which is what appears right before she leaves — and this time it might be *forever,* you never know when your mommy is just not going to come back, it would be so awful. Such a dreadful thing to have to worry about, whenever you see luggage.

Ariel leaned down and hugged the dogs, making it worse, adding to their anxiety; a little whimper escaped from Mallomar. Ariel recognizes that she's selfish this way, with the animals she's responsible for, who owe her unconditional love, which she's determined

216

to collect as much of as possible. This is maybe the only completely credible type of love; all other varieties are suspect, unreliable, temporary, with questionable motives, outcomes that are foregone, disappointing.

Recently she came to the realization that she preferred the company of children and dogs to grown-up humans. Vastly. It's an uncomfortable thing to know about yourself, especially the dog part. Ariel forced herself to examine this, and realized that the things she loved about dogs — their unquestioning loyalty and unrestrained affection, their delight in play, in running around for the sheer joy of running around, their utter lack of self-awareness — these are all the best aspects of little children. The more her own child grew, the more she missed that innocence. Gone forever.

"Okay. But Ariel, why on earth do you now have a *goat*?"

Cyrus the neighbor had purchased Fletcher the goat to keep the company of Shadow the horse, who seemed to be depressed, but it turned out that the horse's lethargy and lack of appetite were due not to ennui but to equine infectious anemia virus, and Shadow died just weeks after Fletcher arrived, and then Cyrus died a few months later, leaving the goat all alone, the mere thought of which made Ariel weep.

"Are you kidding? You're asking me if you can *adopt* that moron's goat?"

This was dead Cyrus's ex-wife on the phone from Scottsdale. They'd divorced two decades ago, after their kids had left home, when they admitted that they hated each other.

"Yes, that's what I'm asking."

This was apparently the funniest thing the old woman had ever heard. "No," she said, when she was finally able to bring the hilarity under control. "I want to travel six thousand miles round-trip to collect my ignoramus of an ex-husband's orphaned *goat* to live with me. In my one-bedroom condo. In a *retirement* community."

"I see. Then —"

"He'll be my *pickleball* partner."

"Okay, thanks. I'll send the paperwork as soon as I can."

"*Paper*work? Are you *insane*?" Then she hung up on Ariel, who related the conversation to Cyrus's estate lawyer Jerry, who wasn't really an estate lawyer, and didn't want to deal with this — not Cyrus's estate, and definitely not Cyrus's orphaned goat.

"Oh, Ariel, just . . ." Jerry buried his face in his hands, and massaged his eye sockets. "I don't . . . Just *take* the goat, will you? Please leave me out of it."

"Thank you, Jerry, thank you," Ariel said, and started to leave Jerry's office, then turned back. "Do you know how?"

"How what?"

"How I should take the goat?"

Jerry's mouth fell open.

"Like, should I use a leash?"

He opened his mouth but couldn't summon an answer. Instead he spread his hands as if to encompass the desk piled with legal files, the bookshelves filled with clothbound case law, the framed degrees from a second-rate college and a third-rate law school, the suffocating levels of student debt, the indignity of failing the bar exam not once or twice but three times, the dispiriting realization that he was a born choker, self-relegating himself to this sleepy small-town practice, prenups and DUIs and mortgage refis, small-fry litigation that ends with boilerplate NDAs. Jerry was intimately familiar with every corner of unremunerative law, but none of it had anything to with transporting orphaned goats.

"Thanks Jerry," Ariel said. "I owe you a drink."

He blinked his assent; this wouldn't be the first time that Ariel paid for Jerry's expertise with a glass or two — or three or four — of bourbon. Jerry embraced all the clichés of the struggling small-town single-shingle barrister, complete with failed marriage, irresponsible nutrition, and functional alcoholism.

Fifteen minutes later Ariel was leading

219

Fletcher down the road by twenty feet of cotton clothesline that she'd plucked from her backyard, which was often strung with clothesline, another housekeeping choice of which her mom disapproved.

"It's your life," Elaine said. "I guess."

"I'll get George," her mom says now, walking away from this fight, thankfully. "Hold on."

Ariel waits while the background noises shift, until it sounds like a television. Of course: Elaine's main parenting strategy has always been to turn on the TV. Ariel tries not to fret too much about the choices her mom makes in loco parentis, while Ariel is away once or twice per year on her business trips. But the TV crutch drives her bonkers.

"Hi Mommy."

A few months ago, George's voice started to crack and change, and now Ariel barely recognizes it, the sound of her own son. But even in its less familiar form, George's voice melts her heart, especially when he calls her Mommy.

"Hi Sweetheart. You doing okay?"

"Yeah," he says. "Mostly."

"You taking your medicine?"

"Yeah."

"But still you're not feeling great?"

"Not great, no."

"On a one-to-ten, how bad?"

"I don't know. Not that bad."

220

Ariel doesn't want to press, doesn't want to force him to complain, doesn't want to reinforce his victimhood, which can be corrosive, can become an obsession, can evolve into the primary way you define yourself. Ariel had fallen into this pit herself, and it had taken so long to climb out. Her child is trying to avoid this fate; she should let him.

"Okay," she says. "If it gets bad?"

"I know what to do, Mom." He sounds exasperated, probably a familiar sound to every parent. It's probably what Ariel herself sounded like thirty years ago. Hell, it's probably what she sounded like just a minute ago, yelling at her own mother.

"Please don't worry, Mommy."

Oh God. Don't worry?

Ariel has started crying again, and she moves the microphone away from her mouth so her kid can't hear it. She takes a deep breath, trying to swallow her crying, to push it down just enough to force a smile so she can say "I won't" and it will sound sincere, this complicated little lie she's telling her son.

"I love you," she adds, wanting to say something that's true. "I love you *so* much."

It hadn't been a deliberate choice. It just happened one night at a time, George crawling into her bed after a bad dream, or with a stomachache, and simply not leaving. Eventually he stopped offering the excuses. She'd be

221

reading — she was always reading, it was a big part of her job but one that she couldn't accomplish during the workday — with Mallomar resting his ridiculously hairy chin on her shin. George would come shuffling in, slink over to the other side of the queen bed, followed by Scotch, who'd plop down on the carpet, curling into a butterscotch-colored ball.

In the morning when Ariel's alarm went off, George would still be there, and she'd let him sleep for another hour while she took care of all the morning things. Then she'd pat his shoulder, he'd ask, "What?" and she'd say, "Time to get up." This had been happening almost every night for years, during which Ariel never stopped questioning it. Was this a healthy degree of closeness, of comfort, of dependency? Or was she screwing up her kid? Or herself?

She found herself unwilling to do anything about it. The truth was she liked it, liked having another life next to her, liked hearing the kid breathe, knowing he was safe, not sick, not nightmaring, not lonely. And neither was she.

When George had been six years old, or eight, when he was four feet tall, fifty pounds, when he sucked his thumb and carried his teddy bear, when she carried him in her arms: Back then it was much easier to answer charitably, to see theirs as a natural way to live, partners in everything, dinner together every night, wake up together every morning. All they had was each other. That was clear to everyone, especially to themselves.

Then he started to pull away. More afternoons away from home, playing with other kids, soccer and baseball and video games. When he was home, he spent more time alone in his bedroom; he no longer did homework at the dining table within sight of Ariel preparing dinner, he no longer watched TV with her at night, he no longer wanted her to read aloud. He resisted public displays of affection, then private ones. He started to keep secrets, withholding information for the sake of withholding, to test out lying, seeing how it works, if you get caught, what are the consequences.

There'd been no dramatic pronouncements, no hard stops, no big blowouts, no new rules. But although gradual, this evolution happened over the course of just a few months. It came on fast, adolescence.

Ariel could still vaguely remember her own experience of pubescence, the imperative to create distance, to define a new self that was separate from her parents. She remembers being unable to avoid hating her parents, even though she hadn't wanted to; at least before they'd given her reason.

She could see this now in her own child. She could even recognize his occasional bouts of self-loathing; she could tell that George didn't understand it, couldn't justify it, didn't know why he couldn't resist the urge to criticize her cooking, her driving, her anything.

"Mom, could you, just, not?"

"Not what?"

"Could you not, like, *breathe* so loud?"

Their tight little team of two, us against the world, had looked impermeable; it had looked permanent. Ariel had known this wasn't true, but for years she'd pretended otherwise. That was no longer possible. But the kid was still crawling into her bed almost every night.

"Hey Sweetie?"

They were seated on adjoining sides of the table, the same positions for every meal, for George's whole life, ever since the high chair. He looked up, wary, already prepared to be angry.

"I think maybe you should sleep in your own bed tonight."

He opened his mouth to answer, and his lower lip trembled. Suddenly he was not the surly adolescent. This was the same look as the heartbroken toddler when she'd informed him that they'd left Teddy on the ferry by mistake.

"Tonight?" he asked.

She'd grilled steak, even though she didn't eat beef. George had been craving protein, red meat in particular, which for most of his life he'd never had. Involuntary dietary limitations had been the subject of one of their bigger recent arguments. He'd won.

"I think maybe most nights."

Ariel could see him trying to understand this, with different developmental stages of himself warring against one another, opposing imperatives. Ariel didn't know which she was rooting for. A big tear rolled down the new peach fuzz of his cheek, which had become leaner, his whole body longer, like a stretched rubber band, thin and taut and dangerously close to popping.

"Why?"

"I think you need space, you're —"

He banged his fist on the table and everything jumped — flatware rattled, plates clanged. His fork, which was speared with a piece of bloody beef, fell off his plate, onto the bare table.

The dogs stood, alert, trying to figure out the problem, looking from George to Ariel and back.

"I think —"

"I hate you!" He pushed back from the table and his chair toppled and Mallomar barked. "I *hate* you!"

Ariel could hear Scotch's claws clatter up the stairs, following George's angry clomping, then his bedroom door slam. Mallomar by her side whimpered, and she reached down to pat him, to try to reassure him. To try to reassure herself.

She stared at the space vacated by her child, his upended chair, half-eaten food. She felt her own lip trembling too. Sitting there at her beat-up cast-off kitchen table, Ariel tried to tell herself that this was the right thing to do, even if it caused everyone involved to cry. But she didn't entirely believe it. She was suddenly so sad about so many things — about every decision she'd ever made, every direction she'd allowed her life to take that had led her here, to this lonely spot where she knew she was going to make her kid cry, and she went ahead and did it anyway, on purpose.

Her life was only going to get more lonely, wasn't it? Everything was only going to get worse.

Ariel had been ignoring too much for too long. She'd justified her willful ignorance because she'd also brought so many things under control, she'd congratulated herself on her achievements, her competence, her confidence. Maybe it's zero-sum. You can't have everything, you need to pick your battles, figure out what you can't live without, make sure those are the ones you win.

She could hear George upstairs, banging around in his room, the anguished barking of the dog. Ariel would not go up there. She would leave him alone in his anger. Space was what he needed, even if it wasn't what he wanted. Sometimes there's a huge difference.

George cried himself to sleep, and Ariel tossed and turned until just before dawn. This wasn't the first time she'd second-guessed herself all through the night. Convinced that none of her choices had ever been good. Determined to make a change, before it was too late.

CHAPTER 19

Day 1. 10:44 p.m.
"Hello?"

"Ms. Turner," he says. "It's been a long time."

Ms. Turner? He's performing. He probably suspects that he's being recorded. Or maybe he's sure of it because he's the one doing the recording himself, to ensure its integrity. These days everything can be manipulated — photos, videos, audios. The only way to counter someone else's manipulated evidence is to manipulate your own, then amplify it. The loudest voice wins.

"To what do I owe the pleasure of your call?"

"I'm in Lisbon. My husband has been kidnapped. The ransom demand is three million euros within two days."

He waits a beat before answering, "That's terrible."

"It is. And I don't have that kind of money. Nowhere near."

Silence.

"I need your help."

More silence. Ariel waits it out.

"Look," he says, like politicians do before they say something disingenuous, "I'm very sorry for this unfortunate thing that's happening to you. I'll be happy to make an inquiry, to double-check that local law enforcement is giving this matter their full attention, and that the State Department is also participating in the appropriate manner. But you know that I can't . . ."

She hears the sound of her own breathing through the earpiece. He hears it too.

"You know that I can't *intervene.*"

"Of course you can."

"What do you think I can do?"

"You can get someone to send in some expeditionary force to rescue him."

"You *know* I can't do that."

"Or you can get me three million euros."

"Are you insane? I can't imagine why you'd think I'd do that."

"*Imagine?* No, you don't need to *imagine* it. You know exactly why I'd think that."

"Again, I'm very sorry for your predicament, but —"

"You don't think I'm calling without any leverage, do you?" She sounds desperate. She is. "You don't for one minute think —"

"Stop talking."

"— that with the paternity records, and the

229

Hamptons police report, and —"

"*Goddamn it!* Stop. Talking."

She stops talking.

"Go to the embassy."

"I was already at the embassy. Twice. And now it's the middle of the night. It's closed."

"Someone will open it."

"When?"

"I guess right now." He sighs. "Go now."

She heads in the general direction of noise, light, people, taxis. She passes an old man walking two dogs, and he gives her a sidelong glance, but no, he can't be CIA or police or kidnappers, not with two dogs. She looks around at everything else, trying to absorb all the details. You never know what's going to be useful; you never know what you're going to be asked to recall.

At the far end of the square, she can see another figure, standing in the darkness beneath a tree, leaning against the trunk. She turns away, as if she didn't notice him.

There's a taxi, and she rushes toward it, raises her arm, hops in.

"The American embassy," she says, and waits for the driver to meet her eye in the mirror, but he doesn't. She wonders if he's the person who's following her; that would make a certain amount of sense.

They hurtle past the occasional nightlife outpost, pools of streetlights illuminating

230

islands of liveliness at bars and clubs, separated by wide seas of empty dark, through which the sticky-seated taxi flies like a rum-running smuggler, and Ariel's heart races like one too, everything accelerating, expanding, beyond her control.

"You can leave your bag and devices here, in a locker. I'll give you the key."

"Thanks, I'd rather keep these with me."

"I'm sorry," the guard says, "but that wasn't an offer."

"Listen," she says, trying to sound calm, measured, "I'm dealing with a really tremendous emergency. And it's possible that I'll get an important call. Extremely important. Can't I just . . ."

She trails off; the guard is shaking his head.

"Please, they're just *phones*. And this is so important."

"My apologies, but regulations forbid it. Electronic devices can be anything. Triggering devices for explosives. Eavesdropping equipment. Virus hosts. They can be actual viruses."

"*Please.* I'm begging."

She's done a lot of begging today.

"I'll tell you what we can do," he says. "I'll keep your devices out here, on this table. If one of them rings, I'll get you out here to answer it."

Ariel doesn't have a choice. She hands over

her things.

"This way."

She walks through a metal detector under the watchful eye of the Marine, into the waiting supervision of another. They walk a few steps down a short hall, then he uses a passkey to unlock a door to a windowless room that's just feet from security, secluded from the rest of the building. Maybe to keep visitors to this room from seeing the embassy staff. Or the other way around. Or both.

"Please have a seat," the guard says. "Your call will come through here. I'll be right outside. If you need anything, press this." He indicates a red button in the wall next to the acoustic-tiled door, which has a rubber seal running all around it. He closes the door behind him with a *whoosh*.

Ariel doesn't need to check the handle to know she's locked in here. She sits in one of the plastic chairs that surround a round laminate-top table, with a substantial-looking communications console affixed to the middle. The phone's wiring disappears into the table's pedestal, down into the floor, with no way for a visitor to access the wires, nor the jack.

She's surprised that this room doesn't have a two-way mirror, but then realizes that no, of course not. This isn't an interrogation room; there must be other rooms in this building for questioning, of both the friendly and unfriendly sorts. This room's purpose is to put people at ease. This is a very secure room, with a very secure phone line. That's why she's here.

Ariel wonders if making her wait is purposeful. Or if there's some reason on the other end that accounts for the delay. But it doesn't matter, does it? Either way she's waiting, her anxiety mounting, unable to think of anything other than: Will this work?

"You're telling me that at this very moment she's *in* the embassy." Nicole Griffiths had been lying in bed with a stack of reports in her lap, on her way to drifting off to a deep, sound sleep. Now she's wide awake. This American woman had not only forced Griffiths to cancel her date with Pietro, she's also going to ruin her full-night-of-sleep consolation.

"That's right," Antonucci says. "I followed her back to the hotel, then twenty minutes ago she emerged and got in a taxi, so I followed that. Imagine my surprise when the taxi dropped her at the embassy. So I waited a couple of minutes, then came inside. The duty guard tells me that he received orders to deliver Pryce to the secure-comms room."

"Orders? From?"

"The Marine won't tell me. Which is understandable."

Her mind is racing around the corner, trying to guess what it could mean that this seemingly random American woman has been directed into a secure location that exists so sensitive communications can be passed among agents, assets, and officers without worrying about intercepts.

"Christ."

It wouldn't be anyone in Lisbon who gave this order, nor Langley, not without Griffiths's knowledge. So this order must have come from Foggy Bottom. Which means that this woman must be more important than she's letting on. Or her husband is. Not just random Americans, apparently.

"We obviously can't eavesdrop on her conversation in there," Antonucci says, "but we can listen to the recordings of any other calls she made. We've been up on her phones for more than three hours now."

"Okay, good. You stay on her, do not let her out of your sight. I'll come in and listen to the recordings. And listen, Guido?"

"Yeah."

"Be careful. I get the feeling that this is a real thing."

The ring is shrill in the dead silence of this little room, and Ariel's hand instinctually shoots out to grab the handset, like the instinct to calm a crying baby. But just as she once forced herself to pause before comforting little George, she now forces herself to

234

take a breath before picking up and saying, "Hello."

He doesn't waste any time. "What the fuck do you want from me?"

"I told you: three million euros for my husband's ransom."

"Three million," he says. "Gee, that's a familiar number."

"Give me a break. It's not a number I conjured out of nowhere. My husband has been kidnapped, and that's the ransom price."

"Again, that's too bad, and I'm sorry that you find yourself in this terrible position. But why is that my problem?"

"You know why."

"No, I really do not."

Here it goes, she thinks, no turning back now: "Because I recorded our final conversation."

He's silent for a second, then says, "I have absolutely no idea what you're talking about."

"That conversation happened before I signed anything. You understand that, don't you?"

"I didn't consent to any recording of any conversation."

"*Consent?* How dare you use that word."

"I specifically took measures to prevent a recording. So any evidence would be inadmissible."

"First of all," she says, "one-party consent."

235

In New York, only one party to a conversation needs to give permission for a recording. Ariel was the one who consented.

"Second of all: Who gives a damn about *admissible*? I'll send the tape to everyone in the world *except* the lawyers. Every news outlet, every hacking collective, every foreign government, every social-media bigmouth."

"This is extortion you're committing right now. A serious criminal offense —"

"Really? In what jurisdiction? I'm in *Lisbon*. At this moment I could not care less about US law or its enforcement."

"— compounded by using the threat of committing another serious crime as the leverage. You will be prosecuted, I can promise you that. You will go to *prison*. And not just for thirty or sixty days of wrist-slapping."

"If — big *if*, by the way — I'm convicted. Unanimously. By a jury of my peers."

"You will serve *hard time.*"

"You know what a jury of my peers will include? Half women. Plus a couple of men who are fathers of girls. You remember how many jurors it takes to acquit, right? Of course you do. You went to law school."

"I will make *absolutely* certain that you serve your time in a very, very hard place."

"Okay, but you know what? I'd be *happy* to go to jail. I'll be a *hero* in jail. But you? Your career will be *over*. And not just your career. Your marriage too, your whole *life*. You will lose *every*thing. So yeah, you go ahead, seek legal remedy. I'll take my chances with a jury, and however many months, and whatever damages —"

Ariel realizes that she has gotten too agitated; she takes a deep breath.

"You will be a pariah," she resumes, much more quietly. Much more menacing. "And you will not recover. Not ever."

"You wouldn't do that."

"Are you really willing to risk everything that I won't?"

"Then why haven't you?"

"This is not a *recreational* situation I'm in right now; I'm not voluntarily doing this. And I'll reiterate: I'm not *going* to do this if you help me get my husband back."

He takes a moment to digest this, and she lets him. The ball is now in his court. But the clock is ticking. And he knows it.

"You said forty-eight hours?"

"A little less."

"I don't have that type of cash on hand. No one does. Except maybe drug lords."

Ariel nearly cries in relief, but gathers herself to say, "You can get it." She knows that a man like him has liquid assets all over the globe that he can convert into cash when business opens in tomorrow's European morning. He'd barely even notice the three million.

"I can't do this," he says. "Not now."

"Of course you can," she counters. "*Because* now."

He pauses again. He hates this, she can taste it through the phone. It's delicious.

"It's impossible. With the holiday, and banks closed, the markets too. This whole thing is impossible. I don't think I can come up with that amount of money, not this fast."

"Okay then, just rescue my husband. Get someone to call in the Marines, the Green Berets, Navy SEALs, I don't give a damn, any US boots on the ground. It's *one* man, in *Lisbon*. This is a problem that someone like you should be able to solve."

"I can't intercede like —"

"Are you kidding? People intercede all the time! For the wife of one of your best friends?"

"*Ex*-wife."

"Listen, you have three options: get me the cash; or get me my husband back; or lose everything."

He's silent. He must be asking himself which of these options is least bad. It's hard to argue that she's right about juries, about jail, about that whole scenario. He has no real choice, and he knows that she knows it.

"Okay," he finally says.

Ariel is worried that her body is going to explode from nervous release. "Okay what?"

"Okay you'll hear from someone."

"Who?"

"I don't know. I have to figure that out."

"When?"

"*When?* How do I know? Have I done this before?"

"Time is of the essence."

"Fuck you. Time is of the essence. Fuck you."

He sighs deeply. This is the last thing he expected to be dealing with tonight. But he has known for years that he'd probably need to deal with her again someday, in some way. Now may not be the ideal moment — now is in fact the worst possible moment — but that's probably why now is the inevitable one.

"No one can know about this," he says.

"Do you really think you need to tell me this?"

"*No one.* Not the Lisbon police, not the kidnappers, not your husband, not — I don't know — not *anyone. Ever.*" Ariel can hear him breathing; she knows that he's thinking through the steps, the additional risks down the line, the ways to mitigate them. "You'll need to sign an NDA, obviously. Before anything else happens."

"Of course."

He's fuming, he must be trying hard not to blow his stack. She wonders if he eventually learned to control his temper. She doubts it.

"Jesus," he says, "this is fucked-up."

"Fucked-up for you? Get over yourself. My husband has been *kidnapped.*"

239

"*Why?* Who *is* your husband anyway?"

"Just a regular Joe who looks like a rich American businessman."

"Is he?"

"Not really. Not like you. He doesn't have three million extra euros."

"Fuck."

Ariel doesn't want to be conciliatory with this man, but she needs to appease him at least a little. She needs him to do this. "I'll pay you back," she offers.

"Damn straight."

"I have money. You know I do."

"I don't know any such thing."

"Yes, you do. But that money is in trust."

She waits for him to ask a follow-up, but he doesn't. He knows what the trust is for, and why, but he probably doesn't want to let her divert this conversation to that narrative. And she's not going to antagonize him by trying.

"Do *not* contact me again."

"Yeah, got it. But listen? If you don't actually get me this money? If my husband is *killed* because of it? Then I'm going to gather all the microphones and megaphones of the world, and I'm going to release *everything.*"

CHAPTER 20

Day 1. 11:41 p.m.
Ariel looks around at the bland furniture, the unadorned walls, the locked door, on the other side of which is a very secure building guarded by armed Marines. Those soldiers are not here for the purpose of helping her; if anything, the Marines would be on his side. It hadn't occurred to her until just now that this might be a dangerous moment, but it is. She's threatening a powerful man while simultaneously giving him the opportunity to silence her. Did she walk herself into mortal jeopardy?

There's no one else here. No reporters waiting for appointments, no assistants watching sideways, no janitors pushing buckets, no diplomats hunched over computers.

No visitors. No guests. No witnesses.

Just a couple of soldiers, with their orders. With their loyalties. With their weapons —

With each passing second Ariel is becoming more and more convinced that she's going to be detained here. She feels her heartbeat accelerating as she approaches the door, and by the time she presses the red button her imagination is dashing toward escape possibilities — out a window, picking a lock, beating down a door with a broken-off table leg — and while she waits for a response she works herself up into a full-fledged panic, completely expecting to be a prisoner —

The lock clicks, the door swings open, and there's the guard, his expression unreadable. "Ma'am?"

"I'm finished here."

He doesn't respond immediately, and Ariel's spirit plummets. Is this the moment when he'll lead her down the hall to a different sort of windowless room?

"After you."

He directs her toward the front, where the other Marine is at the far side of the security checkpoint. Another armed man watching her, guarding another locked door. This one doesn't move as she approaches; he keeps his eyes trained on her.

The building is completely silent, the street sounds buffered by bulletproof glass, double vestibules, hardened walls.

RING!

It's the landline at the security station, light blinking, sound blaring. The guard picks up, returns his eyes to Ariel, who's now twenty feet away. "Yes sir, she's still here."

242

She slows her pace involuntarily.

"Yes sir."

Ariel is now ten feet away from the desk, and she can feel the Marine at her back. She's squeezed between the two. The desk officer puts down the phone, and looks at Ariel again. She wills herself to keep walking toward him, toward the door, toward freedom, even though with each step she becomes more sure that something else is going to happen, she has a vision of this right before it occurs: He holds up his left hand, leaving his right at his side, next to his holster.

"Ma'am?"

Her stomach does a flip, reminiscent of the days when her toddler always seemed to be about to knock over a glass, or a vase, and her body would have this gut response to the impending calamity. She'd tried to tell herself that it didn't matter, a broken mug, spilled milk, but she never really succeeded. There's no talking yourself out of some fears, no matter how petty, how irrational. This fear, though, is neither.

Ariel doesn't trust her voice. Instead she raises her eyebrows at the guard.

"Please wait," he says, with his hand still up in the halt position. "A car has been arranged to take you to your hotel."

Oh God, what a relief. Or is this a relief? Maybe not. No.

"Oh that's okay," she says. "I'll get a taxi myself."

"It's late, ma'am. The car will be here in a few minutes."

Yes, of course: *This* is how it would happen, isn't it? Now that Ariel thinks about it, no one is going to kill her *in* the embassy, and it wouldn't be Marines who did it.

No, it would be a freelancer — a foreigner — who arrives in an untraceable car in the middle of the night. How long would it take to launch this plan? The man she called knew from that first contact that something undesirable was coming, he knew exactly where Ariel would be, he had more than enough time to initiate a strategy after that first call, when was that? An hour and a half ago? Is that enough time for a rich, powerful American to hire a contract killer in Lisbon?

"You can sit here." The Marine indicates a trio of chairs.

"No, thanks, I'm happy to get a taxi myself."

"I'm sorry, but I have to insist. Orders, ma'am."

"Orders? From?"

He motions again toward the chairs. "Please."

Please. It can mean so many different things, can't it? Ariel knows she doesn't have a choice; it's not like she can bust out of here.

244

But once the car arrives, there's no way in hell she'll get into it.

So many of this man's problems would be solved if Ariel's life ended tonight. Not just the immediate problem of her phone calls and her attempted extortion, but the long-term threat of her very existence. A problem that has probably been on his mind for a long time, and increasingly so recently, as various people scratch at the surfaces of his life, looking for what's underneath.

Ariel: She's what's underneath.

If she simply disappears tonight in Portugal, that's something that would definitely be investigated. What would be found? Evidence scattered all over town that Ariel's husband had fallen into trouble, that she went looking for him and predictably fell into the same trouble, got herself killed. The policemen, the embassy, the hotel staff: all witnesses. Evidence might be unearthed, or perhaps manufactured; it's possible that at this very moment drugs are being planted in their suite, bags of heroin, or maybe piles of cash, or dirty handguns, or all of these together, an overwhelming volume of incontrovertible evidence that this American couple came to Lisbon to engage in criminal activities, and what did they get? What they deserved.

RINGGGGGG.

245

The landline seems even louder this time, closer, like an attack. Ariel is holding her own cell; the burner is in her pocket. She expects that both devices were tampered with while she was in the secure room, and that everything she does from now on will be monitored. Every email, every text message, every word she utters, whether on an open line or not, even when the phones appear to be powered off.

"Yes?" the Marine answers.

Another thing to worry about, and there are already so many. She feels all this worry pressing down on her again. How long ago was it when she stood on the sidewalk and sobbed? Just a few hours. She feels like she's on the edge of losing it again. She takes a deep, deep breath.

The Marine hangs up the phone, turns to Ariel. "Your car is here."

For the past minutes she has been studying the map on her screen, plotting routes, alternatives, contingencies. Maybe someone, somewhere, has been able to see that the map on her phone was active. But they wouldn't have been able to follow her eyes, to see why she was using the app.

She strides past the guard with a terse "Thanks," and then she's through the door, out to the quiet late-night street, where there's an Audi sedan idling in front of the gatehouse, parked in the single-carriage roadway that's separated from the wide avenue by a meridian with paving stones and benches and bollards and trees. That's a lot of buffering between the embassy and the traffic, a lot of separation from motorcyclists wielding handguns, from pickup-truck passengers with assault rifles, from eighteen-wheelers packed with explosives. US embassies everywhere are targets, maybe.

The driver pops out, hustles around to open a rear door for Ariel. He's big, not slender but also not fat; he looks solid, strong. He's wearing tight jeans that ride very low on his hips, denim decorated with extravagant stitching. His polo is garishly decorated with an oversize logo, with violent slashes of color and type on the sleeves and back, plus stripes on the collar, which he wears popped. His athletic shoes are an unfamiliar brand, small and tight and multicolored.

Definitely not an American.

With women it's harder to tell; women all the world over follow similar fashions, haircuts, makeup, styles that are copied from one celebrity or another, actresses, singers, influencers, whatever the hell Kardashians are. Global trends, recognizable everywhere, interchangeable. Men's style is more local, more specific. More identifiable. And no American man would be caught dead wearing this ensemble.

Is this a good sign? Or bad? Either way, it's

a positive that the driver emerged to get the door. That makes him farther away from the steering wheel, from the gas pedal.

Ariel's attention is caught by a small car that blurs by on the far side of the meridian, in the main roadway; this wide stretch of avenue is practically a highway. She glances down the avenue to the left, then the right. There are no pedestrians here; this is not a pedestrian area. Also no cars parked anywhere that she can see. There's no sign of anyone in either direction. No one to witness, no one to intervene. It's just Ariel and this driver out here, and the Marines inside.

Okay, she tells herself, when she's just a few steps from the car's open door: *now.*

Ariel sprints. She's heading full-speed in the direction that the car is not facing, toward any traffic that might arrive on the wide roadway. She hears the driver call out, but she doesn't know what he's saying, and doesn't give a damn.

She runs beside the concrete pediment of the embassy's fencing, beyond the end of the compound, now passing a small open-air lot of parked cars and recycling bins, from which her peripheral vision catches some movement but she can't tell what, could be someone shifting in the driver's seat of a dark car but also could be a cat or a bird or a branch rustling in the breeze.

Ariel glances over her shoulder, sees the Audi's driver climbing into his seat. She faces forward again, looks down at the sidewalk, at her feet, concentrating on not tripping on the uneven paving stones, cracks, roots pushing through the pavement.

She can hear the car door slam as she continues past the end of the parking lot, and now the sidewalk is bordered by low scrub next to a concrete wall.

The driver puts the Audi in gear. The car must be pulling forward in the narrow carriageway, at the end of which he'll have to merge onto the wide roadway, which is one-way heading away from Ariel. It would be insane to spin the car around and drive against traffic, irresponsibly dangerous, a maneuver that would be undertaken only if he's maniacally — criminally — intent on pursuit. At any moment speeding cars could arrive on the empty avenue, risking high-speed head-on collision, death. No hired-car driver would do this. Only an assassin would.

Ten yards ahead is an opening in the concrete wall, the entrance to a high-rise compound.

Ariel turns back to watch what the Audi does: Thank God it merges into the roadway, drives away from her. But that doesn't mean she's safe. The driver could speed up, make a right and another right and then around the back of this block, to the rear of this high-rise. How long would that take? While Ariel was sitting in the embassy, examining the map, she estimated ninety seconds, at most two minutes.

Maybe he won't pursue her. She's desperately hoping he won't, because there's no innocuous reason why he would. But she has to assume the worst. Always.

As she runs into the driveway she notices a figure back near the embassy, backlit by the floodlights that bathe the front of the American compound in protective brightness. It's a man. And he's walking in her direction.

No, not walking: he's running. Running after her.

Ariel accelerates past the high-rise's security guard before he has a chance to stop her, into a parking area with angled cars on one side and parallel spots on the other, everything well-illuminated by tall standards.

The guard yells something at her.

She doesn't slow down until she arrives at the end of the wide-open parking lot, and takes the ninety-degree turn around the side of the building along a paved path beneath palm trees.

The guard yells again, more shrill, more alarmed. He's answered by another yelling man.

Around the back of the building she can see tennis courts, a swimming pool on a raised pavilion, palm trees, a salmon-colored wall. This is a fancy apartment building, enclosed within a fortified perimeter, bordered on one side by the American embassy and the Brazilian on another.

Footsteps are pursuing her. More than one set.

That wall is not something she's going to be able to scale. She knows this. The guard knows this. But he doesn't know that she knows, so he probably assumes that the rear perimeter is her destination, that she's going to try to escape via the back, and fail, and that's where he'll corner her, with a weapon-size flashlight in one hand and cell phone in the other, ready to call the police. Or maybe he'll prefer to mete out punishment himself. Maybe he's the type of man who looks forward to that sort of opportunity.

Ariel continues running at full speed beside the tennis courts as if her life depends on it, trying to make it to the far end of the building before the guard comes around the side. She takes the corner without knowing if she has succeeded.

She can't keep up this pace, she's going to keel over. She slows to a jog on the path between the building and the tall wall, a close, claustrophobic space, with no angle to take, no escape to make. Ariel doesn't know if the guard is on her heels or headed toward the swimming pool and the perimeter beyond. She's now just a few feet from the front of the building, and slows to a walking pace, trying to listen for footsteps behind her . . . straining to hear . . .

Nothing. She can't hear any footsteps. The guard hasn't pursued her around this corner, at least not yet. She comes to a full stop, doubles over, trying to catch her breath while she has a few seconds; sprinting is hard. She'll give herself to a count of five to gather her strength for another dash through the parking lot, back out the front gate, across the wide lanes of the hopefully traffic-free avenue, toward the zoo and fast-food restaurants and life and people and hopefully a taxi back to the hotel, or screw it she'll just flag down the first passing car, throw herself on the mercy of a complete stranger. In her experience, strangers are not the dangerous ones.

Ariel unfolds herself, stands upright. She inhales deeply, filling her lungs with oxygen, as if preparing to dive deep underwater. Then she takes one step forward —

CHAPTER 21

Day 1. 11:58 p.m.

There's no way she can get past the man who's blocking the path, standing there just a few feet in front of her. Her only possible escape would be to turn around and sprint in the other direction; she can probably outrun him, she should go now —

But then she recognizes him: It's one of the embassy guys, the one she beat up in the street, a million years ago, earlier tonight. She thinks his name is Antonucci.

"It's okay," he says, putting out his hands in a soothing gesture, as if he's smoothing a bedspread. "You're okay."

Ariel continues to pant, her chest tight.

"It's gonna be okay," he reiterates. "Why are you running?"

She doubles over again, still struggling to catch her breath. He gives her time to recover, then to answer, but she doesn't.

"What are you afraid of? Who?"

Ariel, still doubled over, turns her eyes up

253

at him. She shakes her head.

"How can we help if —"

"Help?" Now Ariel straightens up. "How can you help me at all?" She takes another deep breath. "You people have already proven that you can't. Asking a bunch of irrelevant questions instead of *doing* something. You could at least have found my husband's phone by now. Why haven't you done that?"

"We have."

"What?"

"We found his phone."

"What the — ?" She shakes her head. "Why didn't anyone tell me?"

"It was in a garbage can down by the river. There was nothing there; it was just a place to dump the phone. Probably far from wherever your husband ended up. I'm sorry."

Ariel shuts her eyes tight.

"Locating the phone wasn't the end of it. We're investigating a lot of angles."

"Like?"

"Hey, it's really late. Why don't we go over this in the morning?"

She doesn't answer.

"Why did you run? From a driver who was called, for your safety, by the US embassy?"

What can she say? *I'm running because I'm terrified that the driver might actually be a contract killer hired to assassinate me, to finally eliminate the long-dormant threat of me, a threat that has been resurrected by this kidnapping of my husband.*

"Let's get you back to your hotel," he says. "Come on."

She can see that his face is swollen where she hit him; he should've spent the last few hours applying ice, but instead he seems to have been chasing her around Lisbon. To keep her safe? Or to keep her contained?

"My car is just up the street."

He's right. She has to give up for the night, go back to the hotel, lie down, get some sleep. This was one of the hard lessons she learned while solo-parenting an infant: Sleep deprivation is very real, it doesn't take long to set in, and its effects are brutal. Physical, psychological, emotional, everything all at once. Tomorrow she'll need her wits, that's for damn sure.

"Come on," he repeats.

Ariel begins to cry, again. He notices her tears, and he's trying to decide how to respond, whether to embrace her, or take her hand, or her elbow, or put his arm around her shoulder, but he's probably afraid that she doesn't want to be touched, certainly not by a strange man in an alley in the middle of the night, and he's absolutely right. Instead he offers another empty "It's gonna be okay."

He can't possibly know that anything is going to be okay. But that's what we do sometimes, we lie to each other, even when everyone knows that lying is what's going on.

Sometimes we call this politeness, sometimes we call it optimism, sometimes we call it support, sometimes we call it politics or business or negotiation or public relations or marketing, sometimes we call it just doing our jobs. Sometimes we compound the lies we tell each other with lies we tell ourselves, denying that what we're doing is lying, or denying that lying is bad, or denying that lying has consequences. Denying that facts are facts. Denying that truth has meaning.

It's no surprise that this man is lying to Ariel, and that she's lying by letting him, and that they both know the other is lying, both pretending they don't.

You want to believe that there's only one reality, that we all share it. This is what Ariel used to be certain of: Facts are facts, truth is truth.

But then.

Here's what can happen: You lose faith in yourself, in your capacity to see the world clearly, to understand it correctly. You begin to think that you're somehow broken, that there's some deficit in your intellect that prevents you from being competent in a way that everyone else is competent, some short circuit that renders your brain unable to process facts and emotions, to make appropriate responses.

At first you might be positive — one hundred percent, no doubt — that you understand the events, the physical environment, what time it was, how much alcohol you'd consumed, all these facts seem so clear, so unassailable, indisputable.

But then you're told something different. Told that you don't understand what really happened: No, it wasn't like that, not at all. It's your interpretation that's faulty; you misunderstood. You asked for it — not just figuratively but literally, you actually said this aloud: "I want it."

You know with absolute certainty that this is not true, that you said no such thing. But you are told, with one hundred percent certainty, that you did.

So then what? So then despite yourself, despite your confidence — despite your *certainty* — doubt begins to creep in. Doubt about things that are obviously open to interpretation, subjective matters of opinion. But eventually also doubt about things that aren't. Doubt about facts.

No: It was midnight, not ten.

You'd had six drinks, not two; you were the drunk one, I was sober.

You were asking for it, so I gave it to you.

That's how you lose faith in objectivity, in reality, in yourself.

That's how gaslighting works.

PART III
THE RANSOM

CHAPTER 22

Day 2. 9:17 a.m.
Ariel awakens alone, again. Within seconds her mind is already hyperactive, that peculiar buzzing that comes with stress, too many ideas colliding, haphazard thoughts shooting off in multiple directions with little chance of arriving at logical destinations. This is a disorganized mind, unproductive fretting, and Ariel feels the suffocating clutch of frustration tightening her chest, a panic attack rising in response to this unsustainable situation, and her inability to deal —

Stop.
She shuts her eyes. Deep breath. Think of nothing except exhaling . . .

And again . . .
And then she opens her eyes, and feels a bit better. Not a lot, but enough.

She looks around the room, cleaner and neater than it had been the last time she awoke here, with no last-night remnants of John, of sex. Has it been only one day?

261

Yesterday was definitely bad, but today is probably going to be worse. At least yesterday Ariel had some control, she was the one making fundamental choices — to go to the police, to the embassy, various calls to America, gathering the disparate threads into one ball, giving it a push over the crest of the hill.

Now it's up to other people, and she can't completely rely on any of them. Which is why she needs so many.

Ariel gets dressed in her usual outfit of jeans and a T-shirt. She towel-dries her hair, pulls on her running shoes, swipes a lipstick across her mouth, done.

When she was young, Ariel made so many of her choices — personal, professional, romantic and platonic and sartorial — premised on herself as the center of the universe, the way she looked, the clothes she wore, the places she was seen and with whom, her perceived levels of attractiveness, of status, building blocks of a persona that yearned to be public, to be a person who was envied by strangers.

She'd taken herself pretty damn seriously. But that's youth, isn't it? Young people come from all over the world to New York to take themselves seriously, to clamor for attention, to be known, to be admired, to be envied, to be desired. Ariel attained all of that, only to discover that she didn't want it, and to realize that these traits that we admire and envy — youth and beauty and privilege — these are not accomplishments.

When she left the city, Ariel deliberately ditched those attributes she'd long considered assets; they had become impediments. She gave up her city habits, her city attitude, her city style, including all that hair, all the shampooing and conditioning and drying, the coloring and styling and blowouts, all that time and money that she no longer had. Now she gets her hair cut by Deb, who operates a single chair from the front room of a run-down Victorian at the seedier end of Main.

"That's what you want?" Deb asked, looking at the magazine picture Ariel had dog-eared. "You sure?"

Ariel nodded. She was the single parent of an infant, barely time to shower, much less deal with long hair.

"You know what I call that cut?"

"What?"

"The Commando."

Ariel had already given up manicures and pedicures and facials, the relentless exercise and constant starvation and continuous hydration, the makeup and the jewelry, the form-fitting jeans and short skirts and shorter shorts, the low-cut blouses and side-boob dresses, the complex time-consuming enterprise of constantly maximizing her physical attractiveness, her sexiness, the incessant effort of attracting attention — look at me, please, *please* look at me.

"Yes," Ariel said, "the Commando is exactly what I want."

It's not that she no longer wants to be attractive; she does. But mostly she wants to be attractive to herself, not to every stray lecher who honks his truck horn at her, ogles her at the supermarket checkout, propositions her from a secluded corner of a dark street, every catcall a blatant reminder of how vulnerable she is.

"Let's listen to that part again. The last thirty seconds."

"Sure." Kayla slides the cursor, hits the triangle. Griffiths closes her eyes, sharpens her hearing.

"You don't think I'm calling without any leverage, do you? You don't for one minute think —"

"Stop talking."

"— that with the paternity records, and the Hamptons police report, and —"

"Goddamn it! *Stop. Talking. Go to the embassy."*

"I was already at the embassy. Twice. And now it's the middle of the night. It's closed."

"Someone will open it."

"When?"

"I guess right now . . . Go now."

264

Griffiths opens her eyes. "That voice sounds *so* familiar. Doesn't it?" Voices, out of all context, can be tough to recognize. But sometimes all you need is a little hint.

Jefferson doesn't respond. This is something that Griffiths respects about the young woman: If she doesn't know the answer, she doesn't fill the void with empty words and wild guesses.

"Okay," Griffiths says, "there are a lot of clues to this guy's identity in this conversation. Get started."

"Sure thing. May I ask a question?"

"Shoot."

"Why do we care about the identity of the man who might or might not be providing the ransom money?"

"That conversation sounds a lot like extortion, doesn't it?"

"No doubt about it. But extortion is a crime for the Bureau to investigate, not a matter of national intelligence."

"Unless it is. That depends on who it is who's getting extorted. This guy definitely sounds sketchy to me — paternity records, police, millions of dollars. And most important of all: He's extortable. That in and of itself raises red flags."

Jefferson nods vigorously. She has that look of young people who are ready to work.

"Speaking of sketchy men: Where's Guido?"

Jefferson doesn't miss a beat. "He needed

265

to run an errand this morning."

"Oh yeah? What was that?"

Jefferson shrugs.

"Maybe to get some stitches?"

The young woman's suppressed smile is all the answer Griffiths needs.

"What about Saxby Barnes?" Jefferson asks. "Shouldn't we read him in at this point?"

Griffiths is worried about where this investigation will lead. Until she knows more, she doesn't want the circle to include anyone who might have conflicting motives. Griffiths doesn't know what motivates Barnes, where his loyalties lie, his ambitions.

"No," she says. "I don't think so. In fact I should go gag him, right now. Could you come with me, please?"

"Of course. Why?"

"I want to be extra-sure that there are no future misunderstandings about what Barnes was told, and by whom, and when."

Ariel checks the burner: nothing. Her own cell too, more nothing, just some work irrelevancies, some spam, an invite to a midsummer-break school potluck, one of those opportunities for the alpha moms to bake Instagrammable cakes. For these sorts of events Ariel buys a box of supermarket cookies, plunks it down on the table in its commercial packaging. She doesn't have time to bake on a weekday, and she's not going to pretend otherwise. In fact she's proud of it.

Plus she would never social-share a cake. The bookshop has a few of the obligatory accounts, and Ariel does some lurking. But her name doesn't appear anywhere, and she doesn't do the posting. All of that is handled by Persephone. If there's one thing that girl's generation knows how to do, it's share on social media, and overshare, the type of behavior that not long ago was considered shameful — the insecurity, the hunger for validation, the naked self-promotion, even the explicit sex-tape — but is now accepted, rewarded, celebrated, required.

Ariel does snap the occasional photo — mostly of her child, her dogs, her new goat — and every December she orders glossy prints of the year's best shots, organizes them into a leather-bound album, slid onto the bookshelf next to last year's. A Christmas present to herself, for the future: her past.

Will this year's album include anything from this trip? Maybe the couples selfie with John, the one she showed to the chambermaids. She hopes so. She hopes that one day this will be a story that she'll be able to tell, when the whole thing has become ancient history. But she doubts it.

Breakfast service is coming to an end. Ariel is now the only guest in the big room, sitting at the same table for the fourth morning in a row. Tomorrow was supposed to be their final morning here, before driving out to the coast for a couple of nights at a beach resort.

The television behind the bar is again tuned to English-language international news, a recycled puff piece about the VP nominee, a hagiography of the Ivy League education and the Little League coaching, the charitable giving and service in the National Guard. The point is clear: This is a man willing to sacrifice his time, to donate his money, to risk life and limb, all for the safety and integrity of his community. This man is a patriot.

But what does that mean? The same can be said of the men in Al-Qaeda and the Taliban, of ISIS and the Ku Klux Klan, of the Nazis and the Spanish Inquisition and Attila the Fucking Hun. All held their convictions passionately. All devoted themselves to protecting their communities against invaders or conquerors or infiltrators or infidels, or at least used that rationale as a justification to gain power, to retain it, to profit from it. To subjugate and exclude and exploit.

No, Ariel knows: Fanatic, dogmatic dedication to your community is not what makes anyone a good person. Self-proclaimed patriotism is not proof of anything.

On the screen, this man is wearing a bespoke suit and a smug grin, holding one of those ceremonial checks, a piece of cardboard the size of a beach towel, showily donating a million dollars to adult literacy. This is a charade, and not even a complicated one, nor convincing, just another everyday lie that everyone pretends to not notice. Another strategy for protecting the hefty bulk of his fortune by shaving off a sliver here and a sliver there, giving away little bits to ensure that he can keep the rest. One of the many manipulations available to men like him, created by men like him for the benefit of men like him, the tax structure and capital gains and mortgage-interest deductions, marriage and religion and capitalism and so-called representative democracy, all constructed so men like him could be not only the players but the house as well, everything about the game fixed in their favor, with not only backup schemes but also backups to the backups, and no way for them to lose, not at this game they invented called America.

Ariel has been learning the rules of this rigged game her whole life, trying to figure out what sort of response would be fair and proportionate but also productive. For a long time, all she wanted was simply to not play, to not watch, to pretend it wasn't even there. But that's not really possible.

Recently, though, she came to a different conclusion: There was, just maybe, a way to win. By inventing her own game, and rigging it herself, then making it impossible for someone to refuse to play.

CHAPTER 23

Day 2. 9:53 a.m.
Ariel notices Joao hovering, looking concerned. "I am very sorry to bother you," the waiter says, then waits for permission to bother her.

"Yes?"

"The police are here to see you. May I bring them? After you finish your breakfast, of course."

Ariel wipes her mouth. "Just send them in now, please."

She's sitting beside the French doors again, the curtains, the breeze, the busy square, the whole city going about its everyday business on a Tuesday morning. It's a big room, and she watches Moniz and Santos cross it, and Joao resumes clearing while the kitchen preps lunch, that interstitial period between meals when it looks like nothing is going on in a restaurant, but that's when the whole superstructure is being erected and maintained.

"Good morning, senhora."

She raises her eyebrows at Moniz.

"Yes, you are correct, it is perhaps not such a good morning for you. I am sorry. A habit."

"Is it okay?" Santos indicates the empty seat across from her, John's seat. Ariel nods. Moniz pulls an extra chair from another table.

"I understand that the kidnappers telephoned you?" he says.

"How do you understand that?"

"We were informed by a diplomat from your embassy."

"A diplomat?" Ariel wonders which sort: a diplomat who's really a diplomat, or a diplomat who's really a spy.

"Yes. And these kidnappers, they are demanding a ransom of three million euros. Correct?"

"That's right."

"And you do not have this money, so you are contacting someone in America?"

"Who told you all this?"

"The man is not identifying himself by name. Only that he is calling from the embassy."

"Didn't you ask?"

"I did. He is telling me that it does not matter." Moniz shrugs. "This is true. A name is easy to lie about, especially on the telephone. Are you planning to procure this money?"

"Yes."

"Senhora." It's Santos who speaks now, leaning forward. "This is not seeming like a good idea."

"Of course it's not a good idea. But do you have a better one?"

"Are you trying to ask your husband's company?" Santos asks. "Perhaps they are helping."

"They're closed for the holiday, July Fourth. But I did leave messages yesterday, one in John's private mailbox, one on a general line. Maybe someone will pick up his messages. Like his assistant maybe."

"You do not know?"

"I never call John's office line."

"Never? Why?"

"He said that it's bad form, that no one at his company ever uses business lines for personal calls. That all calls are monitored, maybe recorded; Big Brother and all that. He said I should use the office line only for an emergency. So I've never called his line before."

This is not entirely true. She had in fact called that direct number once, as an experiment. This was soon after they'd met, nearly a year ago, when Ariel started to poke around the edges of John Wright's life. She felt a little like a Gen Z intruder, but not nearly as competent, trying to snoop into the private life of someone who was actually private. She wasn't able to find all that much.

"Tudor Consultants, John Wright's office, how may I help you?"

"May I speak with Mr. Wright, please?"

"I'm sorry, but Mr. Wright is offsite today."

Ariel was expecting this. John had told her that he was going to be out of the country.

"What's this regarding? Perhaps I can help?"

"Oh, no. I'll call back another time."

She didn't. Ariel had already accomplished what she'd needed, verifying that he really was traveling when he said he'd be, and that the man who called himself John Wright had given her a phone number that corresponded to a John Wright who worked at Tudor. But this wasn't the same as confirming that the man she knew really was John Wright.

It had taken her a few weeks to recognize the thing that was worrying her: When someone seems too good to be true, he's not.

Even now, she still hasn't known John all that long; they still haven't spent that much time together. He spends his weekdays and -nights in the city, and his work requires travel on some weekends too. So most of the time, Ariel's life is still just her and George, the two of them together every afternoon, every evening, the boy's routines unchallenged. She'd made this clear to John, from the very beginning: her son would always be her first priority.

"Of course," John had answered. "That's not even a question."

"Also, I should warn you." They were driving back to her house for the first time.

"Yes?" He met her eye, then turned back to the dark country road. "By all means. I appreciate timely warnings."

"I talk to my dogs sometimes."

"Sometimes" was a vast understatement. It's a nearly constant patter she keeps up with the dogs. George had been the one who'd named the little brown rescue Scotch; he was the color of butterscotch, and was supposedly a Scottish terrier, though that lineage was dubious. "Maybe not exactly a Scottie," George admitted, after comparing the dog to the photos in *The Encyclopedia of Dog Breeds,* his favorite book in the world. "Scott*ish,* maybe. Or Scotch. How's that for a name?"

Ariel was going to object that she didn't want people to think she'd named a dog after whiskey, but reminded herself that she didn't give a damn.

"You're a good boy, Mallomar." She says this dozens of times a day. George had named the chocolate-haired mutt too, earlier, back before he had the encyclopedia — back before he could read — when cookies occupied an outsized portion of his consciousness.

"You too, Scotch, though perhaps less *good.* But you are an exceedingly handsome personage." Scotch's facial hair evokes the mustaches of a nineteenth-century Austrian nobleman. "And a fine gentleman."

The dog just looks at her, neither understanding nor not understanding any of the words. What Scotch understands is the tone of Ariel's voice. He wags his tail when she says nonsense like this; he loves everything about her, so much.

Ariel accepts that people might think she's a crazy lady, talking to dogs this way. But years ago she'd stopped caring if people thought she was crazy; she stopped making any attempt to hide it.

Now that she felt the need to explain this part of her personality to this new man, she was reconsidering the wisdom of this deep level of I-don't-give-a-fuck. But it's who she is — who she'd become — and she didn't want to hide it. She'd spent too much of her life pretending the opposite.

"Actually, it's not just sometimes. I talk to the dogs more or less constantly."

John gave her a gentle smile, mostly with his eyes. "I should hope so," he said. This wasn't the same as his high-watt smile, but it was, maybe, better. "Otherwise they get lonely."

Ariel examined John closely, in the soft glow of the dashboard lights, and she could see it there in his smile, the amused recognition of a joke that isn't really a joke but instead a fundamental truth: It wouldn't be the dogs who'd be lonely without the talking.

That was the first time it occurred to her,

just a fleeting thought that scampered across her mind: I could love this man. But she pushed the idea aside.

It had been so long since she'd had a regular sexual partner, or even an irregular one. Back when she'd first fled the city, that was because she was traumatized, and pregnant. Then she was the single mother of a newborn, then of a toddler, her life filled with diapers and vomit and breastfeeding and sleeplessness, none of it conducive to eroticism. Furthermore she was someone who'd receded from social life, from intimacy. Someone who wanted nothing to do with men.

This new life of hers was populated almost exclusively by women. She'd meet other mothers for lunch, or a glass of wine; she'd go to other families' houses for potlucks in open-plan kitchens, where she'd shake hands with the husbands, or kiss some of them demurely on the cheek, but she didn't really talk to them beyond superficial chitchat. The men would stand off to the side, holding bottles of beer by the necks, discussing fishing and football, taxes and trucks. Ariel suspected that they all thought she was gay. She was the only one of the moms who wore her hair this sort of short, plus she was attractive but unmarried, and they'd heard that half her son's DNA had come from a sperm bank. What other explanation could there be?

The few men she interacted with fell into two categories: her friends' husbands, or people she paid — plumber, mechanic, electrician. Ariel wasn't going to have sex with anyone in either category. So for years she didn't have sex with anyone. She was barely able to drum up interest in self-satisfaction, just once every now and then while watching a movie with some carefully choreographed scene with two of the most attractive human beings in the world, with the perfect lighting and music and editing, gasping and moaning and crying out in ecstasy; this type of idealized artistic sex still had the capacity to arouse her. But this cinematic entertainment was a completely different category of activity, utterly divorced from real-life intercourse, the same way that professional ballet has nothing do with falling down a staircase and breaking your neck. Because that's what had happened to Ariel, sexually: She'd fallen down the steps, and broken her fucking neck.

It had taken her such a long time to recover, during which her life had been overwhelmingly defined by no. It was such a huge relief to be able to say yes again. And it wasn't merely the physical act of sex that had been absent, it was the entirety of intimacy that you expect from a romantic partner. She missed it, she needed it, we all do, even if we sometimes pretend otherwise. Ariel had been pretending so many things for so long.

Pete Wagstaff checks the time: It's barely ten o'clock in the morning. Wagstaff knows — everyone knows — that Saxby Barnes is a heavy drinker on a nightly basis; it's never productive to talk to him until he has managed to get himself together. The ideal time is early afternoon, when Barnes's tongue has been loosened by a lunchtime drink or two, but Pete can't wait for that.

"Good morning," Barnes answers. "What can I do you for you today, Mr. Wagstaff?"

"I'm working on that story."

"Mmm."

"I have a few follow-up questions."

"Mm-hmm."

"Can the embassy comment on yesterday's altercation between Ms. Pryce and one of your staff?"

"Excuse me?"

Wagstaff doesn't elaborate.

"I'm sorry," Barnes says. "I simply haven't the foggiest clue what you're talking about."

"Is this really what you want me to write, Barnes?"

Silence, then a sigh. "Off the record?"

"Sure. Off the record."

"I've been *ordered* to keep quiet. Just now, in fact. A few minutes ago."

"Ordered? By?"

Barnes doesn't answer, of course.

"By the CIA?"

Again Barnes hesitates before not answering. "You have yourself a pleasant day, Mr. Wagstaff."

"What about his family?" Moniz asks. "Can they help?"

"No. John's parents died when he was young, six or seven years old. He and his older sister went to live with an uncle who wasn't very nice; they're no longer in touch."

"You are not meeting this uncle?"

"No."

"The sister?"

"I met her just once, at our wedding. She lives very far away."

"Where?"

This question sounds like a whisper of fear in Ariel's ear. "Morocco."

Moniz's eyebrows raise. Morocco is very far from America, though not from Portugal. It is very near.

"This is when? Your wedding?"

"A few months ago."

Moniz and Santos share a look, but neither says anything further.

"Why are you asking about his family?"

"Maybe it is important."

"How?"

"What type of man is your husband?" This is Santos asking.

280

"I don't really know how to answer that. John is a good man."

"What does that mean?"

"He's hardworking, he's considerate, he's honest, he's decent. He doesn't do drugs, he doesn't drink too much, he doesn't gamble, he doesn't beat me or my kid or the dogs. He drives carefully, he plays golf rarely and badly, he cooks acceptably, he cleans diligently. He's not rich, he's not important." She leans forward. "But I just don't understand what any of this could possibly have to do with John's kidnapping."

Santos smiles, trying to project sympathy, to communicate that she understands that Ariel is a woman who loves her husband, who trusts him, who's worried about him, who's in a bad situation. All of which is why the detective looks reluctant, like she doesn't want to ask this next thing that she needs to ask, this question that Ariel didn't see coming:

"Can you think of a reason why your husband's sister would be here in Portugal?"

CHAPTER 24

Day 2. 10:11 a.m.
Time seems to stop.

"What?" Ariel manages to croak out. Her pulse is pounding and her head spinning at this revelation. Or accusation. Or suspicion. "What did you say?"

"Your husband's sister." Moniz has taken over again. "Do you know why she would be here, in Lisboa?"

"No." Ariel shakes her head. "Why would you ask that? *Is* she here?"

"Are you aware that your husband has changed his name?"

Crap, Ariel should have mentioned this. "Yes."

"Do you know why?"

Ariel understands that something important has shifted: The cops are treating her not completely like the victim of a crime.

"His original family name was hard to deal with," she says. "To pronounce. For Americans."

"That is what he told you?" Moniz glances down at his notes. "Reitwovski," he pronounces carefully. "Did your husband tell you at what moment he made this name change? And why?"

"After his military service — John was in the army — he wanted to launch a new professional life with an easier name."

"But his sister, she did not change her name, did she?"

"I don't know."

"No," Moniz says. "On the twenty-one of June, Lucy Reitwovski, resident of Morocco, is arriving on a flight from Marrakesh to Madrid. Since then, she is not departing Spain by airplane. Not unless she is doing this using a different name."

"What does Madrid have to do with Lisbon?"

"It is a short day's drive by car from Madrid to Lisboa."

"Okay. But so is — I don't know — Barcelona. Bordeaux."

"But Lucy Reitwovski's brother is not kidnapped in Barcelona. Or Bordeaux."

Ariel is torn by two competing imperatives: to end this off-the-rails interview right now, or to try to learn more about these cops' suspicions, theories, accusations.

"What are you suggesting?"

"We are not suggesting anything," Detective Santos reinserts herself, trying to defuse

283

the situation. "We are asking questions."

"Why would you think that Lucy is *here?*"

Neither cop responds, leaving Ariel to guess: credit-card receipts, car-rental GPS, toll-collecting technology, surveillance and security cameras, cell phone triangulation, positive-ID eyewitnesses. There are many possible pieces of evidence.

Ariel turns her attention to Santos. "Is Lucy here? Do you know this?"

Santos doesn't answer, and Moniz resumes the questioning: "Do you know of any reason why Senhora Reitwovski *would* be here?"

He maintains eye contact, which Ariel feels like she shouldn't break off, even though she isn't clear on who's challenging whom about what in this faceoff.

"No," she says, "of course not," in the sort of cadence and tone that's meant to sound dismissive, self-righteous even. But Ariel knows she's not on solid ground. These cops have obviously been investigating John's life, which means they've also been digging into Ariel's. She doesn't know the entirety of what they could have unearthed about John, but she's well aware of what they could've discovered about her.

"Your husband, does he talk to his sister often?"

"Often? I don't know about that. More than never."

"Or email? Or text-message?"

284

"Maybe. To be honest, it's not something we discuss." Ariel winces, regretting that "to be honest," which is what people tend to say when they're not.

"Maybe you remember that we don't live together full-time? So I don't know whom he talks to, or when. I don't *quiz* John about his calls."

"Oh yes. I do remember." Moniz glances at his notepad. "And on your husband's previous visits to Lisboa, is he meeting his sister here?"

"What?" Ariel feels panic coming on. "Are you kidding me?"

"Kidding? No, I am not kidding. Morocco and Portugal are very close to each other. Is this a coincidence?"

Ariel feels like she's going to throw up. "What are you saying?"

"Do you know what Senhora Reitwovski does for work?"

"Not exactly."

"No?" He looks incredulous. Or fake-incredulous. "Is it not true that Americans are always talking about their work?"

"Listen, what the hell is going on here? What have you learned? Is Lucy in Lisbon?"

"You and your husband do not share a banking account, is this correct?" Moniz asks.

Ariel takes a second, trying to calm herself down before answering. "That's right. We haven't been married all that long, we haven't gotten around to it."

"But you will?"

"I guess."

"So this number here" — Moniz turns his notepad to face Ariel, and taps his pen on a string of numbers — "and this one here, these are both your bank accounts?"

What the hell is this? "Yes, the top one is my personal. And that's my business."

"This is not much money, in your business account. Is that normal?"

The balance is perilously close to zero, the result of stocking up and staffing up for the summer, and especially for this Black Friday–ish weekend. The shop is always just one bad season away from insolvency, but every year the bottom line is rescued by some unlikely savior, books that don't even seem possible until they're overnight sensations — adult coloring books and irresponsible-parenting screeds, female-friendly soft-core porn and Instagram-friendly poetry. Books that increasingly seem like anti-books, these are the ones that emerge out of nowhere to keep the lights on. But just because it happened last year, and the year before, doesn't guarantee it'll happen this year.

Recently, the shop's most worthwhile innovation has been the espresso machine, which looks like an Italian sports car parked on the big old slab of stained and chipped marble, which itself was a discard from someone's kitchen renovation that Ariel reclaimed from the town dump's reuse center. The books that line the shelves are becoming loss leaders for the shop's real profit center: selling white flour, adulterated with butter and sugar and eggs. Plus of course coffee, which in the summer is often poured over ice for fifty cents more. All of which is why Ariel has to consider the offer from the Brooklyn hipster, with her nose ring and her Tesla and her pile of cash from her tech start-up's buy-out.

"At this moment," Ariel tells the police, "there's an unusually low balance."

"And can you tell me, please, this number? What is this account?"

Ariel hesitates. "That's a trust."

"I am sorry?"

"A trust. An account that I'm the manager of, but not the ultimate owner."

"Who is the owner?"

"My son will be the owner, when he becomes an adult."

"But you are able to withdraw this money?"

"No, not really."

"No?" Moniz asks. "Or not really?"

"No."

"Can your husband access this, as you say, trust? Is that the correct word?"

"Yes, that's the right word. No, John has no standing."

"And how much money is in that account?"

Ariel doesn't like this line of questioning, not one bit. She doesn't want to answer Moniz, but she also doesn't want to stonewall.

"Why does that matter?"

"Perhaps that is for us to judge."

"Perhaps" — Ariel crosses her arms — "not."

Moniz taps his pen on the paper. "What is the origin of the funds? Is this an inheritance?"

Ariel turns to the woman. She was expecting that a female cop would be a natural ally, but it doesn't look that way.

"Why is it, senhora, that you do not wish to answer these questions?"

"Because they're none of your business."

"None of our business? We are not businesspeople. We are police."

"I mean it's none of your concern."

Ariel had hoped that these local cops would be her allies, the only people in Lisbon whom she'd be able to trust.

"Is your previous husband the source of this money?"

Ariel reminds herself that there's no way — none — for the Lisbon police to be certain where the funds originated. Only a handful of people in the world possess that particular fact, and every single one of them is legally prohibited from revealing it. Most of them are lawyers. All of them, in fact, except her.

Which doesn't mean other people can't guess. And with the right sort of research, they might guess correctly. Maybe these cops have already guessed correctly; or maybe someone else has fed them a correct guess. But a guess, even an informed and accurate one, is not the same as a fact, as knowledge. A guess is not evidence.

"I am confused about something, senhora."

A guess, though, can certainly be a very compelling clue.

"Perhaps you can help me to understand."

She doesn't like where Moniz is going, wearing this Columbo-like cloak of confusion. Ariel suspects that the whole thing — his messiness, his distractedness, his air of ineffectuality — is a smoke screen. The rumpled clothes, the food in the beard, all of it an act, the guy an actor. And here she'd been thinking that she was the actor.

Ariel is apparently never going to be too old to learn the same lesson again and again: Everyone is an actor.

"I see that this account is originally opened using a different name." Moniz turns the page of his notebook, glances down. "Can you please tell me who is this person?" He looks up, locks eyes with Ariel. "Laurel Turner? Is this you?"

Ariel remembers everything about the final day she was called Laurel Turner: the confer-

289

ence room in the Midtown office tower with spectacular views of Central Park, of the East River, of the Upper East Side, with lawyers shuffling papers and padding fees.

She glared at the far end of the conference table, not attempting to hide her hostility. This man should be arrested, is what should happen. He should be perp-walked, jailed, compelled to post bail, put on trial not just of law but of public opinion, forced to listen to her open-court testimony, hounded by reporters, picketed, protested, his wife should leave him, his fortunes decline, friends shun him, his life should fall apart, and after all that misery he should spend the next twenty years in a federal prison, surrounded by violent felons who'd rape him on a regular basis.

That's what should happen.

But instead? Instead he was sitting there in his custom-made suit, throwing money at his problem, solving it easily, fully expecting no further repercussions, ever. Just like he'd no doubt solved other problems in the past and would again in the future; just like his daddy had solved his youthful problems. Tutors and coaches, payoffs and bribes. Where's the line between right and wrong?

It was being drawn right here. Except the line is not between right and wrong. Just legal on one side, illegal on the other.

Ariel could barely listen as lawyers explained the nondisclosure provisions, the severity of the penalties, criminal as well as civil. At the time, these penalties were the least of her concerns. She needed the money, she needed to put this whole thing in the past, she needed to invent a new life. She couldn't imagine a scenario in which she'd want to revisit this.

Her gaze wandered up Park Avenue, past identifiable intersections and familiar buildings until she found the right pile of limestone, then four floors down from the top, and there it was: her windows, her curtains, her home.

Her ex-home. She wondered if Bucky was there right now. Would he continue to live in that apartment? Their apartment?

She scrawled LAUREL TURNER on the signature lines, initialed LT in corners, wasted no time getting the hell out of there, tucking her set of signed papers into her bag, rising without saying anything to anyone, just a curt nod at her own attorney, an utterly radiant woman — her hair, her skin, even the silk threads in her jacket seemed to glow, her skin taut from who knows what procedures. It was impossible to guess the age of a woman like this. Some things, like her skin, suggested mid-forties; others, like her octogenarian husband, suggested much older.

Ariel stopped in at the restroom; this might be her last chance for a while. Bucky called yet again, startling her, the loud peal of her flip-phone echoing throughout the tiled room.

She couldn't have that conversation again. It wasn't surprising that her husband was refusing to accept her decision, but Ariel no longer had the patience to try to make him understand. She'd owed Bucky an explanation, of course. And she'd given it, more than once. She didn't owe him anything more.

In the elevator, Ariel tied a scarf over her head, donned giant sunglasses despite the November drizzle through which she walked around the corner to the bank branch where she deposited the cashier's check into an account that was otherwise empty. While inside, she never took off the scarf; the only time she removed the sunglasses was to prove that her face matched her ID, an interaction not recorded by any camera. No one challenged her on the sunglasses indoors on a rainy day. Other people wore wool caps in the summer, fleece vests in heat waves, gym shorts in snowstorms. Everyone too cool for school. Today Laurel Turner was willing to look like one of those people.

She stepped out to the midday sidewalk, and looked for a taxi from behind her sunglasses.

"Hey!" It was a male voice to her right. She turned to see a man fifteen feet away, under an awning, out of the rain, smoking a cigarette. "You're beautiful, you know that?"

She turned back to survey the passing traffic.

"You should smile more."

Ariel still didn't respond, or turn again in this man's direction, but in her peripheral vision she could see him toss his cigarette, start walking toward her.

"Maybe then people wouldn't think you're such a stuck-up cunt."

Ariel flinched. She wasn't surprised that a man had appended some abuse to his supposed compliment; this was not uncommon. But she was surprised at how angry he'd become, how fast.

It was broad daylight, on a crowded sidewalk, with plenty of witnesses; she wasn't going to be sexually assaulted here. But still she felt seized by the grip of terror, scared of being yelled at, or punched in the face, or slashed with a utility knife, or shoved into oncoming traffic. Maybe this man was a psychopath. He certainly hurled insults like one.

Ariel took a long step away from the curb, away from that particular threat. Then she turned to face her assailant. He was such an ineffectual-looking man, unattractive in all the ways that a person could be physically unattractive. But still threatening, because anyone could be threatening. All it took was meanness.

293

This had been happening to her almost every day since she was thirteen or fourteen years old, for two decades now, it was such a commonplace experience as to be almost unremarkable, unless she allowed herself to dwell on it: Why should this be a part of my daily life? Why should I be harassed, menaced, threatened, terrified that someone is going to attack me — verbally, physically, sexually — as a matter of routine?

Occasionally Ariel considered responding to these provocations. She weighed the tiny range of pros versus the vast array of cons, and always came to the same conclusion: Don't say anything, don't antagonize, you can't win, just try to minimize how much you lose. Don't make it your life.

Suddenly she had no more patience, no more turn-the-other-cheek. No more fear.

"Why would you say something like that to me?"

The man was heading toward the office building, but now he froze, and turned back to face Ariel.

"Why would you say that to anyone?"

"Hey, I was just trying to be friendly."

"Friendly?" She took a step in his direction. Then another. "Calling me a cunt, that's *friendly*? What's wrong with you?"

Now she was just a step away from him. Other people on the sidewalk were noticing this interaction, slowing down, stopping. A security guard emerged from the lobby.

"Me? Nothing's wrong with me. What's wrong with you?"

"You. You're what's wrong with me." Ariel realized she was yelling. She decided to yell louder. "You and all the other assholes like you, telling me to smile, yelling that I have a nice rack, a nice ass, that you want to put your big cock in it, and then cursing me when I don't *thank* you for insulting me, for terrorizing me. You."

She was pointing at him now, and yelling very loudly. He was frozen.

"You're what's wrong with me. You're what's wrong with the world."

The security guard put his large body between these two, and that's when the harasser found his voice again, found his courage, and started yelling while the guard restrained him.

"She just started attacking me! Psycho bitch."

The security guard knew there was no way this was true. But he also knew this wasn't his battle to fight; not his responsibility to set anyone straight, especially a volatile man. Volatile men tend to create their own wide orbits of tolerance. No one wants to confront them.

"Come on," the guard says, "that's enough." As if gently reprimanding a small child for a minor lapse in manners.

295

Ariel walked to a taxi that was discharging a passenger. Then she turned back to her assailant, who was still being steered away by the security guard.

"Hey?" she called out. "You should smile more. Maybe people wouldn't think you're such a fucking asshole."

She took the taxi way downtown, to the nucleus of the civic center's bureaucracy. She filled out the simple forms, paid the modest fee. The whole process was easier than expected, this thing that seems like maybe it should be more difficult, or more expensive, or more time-consuming; more something. She shed her old first name in favor of something she'd liked back in high-school Shakespeare; she replaced her husband's family name with her grandmother's maiden name, which no one knew, no one would go looking for. These were puzzle pieces that no one would put together, a new identity that no one could trace.

This was the second time Ariel had changed her name. The first time it had been in the way that's widely accepted — even sometimes required — by taking her husband's name. But she was Laurel Turner for just a few years, living on New York's Upper East Side, summers back and forth to the South Fork of Long Island, a lifestyle defined by recreational shopping and occupational exercising, fine dining and benefit attending and first-class vacationing.

That woman no longer existed. Newly minted Ariel Pryce walked out of the stately neoclassical building on Worth Street, hailed another cab to Penn Station, and boarded the train back to her new town, to the small apartment she'd rented above a wine shop on Main Street, a one-bedroom with big gaps between the wide-planked old floorboards through which she could see down into the shop, hear the music that the owner cranked up after closing, smell the pot that wafted up. For some reason her thermostat was down there, tucked behind the shelf of local rosés; she had to go downstairs to adjust the temperature, wearing her slippers, a flannel robe, nodding sheepishly at the proprietor.

She was just beginning to show. It wasn't noticeable to anyone except herself, a tightness in her jeans, an unfamiliar shape in the full-length bathroom mirror.

Armed with this new name, and the advice of the small-town lawyer Jerry whose shingle was hanging up the street, Ariel Pryce began to build a whole new identity one piece at a time — driver's license, bank account, credit card, each document removing one brick from the old persona to construct the new. By the time she found the ramshackle farmhouse that she irrationally wanted to buy, she'd already taken on the full veneer of a new person, an identity she continued to bolster with a passport, with business documents filed with the town, the county, the state, the IRS, with voter registration and organization memberships, everything. Ariel Pryce was a complete person, documentable and provable.

A few years after changing her name, she tried to find Laurel Turner. She scoured the internet, made calls, searched every way she could think of to find a woman who'd one day ceased to exist. She failed.

But Ariel was an amateur. Professionals, she knew, could find her. Would find her, if they ever needed to.

This was one of the things Ariel wanted to leave behind in the city: the anonymity that allows men — that invites them — to act in ways they'd be far too ashamed of if witnesses knew their names, knew their wives, knew their mothers. Anonymity provides a lot of freedom to act horribly with impunity; witness the internet. Ariel was hoping that small-town closeness would provide the opposite: accountability.

She didn't anticipate the trade-off; the big-city anonymity went both ways. In a small town, no one has anywhere to hide. Not the criminals. But also not the victims.

CHAPTER 25

Day 2. 10:24 a.m.
Ariel has had enough of this questioning.

"Listen," she says to the police, "with all due respect: Why are you wasting time asking about my husband's sister's travel plans? What you should be doing is looking for clues about who *kidnapped* John for a three-million-euro ransom. Seriously. What the hell are you doing about that?"

"We are doing many things about that, senhora."

"Like what?"

"We are reviewing security footage from cameras all over the city. We are cross-referencing motorcycle licenses against criminal records. We are interviewing known members of organized crime. We are locating everyone who has been convicted of kidnapping or kidnapping-related crimes in Portugal at any point during the past twenty years. We are interviewing anyone who was in the vicinity of your hotel yesterday morning and may have witnessed something, anything, that could be of value. We are interviewing staff at hotels, restaurants, museums, cafés, even the tour operator from which you rented your Segways, to see if they witnessed anything unusual, or observed any people who may have been following you or your husband. We are looking for the woman from the café who is thinking she knows your husband. We are investigating *every* angle."

That sure is a lot. More than she expected. Ariel feels chastened.

"And one of those angles, senhora, is the victim's personal life. Including, yes, his sister's location. And his wife's financial assets. And his wife's changed name."

Ariel doesn't know what to say to that. Moniz is right, of course. How could he not question Ariel about all of this?

Just then her phone begins to ring, an unknown number calling from an unfamiliar country code.

"I'm sorry," she says to the police. "I have to take this."

She doesn't wait for their permission as she sweeps her phone off the table, and walks toward the far side of the breakfast room, answering, "Hello?"

"Good morning. Am I speaking with Laurel Turner?"

"Um, yes."

"Hullo Ms. Turner. This is Nigel James, I'm

from the firm of Sinsbury and Lowell, Paris office."

"Okay."

"We represent, um . . . That is to say . . . Sorry, let me start again: You requested a certain sum. From our client."

"Oh."

Now that Ariel realizes what this is, she walks even farther from the police. "Yes?"

"We regret to inform you that the amount you requested cannot, unfortunately, be available."

"Not available? What does that mean?"

"To be clear, my client is not crying poverty. But within the, um, very limited parameters of your abbreviated time frame, combined with the American banking holiday, it is simply not possible to generate that amount of cash. So sorry."

"So sorry?"

"Indeed."

"What the hell?" she says.

"Our apologies."

This is very, very bad. Ariel takes a deep breath, then asks, "How much cash *is* possible?"

"Two million."

A million euros is a pretty big difference, if you look at it as the difference between zero and one million. But between two and three million?

"Is that available immediately?"

"Not precisely. There are a few steps."

"Tell me what needs to happen."

"An agreement needs to be signed by you and our client."

"Do you have this agreement prepared?"

"Not yet. My understanding was that this development — this lesser amount — would not be acceptable to you."

"Well, it'll have to be. Please call me back as soon as the paperwork is ready. I'm not sure if you're aware, but this is incredibly urgent."

"Are we done here?"

The cops glance at each other, then turn back to Ariel, who has returned to the table but not retaken her seat.

"Something has come up that I need to deal with."

Santos offers a curt nod, stands, extends her hand. "Thank you."

But Moniz is flipping through the pages of his notepad. "One moment, please." He finds what he's looking for, hands the pad to Ariel.

"What am I looking at?" It seems to be a list of about twenty names.

"These are the dinner reservations for tables of six or more people this evening at nine, in fine restaurants in the city center. Do you recognize any of these?"

Ariel scans the unfamiliar names. "I'm sorry, no. But I don't think I ever heard the names of my dining companions, so I couldn't recognize anyone anyway."

"Of course."

"But you could call all those people, right?"

"Yes. We are already beginning, but it takes time. We are hoping you are able to help make it go faster. But if not? It is not a problem. We will let you know what we find."

"Good, um, afternoon. Is this Officer Douglas Pulaski?"

"Captain."

"Excuse me, Captain Pulaski. Thanks for taking my call."

"My girl said you're calling from the State Department? I don't get a lot of international inquiries."

"My name is Kayla Jefferson, and I work in Lisbon, where an American businessman named John Wright has been kidnapped, and his wife is trying to come up with three million euros in ransom money."

"Well shit. That seems a bit outside my jurisdiction."

"The wife's name is Ariel Pryce, but she used to be called Laurel Turner. I understand that you were the interviewing officer fourteen years ago when Ms. Turner reported a crime."

Silence.

"Mr. Pulaski? Are you there?"

"Miss, uh, what did you say your name was?"

"Kayla Jefferson."

"Miss Jefferson, I can't talk about this."

"What do you mean?"

"It means I *cannot* talk about this."

"This is a criminal investigation I'm conducting. Someone's life might be at stake."

"If you say so."

"You don't believe me?"

"Tell the truth? No, actually. But even if I did, I still could not talk about this."

"We can issue a warrant." This isn't really true. "Compel you to talk." Kayla doesn't have the power to get a warrant issued to compel anyone to do anything anywhere. Does a rural cop know this?

"I'll be glad to provide you with the name of my attorney," Pulaski says. "You should contact him if you expect to talk to anyone. It sure as shit won't be me."

Ariel retrieves the burner, which has only ever connected to one other number. She calls that one number, and waits for the first ring . . .

And the second . . .

And the third . . .

Voicemail picks up with a greeting in Portuguese that she doesn't understand. What she does understand is that there's no beep at the end. She waits, and waits, and waits, for nothing. Then she hangs up, and approaches the waiter.

"Joao, can I ask a favor?"

"Of course. Anything."

"Could you please translate this greeting? It's a sentence or two."

She redials, and hands the cell to Joao, who listens, then returns it to Ariel.

"I am sorry," he says, "but it is nothing, just the factory setting, which says that the voicemailbox of this number has not been activated."

Ariel feels her shoulders slump, her face fall. She closes her eyes, shakes her head. Now what?

"Hey Pete, how you doin'."

Pete recognizes the voice immediately. And he knows that Myron Baizerman's question is purely rhetorical; Myron doesn't even intone it as a question.

"What do you have for me, Myron?"

"Callin' you back about Ariel Pryce. You ready?"

"Yup."

"Okay, here we go: Ariel Pryce, née Laurel Winston to mother Elaine Winston and father, if you can believe it, Winston Winston the Third. He goes by Bobby, apparently. Anyways, Laurel grows up in Baltimore, private schools, theater-arts major, '95. Looks like she moves immediately after college to

New York City, patchy records for the next decade. Best I can tell, she's one of those actress-slash-model-slash-waitress-slash-whatever's, a few commercials, tiny parts in TV shows. You know the drill."

"Yup."

"So then Laurel marries a hotshot finance bro named Buckingham Turner. This guy has all the pedigree you'd expect from a finance bro named Buckingham Turner. Can you imagine what sort of schmuck you have to be to name your kid Buckingham? What's with these people and their names? Winston Winston the Third. Jesus H. Christ."

Myron has worked in the newspaper's research department for a half-century. It's possible that at some point in the past he was more objective, but in Pete's experience the old coot has always been surprisingly and arbitrarily and vocally judgmental.

"Then Laurel Winston becomes Laurel Turner, Upper East Side socialite, doing the standard Junior League shit. Do you care about all this?"

"Sure. Keep going."

"We even have her pic a couple times in our own society pages. A real looker. During these married years, she earns some token income as a nonemployee from a literary agent named Isabel Reed. For consulting work, which according to the employer meant reading manuscripts."

"A strange career pivot."

"She apparently got this job as a favor from a friend of a friend of her husband. Anyways, fourteen years ago, all of a sudden Laurel Turner ditches everything. Moves a hundred miles to a little village, changes her name, divorces old Buckingham. Buys a farm, gives birth to a boy, names him George. A few years later she buys a bookstore out of bankruptcy, joins the Rotary, becomes a small-town small-business owner. Ariel Pryce has zero social-media presence, zero pics online except old society-page things that got digitized, zero visibility."

"And the new husband?"

"Yeah. A few months ago she marries a business consultant named John Wright. She doesn't take his name, sticks with Ariel Pryce. Not for nothin': This new husband is quite a bit younger."

"And what do you know about him?"

"Him? Zilch. I was assigned to look into her. Not him."

"Okay, can you do a full workup on him too?"

"*Pffft.* I dunno."

"Please?"

"Sorry Pete, I'm gonna need approval first. I got other responsibilities, y'know."

"Come on, Myron. Please?"

"This is not a begging situation, Pete. It's an approval one. I'll have to get back to you."

307

"Okay thanks. So Ariel Pryce: You say she gave birth to a son after she ditched her life?"

"Yeah."

"And this kid is born how long after she leaves the city?"

"Looks like, um . . . six months."

"Which means she was pregnant when she left her husband, her job, her whole life."

"Yeah, looks like it."

"That's a pretty strange decision, isn't it?"

"I'm not a psychotherapist."

"You find the kid's birth certificate?"

"Nah."

"Could you?"

"You got it. And I'm guessin' that the piece of info you want is the father's name?"

The burner is ringing, vibrating, blinking, everything all at once, like a manic child having a tantrum.

"Hello?"

"You called. Do you have the money?" The distorted voice is difficult to make out.

"No," Ariel admits. "Not yet. But soon, I hope."

And the line clicks dead.

CHAPTER 26

Day 2. 11:02 a.m.

"Ms. Pryce? Nigel James again. We have prepared a draft of the agreement. May we forward to your counsel?"

"My counsel? I don't have counsel."

"Well that's irregular."

"It's July Fourth. I can't imagine how I would . . ." Ariel sighs. "Listen, Mr. James: I'm all alone here in Lisbon, my husband has been kidnapped, I need to sign these papers immediately to prevent him from possibly being *executed,* and I'm simply not going to be able to find a lawyer."

James sighs dramatically. "I'm obliged to advise you that it is highly inadvisable to not have representation to review such a matter." He delivers this warning by rote, and with condescension. As if reading rights from a Miranda card to a known career criminal.

"I don't have a choice here."

Ariel knows that the lawyer doesn't truly give a damn; he just needed to fulfill his ethical responsibility, to stave off future complaint.

"Very well. Shall I forward this agreement directly to you?"

Nicole Griffiths walks into the young woman's cluttered cubicle, filled with hardware and peripherals, cords and keyboards, screens of different sizes. It's like a repair shop in here.

"Hey Jefferson, what do you have?"

Kayla Jefferson pushes her headphones down around her neck, and Griffiths catches a few bars of the music before it's clicked off from the keyboard. She's pretty sure it's Bach.

"So that call that was placed to Pryce's cell?" Jefferson points to her screen, a window filled with phone numbers. "The caller used a prepaid phone that was purchased just twenty minutes before the call was made."

"This guy bought it specifically to make this call?"

"Looks like it. That's interesting fact number one. But far more interesting fact number two is where that purchase was made. Look."

Jefferson clicks a different window to bring a map to the front, a familiar grid of right angles intercut with parallel diagonal slashes —

Griffiths realizes that her mouth has fallen open.

"That red pin there," Jefferson says, "is the convenience store."

This changes everything. Griffiths has been suspecting that there was something off about Ariel Pryce's story, her presentation, her husband. But at heart Griffiths didn't truly believe that John Wright's misadventure here in Portugal had anything to do with national security or intelligence. Until now. Now she's almost one hundred percent that it does.

"Do we have security footage of the transaction?"

"Possibly. I'm still working on that. We do know that the call itself was placed from somewhere near the Penn Quarter neighborhood. In this vector here."

Griffiths leans over to look more closely. Half of the federal government is within or just outside those lines, including the Capitol, the Supreme Court, the White House.

"Can we narrow it down any further?"

"Doesn't look like it. Sorry."

"Too bad. And I'm assuming we can't locate the phone's present location?"

"No, it's not active. I'd be very surprised if it was ever activated again."

"So can you show me exactly where the device was purchased?"

"Here, this block. Which is within the same vector as where the phone was located when the call was placed."

"Okay," Griffiths says, standing up straight.

"Let's find out what's in that immediate area. Begin by working out from the smallest radius from the convenience store."

"And I'm looking for what?"

"The homes or offices of powerful men."

All the technologies of Ariel's childhood now seem like ancient history. Her family's kitchen had a black-and-white television on which they could watch three national networks, two locals, plus PBS; nothing more. Their station wagon was the size and shape of a pontoon boat, with manually operated windows and no air-conditioning. Ariel passed handwritten notes in class, torn-up pieces of loose-leaf paper that she folded into the tiniest packets. She used the kitchen's rotary wall phone, twirling the accordion cord around her forearm, untwirling, talking about music videos on MTV, Guns N' Roses, Madonna, the Fine Young Cannibals. She can still remember the advent of fax machines, they were like magic.

But now it feels ridiculous, in the age of wireless streaming, to be feeding paper one page at a time into the hotel's fax machine. Like she's operating a telegraph.

The last page goes through with that reassuring beep.

"Thank you," she says to Duarte, the daytime clerk. "I'm finished."

The tech improvements have certainly

made life easier, power windows and voice-mail and DVRs; air-dropping is definitely quicker than a trip to the post office. But all this convenience comes with plenty of costs, perhaps the steepest of which is the loss of privacy. It wasn't that long ago when private life could truly be private — Ariel's whole childhood, her youth as a struggling actor, her first marriage, this all happened when privacy was still possible, in a world that was largely the same one in which JFK had mistresses and Hoover was gay and everyone who mattered knew but no one else did. A world in which secrets could be kept.

Ariel's wedding to Bucky hadn't been documented online; in those years, almost nothing was. The only public evidence of her nuptials was in the Vows section, a short piece accompanied by a glamour shot of a striking young woman she no longer recognizes.

When that marriage and her entire old life fell apart, social media was just exploding, digital footprints becoming ubiquitous, the internet starting to vacuum up everything — every birthday, every reunion, every gala benefit and awards ceremony and profes-sional milestone — to make every life search-able, discoverable, documentable. There's no longer such a thing as a private life for anyone of any consequence.

Because of the way Ariel left, she chose to maintain digital invisibility even while everyone else started reconnecting on Facebook, sharing vacation pics on Instagram, networking on LinkedIn, amplifying on Twitter, Tindering their way to sordid trysts. Not her.

Ariel Pryce is not completely invisible. But you have to know what you're looking for. You have to know whom. You also have to care enough to look. Almost no one has.

Not yet.

"Oh hi, I was just coming to see you." It's the reporter arriving at the top of the hotel's stairs. "Pete Wagstaff? We met yesterday at the embassy?"

"Yes of course. How did you find me?"

"I'm a reporter." He shrugs. "Sorry for this intrusion."

They're standing in the landing off the stairwell; Ariel can hear footsteps descending.

"I was wondering if I could ask you some questions."

"About what?"

"About your husband's kidnapping."

"I can't talk to you," Ariel says quietly as an older couple pass. "I already told you that."

"Maybe I can be of some assistance?"

"Maybe you can get my husband killed."

Wagstaff looks like he wants to object, but doesn't.

"Listen, you're a reporter, your job is to publish news stories to a wide audience. But if my husband's abduction becomes one of your stories —"

He's shaking his head.

"— if the kidnappers learn that their crime is being investigated by — for all I know — a half-dozen international law-enforcement agencies, how are they going to react?"

"I wouldn't put anyone's life at risk for a story." Shaking his head more vehemently. "I promise."

"Am I supposed to stake my husband's life on the promise of a stranger? Seriously?" She smiles. "Please."

"But —"

"And it's not even up to you, is it?" Ariel doesn't let the reporter defend himself. "You have bosses, and your bosses have bosses who have corporate overlords who have shareholders, and all these people care a hell of a lot more about circulation numbers and click-throughs and ad rates than they do about one man's safety."

Wagstaff can't really argue with this.

"It's not personal," Ariel says. "But if you were in my —"

She's interrupted by the ringing of her phone. "Oh what now." She retrieves the electronic tyrant from her pocket, says "Excuse me" to the reporter, then "Hello?" to the microphone.

"Ms. Pryce? Nigel James again, thank you so very much for returning the signed paperwork so very promptly. But I'm afraid we have a small problem."

For Christ's sake. "What's that?"

"The notary page? That seems to be un-signed. I must remind you that a signature here is not valid without notarization. It cannot be. I do hope you understand."

"You're kidding me."

"I'm afraid not."

"A notary."

"That's right. I believe my covering letter was quite explicit in this regard."

"Where in God's name am I supposed to find an English-speaking notary, in Lisbon, on July Fourth?"

"Please, Ms. Pryce, there's no need to raise your voi—"

"Oh go to hell."

Ariel hangs up on him, and squeezes her eyes shut in the pain of this extra complication, there are just so many. This might be an unexpected breaking point, sneaking up on her just when she thought things were looking better; now they might fall completely apart. Her too.

"I'm sorry," the reporter says. "I couldn't help but overhear."

Ariel opens her eyes.

"I can help."

Ariel appraises Wagstaff, wondering if he's offering assistance because he sincerely wants to help her, or because what he really wants is something else.

"I can take you to a notary right now."

Is this something she can do herself — just start calling notaries? Or would that take forever?

Ariel tries to think of who else might help. The US embassy is, of course, closed. What about the Lisbon detectives? Would they know of an English-speaking notary who'd be available now? That seems unlikely. And all those CIA people, they too are out of the question, Ariel can't knowingly let spies anywhere near this agreement she's going to sign, which would basically violate the very terms of the agreement ipso facto.

Of course it's possible that the CIA has already found her old name, and her old husband, and her old life in its entirety — her old friends and old foes, her old accusations. Maybe they've found her old evidence, her old audio recordings. Her old legal settlements. Maybe they can already diagram the relationships, the phone calls, the demands, the extortion, the consequences. Maybe they already know exactly what happened, how, why, where, when. And who.

Even if so, Ariel still can't volunteer any of this information to anyone, and she can't do anything that could be construed as willingly disclosing privileged information.

"Give me a sec, okay?" She marches into reception. Duarte, who has obviously become

317

fearful of this mercurial American, smiles weakly. "Yes senhora? How can I help?"

"I need to find an English-speaking notary as soon as possible. Do you know of any?"

The desk clerk is clearly reluctant to admit that he can't help a guest, no matter what the request. The truthful answer would be no, but instead he says, "I can find one."

"How specifically would you begin to look for this?"

"I . . ." Duarte looks like he might actually cry. "I will call colleagues who are working at the larger hotels with more business travelers."

Better than nothing, but barely. This might take the young man one minute, but it could also take all day. Duarte doesn't sound very confident, and his plan doesn't sound very promising.

But a *reporter*? That's tough to rationalize. And it might end up being tough to justify. But does she really have any other sensible option?

"No thanks," Ariel says to the clerk, and returns to the stairwell.

"Listen," she says to Wagstaff, "I appreciate your help. But just so we understand each other very clearly: I cannot talk about the details of this situation with you."

"I understand."

Does he? She hopes so. Some men have a

hard time understanding vulnerability, and she can't risk any misunderstandings.

"I have her phone records." Jefferson is standing in Griffiths's doorway, holding a few sheets of paper.

"Come on in," Griffiths says. "Let's have a look."

Jefferson has been annotating a list of Ariel Pryce's phone calls: ER for a half-dozen hospitals, and WRIGHT CELL and WRIGHT OFFICE DIRECT and WRIGHT OFFICE GENERAL for the husband's lines, and Ariel Pryce's own numbers at home, her bookshop, her mother. Jefferson has also drawn helpful lines across the page that indicate Pryce's movements and presumed activity during the course of the past few days — when the woman visited the police station, when she returned to the hotel, the three times she visited the embassy.

"And these pages here" — Jefferson hands over a different sheaf — "these are her text messages."

Griffiths glances at today's, all increasingly urgent entreaties to her husband, except for one to her son. Nothing jumps out. She turns the page. "This is the past thirty days."

"Yup."

"Nothing international, except when she was actually here in Lisbon. Maybe let's go back further? Let's look at everything over

319

the past year."

Jefferson nods.

"Is this copy for me?" Griffiths asks.

"Yeah. And within the hour, I hope to have the same thing for the husband. His carrier is slower to respond." Jefferson lingers in the door. "So are you thinking that this is some sort of a hoax, and Pryce is in on it?"

"Not impossible. What do you think?"

"Nothing's impossible," Jefferson admits. "Or almost nothing. But I don't see it."

"Why's that?"

"The money," she says. "These are not desperate people, neither of them. They both earn decent livings, legally. Although they're not exactly rolling around in piles of dough, nor do they need to engage in a massive international fraud just to make a buck."

"Though maybe they do," Griffiths says, "and we can't yet see why. Maybe they're deep into something. Loan sharks. Betting. Drugs."

Jefferson bounces her head side to side: good but not great point.

"Or maybe their predicament is not even nefarious," Griffiths continues. "Maybe Wright's sister is the one in trouble; maybe Pryce's son needs a new kidney; maybe her mom is about to lose her retirement condo to an online scam. Plenty of ordinary law-abiding people find themselves in sudden need of cash, and do desperate things to get it."

Jefferson nods.

"The truth is that I don't actually believe that's what's going on here," Griffiths admits. "But I'm pretty sure something is."

CHAPTER 27

Day 2. 1:47 p.m.
This was a mistake, wasn't it? Ariel shouldn't
have allowed this reporter to help her, to accompany her to this law firm's reception
room. She should've found an English-
speaking notary some other way.

Ariel perches in a leather chair, and sets
down her contract on the coffee table, which
already holds a potted succulent and a pile of
magazines and newspapers. She can't help
but glance at the front page, a headline in
Portuguese that she can't decipher, but
doesn't need to, it's clear just from the
picture. She's surprised that this is front-page
fodder for a European daily. What will happen when the story actually gets interesting?
It will be a global event, nonstop coverage.

She feels her chest getting tight. She takes a
deep breath, trying to beat back the budding
panic attack. Not now, please.

Pete Wagstaff is continuing to negotiate a
conversation in Portuguese with the recep-

tionist, who has a lot of questions. Finally the reporter walks over to Ariel. "It'll be a few minutes."

Ariel nods. She should take this opportunity to read through the agreement carefully. All she'd done back at the hotel was skim, note the numbers, find the places to sign. But she'd failed to notice that she needed a notary, and what else had she neglected? Cursoriness is irresponsible here. If anything ever has demanded close attention, it's this document.

She reads slowly, carefully, trying to cut through the dense legalese, references to the prior agreement from long ago, its date, its parties. This new NDA is an amendment to that old one, the same terms and penalties and remedies, the same everything still in effect. None of which she has in front of her. None of whose specifics she can recall. And none of which can be provided by anyone — not this notary, not the lawyer in Paris, not even her original lawyer, with whom she hasn't been in touch in fourteen years, a woman who's no doubt spending July Fourth on some beach —

Fuck, she thinks, and "Damn," she mutters, slamming down the small sheaf.

"You okay?" Wagstaff asks.

"No, not really." Ariel stands up abruptly. "I need to confirm a few things. I'm going to step out to make a call." Ariel shuts the door behind her. She checks her watch. It's early in the day for this, but she has no choice. She waits for the international call to connect.

"Ariel?" It's a croaky voice that answers. "Everything okay?"

"No, actually. Sorry for calling so early, but John has been kidnapped —"

"Oh my God. Seriously?"

"— and I need your help with something urgent. It's going to sound strange."

"Of course. Anything."

"I need you to go to the store right now."

"Like, *right* now?"

"Yes, immediately. Throw on some sweats, get in your car."

Persephone lives in her parents' house, a five-minute drive to the store. Hers is a small-town life where she knows everyone — the cops and firefighters, shop owners and bartenders, teachers and doctors and local-newspaper reporters. Everything is at most five minutes away.

"I promise, P., you'll be back home in twenty minutes, go back to bed, whatever."

"Okay."

"When you get there, please call me from the basement. And Persephone?"

"Yeah?"

"This is really, *really* important."

Ariel yanks open the door, and the receptionist and Wagstaff both look up. Ariel's eyes dart immediately to her paperwork sitting on the table, folded in half but in plain sight, right in front of the reporter. She marches over, snatches up the faxed pages.

"You didn't look at this, did you? Tell me you didn't look."

Wagstaff shakes his head.

"Oh God, you did."

"I didn't."

Ariel stares at him, trying to figure out if she believes him. She doesn't. He's maintaining eye contact way too firmly.

"How could you?" She's keeping her voice low; she doesn't want to alarm the receptionist.

"I'm just trying to help."

"You *cannot* write about this. You understand that, don't you? Please tell me you understand that."

"I promise I won't. Not until your husband is out of danger."

"No no no no *no.*" She ruffles the contract. "This? *Never.* You can never *reveal* this. You did not have a right to look. I did not have the right to allow you. I will go to *jail.* And that's actually the *best*-case scenario. Do you understand what could happen to me?"

"Uh, I . . .." he stammers.

Her phone starts ringing again.

"Oh good grief." She looks at the screen, answers. "P., hold just a sec, okay?" She covers the mic, turns her eyes back to the

325

reporter. "Get out of here."

"What?"

"I can't trust you. I never should have trusted you in the first place. Please leave. Now."

Carolina Santos looks up at the young detective who's rushing over. "We found the kidnapped man's client. His name is Jorge Vicente."

"Excellent."

"Two weeks ago, Vicente made a reservation for six people at nine o'clock tonight at Monthana. Do you know this restaurant?"

"I do." But Santos has never eaten there. Monthana is beyond her means.

"Vicente confirms that two of his guests are supposed to be the American consultant and his wife. I informed him that the Americans will not be able to join tonight."

Santos's fingers are already bouncing across her keyboard.

"Jorge Vicente," she reads from the screen, "is chief financial officer of Os Canários Enterprises, which is . . . . Oh who can tell from these websites. Mining? Maybe lumber also." She's clicking around, then shrugs, stands, grabs her jacket. "Let's go," she says to Moniz.

"Should we inform the wife?" Moniz asks.

"Not yet," Santos says. "Let's first hear what Vicente has to say."

■ ■ ■

"There he is," Nicole Griffiths says. "How are you feeling, slugger?"

Guido Antonucci smiles sheepishly. He had to have known that this was coming. He did after all get beat up by a girl. An *amateur* girl. He must be mortified. Griffiths certainly would be.

"I'm good, thanks."

He doesn't look it. His entire face seems to be swollen. But he's here, and Griffiths knows he's ready to work. Now is not when she's going to give him his full serving of shit.

"Guido, can you get ears into Pryce's hotel room?"

"Ugh. You mean right now?"

"As soon as humanly possible."

"This time of day? I dunno. A hotel is likely to be busy."

"True. But on the other hand, there shouldn't be any housekeeping staff wandering around to worry about."

"Good point." He thinks about it. "We wouldn't be able to hide the devices very well. Just a few mics in lamps. If Pryce starts looking, it's not going to be hard for her to find our hardware. Then what?"

"That depends on who she really is, and what she's really up to. If she's just a regular civilian whose regular civilian husband got kidnapped?" Griffiths shrugs. "Then she's not going to be checking any lamps for any microphones."

"But."

"Yeah. If she *does* sweep the room, then we've definitely learned that she's a person who sweeps a room."

"So you're saying a camera too?"

"It doesn't need to be great, Guido. It doesn't need to be at the ideal cinematography angle. It just needs to show us if this is a person who looks for bugs."

Antonucci nods. "I'm on it."

"Thanks. But Guido? I don't think you should be the one to go into the hotel." She swirls her fingers around the front of her own face. "In this state you're a little too conspicuous."

"Okay," Persephone says, "I'm in the basement."

"Good. You know where the toolbox is?"

"Sure."

Everyone in the shop is familiar with the toolbox, the WD-40 for squeaky hinges, the screwdriver to tighten brackets, hammer and nails and picture wire for inscribed author photos and signed book jackets. Fuses for the master board, a putty knife, spackle, drywall tape.

"You'll need the sledgehammer."

"The sledgehammer? Seriously?"

"You see that framed BookExpo poster? Take it off the hook."

"Um, okay . . . done."

"Now take the sledgehammer and smash a hole through the wall, right below the hook."

"*What?* Are you serious?"

"As a heart attack."

"Okay," Persephone says, "I'm gonna put you on speaker. Then I'll swing."

Ariel hears a thud, but not any cracking noise. "Don't be shy," Ariel says, loudly.

Another thud.

"Come on, Persephone, full swing."

Then she hears it, the smash and crack and plop-plop of debris hitting the floor, then a muttered "Holy shit."

"Grab the canvas bag that's in the wall."

"Did you do this? Build this hiding spot?"

Ariel had rented a power saw to cut a hole in the wall. She'd placed the tote — a convention giveaway — inside the wall, resting on a joist. Then she'd pushed the cutout piece of drywall back into place, taped around the edges, spackled over the tape, sanded the spackle, brushed the wall with primer, then two coats of paint. It looks perfect. Looked.

"Persephone, I want you to listen to me carefully."

"This is so awesome."

"Inside the tote, one of those Ziplocs contains electronic hardware; please leave that alone."

That large Ziploc holds a CD and a thumb drive and an inexpensive laptop plus its power cord. When Ariel prepared this packet more than a decade ago, she had no idea when — if ever — she'd need to access this material, and which technologies would be available when that time came, and which would have been tossed onto the slag heap of progress. Hence the redundancies. Her memory was fresh with the recent obsolescence of floppy disks, CD-ROMs, VCRs, tape decks. She'd already lost access to plenty of media due to technological developments, Michael Jackson vinyl and Talking Heads cassettes, videocassettes of Katharine Hepburn movies and DVD boxed sets of *Alias,* now all just different shapes of plastic garbage sitting in her attic. But these are all easily replaceable, and she'll always be able to find a new copy of *No Way Out* in a new format; plenty of businesses are motivated to maintain access to popular entertainments.

The same can't be said for Ariel's private files: her old audio recording of a conversation between two people, nine minutes of talking against background noise that's consistent with the subdued sounds of a posh restaurant during a quiet time of day. Also old scans of a police report, a medical exam, some tests. Those media could also be monetizable, in a very different way.

"The other bag, P., has some hard-copy

paperwork." A legal agreement. Handwritten notes. "That's what I'm interested in."

"You are *so* badass."

"I need you to read to me a few pieces of info from the paperwork."

"Wow. I'm not exaggerating, Ariel, when I say that this is literally the best. Thing. *Ever.*"

Persephone literally doesn't know what *literally* means; she seems to think it means the opposite. Ariel understands the idea of slang, accepts it, enjoys it. But this is something else, this total inversion, like *humble* when you mean *proud,* or *obsessed* for something pleasurable instead of painful. This isn't just harmless slang. This is Newspeak, just like the term *fake news:* not merely untruthful, but a complete repudiation of the very idea that truth exists.

"Listen, P., this is really important: *do not* read the other pages. I am literally — and this is what the word *literally* literally means — legally forbidden from divulging the specifics of what's in that contract. This is all *extremely* private material. And please do not touch the electronics. I need you to promise me."

"I promise."

"Okay, now open the Ziploc. Here's what I need you to tell me: the names and dates that are on the top of the agreement. Who the parties are."

Ariel of course knows that someone might

be eavesdropping right now, or will listen to a recording of this conversation later. But it would be wantonly irresponsible — it would be criminally negligent — for her to not check this information before signing a new contract.

She doesn't have a choice.

Ariel wakes every day to find that new words have been invented while others have been redefined, the language has been co-opted and distorted, weaponized, in an intersectional world of safe spaces and trigger warnings and microaggressions, of tokenizing and othering, Columbusing and whitewashing, centering and amplifying, mansplaining and manspreading, calling out and canceling, everyone rallying their point of view incessantly, to broadcast their complaints stridently, to yell relentlessly at anyone who disagrees.

It's an ever-expanding lexicon of grievance. Ariel doesn't think any of it is convincing anyone of anything that they didn't already believe, not converting anyone to any cause. Instead she's pretty sure it's accomplishing the opposite — demonizing, alienating, repelling, infuriating everyone whose eyes really do need to be opened, driving ever deeper wedges.

It had taken her a long time, but Ariel had eventually accepted that problems can't be solved by pretending they aren't there. She's also pretty sure that they can't be solved by giving them abstruse labels to use as bludgeons with which to beat everyone over the head. Problems are solved by changing minds, not by making enemies.

"Thanks," Ariel says. "And Persephone?"

"Yeah?"

"I really need to trust you here: Please do not look at the rest of the agreement."

"I promise. I will not even glance at it. Literally."

Persephone is Ariel's primary guide to the idioms of ideologies; it's the one thing contemporary grad school is definitely good for. They listen to NPR together, and Persephone tells her boss what the hell everyone is talking about.

At first, Ariel had worried that Persephone might turn out to be just another problem in her life. But she forced herself to take a step back, to try to see the young woman clearly, not as the person Ariel wanted to see, but as the person she really was. Not an enemy to reject, but an ally to nurture.

CHAPTER 28

Day 2. 2:04 p.m.
Everything is finally moving along, until suddenly it isn't. The notary is shaking her head.

"Who is this, please?" She's pointing at the paperwork. "This Laurel Turner?"

Ariel's spirits plummet, and she covers her face in both hands.

"You are Ariel Pryce, yes? But this document is for Laurel Turner. I do not understand."

Of the many challenges to her credibility, Ariel had failed to anticipate this one. "I changed my name a long time ago. These papers use my old name."

The notary seems to be taking this as a personal affront.

"I'm sorry. I don't have any identification with that old name."

"Nothing?"

"No. Not with me."

The notary sighs. "This," she says, "is a serious problem. Very serious."

Kayla Jefferson puts the printout of phone records down on her station chief's desk.

"Oh my goodness," Griffiths says, thumbing through the pages. "This is a lot."

"Yeah, it looks like John Wright uses this cell for everything. I check-marked in blue the things that look like client calls. Green is travel — hotels, restaurants, cars, a place where they rented Segways."

"Sorry: rented segues? What the fuck does that mean?"

"You know those things." Jefferson holds her fists in front of her, as if clutching handlebars. "Like upright scooters? People zoom around on them, looking like idiots?"

"Ah. Right."

"Red checkmarks are personal contacts. No checkmark at all means we don't yet know what the relationship is to Wright. Still working on those."

Griffiths turns a page, and Jefferson points at something. "This incoming call is a mechanic's garage near Pryce's farm. And this one here is Wright's sister in Marrakesh."

"Marrakesh?" Griffiths turns another page, then flips back. "His sister lives in Morocco?"

"Looks like it."

"That's a strange place for an American woman to live, isn't it?"

335

"Is it? There are a lot of American expats in Morocco."

"*Hmm.* Let's take a look at this sister."

"You got it."

"Also that mechanic. Could you see what that's about?"

Jefferson nods.

"Anything else?" Griffiths asks.

"Yeah: Just a few minutes ago, she had a really weird phone conversation with I think an employee of hers."

"Really weird? How so?"

"You're going to want to listen to it."

"Hi again Mr. James, this is Laurel Turner. I just realized that I have a small problem with the paperwork. I'm no longer Laurel Turner, I changed my name, I don't have any ID in that name. So the notary can't endorse my signature of this agreement."

"I see."

"Can you please redraft with my new name?"

"I'll have to check with my client."

"Please," Ariel says, "can you hurry this up?"

Ariel wonders if James knows his client's identity, or if this lawyer is just another unaware cutout, a subcontractor of a subcontractor, anonymous outsourced legal help buffered by multiple layers of insulation.

"Do you have any idea what's going on

336

here?" Ariel asks.

"Listen, Ms., um, whatever you say your name is. That's really none of my concern."

Twenty minutes later, Ariel can barely keep herself from launching across the desk to throttle the notary, who seems to be purposefully turning the pages in slow motion, double-checking who the hell knows, eyes back and forth between Ariel's passport and the agreement. As if inventing new ways to waste time, like a taxi driver running up the fare on a tourist.

"Very well," the notary says abruptly, signing with a dramatic flourish. "We are finished."

"Oh thank God."

Ariel gathers up her pages. Is this woman a possible leak? Is she bound by confidentiality? Did she as promised attend to nothing except her specific responsibility, which was verifying Ariel's identity, ensuring that the person signing the paperwork is the person referred to in it? Is she obligated to turn a blind eye to everything else? Has she? Will she?

The triggering event's details — the very existence of it — are all omitted from this paperwork, all buried deep in the past. But this document could certainly be a start. It could be a shovel.

■ ■ ■ ■

"Thank you for taking the time to see us."

"Of course," Jorge Vicente says. "How can I help you?"

Detective Carolina Santos looks around the wood-paneled walls hung with gilt-framed oil paintings: a hunting scene, a whaling boat in action, farmers tending an orchard. All pictures of men in the process of exploiting the earth. She sighs at the obviousness of it.

"We have a few questions about John Wright," Moniz says.

"This is just terrible." Vicente looks from one detective to the other. "I feel — I do not know — *embarrassed* about this happening to an American here. As if it is our fault."

"I agree," Moniz says. "It is humiliating when crime happens here to foreigners, especially to Americans. As if their worst prejudices are justified. We police take this personally."

"I can imagine."

"We do not want to take up too much of your time." Moniz opens his notepad. "What is the purpose of Mr. Wright's visit to you?"

"He is here to help us prepare for a round of financing."

"Financing for what? If you do not mind the question."

"It is no secret. We want to raise four

338

hundred million euros to purchase a tract of land from one of our competitors that has fallen on hard times, and is thus willing to sell. This purchase would be a big change to the scale of our business."

"Would this purchase generate any ill will? Are there other competitors who also want to buy this land?"

"Yes. They too are welcome to make bids. But this is a size of investment that is not appropriate for everyone. Though maybe I do not understand what you are asking, exactly?"

"Would any of your competitors be desperate to stop your deal from going through?"

"Oh, I see." Vicente shakes his head. "No. Certainly not desperate enough to kidnap a consultant to — what? — delay our financing?" He shakes his head more vigorously. "No."

"Can you imagine anyone else who might want to kidnap this American? For any reason at all?"

"No."

"Does he strike you as a natural target for kidnapping?"

"That is the strange thing. When your colleague told me about the kidnapping, I thought, why would anyone kidnap *him*? You have seen the wealth on display here, especially the British and the Russians with their yachts, their villas in the Algarve. There are so many foreigners in Portugal who look like

339

lucrative kidnapping targets. But John Wright? He is not one of them."

"Thank you," Moniz says, then turns to Santos, giving her a chance to ask follow-ups.

"Is there anything unusual about Mr. Wright's visit?" she asks.

"Such as?"

"I do not know. Anything. Is it last-minute? Did he make any special requests about the dates, or the schedule, or accommodations, or dining? Anything?"

"Well, now that you mention it: This visit of his, I think it is not one hundred percent necessary. Mr. Wright was here just a couple of months ago, and also a few months before that. We have already done the important work, and we are now at a very final stage of preparing our materials, which I think we could easily do by telephone and email. He does not need to be here."

"Perhaps this visit is more for the purposes of relationship-building?"

"Yes, perhaps. But our relationship is well-established at this point."

"Is it celebratory?"

"That would be premature."

"Do you have a guess of why he wanted to come?"

"No."

"Maybe something to do with his wife?" Santos suggests.

"His wife?" Vicente makes a face: It's possible. "Maybe. I was surprised to learn that he was planning to bring her along on this visit."

"Surprised? So her presence was not your idea?"

"My idea? Why would I want him to drag his wife across the ocean? In truth I was a little bothered by it. This wife necessitates organizing a dinner, with my wife, and my colleagues, and their spouses . . ." Vicente waves his hand, it just goes on and on, the pain in the ass.

Santos smiles: There is the first confirmed, definitive lie.

"Thank you for your time," she says.

"Well, now we know," Santos says. They are back on the sidewalk, where it is very hot, and very bright.

"What do we know?"

Santos is squinting, fishing around in her bag for her sunglasses, which are nearly as big as ski goggles, darkening every corner of her field of vision, from every angle. Moniz suspects that those giant things, meant to protect her, probably make it harder to actually see clearly.

"We know that Wright lied," Santos says in her most sanctimonious tone. "He claimed to his wife that it was the client who wanted her to come with him here. And the client just denied it."

"Perhaps," Moniz says.

"Perhaps? What do you mean? Perhaps what?"

"Perhaps it was Wright who lied. Perhaps not. We do not know for certain."

Santos turns to him, but Moniz can't read her face behind those glasses. Maybe that is the point.

"Perhaps," Moniz continues, "Wright never said any such thing to his wife. The only reason we think he did is because that is what the wife told us. Perhaps she is the one who is lying."

Moniz can see that Santos is about to object, but her ringing phone interrupts her. "Hello Erico," she says, then listens for a few seconds. "Thanks. We will be right there."

In the notary's bathroom, Ariel stares at herself in yet another mirror, taking deep breaths, alone, trying to get her pulse to slow, her nerves to settle, her brain to quiet. She feels so many different panics within her, so many different threats converging.

"Okay," she mutters to herself. "That's finished."

She knows that as a matter of theory she's on solid legal ground. All her actions have been rational, all defensible. She hasn't violated the terms of her agreement; she hasn't induced anyone else to break any law. Even though she's in a situation of extreme

342

duress, she has acted as carefully as could be reasonably expected. She has made all the logical choices that any sensible person would make. Every call, every contact, every request.

But Ariel is not responsible for the choices that other people make; never has been. If this notary gets too nosy? Or the reporter? Ariel did what she could do. She's trying to make the best of a horrible situation that she has been thrust into. Same as she did back then, back when this all began, when she was standing in front of a different mirror, trying to settle herself in a different bathroom, in a place where you have the expectation of complete privacy, a safe space in the only sense that the phrase existed back then: a physical one.

But it wasn't.

In the small town where Ariel lives, one of the many service categories that doesn't offer a lot of options is legal help. There's really just one attorney. Yes, there are other lawyers in adjoining villages, and if Ariel hated Jerry she could cast a wider net. But she likes Jerry, and has entrusted him with the purchase of the farm and the bookstore, with some complications arising from her name change, with her estate planning when George was born, the trust, a life insurance policy, everything.

Jerry is reasonable about his fees. In a town

like theirs, in a business like Jerry's, his liveli-hood relies entirely on referrals and repeat business. If he ever gouged anyone, everyone in town would know; a quick way to kill a career. In the same vein, Jerry is often willing to provide incidental legal advice in exchange for a night's bar tab. This is how Ariel repaid Jerry for his help in her acquisition of Fletcher the goat from the disorganized estate of her neighbor Cyrus.

"Thanks again, Jerry." She was still sipping her first glass of white wine; Jerry was deep into his third bourbon.

"My pleasure." Jerry raised his glass to her. "Just please don't mention it to anyone."

"Mention what?"

"My, um, role in the *ex parte* transfer of the orphan goat from the deceased's *intestate* estate. In fact, I'm-a have to insist on you signing a confidentiality agreement."

Ariel laughed at the absurdity.

"I'll draft the nondisclosure in the morn-ing."

Then something occurred to her that was even more absurd, but also a lot less so. "What do we do about George?"

"George?"

"My son? How do we prevent him from talking?"

Jerry rolled his eyes dramatically. This prob-ably happened to him every night, sitting here drinking his dinner. People asked him ridiculous questions.

"George is a minor. We can't force the NDA onto him."

"So he's free to tell people? About the origins of our ownership of the goat?"

"Well, there's nothing we can do about the minor. And, alas, the NDA doesn't negate the existence of the facts."

Jerry was now holding up his glass as if it were a classroom prop. Or maybe this was a courtroom he was imitating? Who knew. Probably not even Jerry.

"Which is essentially this: You, a person now doing business as Ariel Pryce, broke US code . . . y'know what, I'll have to get back to you on the *exact* case law . . . committed theft of livestock —"

"Is Fletcher livestock? I think he's more like a family pet."

Jerry waved off the objection, continued, "From the estate of Cyrus Latham, Jr. That is a fact. But the signatory to the confidentiality agreement — you — will be forbidden from sharing that fact with anyone. From introducing that fact into the public sphere. From *disclosing* that fact."

Ariel laughed, egging him on. She wanted to hear where this ended.

"A nondisclosure agreement, madam, does not *change* history. It merely gags certain *witnesses* to history. But if a nonsignatory discovers these same facts on his own, without assistance from signatory parties?" Jerry shrugged.

"What?"

"There's nothing a nondisclosure agreement can do."

Jerry finished his drink with a flourish.

"Facts are still facts," he said. "Truth is truth."

CHAPTER 29

Day 2. 4:11 p.m.
When the room phone rings, Ariel is standing on the narrow balcony, surveying the square in front of the hotel.

"Senhora Pryce, there is a gentleman named Guy Cicinelli here to see you. From the office of, um" — Ariel hears a man's voice in the background — "from the office of Nigel James?"

"I'll be right there." Ariel hustles down the staircase again, rounds the corner into reception.

"Guy Cicinelli," he says, advancing on her quickly. He's a young man in a young man's tight suit, narrow collar, pointy shoes, studiously akimbo hair. He's carrying a serious-looking briefcase in one hand, the other hand extended for a shake. "A pleasure."

"Is that for me?" she asks.

He flashes a smile so quickly that she almost doubts it was ever there. "Not entirely." He lowers his voice. "Would you mind if we conducted our meeting in your room?"

Mind? Yes, she sure as hell would mind, and he can see this on her face.

"I'm afraid we need some privacy," he continues. "This is not merely a handoff."

Ariel's mind scurries around the public spaces in this hotel. "How about the restaurant?"

"I really must insist." Again that fleeting flash of a smile. "Perhaps you'd be more comfortable if you rang Mr. James to verify my identity? By all means."

Ariel realizes that if there's ever zero chance that a man is going to hurt her, it's this man here. "That won't be necessary," she acquiesces, then leads him up the stairs. She can feel the hairs on the back of her neck standing up. She unlocks the door, and shows in Cicinelli.

He examines the foyer, then closes the door behind him, engages the security chain. "Are you alone here?" he asks. "You won't mind if I double-check?"

"Go ahead."

"I should warn you that I'm armed. It's for my own protection, and yours as well."

"Okay."

"And I'm going to unholster my weapon now."

"Um . . . all right."

He yanks a large handgun out of his jacket. Even though Ariel knew it was coming, the sight of the gun scares the crap out of her; she can feel her heartbeat accelerate.

Cicinelli strides into the bedroom, weapon held carefully in front, with the barrel pointed down. He's ready to shoot someone, but not the wrong someone.

This is a scary person Ariel is alone with; she's second-guessing the prudence of letting him in, letting him lock the door. She can hear his footsteps in the bathroom, then back out, then he turns the corner to examine the kitchen, clearing the entire suite.

"Right."

Cicinelli is apparently satisfied that this isn't an ambush, a setup, a scam. He reholsters his alarmingly large gun, and places the metal briefcase on the glass-topped dining table with a soft *clang*. He spins the bag around, uses an electronic touchpad to unlock it. Removes a laptop with a small electronic device already attached to an external port.

"Is this network functional?" He points at a laminated card that explains the wifi.

"Yes."

He bends over to type, fingers flying. "Right." He removes a small peripheral from the bag, plugs it into an external port of the laptop. "If you don't mind?" He nods down at the glass-screened device, like a smartphone, except square. "Fingerprints. To confirm your identity."

She rests her fingers on the screen, waits

while the whorls are scanned. A beep sounds.

"Thank you," he says, and turns back to the keyboard. He is one fast typist. As well as being an armed man carrying two million euros. "It'll be just a minute to transmit and verify."

Another beep sounds, and Cicinelli says, "Right." Then he reaches back into the briefcase, and pulls out a neat bundle of cash bound in a paper collar stamped €10,000. He places the packet on the table, then reaches into the case and removes one bundle at a time, counting off — four, five, six — as he stacks a small edifice, until he concludes, "And that's ten, yeah?"

Ariel nods.

"Each packet is ten thousand euros, so this pile of ten packets is one hundred thousand." He continues to remove packets quickly, his hands whirring like a juggler's, building a fresh stack next to the first. Ariel joins him in this kindergarten-type project, building pile after pile of money until the bag is empty, and on the table are two rows of ten stacks.

"Right," Cicinelli says. "That's twenty stacks there, each of one hundred thousand euros. Which equals two million. Yeah?"

"Yup."

"Please examine one at random."

Ariel slides off a band of paper, flips through the crisp green-and-white bills. This is a lot of cash. She nods.

Cicinelli has now removed a few pages of good old-fashioned paperwork from the bag. "Sign here, please, and here, and here, acknowledging receipt. And then in the same spots on the second copy too. That one's yours."

Ariel is getting a receipt? Like she just bought a microwave at Best Buy. This strikes her as insane. Then it strikes her as completely rational, and obvious, and inevitable.

"This is for you." He unfolds a generic white plastic shopping bag, stuffs the cash into it. "There, fits perfectly." He hands the bag to her, like a salesman at a boutique.

"Thanks."

"Right," he says again. "I believe we are finished. Agreed?"

"Yes."

"Very well." Cicinelli picks up his case, appraises her. "Do you know what you're doing?"

"No," she says. "Definitely not."

"Do you mind me asking what you intend to do with this cash?"

"Pay a ransom. My husband has been kidnapped."

"Oof. That's a bad one, innit?" Cicinelli reaches into his jacket and Ariel recoils, knowing what's coming, and sure enough he draws his gun.

What?" she yells.

"No," he says, holding the weapon upside

down. "I'm not . . . just, er: Do you want this?"

Does she?

"It's new, it's clean, it has no connection to me, nor to anyone else."

Huh. This is interesting. But is it useful?

"Do you know how to use a pistol?"

"Not really." She shakes her head at this man with his French first name and Italian last, English accent and German gun, brief-case full of euros.

"Here, look, it's easy." He shows her the mechanism, loading the chamber, the safety. "That's it. Point, squeeze." He shrugs. "Not complicated."

Easy. Not complicated. Does he really think that? Ariel looks at this large piece of danger-ous hardware, which she absolutely does not want. Her only reason for pause is that she's worried how it will look to decline, to be too dismissive about arming herself. It might look like she wasn't worried about the ransom exchange, instead of looking like she's wor-ried about escalating the tension with un-necessary firepower.

Then again, who cares? Cicinelli is just a messenger. She doesn't need to worry about any suspicions he might have.

"Thanks, that's very kind of you. But I don't know how to . . ." She points at the gun. "While the kidnappers probably do. Plus I wouldn't want to give the appearance that

I'm thinking about double-crossing anyone, robbing anyone. So I don't think this is such a great idea. For me."

Cicinelli stares at her, weighing her reasoning, wondering if he should argue. "Of course. You're probably right."

"But thanks for the offer."

Cicinelli nods, turns, unlocks the door. "Best of luck to you."

Ariel secures the safety chain behind him, then leans against the door, and faces her room, the window, the cityscape beyond. Here she is, alone in a hotel suite with two million euros, waiting for the phone to ring. The end is near.

The end, at least, of this part.

Pete Wagstaff accepts that a certain amount of anger will be directed at him. What he does for a living often involves betraying people's trust: He digs for their secrets, then exposes those secrets. He gets people to say things they don't want to say, on the record, then he's the one who actually puts those things on the record; he is the record. And though he's accustomed to the resultant anger, still he sometimes feels plenty shitty about it.

Now is one of those times. He actively curried this poor woman's confidences; he put himself in the path of being able to help her, specifically so he could exploit her. This is without question ethically dubious, at best.

It's also just not nice.

But the First Amendment isn't there to be nice. The point of a free press is not to make friends.

Wagstaff was very careful when photographing her document. Careful that everything was readable. Careful that the receptionist didn't see him doing it. Careful to return the papers to their original position so Pryce wouldn't know that he'd touched them. But she did anyway. Sometimes you don't need any proof to know you're right.

He's having a tough time gleaning much from this agreement. It seems to be an amendment to an old contract, dated fourteen years ago, with all the same terms and penalties still in effect, but none of them enumerated in this new paperwork.

Ariel Pryce is one of the parties. The other signatory is a vaguely named LLC with a physical address in Grand Cayman that's probably shared by hundreds or thousands of other LLCs and partnerships and corporations that all want to obscure their owners' identities, to protect their assets, to minimize their tax exposure and legal liabilities, to hide in the shadows that were created by lawyers for the express purpose of hiding.

This shield is something that Wagstaff knows can be investigated, cross-referencing the mailing addresses and phone numbers and court filings and real-estate transfers, law firms and private bankers, stripping away one cutout after another, working backward through the maze. That would be a lot of legwork, all with no guarantee of finding a definitive answer, and no guarantee that the answer would be of any interest to anyone. But that's what reporters do, isn't it? That's what investigation is: looking without knowing what you're going to find. That's how you discover the truth.

"Okay," Jefferson says, "I've now ID'd a bunch of the other people from Wright's phone records."

Nicole Griffiths runs her eyes down Jefferson's annotations — COLLEGE ROOMMATE, WORK FRIEND, COUSIN. She turns the page, then back. "Huh. The calls to his sister."

"In Marrakesh."

"They're very regular, for a very long time. Nearly every week. And then suddenly they stop." Griffiths flips the page again. "Completely. The last call was three months ago. Not one since."

"They had a fight? Or maybe the sister got a different phone, with a non-Moroccan number. Maybe one of these that we haven't yet ID'd."

"Possible." Griffiths examines the pages again. "But none of these other numbers are called as regularly. Why would Wright stop talking to his sister three months ago?"

"That's when he got married. Maybe something happened?"

"Oh something definitely happened," Griffiths says. "We need to find out what. Let's learn more about this sister. What about that mechanic?"

"Sorry, that's a dead end. The mechanic says he doesn't know anyone named John Wright, didn't place a call to anyone by that name."

"Yet he did."

"By mistake, maybe?"

"Maybe not, Jefferson. Press a little further. And anything more on that LLC that Pryce discussed with her employee?"

"No, sorry. I can't get almost anyone in Langley on the phone. It's still pretty early back home, and it's the Fourth."

"Okay, stay on it."

"My God!" this stunning woman exclaims. "He has been kidnapped? That is horrible."

"Yes it is," Carolina Santos says. "And you are certain it was the same man?"

"Absolutely. But he was with his wife, so I decided to pretend I was wrong." She shrugs. "I did not want to make trouble for him."

"Tell me, please, how is it that you met?" Santos asks. Moniz seems to be too busy staring at the woman to ask any questions.

"At a club."

"You saw each other how many times?"

"It was just the one night." She says this without the least hint of shame. Good for her, Santos thinks. Maybe there's some hope for the world.

"How long ago was this?" Santos wants to know what type of cheating John Wright was doing.

"Last fall. September? Maybe October."

At that point Wright was already dating Pryce, but they were not yet married. Bad, but not as bad as it could be.

"And you are positive he told you his name was Luigi?"

"Yes. I was drunk, but not that drunk."

The fake name bothers Santos, especially for a man who had already changed his name once, who is married to a woman who had also changed her name. That is a lot of hiding that these people do.

"Does he have any identifying marks that would prove he is the same man? Tattoos, scars . . . ?"

The woman cocks her head. "Well . . ."

"What?"

"His penis is circumcised."

Moniz coughs, and blushes. If Santos did not know any better, she would say that her partner is a little in love with this woman. She supposes there are many different ways to love. Hate is much simpler.

Ariel answers the burner on the first ring,

"Hello?"

"Do you have the cash?"

She almost admits that she doesn't have all three million, but instead says simply, "Yes."

"Good. Do not take it with you now. Leave the hotel, walk left, then take your first left-hand turn. You will find a souvenir shop. Purchase two matching duffel bags, both in black, that are large enough to hold all the cash. While you are still in the store, put one bag into the other. This is important. Then take the luggage to your room. Put the cash into the bag that is holding the other one. Do you understand?"

"Yes. Then what?"

"Then wait."

CHAPTER 30

Day 2. 5:55 p.m.

The indispensable disposable phone in Ariel's hand rings again. She reminds herself to stay calm, to remember to breathe, to say hello.

"Hello," she says.

"You are ready?"

"Yes."

"Is the bag ready, packed with the other bag?"

"Yes."

On her own initiative, Ariel had also made another purchase at the gift shop: a brand-new mobile, which is plugged into its charger but not yet activated.

"Take the bag, leave the hotel, walk across the square. Keep this phone in your hand. And leave your personal phone in the room. This is very important. Leave right now."

Carolina Santos is well aware that her partner is one of those people who always knows which direction is which. Even if António

Moniz is walking through a windowless hallway in an unfamiliar building, he would be able to tell you that he is facing south-southwest. This preternatural skill — or instinct? — does not have anything to do with the mechanical operation of a motor vehicle, the steering, the speed management, the situational awareness. But it is not as if they engage in high-speed car chases through the streets of Lisbon. For the most part, being a good driver as a police officer means knowing where you are, and where you are going, all the time. Moniz does. Santos does not. So she reluctantly admits that this makes her partner a superior driver. Which is why she is sitting in the passenger seat while he is behind the wheel.

For the past hour they have been parked across the square from the hotel, watching. There is no way that the ransom handoff is going to happen *in* the hotel. No kidnapper would walk into a potential trap like that, not one who was sane and competent enough to successfully kidnap someone in the first place. So the American woman is bound to come out, sooner or later, to deliver this ransom somewhere else. She is bound to take evasive maneuvers of some sort.

The police are ready. Moniz and Santos are waiting here in this car, another detective is around the corner with his eye on the hotel's back door, and four others are stationed at strategic chokepoints nearby. Plus uniformed officers are strewn around the neighborhood, on alert.

"I still do not see any American watchers. Do you?"

Moniz shakes his head. "Are you expecting the CIA?"

Santos shrugs. She does not know what to expect from this situation. "Tell me, António, what is it that you suspect of the Pryce woman?"

"Specifically? Nothing. But I want to be careful not to jump to conclusions. Yes, Senhora Pryce seems to be a beautiful, sympathetic woman who finds herself in an unfortunate situation. Perhaps too sympathetic? Perhaps too unfortunate?"

"You are not blaming her for her good looks and bad fortune, are you? Tell me you are not doing that."

"Definitely not. But the whole package of her, combined with the fact that she showed up to us so early in the day, plus that she has not been completely forthright about everything, the bank accounts, even her own name —"

"No one is completely forthright about everything."

"Of course. And no one is completely innocent about everything. And when I asked her why the sister is in Lisbon?"

"But the sister is *not* in Lisbon."

361

"There you go again, Carolina, jumping to conclusions. It is true that we have no evidence that the sister is in Lisbon. But she could be. And the way Pryce responded to my question?"

"That was pure surprise."

"Yes. But surprise at what?"

"You were badgering her about every —"

"Look," Moniz interrupts. "Is that her?"

A woman has just stepped out of the hotel with a bag slung over her shoulder.

"Yes." Santos moves the dangling microphone to her mouth. "Pryce is on the move. Tomas? Do you see her?"

"Yes."

"Okay, Tomas, Erico, both of you remember: If you think you have been made by Pryce or by anyone else, you must say so. Francisco and Mariella are ready to tag in."

The street is teeming with commuters, and the ludicrously hazardous streetcars are careening around, taxis and mopeds zipping with goose-like honks around the square, this loud place with hundreds of people coming and going and staying, a hard-to-monitor population that definitely includes some men and maybe women who are watching Ariel — the CIA, or the Lisbon police, or the national security service, or reporters, or kidnappers, or some combination of any of these, or maybe all, earpieces for instructions, handguns for interventions, vans around the corner, satellite feeds, cell phone intercepts —

Ariel's eyes jump around, looking for people who are looking at her, but she fails to identify a single one; they're all doing a good job of pretending. Or she's doing a bad job of detection.

When she arrives at the far side of the square, the phone rings again. "Yes?"

"Across the street to your left. Do you see that café?"

"Yes."

"Walk into it. Keep this call open. Tell me when you're inside the café."

Ariel weaves through the traffic, enters the busy, well-lit place. "I'm inside."

"Go to the toilet."

She looks around, finds the sign, the corridor, the door. She turns the handle, but the door doesn't open. "Damn," she says. "Someone must be in there. It's locked."

"Wait."

The thirty seconds feel like forever, then a woman emerges, and gives the crazed-looking Ariel as wide a berth as possible within the confines of the narrow corridor.

"I'm in the bathroom."

"Lock the door. Do you see the shelf above the sink?"

"Yes." It's filled with the type of supplies you expect in a commercial bathroom.

"Reach behind the paper rolls on the right."

"What am I looking for?"

"You will see." And she does: a cell phone connected to earbuds. "Do you have it?"

"Yes." This new device immediately starts to ring.

"Put on the headphones, and answer."

Ariel does.

"Now end the connection on the old phone, place it behind the rolls, and leave."

She wends her way among the tables. "I'm outside."

"Do you know the Elevador de Santa Justa?"

"I do." It's just a few blocks away, a hundred-plus-foot-tall elevator that saves pedestrians the trouble of walking up a long staircase on a steep hill that separates one neighborhood from another.

"Go there, and ride to the top."

Ariel walks quickly, neck swiveling left and right, back and forth, alert not just for tails but for muggers, for assailants of any sort. Lisbon is not a dangerous place, but now would be a very bad time to stumble into random danger. She notices a pair of teen-aged boys loitering in a doorway, their heads down but eyes up, darting, shifty; a lupine pose, predatory. But these boys don't notice Ariel. Whatever they're hunting for, it's not someone like her.

After just a few minutes' walking here it is, the upper approach to the *elevador,* reminiscent of a smaller, utilitarian Eiffel Tower. Beside the elevator is a long staircase, at the bottom of which is the entrance. Ariel surveys the scene from the top of this crowded staircase, one side of which is filled with a thick throng that Ariel realizes is a queue, maybe a hundred people are waiting to ride this odd attraction, to enjoy the view from the platform at the top.

She groans; this is going to take forever. But Ariel doesn't have a choice, so she installs herself at the end of the line, beside the busy flow of foot traffic, people going up and coming down, shopping bags from Nike and Foot Locker, Mango and H&M and Sephora, the same stores as everywhere. New groups quickly fill in the queue behind her — it's good late-afternoon light for photos from up top — one group after another, a sunburned family with cockney accents, and behind them a half-dozen elderly Japanese, and behind them a trio of teenaged girls posing for selfies, peace signs, duck lips, shrieking at one another, screaming for attention shamelessly, indiscriminately.

Ariel tightens her grip on the strap of the cash-filled duffel bag. This would be an easy place to mug her; a hard place for her to give chase.

This queue can't be the handoff spot — it's too public, too obvious, too monitored, too soon. She hasn't yet been instructed to make any evasive maneuvers. Whoever was watching her at the hotel is still watching her now, probably perched behind her at the top of these steps, with maybe a partner who rushed to the bottom and is now peering up, standing guard. Ariel is wedged in here, in the midst of this dense crowd, all this activity, all this humanity.

Without warning the line begins to move haltingly toward the ticket counter, four steps down then pause, another three steps then pause. Ariel descends carefully until she hears a new instruction in her ear: "Step out of the queue now. Walk down the steps."

Ariel obeys the instructions, walking faster than the people descending beside her.

"There is a taxi at the bottom. Do you see?"

"No." Panic, and then she does. "Yes, now I see."

"Get into it. The driver is expecting you. Ask for the rua de São Paulo tram stop."

"Pryce?" the driver asks through the window. Ariel nods and gives the destination as she's climbing in. The car swings around a turn, and descends a steep incline, and quickly they are out of the shopping district, into an area that's grittier, the sidewalks narrower, the buildings close to the roadway, the feeling claustrophobic. This would be a good spot to stage an ambush, roadblocks, cross fire.

"Tell me when you have exited the taxi."

At the bottom of the hill the car merges onto a busier street, less worrisome looking, and within a few fast blocks they come to an abrupt halt. A short trip.

"Obrigada," Ariel says, handing a bill to the driver. Then to the phone, "I'm out."

She glances back against the one-way traffic, looking for a tail. She doesn't see anything at first, but then she does, a moped fifty yards behind her, slowing, pulling to the curb.

"Walk past the tram stop, to the yellow building."

She looks up at the dirty graffitied structure, an open arched doorway, a sign that announces ASCENSOR DA BICA. "I'm there."

"Walk into that building." A dim industrial space, the lower terminus of a funicular. A car is waiting, doors open, a handful of people already seated. "Board the *ascensor.* Watch for anyone who arrives after you. Tell me when the gates close."

Ariel is on the lookout for the man who followed her on the moped, but he never arrives. A few other passengers do in the minute before the doors close.

"Okay," Ariel says, "we're moving."

"Look around at those passengers who boarded after you." A middle-aged woman carrying groceries, an older man with a newspaper, a young couple. "One or more of those people might be following you. Can you tell which?"

367

"No."

The tram creaks its slow way up the steep hill.

"Tell me just before you pass the first street that intersects the tracks."

It's coming up already. "We're just about there."

"Now jump off."

What? There's a folding gate blocking the doorways. "I can't do that."

"Yes you can. It is not difficult. Do it. Right now."

She stands, and it's just two strides to the gate, and sure enough it's not that hard to swing one leg over the gate, which she does as someone behind her says something loudly that Ariel ignores, now folding her second leg over the gate while holding the edge of the cable car, and now her butt is balanced on top of the gate, and there's nothing to do but do it —

"This is definitely the correct transaction?" Griffiths can't hide her disappointment. She was hoping that this would be the big reveal, there he is, the man in DC who's being extorted for millions of dollars by Ariel Pryce. But instead Kayla Jefferson's screen shows a woman standing at the counter of a convenience store, buying a prepaid cell phone, with cash.

"No doubt about it," Kayla says. "Sorry."

"Okay, so what can we learn here? Let's rewind . . . There, her open wallet. That's an American Express green card. And it's in a Louis Vuitton wallet."

"Or a fake."

"Good point."

"It looks like she's wearing a lanyard under her jacket," Kayla says. "I can't think of anyplace that uses that color of ribbon. Does it mean anything to you?"

"Pink?" Griffiths scoffs. "Yeah, to me it means that she bought her own lanyard to hold her ID card. Any exterior footage?"

"Not from the convenience store, no. But I have calls in to other businesses on the block whose cameras might have an angle on the door. I'll let you know when we hear back. But —"

"Yeah, yeah, I know, I know: July Fourth. I'm not holding my breath."

Ariel lands awkwardly on the steep street, stumbles, falls onto one knee and plants both palms to steady herself, and more people are yelling at her from the tram, but she sees over her shoulder that the yellow car doesn't stop, the operator shaking his head in consternation, all the other faces at the windows, everyone tsk-tsking.

"Are you injured?"

Ariel gets to her feet, pulls the duffel over her shoulder.

"Not really."

"Did anyone get off the tram to follow you?"

"No." She rubs her knee, confirming that it hurts. With all the adrenaline, it's hard to tell.

"Good. Walk on that intersecting street, make your first right, it will be just a few seconds."

"I've turned."

"Now your first left. There is a place called Bar Porto. Do you see it?"

"I do." There are a few groups of young people out on the narrow street, beer bottles and clove cigarettes, sandals and harem pants and patchouli oil.

"Go into the bar, walk through the front room to the hall, then turn back to face the door."

It's a dimly lit space with lights strung from the ceiling, and barrels for tables, and the scent of something musky. At the far end of the room is a beaded curtain to a short hall, and a flimsy-looking door labeled WC.

"Should I go into the bathroom?"

"No. Just watch the front door for any tail."

The bar is crowded, but no one is paying Ariel any mind except the bartender, who nods. Ariel nods back, then cuts her eyes to the door as the form of a man appears, and pauses, and —

Oh no, she thinks.

— and keeps walking.

"Has anyone followed you in?"

It has been maybe fifteen seconds since she entered. "No."

"You are sure?"

"Yes."

"Past the toilet are two more doors. Open the final one, and walk through it —"

And then Ariel is in a narrow alley, stone walls close on either side, trash cans, a wooden crate filled with empty beer bottles.

"— and shut the door behind you."

One end of the alley is a dead end, and in the other direction is a bend. Ariel can't see what the bend opens to, but it must be a street. That must be where she's going.

"And now what?"

The voice doesn't reply, but the answer is suddenly obvious: Someone has appeared at the bend, filling the narrow space, closing in on Ariel, very quickly.

"Hey Pete, how you doin'."

"Myron. Thanks for getting back to me."

"No problem. First off, about that LLC in Cayman, I gotta warn you: This is not an easy lift. It's probably gonna take weeks, or months, possibly never. These legal shields are set up specifically to be opaque, that's the whole point, usually by people who know what the hell they're doing."

"You said *probably* going to take a while.

371

Which means it might not?"

"The exception is if the legwork has already been done by someone else who took the time to investigate this particular LLC, or another entity affiliated with the same law office, or bank, or local corporate governance. Then it could be a matter of days, or even hours. But don't count on it."

"Okay, thanks Myron. I'll be patient."

"Like hell you will."

"And what about the birth certificate?"

"Yeah, I suspect you're not going to like that answer either. But it's not uninteresting."

CHAPTER 31

Day 2. 6:22 p.m.

Ariel watches the rapidly approaching figure, a woman wearing all the hippie regalia — a handwoven blouse and baggy linen pants, Birkenstocks and a nose ring, white-girl dreadlocks and big round sunglasses à la John Lennon. She's shedding the straps of her dirty, battered backpack, which is no book-bag type of thing but a big complex piece of serious outdoor gear, with a sleeping bag clipped to the bottom, even one of those splatterware enamel bowls.

When she's just a few feet away, the woman swings this pack in front of her, lowers it to the ground, and kneels behind it. She points at the duffel on Ariel's shoulder.

"When do —"

"*Shh,*" the woman hisses, shaking her head.

The man in her ear says, "Open your duffel, remove the empty bag. Put the empty bag on the ground. Quickly."

Ariel does this. The woman reaches into

her big pack to remove a small pile of newspaper, which she places into Ariel's empty duffel, then another pile of newspaper. She zips closed the newspaper-filled duffel, and points again at the bag that still contains the two million euros.

"Put the cash into my colleague's backpack."

"Listen," Ariel whispers, "I have to tell you: I don't have all of it."

"What?" Pause. "What do you mean?"

"I have two million here, not three."

"Fuck. *Fuck.*"

"I tried, I really did. I'm sorry."

"Sorry? *Sorry?* Who gives a shit about *sorry?*"

"I know. I know."

"We were very clear. *Very* clear."

"You were," Ariel says quietly. "And I tried my hardest. But I just couldn't get all three. It's so much money, and such a short amount of time."

"So maybe we will return only two-thirds of your husband."

"*Please.* It's not his fault." She can hear breathing on the phone. She presses on, "But here we are. So wouldn't you rather have two million euros right now, and walk away safe, than have no money, nothing except a hostage, with the police and the CIA and Lord knows who else hunting for you?"

Ariel glances at the woman, her eyes narrowed behind the round shades, with her own earbuds plugged in. She too is listening to both sides of this conversation.

"Fuck," the man says again. "Fuck," less explosively. Then, "Okay."

The hippie woman gets back to work quickly, zipping closed her backpack with the cash inside. She wants to get this over with.

"When do I get my husband back?"

"Very soon," the man answers in her ear.

"Very soon. What does that mean?"

"It means: very soon."

The woman still has not said a word. She hoists her backpack.

"Take that duffel filled with newspaper, and walk to the end of the alley, and out to the street, and turn right. Then walk straight."

The woman is now wearing her backpack again, and puts one hand on the bar's back door —

"Hey, wait a —"

She ignores Ariel, steps inside, closes the door behind her. Ariel is all alone in the alley.

"What the hell is going on?"

"When we have verified that your payment is as promised, and that our messenger is safe, then your husband will be released. Remember: Turn right at the end of the alley, then straight."

"Then what?"

He doesn't answer.

"Then what?"

■ ■ ■ ■

Kayla realizes that she's been staring at her screen for pretty much ten straight hours; it hasn't felt that long. This is a big part of what attracted her to the CIA in the first place: the research, the detective work, the chipping away at impermeable-looking shells, finding cracks that can be widened, exploited. Kayla never wanted to be an analyst, sitting around Langley, doing nothing except research. She loves being here in Lisbon, out in the field, hunting for human intelligence; she relishes the opportunity to recruit assets. But that doesn't mean she dislikes this part. She likes all of it.

For the past half-hour she has been opening up one file after another of security-camera footage from Washington, DC, and so far it's only this one clip that has yielded anything useful. Maybe one is all she'll need. She wishes she could have gotten further with this piece of evidence, but she has come to a dead end, at least for now, and it's time to loop in the boss.

Griffiths answers on the first ring. "Tell me you have good news, Jefferson."

"Sort of. A coffee shop has an exterior camera that faces the general direction of the convenience store. It's too far away, plus at a bad angle, to give a useful view of anyone

376

coming in and out. But it has a good view of the street itself. And in the minute before the purchase of the burner, a car pulled up and discharged a passenger, then the car waited, and a couple minutes later someone got back into the car, which then drove away."

"Tell me you got the plate. Please tell me that."

"Yes ma'am. It's a ride-share."

"Okay then! We're in business. This should be a piece of cake."

"It should be. But I've butted up against a privacy policy. They're saying they need a warrant. And, y'know, it's July Fourth."

"Fuckers."

"Well, I don't know about that."

Kayla doesn't want to wade into the quagmire of debating the founding principles, on Independence Day itself, with her boss. But Kayla's reverence for civil liberties is rigid. This occasionally puts her at odds with her work in intelligence, a field that's largely premised upon intrusions into privacy and the suspension of civil liberties, or at least a willful disregard for them. She suspects that this paradox is going to be a challenge throughout her career.

"What in God's name do you want to do that for?" This is what her father had asked when Kayla said she'd applied to work at the CIA. Shawn Jefferson put no trust whatsoever in any organization that gave white men guns and permission to use them. You also wouldn't catch him waving any flags, singing any anthems, reciting any pledge of allegiance. Shawn didn't know where in hell his daughter came by her patriotism.

Griffiths doesn't argue with her, not this time. Instead she asks, "Why don't you have a chat with the driver himself?"

"Will do," Kayla says. This is where patriotism gets trickiest, isn't it? When the patriotic impulse crashes against the very ideals that America is supposed to represent.

"I have located Pryce again," Officer Tomas announces. "She just emerged from an alley and is now walking west. She is still carrying the money."

"How long was she out of sight?" Santos asks.

"Ninety seconds, perhaps two minutes."

That's certainly long enough. "But she still has the money? You can see the bag?"

"Definitely."

"Which means that hailing the taxi, and boarding the tram, and jumping off it, and running through this quarter, and ducking into and out of this alley: That was all an evasive maneuver that in the end failed to evade you?"

"It looks that way."

Santos doesn't believe it. "Text us the nearest address to the alley." She turns to her partner. "Dispatch uniformed officers to interview anyone nearby, immediately. Ring every doorbell. Everything very fast."

Moniz obeys, gets on the phone to the station.

Should Santos order the whole area to be closed down? She has only seconds to make this decision, to try to cordon off a three- or four-block perimeter, something that would require — what? — two dozen officers who'd need to arrive inside of two minutes or it would be a complete waste of effort.

Is that even possible? Yes, if the justification was that police needed to close in on the assassin of the president. But for this? For the kidnappers of a low-profile American businessman? No, it's out of the question. Even if the tactic were successful — big *if* — Santos would be excoriated for the waste of resources, for the inconvenience to the populace, for the intrusion of mass interrogations on a quiet Tuesday evening, with no immediately apparent emergency — no gunfire, no hostages, no bank robbery, no large-scale threat to anything. Portugal's long history of authoritarianism is still a fresh memory for many, especially among those who now wield the reins of power, people who have very little tolerance for anything that smacks of a police state. The dictator Salazar didn't die until 1970, after having been prime minister for thirty-six years.

No: Closing off this corner of Chiado is much more likely to get Santos reprimanded than praised. Maybe even fired. Her chief was a teenager back in '74 when the military coup finally overthrew the Estado Novo; he often mentions his memory of the soldiers who put carnations in the muzzles of their guns.

"Okay Tomas," Santos says, "stay with her until the next corner, then Erico, you step in."

But her heart is not in it. Santos is fairly certain that they already missed the ransom handoff. Was it in the taxi? The tram? The bar? Or maybe this whole thing has been a ruse? Maybe the money was left back at the hotel, and the entire countersurveillance route was just a way to draw the police away, a complex misdirection. Maybe the police have been looking the wrong way the entire time.

With each step, Ariel is increasingly aware of the pain in her knee from her tumble out of the tram. She's limping under the weight of this pain and this duffel filled with yesterday's news, and her adrenaline level is falling, her energy flagging, her middle-aged body breaking down. She's feeling like she can barely take another step, she'll never be able to reach the next corner. But she does.

As she waits for a traffic light, Ariel looks back. She can see a few people — a couple who are a block behind, and a lone man even farther. But at this point it doesn't really matter who's following her.

It has been five minutes since the handoff, then ten, and now she enters a different-looking neighborhood on the far side of a hill, and the low sun is directly in her eyes, forcing her to squint while she limps, feeling like she's going to collapse.

But she has to keep going.

"Jefferson. That was fast."

"I suspect that Anton Dupree, recent GW dropout, is engaged in some low-level illegal activity. Enough to be intimidated when I told him that we know what he's doing, and we're willing to look the other way, we just need a small piece of information in exchange."

"Good thinking. And what is it that Anton is doing?" Griffiths asks.

"I have no clue. If I had to guess, I'd say that it's street-level dealing of recreational drugs. But anyway, he was quick to give up the name of the passenger he took to and from the convenience store, as well as the address where the round trip originated and ended. I just sent the coordinates to you. You're going to want to be sitting down for this."

Ping.

Griffiths opens the map, zooms in, and her

mouth falls open.

"Holy shit," she mutters. "I knew I recognized that voice."

The street ends.

"What the — ?"

Ariel stands there, seeing no obvious next move. She retrieves the burner, and calls back the last number that dialed her, the only number that ever called this phone. No answer; it doesn't even ring. That device probably no longer exists.

The street she has been walking has ended at a perpendicular avenue. She glances in both directions, down the hill toward the river, uphill toward the city's sprawling untouristed interior. Neither direction makes more sense, nor less.

Ariel looks around at the apartment buildings; nothing screams out at her. She's standing next to a ten-foot-high concrete wall with a large metal sliding door, the sort of door that looks like the gateway to a parking lot, with a small window at eye level, for safety. From one side, you can look through and see the other, make sure no one is lying in wait.

She looks through.

"There's no father listed on George Pryce's birth certificate."

"None? So the birth certificate doesn't say *unknown* for father?"

"Nope, it doesn't say nothing. That line is just blank."

Pete Wagstaff mulls this over. "That means Ariel Pryce knows who the father is, but for some reason did not name him."

"Sure, that's possible," Myron says, though it doesn't sound like he agrees. "It's also possible that she did not know who the father is, but also did not want to commit to that uncertainty on a legal document."

Wagstaff feels like he has learned something important here, but he doesn't know what exactly. "Maybe we can come at this from a different direction."

"How's that?"

"We know what NDAs are for, right?"

"Uh . . ."

"NDAs exist to hide bad acts. Things that might be subject to criminal prosecution, or at least civil judgments."

"That's one reason. But there are others. Like to protect proprietary information in business, or science, or the terms of any contract in any field. Or to enforce silence about illegally obtained information without resorting to criminal prosecution. Or simply to keep a secret that's embarrassing but not illegal. There are plenty of NDA scenarios that don't involve crime, and plenty that might be to the mutual benefit of all the parties involved."

"You're right, Myron. But what's the most

common?"

"I don't know. And I'm pretty sure that neither do you."

"Certainly the most well-known involve inappropriate or illegal sexual relationships."

"You're getting way out in front of the facts, Pete."

"Maybe. But look at this combination of events. Fifteen years ago —"

"Fourteen."

"— this woman must have been *spectacular* looking. I mean, she's a knockout now, so I can only imagine. Tell me how many NDAs signed by beautiful young women don't involve sex?"

"Well, sex, that's pretty broad, isn't it? Sex encompasses a lot of different relationships."

"NDAs signed between beautiful young women and anonymous entities."

"There you go again with wild conjecture."

"All of a sudden this beautiful young woman ditches her entire life — her husband, her Park Avenue lifestyle, her home — while at the same time signing an NDA with someone who's hiding behind an LLC. This happens at the *exact moment* when she becomes pregnant. Then when the child is born, she declines to name the father on the birth certificate."

"Yes, fine, I can see what you're saying, and that's a plausible scenario. But I don't think that I of all people should have to warn you that it's all conjecture."

"And then fifteen years later —"

"It's fourteen years, Pete."

"— when this woman finds herself in emergency need of a tremendous amount of cash, she signs *another* agreement with the *same* entity. Come on, Myron. You and I both know what went on here: This woman had a kid with someone who wasn't her husband, and signed an NDA to keep the paternity a secret, in exchange for money."

"We don't know that. And even if we did, what's the crime? Where's the story?"

"I don't know. But now she has come back to this unnamed father for more money, and not only does he have it — which means he's rich — but he also agrees to provide it, which I think means one of two things. Either she still has a relationship with him, which seems highly unlikely, right? A decade and a half later, new husband, a lot of water under whatever bridge they crossed together."

"Or?"

"Or she's blackmailing him."

Myron doesn't answer for a moment, then says, "Okay: Prove it."

"Okay," Wagstaff says. "Help me."

"You're positive?"

"Me? Uh-uh, hell no." Kayla Jefferson shakes her head. "I'm just relaying what the analyst in Langley told me. He said *he* was

385

positive."

"And just to be clear, the thing he's positive of is the ownership of this LLC in the Caymans that paid Ariel Pryce three million dollars, fourteen years ago?"

"That's correct."

"Jesus," Griffiths says. *"Jesus."*

Jefferson just stands there, looking like a private who has arrived to tell the general that the missiles are already in the air. "What do we do about this?"

"I don't know. I have to think."

"Should I leave you?"

"Yes please. And Jefferson? Not a word of this to anyone. Not even Guido. I'll tell him, if he needs to know. You understand?"

"Yes ma'am," the young woman says, and pulls the door closed behind her.

Nicole Griffiths's eyes drift back to the computer screen, the map, the bright red pin. But all her focus is elsewhere, gaming out the situation, running conversations up the chain of command, then sideways from Langley to Foggy Bottom and back to Lisbon. She needs to consider this very carefully, from every angle. But she also needs to do this quickly; she's suddenly sure that she has very little time.

She starts jotting a list of names, putting asterisks next to the political appointees as opposed to the career diplomats, trying to chart a path of communication that has the best chance of keeping this investigation as clean as possible for as long as possible, while at the same time covering her own ass as much as possible.

It's a challenge. She tries to convince herself that she doesn't have a dog in this fight. It's not a matter of politics, nor policy, nor preference. It's a matter of national security, which is the basis for her job, her career, her entire fucking life.

Griffiths has arrived, unexpectedly, at a life-defining crossroads. In this line of work, you never know when it's going to happen: You go into work for a normal day and find yourself in the midst of a full-blown crisis. For most people in the CIA, this never happens. Until today, Nicole Griffiths had been one of those people.

After ten minutes of debate, she feeds her sheet of notepaper into the shredder. Then she places the first call; there will be a few. And this has to happen on July Fourth, of all days? People are at barbecues, at beaches, on sailboats in the Chesapeake, day-drinking in poolside chaises. They're not expecting a call like this, certainly not from Lisbon. From Riyadh, Baghdad, Jakarta, Khartoum? Maybe. But Lisbon? They're going to laugh her off. At first.

"Okay," she tells herself as the first ring sounds of the first call. It's not just the reporting that Griffiths is worried about, nor the impartiality of the investigation, nor the orders that she's going to be given, by whom, to do what. She also has an indistinct suspicion that she — that everyone — is somehow being played.

"Hello sir," she says. "I'm sorry to inform you that we have a situation here."

The big metal sliding door is unlocked. Ariel pushes hard, and the door rolls with a squeak on thick rubber casters, and her eye is drawn across the small parking lot —

There he is, seated in a folding chair under a leafy tree that shields him from the apartments above. His wrists are bound with rope; his ankles are tied to the chair's legs. He isn't moving.

Ariel starts rushing through even as the door is still rolling open.

He's wearing a hood made of thick burlap, like a potato sack. Even from thirty yards away, Ariel can see the dark blotch at the temple, and knows immediately that it's a bloodstain.

PART IV
THE ESCAPE

CHAPTER 32

Day 2. 7:51 p.m.
Ariel has no awareness of moving her legs but she can see that she's closing in quickly on the slumped figure, just a few steps now, then none, she's reaching out for the hood, and she pulls, yanking harder through a snag of his thick hair, revealing his face from the bottom up, so the first thing she notices is that his mouth is gagged, and the second is that his cheek is bloody, and now the hood is up over his eyes, so the third thing she registers is that his eyes are open, blinking in the light.

He's alive, thank God. He's safe.

"I'm glad I caught you."

The ambassador is pulling on his jacket. "What can I do for you, Ms. Griffiths?"

They don't have a good relationship. Nicole Griffiths thinks of Tanner Snell as an incompetent, aggressively stupid business crony of an illegitimate president; the ambassador probably thinks of his CIA station chief as a hypersensitive uppity pain in the motherfucking ass.

"I need to give you a heads-up about something."

The ambassador's personal aide turns a page on his pad, ready to take notes.

"Off the record," Griffiths adds. "And in private."

"Landry, give us a minute," Snell says, without thanks or apology or any show of politeness. It must be a real treat to work for this guy. "I'm due at a dinner," he says to Griffiths. "So?"

She waits for the door to close completely, then says, "There might be a thing."

"Oh yeah?" Snell's resting-douchebag face is almost a work of art. "What sort of thing?"

"It might be big, and it might involve Langley."

"Oh good God Almighty. What are you talking about?"

"I can't actually say anything more. This is just a courtesy heads-up." Griffiths shouldn't reveal any details to this loyalist kleptocrat; neither should she refuse to alert him to a pending clusterfuck. So she has settled on this middle ground, which will also have the bonus of pissing off Snell no end.

"A courtesy? What type of goddamned courtesy is this vague bullshit?"

The fuck-you type, Griffiths thinks. "The

392

courteous type. Don't be surprised if there's some big action over the next hours or days. Please do your very best to stay available."

"Available?" He snorts. "I'm always available."

"I guess what I mean specifically is: Stay sober." Take that! "Also, you might want to stay away from your Brazilian mistress." And that! You smug jackass. "Her bed in Belém is not where you want to be found if Washington calls."

Ariel can see that the wadded-up cloth gag is secured by duct tape around John's head; she knows firsthand how horrible a gag is, how uncomfortable, how frightening, how degrading. She can't see any choice but to rip off the heavy tape, which must hurt like a son of a bitch — John's eyes roll over, and he grunts something from low in his chest, like the distant rumble of thunder. She plucks the wad from his mouth. Plenty of hair has come off on the tape.

"Ow," John says.

"I'm sorry. Oh God. Are you okay? Are you hurt?"

"I'm okay."

She's trying to untie his hands but is having trouble with the knot. "I'm sorry," she says again. "I can't get this. *Shit.*"

"I'm okay," he repeats.

And then the knot is free, but there's blood

— why is there all this *blood,* and she hears herself asking "But what is this?" while swiping at his cheek with her fingers. "What *is* this?"

"I got punched. It's just a cut." He rubs one wrist in one palm, then the other.

"Are you in pain?"

"The cut? It burns a little. But hey, look at me: It's over."

Ariel realizes that she's crying. She nods, and drops to her knees to unbind his feet, which she manages easier than the wrists.

John gets up, shakes out his legs, bangs his toes on the ground. "My foot's asleep."

She expected to be relieved at this moment — of course she did — but she's surprised by the depth of her emotion, it's a visceral, full-body experience. She's unable to stop shaking and sobbing.

"Oh God," she says, and collapses against John's chest, wraps her arms around him, squeezes tight, puts her cheek on his shoulder. They stand there for a few seconds, in a tight embrace, then she pulls back, places her hands on his waist, and stares into his eyes. "*Are* you okay?"

"I am."

"The blood on the hood," she says. "For a second I thought . . ."

He shakes his head. "I'm fine. Are *you*?"

It's a good question. Ariel can't for the life of her come up with the answer.

394

CHAPTER 33

Day 2. 7:59 p.m.

"Look," she says, "a taxi. Hey! *Hey!*"

The car stops. The driver glances at John's bloody face, pauses for a second to consider it, then nods. Ariel and John tumble into the back.

She takes his hand. It'll be just a short ride to the hotel, during which Ariel knows they should remain silent. This is not a conversation they should have within earshot of anyone, not even a taxi driver, if that's what he really is. This guy might actually be a cop. Or CIA. And even if he's neither, he could quickly become an asset of either.

Ariel stays quiet, and so does John. He understands.

As the car pulls around the square, Ariel sees that Moniz and Santos are already waiting in front of the hotel.

"Okay." Ariel takes a deep breath. "Those are the detectives who've been handling my case. Your case. They probably want to talk to you, right now."

John nods.

"We could tell them to leave us alone for tonight. We can do that, you know."

"No." John shakes his head. "Let's get it over with. If the cops are going to have any chance of catching these guys, we should do it now."

Moniz is already approaching the taxi as it pulls to a stop.

"John Wright?"

"Yes."

"Good," Moniz says, nodding, looking relieved. "This is good." He examines John's bloody face. "You are injured? You are in need of medical attention?"

"No, it's not serious."

"Good. I am Detective António Moniz, and this is my partner, Carolina Santos."

They all shake hands on the sidewalk. A few passersby have noticed this odd foursome. Someone snaps a picture.

"Let us go inside," Moniz says, and they all step into the entryway. "You must be very tired, senhor. And very happy to be back here, with your wife."

"I am."

"You were carrying a bag, senhora?"

Ariel shakes her head. "It was a decoy filled with worthless newspaper. I handed off the ransom bag a long time ago, in an alley."

"I see," Moniz says. "I am sure you want to

rest, both of you. But I am also sure you want us to catch the people who abducted you, senhor. So I am afraid we cannot wait to ask you some questions."

"Of course. But can you give me a few minutes to take a shower? And get something to eat?"

"Please. We will be happy to gather some food for you from the *taberna*."

"That would be great. Thanks."

"I will return in fifteen minutes? Or twenty?"

"Why don't you give us thirty."

"My pleasure. And these policemen" — Moniz indicates a couple of uniformed cops who are standing near a squad car — "they will wait here. For your safety."

Just another one of those lies that we pretend isn't. Ariel and John nod, tacitly contributing to the pervasive culture of dishonesty, reinforced every time we hear a blatant lie and refuse to challenge it. Refuse even to acknowledge to our own selves that it's a lie.

Tonight is going to be an important night. Sometimes you think you know this in advance: a hot date, a long-awaited reunion, a milestone party. But in Ariel's experience, such eagerly anticipated events have never turned out to be noteworthy. Her important evenings have all snuck up, cloaked in the disguise of the mundane.

That horrible night was one of those, starting like so many others in front of a full-length mirror, trying to rally the enthusiasm to spend the evening with people she didn't particularly like.

"Get it together," she muttered to herself. "This is your *job.*"

She also had a paying job, sort of, a part-time freelance position reading manuscripts that had been submitted unsolicited, unwanted, and unacceptable to a literary agent named Isabel Reed. Ariel had been doing this work for a couple of years, and hadn't once unearthed that fabled hidden gem that clawed out of the slush pile to find its way to a book deal. But even if all the manuscripts were crappy, Ariel still loved reading these mysteries and thrillers and police procedurals.

Ariel's employment was optional, and unlucrative, and came to her as a favor that someone did for someone else, who wanted to do something for Bucky; New York was an endless web of overlapping circles of favors. But Ariel knew that her real job — the one she was obligated to do, every day — was being the wife of Buckingham Turner. Although she loved Bucky, she did not always love the job of being his wife.

She quarter-turned in the mirror to examine herself from the side. She smoothed her hand across her stomach, still flat.

One of this job's chief responsibilities was being an attractive, charming companion at parties, and no party was more important than Charlie Wolfe's summer bash, a dinner thrown on a wedding's scale and budget, with two hundred guests at eight-tops on the lawn that faced the moonlit ocean; Ariel would not have been surprised if the party's date had been chosen for optimal moonlight.

Arranged seating was boy-girl and spouses separated, but after the entrées were cleared, Ariel's table reorganized itself by gender, and she found herself surrounded by the usual crowd. At the other end of the table the men were talking finance, or baseball, or the finances of baseball, while taking occasional bites of gold-leafed torte, drinking Armagnac and port, getting expensively drunk.

Charlie Wolfe's parties were legendary for their conspicuous consumption, with raw bars and Champagne magnums, plated dinners of lobster tails and filet mignon, with money thrown at caterers with no mandate other than to impress. But Charlie was neither a stockbroker nor a tech bro, so there were no hookers, no piles of cocaine; not that sort of scene. Just plenty of the legal intoxicants, imported high-end luxury-lifestyle markers, the exact sorts of things you'd expect to be consumed by the one-tenth of the one percent at a South Fork oceanfront estate, this was behavior to be envied, this was how you courted the coveted high-net-worth demographic in the pages of *Vogue* and the *Wall Street Journal* and *Elite Traveler: The Private Jet Lifestyle Magazine*.

This party didn't conform to anyone's vision of a dangerous environment.

Ariel knew better. She knew that she had to be careful, always. She also knew that sometimes careful doesn't suffice.

"Adorbs." One woman was admiring another's bracelet, vintage Italian from the sixties, all the rage those days, the sort of micro-fad that can be wildly fashionable among a tiny population who can afford forty-thousand-dollar pieces of jewelry, while no one else in the world is even aware of the trend. All the women at the table appreciated how the gold accentuated the tan of a forearm that was well-toned by tennis and sailing. These bracelets enjoyed renewed popularity every summer.

None of these women had consumed more than a forkful of torte, though a few had picked at the decorative berries. Someone was raving about her new Botox guy, and then the discussion turned to more invasive, more dramatic procedures. These women all had the same job as Ariel, with the same job requirements.

Ariel glanced at her husband, who was having a great time, no way he'd want to go home yet, and she couldn't be that wife, the sort who asked to leave. That wasn't acceptable performance of her job. Ariel realized much later that this was her mom's definition of wife, and her dad's, Bucky's too. But not her own.

"Ezra's test scores are off the charts," Stacey said. "Literally."

Other mothers were nodding in agreement, none of them apparently understanding what the word *literally* meant, or how charts work, or, possibly, both.

Ariel took a sip of water. Her alcohol consumption had been limited to one glass of Champagne before dinner, which she'd surreptitiously dumped most of into a planter of lavender. Ariel wouldn't drink tonight, but she also didn't want to be seen to be not drinking, she didn't want anyone to ask about it, she didn't want to lie, a common enough lie that everyone sees through. She could imagine the exclamation months later, "*Of course!* You weren't drinking at Charlie's party! I remember!" At any given party, some woman or another isn't drinking, and all the others are noticing.

Another part of Ariel's job — a large part, perhaps the largest — was bearing children.

"I want lots of kids," Bucky had told her, a couple years earlier, when they'd been in that final pre-engagement stage during which both understood that a proposal would be forthcoming unless something went awry. They were vetting each other. Due diligence.

"What does *lots* mean?"

"At least three. Probably four?"

"*Four?*" Ariel laughed, uncomfortably. Four sounded excessive. Ariel was younger than Bucky, hadn't met all his friends yet, their wives. She didn't know yet that it was trendy among a certain crowd — his crowd — to raise big families in the city, in big apartments.

"You really like kids that much?" She was trying to sound curious, not contradictory. She didn't want this to become a disagreement.

"Of course!"

Of course? Ariel wondered what Bucky thought he meant. He didn't have younger siblings, nor nieces or nephews. He'd never been a teacher, nor a tutor, nor a mentor, nor a babysitter. Bucky's sole experience with children had been being one.

"How do you know?"

Bucky was as a rule so sure of so many things, and Ariel was not. This supreme self-confidence had been one of the things Ariel had admired about him.

"Are you kidding? What's not to like?"

Four kids would mean that she'd spend the better part of a decade pregnant or nursing or changing diapers: Four kids would mean, in all probability, not having a career. That's what's not to like. But at the time, she couldn't see this forest she was planning to inhabit, because the tree directly in front of her was about to sprout a giant engagement ring and a couture bridal gown and a destination wedding and a Classic 6 in a good building.

Ariel wasn't looking for reasons to ruin this. She wasn't running out of time, not quite yet, but she would be if things didn't work out with Bucky Turner, who was smart and funny and charismatic and handsome, plus already rich, and well on his way to being much richer.

"A big family," Ariel said, conjuring up her most enthusiastic smile, "sounds great."

She chose to believe that Bucky was telling the truth. She chose to pretend that so was she.

CHAPTER 34

Day 2. 8:17 p.m.

At last they step into the suite; it feels like years since they were here together. John staggers across the living room, collapses onto the couch. Ariel fastens the security chain, then leans against the closed door, the peephole, these reassurances of safety.

"My God," John says. "I never thought I'd be so happy to see a hotel room."

Ariel slides to the floor, her back against the door. She closes her eyes, and drops her face into her hands. She allows a quiet sob to escape into her palms.

"Hey?" he says. "Are you okay?"

She's not. His question gives her permission to not be, and she sobs again, louder.

"Hey" — he's coming over — "hey, it's okay" — and dropping to his knees, putting his arms around her. Now she can let herself go, and her whole body convulses.

"*Shhh,*" he says. "I'm okay, you're okay."

He's right, she knows it. But she can't stop crying.

"It's all okay."

John sits beside Ariel with both arms around her shoulders. He doesn't say anything more. He just lets her cry until she's all cried out, when she looks up at him, at his beaten face, and asks, "Are you sure you're okay?"

"I'm just so relieved to be free."

Ariel wipes her tears away.

"So what happened?" he asks. "Why am I not dead?"

"I paid the ransom is what happened. Two million euros in cash."

"Holy shit. Where in God's name did you get that type of money?"

Ariel shakes her head slowly, then faster, then she drops her face back into her hands.

"No," John says. "Not him. You didn't."

She's crying again. "What else was I going to do?" Her voice is muffled through her hands, through her tears.

"Oh my God. I'm so, so sorry. Was it awful?"

"Yes."

Ariel really has become a weepy sort these past days; she has gone years without crying, and now look. She straightens up, wipes her eyes again.

"Not only was he a complete asshole — of course — but for a while there I was worried that he wouldn't give me any money at all. I couldn't stop thinking that they'd *kill* you."

John squeezes her tighter. "I'm so sorry." He kisses the top of Ariel's head. "Thank you. I'm astounded he agreed to it. I'm assuming it wasn't just because you asked nicely?"

"No, of course not."

"What did you do?"

"I threatened him."

John pulls his face away to get a full look at his wife. "Threatened how?"

"How do you think? I told him that I'd release the recording of our last conversation. That I'd expose everything."

"My God. Did you really?"

"What else could I do?"

"And how'd he react?"

"He went nuts. But he had no choice. He couldn't risk it."

"Christ."

"I know."

They sit for a few seconds in silence.

"Are you worried?" he asks.

"About what?"

"About what he'll do next?"

"Not really. At this point in his life, he can't do anything to me. Nothing as bad as what I can do to him."

"Mr. Ambassador?" Saxby Barnes is both excited and terrified to have been summoned to the ambassador's office. This is something he has dreams about. Also nightmares.

"Barnes: Do you know what the hell Griffiths has gotten herself into?"

"I'm not exactly sure what you're referencing, sir."

Tanner Snell stares at the ineffectual drunk who serves as liaison between the consular and intelligence. He really should fire this buffoon.

"Are you talking about the kidnapping?" Barnes suggests.

"Maybe." The ambassador squints. "What's the kidnapping?"

"An American businessman went missing yesterday morning. His wife came to the embassy for help, before she knew that he'd been abducted. Then she got a ransom call, and last I heard she was planning to try to get the ransom together."

"What do you mean, the last you heard?"

"I was told to butt out."

"By?"

"Griffiths."

Snell groans. "Do you know anything about this kidnapping that might turn it into a thing?"

"No sir I do not."

Snell glares until the guy understands.

"But I will definitely try to find out," Barnes says, "and get back with you as quickly as humanly possible."

Ariel takes a closer look at the wound on John's cheek. "Come on, let's get this cleaned up." She leads him to the bathroom, turns on the hot-water tap, places a washcloth underneath.

"Ow," he says when she places the cloth against his cut. She wipes away the dried blood, and can see that the cut is not very large after all. It's the swelling that's really going to hurt. "We need to get you some ice."

"I'm going to shower." He starts unbuckling his belt, turning away. Not exactly shy, but close to it.

So is she. They've barely been together, in the overall scheme of things. Ariel and Bucky had lived together full-time for years, they'd had sex hundreds of times, maybe more. After all that intimacy, Ariel would've thought that she really knew Bucky. That he really knew her.

This had been a large part of her devastation: realizing that she'd been so wrong.

A year after she married Bucky, Ariel pushed the birth-control pills to the back of a bathroom drawer. She'd spent the better part of the previous two decades worrying about getting pregnant. It had never occurred to her to worry about not getting pregnant.

It had now been a year of failing. Though maybe last night had finally done it, or the night before, or before, back-to-back-to-back evenings of clinical sex, a chore that made Ariel feel like another type of failure, on top of the long-term failure of her old acting career, and the more recent failure to find a satisfying replacement to occupy her time. And now? She was no longer good at pretending to enjoy sex.

She was also no longer good at pretending to enjoy Bucky's friends, and the parties they threw.

"Every summer," Ariel heard one of the men saying, off to her left, "we rent a boat in the Mediterranean, fully staffed. It's such a great way to get quality family time."

"Couldn't agree more." Another guy was nodding along. "Love it. So what's the biggest boat you've ever rented?"

To Ariel's right, Tory Wasserman was on a different subject with the women: "Slade had his surgery at Mayo."

The age difference between Ariel and Bucky was not an embarrassing amount — they could still be thought of as the same generation, maybe — but his friends and their wives were having back surgeries and facelifts while Ariel was still going to her college friends' weddings.

"They're the best. The absolute best." Slade had slipped a disk. "Then we got one of those handicapped tags, you know those things? So now I can park *anywhere.* I drive around the city *so* much more. I barely take taxis anymore."

Tory was beaming, waiting for people to praise the cleverness of her pathology. They did.

Ariel suddenly felt sick. She looked around at these people bragging about their privileges, their genius children, their rented yachts and obscure jewelry and name-brand physicians who inject poison to paralyze their foreheads.

She could see how it happens, one small decision at a time until self-care is all you do, and all you are, and one day, without even realizing what you're saying, you find yourself bragging about your achievements in self-objectification, about the Le Cirque chef you import for the summer, about the car and driver who takes you gallery-hopping, the increasingly clever and enviable ways that you invent to spend your husband's income.

Little by little, Ariel had given up trying to find her own tribe, and instead had simply joined Bucky's, she'd taken on their stripes, pretended to be one of them, this network that spun out from her husband's upbringing, his schooling, his professional orbit. His people had become hers, the men from Bucky's job and the women who married them, bore their children, wore their wealth on their ring fingers, carried it in the crooks of their arms.

This was not who Ariel had ever intended to be. She did not want someone like Tory Wasserman to be one of her closest friends.

"Excuse me," Ariel muttered to no one, walking away from those people, from everything. She could not allow herself to become one of them. But she was worried that it was already too late.

Ariel had always felt like an intruder, like her membership in the club was provisionary. One false move and they'd kick her to the curb, with her unconvincing degree from her unimpressive college, her unsuccessful career as an actor and her unremarkable years afterward, accomplishing nothing much besides staying in peak physically attractive condition and marrying an eligible man, but failing to bear him children. Then she'd be lying in the gutter, thirty-three years old, broke and alone, unemployed and unemployable. Then what?

Walking away from that table, all she'd wanted was to hide for a few minutes, a brief respite from pretending to covet someone else's red-soled shoes.

The nearest bathroom was just inside the crowded veranda. Ariel couldn't bear to run into yet someone else who'd be bragging about all the ways that rules did not apply to them — traffic, parking, taxes, waiting lists, sports, all those rules were for other people, people who weren't smart enough or rich enough to figure out how to cheat. So she headed down a flagstone path lit by tiki torches to the poolhouse, flickering candles and overstuffed couches and a wet bar and a huge-screen TV and a billiards table and a couple of pinball machines.

The bathroom of this fully tricked-out man-cave was of course huge; everything was huge, huge was the point — huge furniture, huge windows, huge car, huge bank account. The huger the better. The messaging was not subtle.

Ariel opened the medicine cabinet, shook out and swallowed a couple of Tylenol.

She examined herself in yet another mirror. She cradled her palms around her flat belly, wondering what it would look like, feel like. Wondering if this was part of it, if it had already begun, this moodiness, her sudden nausea a minute ago.

Wondering if she was, in fact, already pregnant.

But no, she scolded herself: Don't do that. Over the past few months she'd made a deliberate effort to wean herself off the self-defeating habit of premature pregnancy tests, which had accomplished nothing other than making her deeply unhappy. Yes, it was possible that at the moment she was already pregnant; it was also likely that she wasn't. And if she was, she'd be keeping the pregnancy to herself for a good long while, past the first trimester. Bucky hadn't reacted well to her miscarriage, in fact he'd been horrid — disappointed in her, angry, *accusatory*, as if she'd tried to home-cook an important dinner party and everything had turned out inedible, humiliating him, when she should have just hired a caterer like everyone else.

"Have you been exercising too much?" he'd asked. Ariel wished she could pretend that he was joking, but there was nothing remotely funny about it. "Eating shellfish?"

Blame was one thing, she understood blame, everyone always wants to assign the blame for any negative outcome. But this was something beyond blame.

"How much have you been drinking?"

This was pure emotion, and the emotion felt a lot like hate. That conversation should've been Ariel's first clue, but she'd chosen not to see it that way; in truth there'd been other clues. But afterward she made excuses for Bucky: this had been in the depths of winter, and the gloomy season was part of the bad circumstances and bad timing of the bad news, all contributing to her husband's bad response; maybe he suffered from seasonal affective disorder, which everyone was discovering back then, like ADD a few years later; people were coming out of the woodwork to self-diagnose. Or maybe Bucky's behavior was not way outside normal parameters; there's a large segment of the male population whose first instinct, always, is to assign blame to someone else — whoever happens to be nearest, or femalest.

Ariel's instinct was to shoulder the blame. The longer she failed, the more the concept of failure established residency in her consciousness, and her biological failure expanded into a moral one, as if this were a question of insufficient effort, like getting a C-minus on a math exam, or crashing a car. A thing she failed at because she hadn't practiced enough, concentrated enough, tried enough. Cared enough.

Maybe, Bucky accused, she didn't want to have a baby with him after all.

Maybe, Ariel eventually thought, he was right.

She adjusted her hair. She touched up her makeup. She practiced her smile in the mirror, for — what? — it might as well have been the millionth time, uncountable. How much of her life had she spent trying to figure out how to make herself more beautiful?

"Bucky," she said, quietly, to her reflection. "Can we please go home now?"

No. There was no point asking, it would only make him angry.

Ariel sighed, resigned to returning to the

414

party, to grinning and bearing it, to letting it slide. This too was part of her job, letting it slide. This was discussed, the things you had to let slide.

She opened the door —

CHAPTER 35

Day 2. 8:42 p.m.

Ariel sits on the couch, surreptitiously listening to John leave brief messages for his assistant, his boss, a colleague, all promising to be back in touch tomorrow. His final call is to his client here in Lisbon, explaining, apologizing, and ultimately promising that he'll be at their offices tomorrow. Ariel doesn't think he should be promising anything of the sort, but she's not going to interrupt to tell him so. She doesn't want him to know that she's eavesdropping.

She too needs to place a reassuring call, to her mom: problem solved, sorry for the alarm, for the inconvenience, for the panic.

"Please go back to my house as soon as you can," Ariel says. "I was just being extra-cautious. And maybe a little irrational."

"Honey, are you sure it's safe?"

"Yes. And can you put George on for a minute?"

"I'll go get him."

"Actually, Mom, wait: Why did you just ask if I'm sure it's safe?"

"Well, I just got the strangest call."

Ariel feels her whole body tense. "What was that?"

"From a reporter in Lisbon, a few hours ago. Let me see, I wrote his name somewhere . . ."

"Was it Pete Wagstaff?"

"That's it! How did you know?"

"What did he want?"

"That was the strange thing. He was asking about Bucky, and why your marriage ended. Why would a reporter be interested in any of that?"

"What did you tell him?"

"What *could* I tell him? I don't know anything about why your marriage ended, do I?"

"Did he ask about anything else?"

"Well . . . Give me a second, I need to . . ." Ariel can hear the *squeak-slam* of a screen door. "I needed to get away from George." Elaine is now talking in a low voice. "The reporter asked if I knew who your son's *father* is. I said no, you'd gotten an anonymous donor. And he asked if I was *sure.*"

Oh God, Ariel thinks: She does not want to talk about this with her mother. Then she realizes something else: "Mom, why did you have your phone on? Didn't I ask you to keep it powered down?" Ariel hears knocking on her door, which she starts walking toward.

"Well, I turned it on just for *one* minute, to check messages."

"But —" Ariel is about to explain that a minute is plenty long to locate a cell, but there's no point.

"And after I checked my messages, I forgot to turn the phone off again."

"Mom could you hold on one sec?" Ariel opens the door to find Moniz and Santos there, as expected. "Sorry," she says to the police, "can you give us a couple more minutes?"

"Certainly."

Ariel shuts the door. "Okay Mom, can you get George now, please?"

"Yes. But Honey? Why would a reporter ask that? About George's father?"

Ariel was well aware of her mom's views on marriage, on sexual assault, on a woman's place in the world, what it means to be a wife; she'd learned the hard way. So she hadn't told Elaine the truth about her pregnancy. In fact she hadn't told anyone. Then she'd gone ahead and signed away her freedom to tell anyone anything about it, ever. Certainly not over a telephone line that might be bugged by the CIA.

"I don't know" is what she tells her mother, with butterflies dancing in her stomach.

"Oh my God!" Ariel startled, recoiled, released her grip on the handle of the bathroom door.

Charlie Wolfe grinned, swayed. "Hello there, sexy lady."

She didn't like the look of this, nor the sound. "Charlie, you scared me."

"Sorry, didn't mean-a."

He was plastered. But why not, it was his party, and being inebriated was not a crime. Ariel chose to afford him the presumption of innocence — he was blocking the door because he was drunk and confused, he'd come to this out-of-the-way bathroom because he needed to snort a line, make a call, take a dump. Though Ariel's racing heart told her that these guesses were all bullshit. Experience told her.

"Excuse me," she said, nonconfrontational. Charlie wasn't merely the host of this bash, he was also her husband's most important business associate, a man who was flinging open doors for Bucky, allowing piles of cash to tumble in. Bucky's business was on the cusp of everything that was about to blow up — digital media, social networks, partisan news, fake facts — and this drunk man blocking the bathroom door was helping it happen.

Charlie pushed back his hair, and Ariel noticed that his wrist was adorned with a couple of those rubber bracelets that profess support for some cause, self-adornment to

419

display what a generous person he was, plus a rustic leather strap to display how cool, how laid-back, how fond of some unspoiled exotic beach. Tulum, probably. Everybody loved Tulum.

This was a man who'd bought a gala table in support of childhood literacy, he'd been the only one who'd raised his hand when the live-auctioneer asked if any of the assembled wonderful people could see their way to a hundred-thousand-dollar gift, and Charlie had looked down faux-sheepishly — *humbly* — when the room erupted in applause, with Ariel right there at his table, so she'd been one of the first of the little-black-dressed women and dinner-jacketed men obligated to rise, to clap, to gaze in ersatz admiration at this entrepreneur-philanthropist-douchebag until he reluctantly — *begrudgingly* — rose to acknowledge everyone's standing-ovation acknowledgment of his altruism.

"What's the rush?" he asked. "Why dontcha stay here with me?" He took a step toward her.

"No, Charlie, I don't think that's such a great idea."

Ariel put her hand up — halt right there — but he didn't. Instead he took another step forward, blocking the door completely.

"C'mon. Jussa minute or two."

"No," she said, "I should go."

But he didn't get out of her way. Instead he

took another step forward, through the doorway, and now her outstretched hand was just inches from his chest.

"Could you move, please?"

Ariel didn't want to touch him, so she pulled her hand back, dropped her arm to her side.

"I need to get back to my table. To my husband."

Charlie ignored this. He lowered his hand to his crotch, and stroked his erection through his linen pants. "Whaddya think?"

"No," she said, feeling her fear give way to panic; this was happening awfully fast. Was now the time to scream? "Please let me get by."

"I know you want this." He was nodding in agreement with himself. "You've always had a thing for me, haven't you?"

There was absolutely no way he could have believed this. Ariel had never flirted with Charlie, never encouraged him by any stretch of any imagination, no matter how distorted.

"No Charlie, I really don't." How many times had she already said no? "Now please get out of my way or I'll scream."

"Oh" — arrogant smirk — "I bet you will."

One of his hands was flapping around behind him, and Ariel realized too late that he was searching for the doorknob. He pulled the door closed, then she heard the click of the lock, and now full-on panic was coursing through her body like an electric shock, making it hard for her to think, and she blurted out, "Bucky is going to come looking for me," an obvious lie.

"No." Charlie shook his head, steeled his jaw. "He isn't."

She would need to scream very loudly, as loudly as possible, but people would hear, wouldn't they? Someone would come running, a couple of men probably, she could envisage them bursting through the bathroom door, coming upon this impossible-to-misinterpret scene —

But then what? Charlie owned all these people, the businessmen out there, the politicians, the bankers, the socialites, the caterers.

Ariel could see exactly what would happen: She'd be the one portrayed as the aggressor, the seducer, the slut. The drunk social climber who'd fallen on her face.

"I told Bucky I'd be right back." Ariel shuffled backward, away from Charlie, bumping up against the vanity, running out of room. Running out of time.

"No, you didn't."

"Please," she said again, "don't."

She searched his eyes, begging for leniency, looking for the humanity in there, but what she found was the opposite, an unmistakable clarity, a sober intensity. Suddenly Charlie didn't seem drunk at all. What he seemed like was a cold, calculating monster.

He reached for his belt buckle, and everything seemed to be happening faster than reality, as if a sped-up film, skipping frames — the frame where she says *Get the fuck away from me,* the frame where she kicks Charlie in the crotch, the frame where she bursts through the door, runs to Bucky, collapses into his protective embrace. All those frames are missing. None of that will happen.

In the minutes and hours and days and months and years and decade to come, Ariel would revisit this moment again and again, ask herself what she should've done differently. Not come to this party in the first place? Not slunk off to the poolhouse to wallow in self-loathing self-pity? Should she have punched Charlie in the nose, clawed at his eyes? Taken his cock in her mouth to bite down on it? Should she have screamed at the top of her lungs, again and again until her throat was hoarse and the sound unbearable and the cavalry came rushing?

But then what?

Then this is who Ariel would have become, for tonight and tomorrow, for the rest of her life: the woman whom Charlie Wolfe assaulted during his summer party.

No: *allegedly* assaulted.

Kayla Jefferson is on the phone again.

"I finally got the full report on John Wright, born John Reitwovski. A few interesting details jump out. First, he did Army ROTC, and served his commitment in Afghanistan."

"Interesting indeed," Griffiths agrees.

"Not as interesting as his next move, which is why it took so long to get his details. He resigned his army commission when he was accepted by us."

"Us?"

"John Wright," Kayla says, "was CI-goddamn-A."

CHAPTER 36

Day 2. 9:03 p.m.

"Thank you for giving us this time." Detective Moniz extends a plastic bag. "Sandwiches." He looks at Ariel. "For you too."

Two nights in a row, these cops have bought her dinner. That's nice. But that doesn't mean she can trust them.

"Thank you," she says. John unpacks the bag onto the table, while Ariel collects plates, napkins, utensils: methodical but mindless domesticity, automatic muscle memory.

"Did they feed you?" Moniz asks. "Your kidnappers?"

"Yes, plain bread with ham." John has a bite of sandwich, then another.

"For every meal? Breakfast also?"

John stops chewing, stares at the cop with unmasked hostility. "I can barely stay upright, and you're asking me about my kidnapping's *meal plan*? Is that really why you're here?"

"Please, Senhor Wright, calm down. We are trying to look for clues. You might be surprised where we find them."

Moniz opens his notepad. Santos is, as always, listening and observing, not asking and writing.

"Including, yes, meals. Including everything. But I understand that you are tired, and scared, and injured. So we will do this quickly, then we will leave you. Okay?"

John nods. He looks ashamed of his outburst.

"Excellent," Moniz says. "If you do not mind, from the beginning, please."

John nods, puts down his sandwich, wipes his face, his hands. "Yesterday — was it really just yesterday? — I woke up very early. Too early."

"What time is that, please?" Moniz has started writing.

"About five-thirty. Lying in bed, I realized I wouldn't fall back to sleep, so I took a shower, got dressed, left to take a walk, maybe grab a coffee, buy some *pastéis de nata* for my wife." He turns to Ariel. "She loves them, and there's a famous bakery nearby. I left a note for her on the pillow."

"I didn't get it," Ariel says. "It must've fallen off the bed. A chambermaid found it later, when she made up the room. But that wasn't until the afternoon, by which point I was losing my mind. I had no idea where you were, anything . . ."

"I'm so sorry."

426

Moniz turns to Ariel. "Do you normally remain asleep while your husband rises?"

"No."

"But you did yesterday?"

"I'd taken a sleeping pill the night before, to adjust to the time change. It knocked me out."

"What is the name of this pill?"

"I don't know . . ." She glances at John.

"Ambien," John says.

"You are sure? There is no other pill you could have given to your wife? Perhaps by mistake?"

John recoils at the implicit accusation. "No. The only pills in the canister are Ambien."

"And then, you left the hotel at" — Moniz glances down — "a few minutes before seven."

"Yes. There was a car in front of the hotel, and as soon as I stepped outside, the back door opened. A man climbed out, said to me, Mr. Wright, there's an emergency, something very sensitive that can't be discussed on the telephone. I assumed it had to do with my client, because of course that's why I was — why I *am* — here. This guy looked around, as if searching for eavesdroppers, then asked if I'd mind getting into the car for a minute, so he could explain."

"Did you know this man? Recognize him?"

"No, I'd never seen him before."

"And what did he sound like? Was he speaking English?"

"Yes. With a Portuguese accent."

"And you entered this car?"

"I did. But as I was bending over, I felt a sharp pain in my rear, and I thought what the hell, and I may have said hey or something, and I felt myself falling forward, and I was dizzy, then that was it: I was out. When I came to, I was alone in a room with no windows, one door, nothing except a bed and a pillow. I tried the door handle, but it was locked. I banged, and a few seconds later I heard a man on the other side say, Sit on the bed. I didn't move immediately, and he said, We are watching from a camera. I looked around and saw it mounted on the ceiling. So I sat, and the door opened. Two men were in a hallway: one right at the door, the other ten feet behind. The second man was holding a gun, pointing it at me."

"What did these men look like?"

"Both wore black pants, long-sleeved black shirts, balaclavas that covered everything except the eyes, and sunglasses. I couldn't see anything else."

"That is a pity. What size are these men?"

"Both about six feet."

"The two are the same exact build?"

"More or less."

"Interesting."

"One of them said, You've been kidnapped. We don't want to hurt you. We've asked for

428

ransom within forty-eight hours."

"This is exactly what they said?"

"I'm paraphrasing."

Ariel steals a glance at Santos, who's looking around the room, taking in the details, or pretending to. Ariel had assumed that Santos would be a natural ally, despite plenty of evidence that not all women believed in female solidarity, or agreed on what it might mean. Ariel was reminded of this every Election Day. And she's reminded right now by the cold hard stare of this Portuguese detective, who's clearly not giving anyone blanket credibility, regardless of shared biology.

"So I ate my sandwiches," John continues, "and drank my water, and once in a while I went to the bathroom. I also slept, but I don't know for how long, or when. There was no way for me to keep track of time."

"And your interactions with the men?"

"Honestly, there wasn't much. Only when they brought me meals, and took me to the bathroom."

"No questioning? They are not wanting any informations from you?"

"I guess not."

"Is it always the same two men?"

"Hard to know. They looked so similar, with their heads covered, and sunglasses. For all I know there were a half-dozen of them. They barely spoke, so I couldn't get a sense of their voices."

Suddenly Santos cuts in. "Tell us about the bathroom."

"The bathroom?" John is surprised at this question, and by the person asking it. The bathroom is a private place, the only truly private place, a place so private that we don't even discuss it.

Or at least that's what it's supposed to be.

"No!"

She felt Charlie lift her, roughly, and as her feet left the floor she felt the immediate loss of balance, of any hope of control —

"Stop!"

— and then he had already shoved her dress up over her waist, he was pawing aside her panties, and she felt the harsh exposure of her unprotected skin against the cold marble.

"No, Charlie," she said, and caught a glimpse of herself over his shoulder, in the mirror on the opposite wall, where she could also see Charlie's face in the mirror within the mirror, the infinity effect.

"*Please* no."

He didn't even acknowledge her plea, just pushed himself in, but she was dry, unreceptive, and she felt a tearing, a burning.

"Ow," she heard herself say. "You're hurting me."

He ignored the pain in her voice, and pushed more deliberately, more forcefully. More viciously.

430

She continued to watch the woman in the mirror struggle, saw her trying to twist herself away, to shove him off and out of her, but she had no leverage. Ariel's arms felt useless against this man who was twice her weight, like a completely different species of animal.

Her strength was draining fast, her arms burning from the effort of trying to push him off, as if she'd been attempting to lift a sequoia, a failure so abject that the tree didn't even realize anyone had been trying. She felt the back of her head banging against the mirror, the faucet digging into the small of her back. Tomorrow there would be bruises, but they'd be hidden by clothing, by hair. These wounds would be invisible. The others too.

In the mirror Ariel saw herself begin to cry, she heard it too, and in response Charlie yanked a hand towel off the rack, shoved it into her mouth, and she felt a burst of energy to renew her struggle against this fresh outrage, tried harder to push him away but failed again, tried to spit out the towel but gagged instead.

It wasn't sex that was happening here, this was just violence — taking something, hurting someone. She couldn't believe that he was enjoying this. She almost couldn't believe that it was actually happening, and she turned her eyes away from the infinity mirrors to look directly at the one real Charlie, his head lolled back with each burning thrust, his eyes clamped shut, his jaw jutted out in self-assurance, in challenge, in the arrogance of savage conquest.

She could see gray hairs sprouting from his nostrils, the saggy wattle under his chin. His breath was hot whiskey; he emitted the rancid sweat of a habitual drunk, comingled with cologne. She felt nausea rising up within her, the acid onslaught of bile, and she knew she'd throw up if she continued to look at him, so she turned her eyes back to the far wall's mirrors, where an infinite number of Ariels were trapped, being raped by an infinite number of Charlies, forever.

"Operations or Intelligence?" Griffiths asks.

"Ops." Jefferson hands her the report. "John Wright's first overseas assignment was a year-plus in Belgrade, then he abruptly resigned. Apparently changed his mind about how he wanted to live his life."

"And his polygraph agreed?" Griffiths is turning pages.

"Looks like it. There were no red flags on any of his polys."

"Any red flags at all?"

"Nope. At least, none in the paperwork. But I'm planning to call some of his old colleagues."

"Definitely do that. My suspicion of this guy just ratcheted up pretty fucking high. He served in the army in Afghanistan, then in the CIA in Serbia, then he gets kidnapped in Portugal? That's a lot of international intrigue in the background of a middling business consultant, isn't it?"

"I'm on it," Jefferson says. "Also, the mechanic situation is interesting. That's a guy named Billy, who checked his sales receipts for the period around the phone call, and didn't find anything to do with anyone named John Wright. As far as Billy can remember, the only possibility is a follow-up call to a guy a couple weeks after a sale, to see if everything was working out."

"That sounds unusual."

"It is. Apparently the sale in question was a used motorcycle to someone who didn't seem to have an excess of familiarity with that particular type of bike, so Billy was concerned for the guy's safety. And Billy admits that although record keeping is not his forte, he doesn't tend to just *lose* bills of sale. This one, though? It's completely missing."

"Huh." That too is pretty suspicious.

"Even without the records, Billy was able to recall two important details about the transaction: one, the guy paid twenty-five hundred dollars; two, it was in cash."

"You said *that particular type of bike.* What does that mean, exactly?"

The phone rings, Antonucci calling.

"I don't know," Kayla says. "It's just what the mechanic said."

433

"Please find out."

Griffiths picks up the phone. "What's up, Guido?"

"I think you want to come listen to what's happening now in their hotel."

"My room was at one end of a hall. At the other end, maybe twenty feet away, was a door I never saw open; I assumed that was the exit. The bathroom door was in the middle of the hall. Just a toilet, a roll of paper on the floor, and a sink. But no shower, no tub, no window, no soap, no towel, no mirror, no nothing other than the toilet, the paper, the sink."

"This is on the left side of the hall? Or the right?"

Ariel feels a churn in her stomach. She doesn't like this line of questioning, the challenge that's implicit in its specificity, in its irrelevancy. This detail can't matter for the investigation; the only reason for asking this question now is to ask it again later, and see if the answers match. This question is a trap.

"As I walked away from my room, on the right."

"Please, tell me about this." Moniz indicates John's injured face. "How is this happening?"

John grimaces in what looks like shame. "It was stupid, I don't know what I was thinking. I'd been asleep for a while, and when I woke I really needed the bathroom. So I knocked on the door, and when it opened I saw there was only one man instead of the usual two, and it occurred to me that this was my chance. That I should try to over-power him."

"He is armed, this man?"

"Yeah, but I thought if I could get his gun away . . ." John shrugs. "So I went to the bathroom first, because, well, because I had to. Also I thought it would lull him, that I wasn't attacking immediately. When I was finished at the toilet I didn't flush, I just flung the door open, hoping to surprise the guard. He was standing a few feet away, and the gun was tucked into his waistband, and I could see that he wouldn't have time to raise the weapon, so I rushed him, tried to body-slam him against the wall, but he shunted me aside, and I lost my balance. He punched me in the side of the head. I stumbled backward, and he hit me again in the front of the face, really hard."

"This was a punch made with the left hand, yes?"

John looks at Moniz blankly.

Ariel feels a nearly physical urge to stop this interview, but she knows she should let this ride out as long as possible, to try to glean what the cops are thinking. What they'll do next.

"Your injury is on the right side of the right half of your face, so a person facing you" —

Moniz raises his left hand slowly, forms a fist, moves it in slow-motion in the general direction of John's face — "must be using the left hand to be hitting you in that location. That angle."

John closes his eyes, remembering. "Yes." He opens his eyes. "It was the left hand."

Moniz writes something. "And then?"

"And then I fell, and he was standing over me, still wearing sunglasses, now holding his gun again, aiming it down at me. He said, That was stupid."

"Yes," Moniz says. "If you do not mind me saying it, I agree. Why are you doing that?"

"Honestly? I really don't know."

Ariel hates that John keeps saying *honestly.*

"I was kidnapped, and I thought this was a chance to escape. Maybe my only chance."

"But why did you believe that you needed to escape?"

John looks confused.

"Did you not think that the ransom would be paid? By your employer? Or by your wife?"

"Well, honestly" —

Will he just stop saying that?

"— because of the holiday I was worried that my company wouldn't be reachable, and Ariel would have to handle this all herself. She doesn't have that type of money —"

"Excuse me, please," Santos interrupts again. Ariel is really beginning to dread this woman's interruptions. "Are the kidnappers

436

telling you how much ransom they are demanding?"

"No. But Ariel doesn't have *any* type of ransom level of money."

"How are you knowing this?" Santos asks. "How much money do you believe your wife is able to secure? For a ransom?"

"I don't know."

"No?" Santos looks briefly at Ariel, then back at John. "You do not know how much money your wife has in banks? In investments?"

John doesn't answer immediately, and Ariel jumps in. "Why are you asking about this?"

"I am just trying to understand your husband's thoughts."

"What do his thoughts about my bank accounts have to do with his kidnapping?"

"Nothing," Santos says. Then adds, "Perhaps."

Now Ariel can put a name to the prickle in her stomach: fear.

"Do you enjoy your work, Senhor Wright?" Moniz takes over again. The ping-pong questioning is making Ariel feel like her head is spinning. That's probably the point.

"Mostly."

"Do you ever think about quitting?"

"Who doesn't?"

"Me." Moniz smiles. "I love my work. I hope to do my work until the day I die."

"Well then you're very lucky. Or something."

"Have you calculated how much money you need to go on the retirement?"

"To retire? No, not specifically." John has a quaver in his voice. All this cage-rattling has worked. "I'm pretty young for that."

Ariel has been in this sort of predicament before: certain that something terrible is about to happen, but unable to do the necessary thing to stop it, reluctant to admit the defeat, to make the decision to confront. She has always ended up regretting it, putting off the uncomfortable that would stave off the unbearable. She has always thought, later: I should've done something when I had the chance.

When he was finished, Charlie yanked the towel from Ariel's mouth, used it to wipe off his dick.

She was rubbing her jaw, her face muscles aching from the wadded-up terry cloth, in addition to all the other pains in all the other parts of her newly battered body. She watched as Charlie zipped up, preened in the mirror, smoothed his hair, adjusted his mouth into something that looked like a smile, putting his party face back on — just a fun-loving guy on a Saturday night, wearing those goddamned bracelets.

"I'm-a go out first, okay?" Charlie was slur-

438

ring again, and Ariel could see him constructing the narrative, the justifications, the
excuses — sure, okay, maybe he was a little
drunk, but he had definitely not misunderstood Ariel's overtures, she'd been coming
on to him forever, and then she'd gone ahead
and followed him to this out-of-the-way
bathroom, what the hell was he supposed to
think she wanted? Exactly what she got.

"Okay?" he asked again.

Ariel couldn't find any words, just stared at
him, aghast, until Charlie turned his eyes
from his reflection, met hers. It was just for a
second, but that was long enough for her to
see it, even through the thick cloud of her
anguish: the lie.

At that point it had been nearly two decades
since Ariel's first sexual assault, two decades
during which she'd come to understand what
gaslighting was. She knew it was purposeful;
she knew how it worked. It worked like this.

Did Charlie know he was a monster? Did
he make a concerted effort to hide his monstrosity from everyone, maybe even from
himself? Did that explain the ostentatious
philanthropy? The cool-dude bracelets, the
do-gooder galas, the twenty-dollar tips he
doles out to bellhops, to garage attendants,
and especially — extravagantly — to coat-
check girls? There, see: I'm a good guy.

Did he actually believe this, himself? Or did
he know full well that what he was doing was

a con? That he was trying to hide what he really was.

"You," Ariel said, "are a fucking monster."

440

CHAPTER 37

"How did it end?" Moniz asks.

John sighs in relief. He too had grown uncomfortable with the cops' line of questioning, and is thankful to be back on the more secure footing of straight-up factual chronology.

Ariel is not. She's worried that this is merely a tactical retreat, a feint, after which the interrogation will swing back. She's worried that John should have a lawyer present for this inquiry, an American lawyer, and it should be happening in the American embassy. If only she could trust the integrity of the American embassy. Of American lawyers.

"They told me to sit on the bed, as they always did before opening the door. Then one man said that I was lucky, my ransom had been paid, I was going to be let go. But I had to wear a gag, and a hood. He said that now was not the time to be a hero; I was just a few minutes from freedom. So I sat still while he filled my mouth with a gag, and put a heavy, itchy hood over my head. Then they led me down the hall, and maybe twenty more steps, then I could feel fresh air. I was bent over and shoved into a car. We drove for about thirty minutes, then I was pulled out of the car, walked a few steps. I was pushed into a chair, I felt my feet being tied together, my hands too. Then I heard footsteps receding, a car door slam, the car shift gears and pull away, and a big door slide shut."

"You can find this place?"

"I can," Ariel jumps in. Everyone turns to her. "I know exactly where it is." One of the things that Ariel has learned: how to be a credible witness. Certainty is critical. Certainty is everything.

"Good." Moniz nods. "And the hood that you were wearing?"

"It's right there," Ariel says, pointing at the kitchen counter.

"Would you mind if we . . . ?"

"Go ahead."

Ariel has taken over the role of witness, deflecting attention away from John. His energy seems to be flagging; the fight-or-flight response is exhausting. Afterward, you're always at least a little confused, and not necessarily capable of making the best decisions. Though you don't realize this at the time. Nor, possibly, ever.

442

■ ■ ■ ■

Ariel was trembling, assessing the damage, triaging, like a field medic who'd come upon her own injured self at the end of a bloody battle.

She didn't want to walk through the party looking like she'd just been raped. She wiped away her smeared lipstick and mascara, her unsteady hands doing an inefficient job. Took a swipe at fixing her hair, but this seemed to do more harm than good. She adjusted her panties, smoothed her dress, winced when she suddenly became hyperaware of Charlie's semen, warm and slick, the idea making her sick, a ferocious attack of nausea, and she spun to the toilet to throw up, another violent wrenching that hurt her whole body.

Then Ariel stood, started cleaning herself again, wondering: What should she do now?

She could storm back to the party, yell it out for everyone to hear. But then what?

Or she could make a 911 call right here in the bathroom, then go wait for the police by the front door, where a couple of Maseratis and a Lamborghini had been valet-parked in the most visible locations, posing for the other guests. *There he is,* she'd say to the cops. *That fucking monster over there.* But then what?

Or she could make her way to her husband,

whisper, *Could I talk to you?* After she explained, maybe Bucky would call the police himself. Or maybe he'd march over and punch Charlie in the face. Either way: then what?

Or she could pretend like the whole thing never even happened, just as her father had once counseled. But then what?

Then what? Then what? Then what?

She didn't know if she'd be able to walk, but she managed, barely, unsteady, with a loud din in her head, as if different parts of her were all yelling at once about everything that was wrong, the pains in her body, in her psyche, the shittiness of the predicament, and she still was unable to decide what specifically to do, other than knowing this one thing for certain: She needed to get the hell out of that party, immediately.

Ariel staggered among the tables, drawing one glance after another, feeling as if her whole body were cloaked in the assault, soaked in Charlie's sweat, his spit, his semen, as if everyone could see it on her, smell it, and she was hit with another wave of nausea, and needed to lean against a chairback, and someone at the table asked, "You okay?" and she muttered, *"Mmm,"* then resumed her slog across the lawn.

"Bucky?" she croaked out quietly, her voice weak, hoarse.

444

He looked up from telling some story. People seemed to be anticipating a punch line.

"I'm not feeling so great."

Bucky didn't respond immediately, and Maggie Mitchum flung herself into the silence, said to her husband, "Come on, Aubrey, let's blow this joint."

The two couples had carpooled so only one person would need to remain sober. It certainly wasn't going to be either of the Mitchums, nor Bucky. These three were all people who were never sober at the end of a party, not even on nights when they intended to be.

Another function of Ariel's job.

"Okay," Bucky acceded, with obvious reluctance. He started shaking hands.

"Hey," Maggie whispered. "Are you okay?"

Ariel was afraid that if she tried to speak again, she'd lose it. She just nodded.

"You sure?" Even drunk as Maggie was, this woman whom Ariel barely knew could still see that something was wrong, while Ariel's own husband had no clue.

"Mmm," Ariel said again, lips clamped shut, trying to prevent herself from crying, from sobbing, from throwing up again, from breaking down completely in front of everyone.

"I just gotta say good night to Charlie," Bucky said.

Oh there was absolutely no fucking way in hell.

"I already did," Ariel managed to say. "I'll get the car."

She held out her hand for the valet ticket, which Bucky fished out of the fifth pocket he searched: a seashell with a hand-painted number on it, very beach chic, like everything here, the luxury, the elegance, the fancy people in their fancy dress. This certainly didn't look like the scene of a violent felony.

"Mr. Wagstaff! Saxby Barnes here."

"Hey." Wagstaff begins to walk toward the far side of the square, away from the hotel. He'd been sitting near a man who looked like he could have been American, possibly CIA. Wagstaff doesn't want that guy to hear this conversation. "What's going on?"

"I'm wondering what info you've been able to dig up, on that story we discussed?"

"Such as what, Barnes?"

"I don't know. Such as anything."

Wagstaff isn't sure what Barnes is digging for, and he's not going to just give him the whole story.

"You have to be more specific, Barnes."

"The ambassador is concerned that something about this situation might turn out to be problematic."

"I see," Wagstaff says. "Okay. I might have something to share with you, Barnes. If you

446

have something to share with me."

Barnes doesn't answer, but Wagstaff knows he can wait out the embassy functionary. Pete has been doing this much longer, and he's much better at it. You don't need to be employed by Langley to be a good spy. In fact many of the best spies aren't. Plus at this moment Barnes needs him, but Pete does not need Barnes.

"Okay," Barnes caves. "But you can't use me as a source, or even on background."

"Understood."

"Ariel Pryce visited the embassy very late last night, when everything was shut down, to use the secure-communications room. No one I've spoken to knows why."

"You're saying that this was not at the direction of the ambassador?"

"Definitely not."

What does this mean? It means that Ariel Pryce was summoned to the embassy by someone powerful who either works for the federal government or has deep connections. This is a good tip from Barnes. In fact, a great one.

"So what is it that you have for me, Mr. Wagstaff?"

"The birth certificate of Pryce's thirteen-year-old son lists no father. And I'm almost positive that she signed an NDA about the paternity."

Barnes doesn't respond for a few seconds,

then asks, "So that means what?"

This guy really is a simpleton.

"So, Barnes, the person who provided the ransom, and the person who's the father of Ariel Pryce's child? They're the same person."

"Huh. Do you have any idea how we might identify this gentleman?"

Wagstaff looks up toward the woman's hotel room, all the windows open, curtains fluttering. She's in there right now with her recently rescued new husband, and two Lisbon detectives, trying to keep the lid on this explosive secret that she's apparently been hiding for the past decade and a half. And Wagstaff is about to light the fuse. His heart is already racing.

"No," he lies to Barnes. This is something he needs to pursue himself, far away from anyone who might want to stop him. "No idea."

CHAPTER 38

Day 2. 9:42 p.m.

"Senhora, how did you procure the ransom?"

"I'm sorry, I can't tell you."

The detective waits for more of an explanation, doesn't get it, and Ariel chooses not to fill the silence.

"I do not understand," Moniz says. "You do not know where the money came from?"

"Yes, of course I know. But I'm legally forbidden to reveal it."

"Even to the police?"

"There are no exceptions."

Moniz shakes his head. "I still do not understand."

"I signed a legal agreement promising that I would not divulge any details about the interaction. That I will not divulge even the *existence* of the agreement. To anyone, ever. So right now, by telling you this, I'm already breaking the terms of the agreement."

This cop should not want to induce Ariel to break the law; that's not what cops are for.

"This is common in America." Ariel knows she needs to make this abundantly clear, so the police know why she's refusing to answer. She turns to Santos. Although Moniz is doing most of the talking, Ariel is pretty sure that Santos is the one who needs to be convinced.

"It's called a confidentiality agreement, or nondisclosure, NDA. Have you heard of this?" Neither cop responds, so Ariel continues, "The rules are rigid, the penalties severe. If I broke the terms, I'd be ruined financially, and I'd probably go to jail." She levels her gaze at Santos; she needs this woman to understand this part. "I'd also face other dangers. To my personal safety."

Ariel assumes that both cops know what she's communicating; they're cops, after all, they know what men do to women, what men do when angry, what powerful men are capable of. This is the job of being a cop. Ariel needs them to understand that she's scared; they should be able to figure out why.

"You have reason to fear this man?" Moniz asks.

"I didn't say it was a man."

"This man has hurt you before? Or threatened you?"

Ariel doesn't answer.

"But it was not your ex-husband who provided the money?" Moniz glances down at his notes again. "Buckingham Turner. He seems to be wealthy."

"He is, and I did try Bucky. But he doesn't have all this cash just lying around."

"Yes, three million euros is a large amount of cash."

Ariel thinks about correcting Moniz, but decides against it.

"There are not many people who are having these funds available on such short notice. So it is very lucky for you, yes? That you are able to find someone with this unusually large amount of cash, as you say, just lying around."

"Lucky? You think lucky is what I've been?"

"These kidnappers, they are committing a complicated crime with no witnesses, no clues, no mistakes at all. A very well-planned crime. Yet these very careful kidnappers are failing to consider how difficult it is for you to find this large amount of ransom in such a short time. Difficult especially for an American, during an American holiday. These are large obstacles, yes?"

Ariel shrugs.

"And these large obstacles are foreseeable, and avoidable, for very careful criminals. Do you think the kidnappers are considering these obstacles?"

"I don't know what the kidnappers considered. Obviously."

"You and your husband are not known to be wealthy. Not in this way, with three million in cash. Yet this is what the kidnappers are demanding."

Ariel just stares at him. If these cops truly believed that something irregular was going on, and had any evidence, then this conversation would be happening in the police station.

"So yes, senhora, I do say it is very lucky that you are able to find such a person. Do you not agree?"

Ariel has given a lot of thought to the concept of luck, to what it means to be which types of fortunate, to how providence should inform behavior. She has often looked like a very fortunate person; she has often been one. She certainly looked fortunate driving that giant luxury SUV, a car that cost more than the average house in America, wearing a runway-ready dress and seven-hundred-dollar shoes, dripping with collectible jewelry, on her way home from a party filled with the rich and famous and powerful that would be detailed in next weekend's social pages for the masses to leaf through, envious, God I wish I were one of those lucky people.

Ariel was one of those lucky people. Yet here she was, chauffeuring her husband and their friends along the quiet backroads of the Hamptons while her whole body was still shaking from a sexual assault that ended only minutes ago. Her hands were so jittery that

452

she could barely grip the wheel; she kept doubting which was the gas pedal and which the brakes. She was halfway worried that she'd crash into a tree. She was halfway hoping for it.

She somehow managed to find the drunken Mitchums' crushed-oyster-shell driveway, then she spun the black Range Rover around, back into the dark night, while Bucky prattled on, who knew what he was even talking about, he seemed to be getting drunker by the second as his final drink was still being absorbed into his bloodstream.

She realized that she could not tell him tonight; Bucky wasn't in any condition to process the narrative, nor to do anything constructive with it. He could not be part of any solution tonight. More likely he'd be an additional problem, irrational and unmanageable and possibly violent. Bucky was a messy drunk, intellectually and emotionally.

Sexually too.

Suddenly this horror stuck: What if Bucky wants sex tonight? They were trying to conceive, of course. Plus he was, as a rule, a horny drunk.

Oh God no.

Ariel desperately needed a shower, immediately; she needed to rid her body of every toxic trace of Charlie. But she didn't want Bucky to misconstrue the motivation behind her nakedness, nor even to construe it correctly. So she snuck off to the ground-floor guest room, marched toward the en suite, and froze in the doorway.

Another bathroom.

Could she do this? Should she? She felt her whole body vibrating again as she tentatively crossed the threshold, as she switched on the lights, terrified of this brightly lit sterile space, terrified that she was about to wash away crucial physical evidence of the crime scene that was her body, but also terrified of the alternative, of trying to survive the night without at least making every effort to cleanse herself of the violation, even knowing that she wouldn't succeed.

She had no choice. She peeled off her dress, she would've peeled off her skin if she could, which is what it felt like she was trying to do, scouring herself everywhere, using a loofah as if it were a Brillo pad, rubbing raw flesh that was already bruised, abraded, violated, it was pain on top of pain, horror at what she was now doing on top of horror at what had been done to her.

Ariel eventually crept up the stairs, listening carefully, and thankfully she could hear her husband's snoring before she got to the top. She slunk into their bathroom, brushed her teeth, flossed. She had a good smile, it was one of her most notable features, and of course a smile was a function of healthy teeth, whose foundation was healthy gums, so she flossed every goddamned night, even apparently on nights when she'd been raped.

She glanced at Bucky splayed in bed, not even half-covered by sheets, shirtless, hairy, beastly.

No, she absolutely could not get into that bed.

She returned to the bathroom, popped a Xanax, then on second thought another. She decamped for the den via the kitchen, where she pulled a four-hundred-dollar chef's knife from the block. Then she sat in the dark, willing herself not to fall apart while also suspecting that it may have been too late for that. Maybe this was what a fallen-apart person looked like, clutching a blade in both hands, staring at the door, her whole body buzzing in anticipation of the next assault, even though she knew that it wouldn't be here, and it wouldn't be tonight.

After a couple of hours, rational thoughts began to form, all coalescing around one central question: What should she do now? Should she drive over there, wake up Charlie's wife, tell her? Or wake up Charlie, beat the crap out of him with a golf club? Or drive to the police station? Or call the police?

Now that she'd had time to think, it felt like such a failure, doing nothing. She should do *something*, shouldn't she? But she could not force herself to decide what to do. Every option was bad — started with the same unspeakable thing, and ended with something unacceptable. Ariel had no good choices. She needed to figure which was least bad.

At three in the morning, it occurred to her that she needed to take a pregnancy test tonight, when it would still be absolutely clear who the father was if the result was positive. So she crept back upstairs, and peed on a stick, and waited, and broke down in tears.

"Your wife does not often accompany you on business trips." Moniz looks to Ariel, then back to John. "This is the first such trip, yes?"

"That's right."

"Why this time?"

"Business trips are lonely, and difficult. I figured if I could turn that into something fun with my new wife, I should."

"Yes, but why *this* specific trip?"

"I'd been to Lisbon a few times before, I know the city pretty well, so I wouldn't mind missing out on some of her adventures while I had to work. It's a short flight, it's convenient, it's inexpensive, it's beautiful, and honestly I just thought she'd love it. A lot of reasons."

"But it is not because your clients are interested to meet your wife?"

John doesn't answer immediately.

"Is that not what you are telling her?"

"Yes." John swallows. "That's part of it too."

"Are your clients asking you for this? To bring your wife to Lisbon?"

"Well, no. Not explicitly."

"Please forgive me. Perhaps I am not understanding. How do you know that this is what your clients want?"

"I have a lot of experience doing business in Europe. This is common."

"Is it?" Moniz looks again at Ariel, then back at John. "So you are assuming."

"Yes."

"But that is not what you are telling your wife, to convince her to join you."

"I didn't want her to feel guilty about taking the time, and spending the money, and being away from her child, her business. I guess I was sort of tricking her into a vacation, which she otherwise refuses to do."

"So you are lying to your wife."

"Well, *lying*? That's a strong word. A romantic ruse, is how I'd put it."

"Yet it is not turning out so romantic, is it?"

"Senhor." Santos jumps in again. All eyes turn to her. "When is the last time you are speaking to your sister?"

John is a deer frozen in the headlights. "I'm not sure. A couple of months?"

"Do you know her current location?"

"No."

"You are having recent contact with her? Text message? Email?"

Ariel doesn't like where this is going, not one bit. She wants these cops to leave, she wants to go to the airport, get out of this town, this country, she wants to be home with George, away from this whole misadventure. Why the hell did they come here? This was such a monumentally bad idea.

"John, can I speak to you a minute?"

"You are exhausted," Ariel whispers, behind the closed door of the bedroom. "You have been through a horrible experience. You are traumatized, you are in pain. You need a break, you need sleep."

John is looking at her, searching. "But I don't."

"Yes." Ariel glowers at him. "You do."

"But . . ." He turns toward the bedroom door, the detectives sitting out there, waiting with their notepads, with their suspicions, their handcuffs, their guns.

"But I have nothing to hide. So I don't want to look like I do. And honestly —"

"Don't say *honestly*. Please, just stop using that word, forever. It's what liars say."

"And it's guilty people who refuse to talk to the cops."

"No, it's what rational people do when they realize that the cops are not on their side. I'm serious, John: We need to shut this down, right now. I don't know what exactly these cops suspect, but I don't think we should just

458

wait around to find out."

He sighs; he knows she's right.

"Remember: Everyone will understand that you can't talk about this, just like everyone will understand that I can't divulge the name, and neither can you. And anyone who doesn't understand? That's someone we shouldn't be talking to anyway. We'll just go home, and get you a lawyer, get me a lawyer, and we'll shut the hell up about who provided the ransom money."

He nods.

"I've been keeping a big secret for a very long time," she says. "The hardest part is the beginning. Remember that. It will get less hard."

The three CIA officers are all in the same position, sitting with their elbows on their thighs, leaning forward, listening intently. For good measure, Griffiths has her eyes closed. She doesn't want to be distracted by Antonucci's workspace, which is so irresponsibly disorganized that it sends shivers of unease down her spine; this is the stuff of nightmares. It's extremely important to Griffiths for workspaces — for everything — to be organized. This is one of the things that makes her an effective manager of intelligence operatives and assets. It's also maybe why she has never been married, not even close, and is pretty sure that she never will be.

459

Now there's silence over the speaker. The American couple has apparently ended their private conversation away from the Portuguese cops.

Kayla Jefferson has been scribbling madly during this interview; there's a lot of intel to follow up on. Guido Antonucci has taken fewer notes. He's the muscle, despite the evidence of his beaten-up face. He closes his notepad and stands.

"You know what to do, right?" Griffiths asks.

"I'm going down there to keep an eye on them."

"Hit the head first. And definitely bring something to eat and drink. You'll probably be there all night. Or at least we hope so."

Antonucci leaves his cubicle; the women stay, to continue to eavesdrop on the police interview.

"Have you made a decision yet?" Jefferson asks, quietly. She wants to know what Griffiths is going to do with the revelation about the owner of the LLC. Which is a revelation about everything.

"It's not my decision," Griffiths says. "So I've started to run it up the chain. I'll let you know. Or maybe I won't. That too may not be my decision."

"Listen." Ariel looks both cops in the eye. "We appreciate all your help, we really do.

But I'm exhausted, and my husband is exhausted, and we really need this day to end. I'm sure you understand. We'll come to your station first thing in the morning to answer any other questions you might have."

Ariel hasn't sat down again. Moniz takes the hint, and rises, followed by Santos, who says, "Just one last question, Senhor Wright."

After just a couple of days, Ariel knows how these cops operate. Both of them are staring intently at John. Ariel doesn't know what this question is going to be, but she braces herself for something catastrophic.

"Your sister" — Santos says — "is she left-handed?"

461

CHAPTER 39

Day 2. 10:04 p.m.
Ariel shouldn't say it aloud. John already knows it, and she already knows it, so actually saying it would serve no purpose other than to create antagonism.

John does it for her: "Well," he says, "you certainly did tell me so."

Despite the tension of the moment, despite the exhaustion, despite the fear, Ariel smiles. She's surprised at how much love she feels for this man.

"That was fucked-up," he says.

"It was," she agrees. From behind the sheer linen curtain, she watches the detectives step out onto the sidewalk in front of the hotel.

"They really think I staged my own kidnapping?"

"I don't know." Ariel scans the square again, another inventory. "Maybe they don't actually believe it, but are just poking around to see if your story holds up, on the chance that it doesn't."

She moves to the dining table, opens his laptop. "Can you log in, please?"

"Sure. What are you doing?"

"I'm going to see if we can get on an earlier flight."

There's no debating the suspicion that was coming off the police tonight; there's no reason to expect that things will be any better tomorrow. Just because today was awful doesn't mean tomorrow won't be worse.

"So we're not going to the police station in the morning?"

"Are you out of your mind? We're going to the airport in the morning."

Ariel woke after just a few hours of sleep. She struggled to rise from the couch, in physical pain at various sensitive spots, and in mental anguish in every corner of her consciousness, and utterly exhausted. She walked in a stupor through the fully furnished McMansion rental, filled with things she didn't need or want, the deluxe and oversize everything, the cathedral ceilings and walk-in closets and en suite bathrooms with double vanities and soaking tubs.

She took another shower, maybe the longest of her life, but she still didn't feel clean; maybe she never would again. She swallowed a couple of painkillers, stared at herself in the mirror. *What are you going to do?*

She found her husband's hastily scrawled note on the kitchen counter:

LEFT FOR GOLF, HOME FOR LUNCH, LET'S HEAD BACK TO CITY MID-AFTERNOON

— LOVE, B

Golf: Bucky would be playing with three other guys. One of them might even be Charlie himself.

The kitchen appliances were massive too — a refrigerator the size of an SUV, a ten-burner stove. Who needed ten burners? Ariel barely ever used one, like now, making tea to take to the patio that faced the pool, sit in the shade under the striped umbrella, the terra-cotta paving stones surrounded by a palace guard of blue hydrangea, a staggering array of big blooms sagging on thick woody stems, too big and showy for their own good, like this whole property, her whole life. Like herself.

The rent here was three hundred thousand dollars for the season, Memorial Day through Labor Day. Fifteen weeks. Fifteen Saturday nights. Twenty thousand dollars per Saturday night.

What do you do the morning after you've been raped?

"Well," Moniz says, "I am man enough to admit it: You were right."

"What was that? I did not quite hear."

464

Moniz smiles. "I said you were right." He looks around the square, all these people, all this life. How many of them will commit crimes tonight? How many will be victims?

"Should we call a judge?" he asks. "Try to arrest Wright now?"

"Oh I wish. No, we cannot do that without discussing with the American embassy."

"Yes we can. The American embassy has no jurisdiction."

Santos snorts. "Do not be naïve, António. Jurisdiction has nothing to do with it. If we arrest Wright without first getting the embassy's sign-off, and then it eventually turns out that we are wrong? *Pffft.*"

This is the thing that has always frustrated Moniz about working in law enforcement: Police are sometimes more worried about stepping on the wrong toes than about crimes going unpunished. The more senior the police, the more they are concerned for their own skin.

"But we are not wrong," Moniz says. "John Wright is as guilty a man as I have ever seen."

"Now who is jumping to conclusions?"

They have arrived at their car. "I will call the embassy first thing in the morning, they will send someone to meet us at the station, and we will arrest Wright as soon as he arrives."

"What if he does not show up? What if they run tonight?"

"I will station a team here to keep an eye. And I will have someone monitor the airline records. We will know if they run."

Pete Wagstaff watches the cops drive away, then minutes later the hotel room lights go out. Wagstaff has been standing in this square a long time, waiting for something to happen — an arrest, an escape, another bizarre altercation like when the woman beat the shit out of that CIA operative. But it looks like there will be no further drama tonight.

This stakeout, though, has not been a complete waste of time. Wagstaff has used the opportunity to come up with a plan of attack, to think through the lists he'll generate, and how. He suspects he'll end up with thousands of names, so he has also started to figure out which categories he'll be able to rule out, to narrow down the possibilities. It will be a lot of work, yet he's excited to do it. He's confident that it will be worth it, that the payoff will be immense.

He'll be up all night. He hops on his moped, headed toward home. First he'll stop at Luisa's bar to buy a gram of blow.

Ariel doesn't need the midnight alarm; at a quarter to twelve, her eyes pop open. She lies in bed for a minute, listening to the steady rhythm of John's breathing. Then she gets up.

466

She doesn't turn on any lights. She walks to the window again, and shields herself behind the curtain to make another survey. There's still one other car that has been sitting there all night, parked on the far side of the square. She's pretty sure that this nondescript little Ford is occupied by one of those CIA men, the one she pummeled. But it's hard to be certain from this far away.

Ariel walks into the kitchenette, pushes aside the coffeemaker to retrieve the new disposable phone that she bought around the corner with the matching duffels, and hid back here, out of the view of any prying that the cops might do. She pops the SIM card into the never-used phone, holds down the power button.

Her pulse is already beginning to race.

Moniz walked in the door only five minutes ago, and already Santos is phoning him. "Sorry," he mouths to Julio, who rolls his eyes and leaves the room.

Santos doesn't waste time with any preliminaries: "They were originally ticketed to depart Lisboa on Friday. But a half-hour ago, they changed their reservation to tomorrow's early-afternoon flight to New York."

"Do you think they are still intending to come to the station in the morning?"

"Probably not. So I will make sure that there is a patrol car at the hotel at all times."

"Is that enough?"

"We cannot arrest them now, António."

"But this is evidence that they intend to flee."

"No, this is evidence that they intend to shorten their trip."

"Why are you giving them the benefit of the doubt?"

"I am not. What I am giving is the benefit of protecting ourselves from a career-ending mistake. We cannot go around dragging American citizens out of their hotel beds in the middle of the night, especially on the suspicion of committing an outlandishly complicated — and nonviolent — crime based on nothing except our suspicion that they behaved evasively during stressful questioning. Do you not understand this, António? We do not have any actual evidence. Not yet."

"Hey," Guido Antonucci says. "Sorry if I woke you. But I thought you'd want to know this immediately. Pryce just stepped out onto her balcony to make a call."

"To?"

"That's the thing: We don't know. The phone she used wasn't her own, nor was it the kidnappers' burner. And of course out on the balcony it was beyond the range of our microphones."

"Fuck." Griffiths pushes herself up to a sitting position. She was asleep twenty seconds ago, but now her mind is operating at full speed. "*Fuck.* Are you alone at the hotel?"

"Yeah."

"Okay, call Jefferson, get her to join you down there as soon as humanly possible, on her bike. I'll be there too."

As Ariel does a quick brush of her teeth, she examines the amber canister with John's name and address in typescript on the label, the milligrams, the dosage. Do the cops think he drugged her? Slipped her something so she'd sleep through his early-morning departure, so he could participate in his own kidnapping without his wife witnessing it? The police are giving John a lot of credit for cleverness that Ariel knows he doesn't have.

She takes a seat on the edge of the bed. "Hey," she says, softly.

"*Mmm.*"

She places her hand gently on his chest. "Time to get up." The same thing she has said to her son, in the same tone, hundreds of times.

John's eyebrows raise but his eyes are still closed, and he yawns, then his eyes blink open.

"Five minutes," she says.

It was very quiet. Ariel couldn't hear any sign of neighbors, and the street was an out-of-the-way cul-de-sac with no traffic. The birds had settled down for their midmornings. Even the swimming pool's pump was bunkered way back beyond a thick barricade of boxwood; inaudible. The only sounds Ariel could hear were the occasional *glurp* of a circulation bubble in the pool, and the *thrum* of the crashing waves, rolling across the half-mile of potato field between this house and the Atlantic Ocean.

Everything else was still, silent, pristine, perfect. But all this perfection had a cost, of course; nothing was free. What cost was Ariel willing to bear?

Everyone knew that to live this sort of pampered life, it was an absolute imperative to be thin. So Ariel had to diet more or less constantly, she had to exercise every day, she had to abstain from this or that or the other. She hadn't consumed a full sandwich in years; she couldn't remember the last time she'd eaten French fries.

These were costs she could accept. She liked kale.

She had to be phonier than she would have preferred; she had to be saccharine-polite to some people she loathed. She could not use profanity. She had to arrange her hair and apply makeup just to step into the elevator, much less out onto the stage of the East Side.

Okay, okay, okay: Ariel accepted all this.

"That's how life works," her mother had

counseled, again and again, about everything, salad forks, legs crossed at the ankles, bread-and-butter notes. Her father too, young ladies don't do this, young ladies don't do that, all these things your parents tell you that you're supposed to simply accept — religion, politics, manners. What does it even mean to have good manners? It means to do what people expect you to do.

"Manners are what's necessary for the smooth operation of a civilized society." Her father liked to trot out this bon mot when there were guests around. This was the same person who'd advised his daughter to just forget about a sexual assault. But he knew his manners.

Even her tea was perfect, imported from New York after imported from London after imported from India, brewed with water from a state-of-the-art reverse-osmosis filtration system, Tiffany cup and saucer, shiny sterling silver spoon. She felt an impulse to fling it all into the pool.

And last night: Was that one of the costs? Could she bear it?

She knew that this perfect life was bankrolled by entitled men who took whatever they wanted as an entertaining type of challenge. In these lives of sporting aggression, where were the lines between what was illegal and what was merely boys-will-be-boys, locker-room talk, fun and games? In sports and law and hostile takeovers, in shock-and-awe bombing campaigns and drone strikes, in big-game hunting and stand-your-ground laws: Rules of engagement separate the illegal violence from the legal, from the encouraged violence, the celebrated violence. Is it a surprise that all this sanctioned violence leaks into other spheres?

All the lines were, to some extent, arbitrary. The difference between tackle football and a bar fight and aggravated assault.

There was a point in her life when Ariel was amused by testosterony vigor, maybe attracted to it, strong men, strong-willed, strongly held opinions. That's what men are supposed to be, isn't it? That's what women are supposed to love. And she did love Bucky. But it wasn't because he was so hard. It was because occasionally he was soft.

Maybe last night could have been expected. Maybe a self-described apex predator like Charlie Wolfe would of course — *of course* — want to screw his business partner's wife. Because that's how he wins, isn't it? That's how he proves he has won.

Winning in complete privacy is meaningless. Without at least one witness, it isn't really winning.

Ariel was the witness.

CHAPTER 40

Day 3. 12:07 a.m.
They bring nothing. No luggage. No change of clothes. No laptop, no chargers, no headphones. They leave the hotel as if they'll be returning after a drink or a bite, with nothing except the clothes on their backs, their wallets, their phones, and Ariel's cell and untraceable new burner. And their passports.

Wagstaff does another line, just a small one, then runs his fingertip across his gums, an aspect of cocaine that he enjoys almost as much as the mental and emotional parts: the immediacy of the physical numbness, the confirmation that yes, this is a powerful fucking thing he's putting into his body.

The lists are spread on either end of his dining table, printed from various websites. Wagstaff has found very few definitive facts about Ariel Pryce's life back when she was named Laurel Turner; the world was different then, not much was real-time documented online. But in the years since, some useful things have been digitized: the old membership roll of a private club to which she belonged; a list of patrons of a historical society where she was among the Platinum Donors Circle; a literacy organization whose annual gala made the society pages of Wagstaff's very employer, with a red-carpet photo of Mr. and Mrs. Buckingham Turner plus another couple, the four of them looking as glamorous as movie stars. It's hard for Pete to reconcile the young long-haired Laurel Turner in that photo with the frantic middle-aged Ariel Pryce here in Lisbon. It's not the physical differences so much as everything, the whole package, that makes them seem like completely different people.

These three lists are all that Wagstaff could find of Laurel Turner's participation in New York society. The names on these rolls were her friends and acquaintances, her world, the women she lunched with, the husbands she flirted with.

The husbands, of course, are the point.

Buckingham Turner, on the other hand, is an extremely visible person these days, with an exponentially larger archive of photos and lists — boards of directors, club rosters, alumni gatherings, reunions, weddings, social-media connections. It's easy to chart the social web of a man like this, at a moment like this.

Not his ex-wife. She has obviously gone out of her way to keep a low profile. Nonexistent.

His and her lists are on the left side of the table: these were the possible men in Laurel Turner's life a decade and a half ago. On the right side, Wagstaff has compiled lists from contemporary DC: the administration from the president down through a few layers of senior staff; the top echelons of the CIA and the FBI; every member of the Senate and House; every cabinet secretary and undersecretary. Only the men, of course. These are the possible people whom Pryce extorted for the ransom.

Wagstaff surveys this hastily secured territory, a landscape of perhaps a thousand names. Now it's time to start heading in the other direction, to winnow these lists. When that's eventually finished, he'll look for the overlap between the left side of the table and the right. The anticipation is delectable. How many names will there be? A dozen? Two dozen? A hundred?

He does another line.

The crowds have thinned but not disappeared, there are cars and mopeds driving around, people are drinking and smoking and laughing, hanging out in the square, loitering in front of the entrance to a dance club. Lisbon is a late place, even on a Tuesday night.

"There," Ariel says, and John sees it too, and raises his hand, and yells, "Taxi!" One of the few words that's the same in English and Portuguese.

"Time Out Market, *por favor.*"

As they settle into the backseat, Ariel keeps her eye on the CIA car that's parked on the far side of the square. Sure enough, the sedan pulls out of its parking space, not even trying to be subtle. Ariel continues to examine other vehicles, all around the square, and just before the taxi turns the corner she sees it.

Crap. She was hoping it was just the CIA who'd be watching, but it looks like the Lisbon police are still at it too. Which confirms to Ariel that she and John are making the right choice. It's always satisfying to get positive feedback immediately, even for bad news. At least you verify that you were right.

On the other hand, this will make it that much harder to execute the plan. And that much more crucial to succeed.

"Can you wait around this corner? Five minutes." John holds up his hand, five fingers extended.

The taxi driver looks dubious. Ariel extracts a hundred-euro note, rips it in two, extends one half toward him. "The other half when we return."

The driver nods, takes the half-note.

Ariel and John walk into the market, big

and loud and packed with people lined up at dozens of food stands to order tapas and croquettes, stews and pastas, burgers and sandwiches, beer and wine and white port spritzes, cakes and pastries and chocolates and ice cream, hundreds of people carrying trays and glasses and plates, it's a madhouse that Ariel and John are rushing through, and then around a corner and into the busy corridor where Ariel drops her mobile into a garbage can and then they exit through a side door, around the building quickly, back into the still-waiting taxi —

"Teatro Nacional, *por favor,* rua Duques de Bragança."

Ariel doesn't see any trace of the CIA car, nor the police, nor anyone else who seems to be watching. But that doesn't mean that they aren't there. It might just mean that they're better at hiding.

And then she does see something, a familiar-looking woman sitting on a moped around the corner, talking into a mic dangling from earbuds, and Ariel senses other movement from another direction, and swivels her head around until she sees another car pulling away from another curb.

"Damn," she mutters, and then to the driver, *"Rápido, por favor,"* guessing at the Portuguese, hoping that even if she's not completely right, she's close enough, which is usually good enough.

■ ■ ■ ■

"Oh Christ." Griffiths spins her moped in a tight circle. "Jefferson, do not lose them." She too is riding a moped. For surveillance in a place like Lisbon, there's nothing better.

"Guido, where the fuck are you?"

"Still in the market. Go ahead without me. Note that you've got company."

"Lisbon police?"

"I think so. At least two plainclothes in a car, and one uniform tracking on foot."

"Good God."

Three cops, in the middle of the night, vehicular pursuit — that's a lot of manpower — and suddenly Griffiths has an epiphany that her mission just tilted on its axis: There's no fucking way she can allow the Portuguese police to arrest Ariel Pryce and John Wright.

She accelerates up the hill.

"Obrigada."

Ariel tosses the other half-hundred over the seat, then she and John spring out of the taxi. She glances back down the one-way street, and sees the same silver car in pursuit, followed by the same moped.

On the right side of the street, a stone staircase leads down to the national theater and a broad plaza; on the left, stairs lead up to a different street, a one-way in the other

478

direction. These are the stairs that Ariel and John sprint up, taking two steps at a time.

"Hurry," she urges him as they reach the top step, and "This way" as they turn left, quickly out of sight to whoever's pursuing below, and directly into the roomy backseat of the waiting Mercedes, which pulls away from the curb even while John is still pulling the door closed, speeding down the street, around one corner and then another and then accelerating on a straight wide street.

"Okay?" asks the driver, the same man who drove them from the airport on Saturday morning, forever ago. This is the person Ariel called from the balcony, confirming the pickup for twelve-fifteen A.M. that she'd arranged earlier, but changing the location. And the destination.

"It will be a long drive," she'd said. "Four hours? Something like that."

"Yes, that is long. To where, please?"

"Five hundred euros," Ariel answered. "In cash. Plus we pay for the petrol and tolls."

She imagined the driver debating with himself, maybe whether to negotiate, and if so for what; maybe whether to do this at all, whether these Americans were criminals, whether this might be dangerous, or illegal, or both. On the other hand: Five hundred euros, tax-free, was a lot of money. So maybe it would be better to not ask any questions. Maybe that's always the case.

Ariel was prepared to pay more, if necessary. Whatever it took to get out of there.

"Okay," he'd said.

"Can you be waiting at midnight? We might arrive early." Ariel wanted to make sure that the driver wouldn't be late.

Now she leans across the seat, and places the five hundred euros on the center console. The driver glances down at the green bills. "Where, please?"

"Just go straight," Ariel says. "I'll let you know what to do when you need to do it."

He nods repeatedly, as if this is a good idea. As if he too is happy to operate on a need-to-know basis. Plausible deniability.

Ariel watches the late-night streets fly by, and within minutes they're ascending the longest bridge in Europe. She keeps turning to look out the rear windshield, expecting to see blinking lights closing in.

They're not out of the woods yet. Maybe never will be.

"No no *no*. Tell me this did not just happen."

Griffiths is standing astride her moped, facing the wrong way on the one-way street that she just sped down rapidly, dangerously, illegally, and all to no avail: There's no sign of the Americans.

"Where the hell could they have gone?"

Jefferson has abandoned her bike, is walking quickly up the lively street, busy restaurants and bars, people everywhere. "Any-where," she says into her mic. "There are thousands of places they can be. They could also have gotten into another car."

"Fuck. And their devices are still in the market?"

It's Antonucci who answers. "Yup. Ditched somewhere."

No phones, no luggage, no computers. Which means that not only have they fled, but they did it expecting that they were being watched. Expecting to be chased.

"Jefferson, let's you and me keep looking around here. Guido, get yourself to the airport. If they show up, call me immediately."

"What about Mazagón and Cádiz?" The ferries to the Canary Islands.

"I think not. Then they'd be trapped in the Canaries, which isn't any closer to the States, and isn't a particularly easy place to hide. But Tangier is another story. A quick trip, at the end of which they can disappear in Africa. So let's alert Rabat to be on the lookout."

"Okay. But why don't we just let them go?"

It's a good question; she can understand how it would seem like a reasonable option to Antonucci. Griffiths doesn't want to explain the whole thing to him, her whole array of fears. And she doesn't need to. Guido works for her. But she doesn't want to be imperious about it.

481

"It's a matter of national security," she says, which has the benefit of being true.

CHAPTER 41

Day 3. 2:00 a.m.

This time Ariel does need an alarm. The new phone trills and vibrates an unfamiliar sequence, jarring Ariel awake, and for a second she doesn't know where the phone is, or even what it is, then she finds the thing lying on her stomach, and turns it off, and tries to get her bearings.

John stirs, but doesn't open his eyes.

Ariel looks out the window. "Are we still in Portugal?"

"Five more kilometers," the driver says.

"When we cross the border, continue on the A-5. When we approach Mérida, please wake me up."

John shifts position, but remains asleep. Ariel hasn't been in the backseat like this with a man in — what? — maybe never. The last time she got into a car with a man for a long drive was fourteen years ago. Or at least she'd expected it to be a long drive, just like she'd expected it to be a long marriage. Both turned out to be brief.

"What?" Bucky glanced at Ariel, then back to the road. "What did you just say?"

They were in stop-and-go traffic on the Montauk Highway, short bursts of movement that interrupted long stretches of crawling. It was going to be an interminable drive to the city, three and a half hours, maybe four. Ariel had waited a few minutes after they got in the car, for no reason other than to delay starting this conversation she didn't want to have. But she knew that with each passing minute it was going to get harder, and eventually impossible. So she jumped in without looking down, and blurted it out, too fast and too unexpected for Bucky to absorb.

She took a very deep, very long breath, and started again: "Last night. I went to the bathroom, and Charlie barged in, and locked the door, and raped me."

"Oh my God." Bucky flicked his eyes to her again, longer this time. "I'm so sorry. Here, let me pull over."

"No," Ariel objected. "Traffic is only getting worse. Keep driving."

Ariel wanted Bucky to need to face the windshield instead of staring at all her humiliation, all her pain. She didn't want anyone, even her husband, to see all that. Ariel of course expected Bucky's full support, but

484

empathy is not the same thing as sympathy, and she was worried that the space between the two might get filled by something poisonous.

"Are you okay?"

"No," she said. "Not really."

"And by *raped,* you mean . . . ?"

Ariel took another deep breath to steady herself, but it didn't do much good. "I mean he forced his penis into my vagina, again and again, until he ejaculated. *Inside of me.*"

She stopped trying to fight back the tears.

"My God. When?"

When? "During dessert."

Ariel had a sinking new feeling, in addition to all the other unbearable emotions that had been coursing through her. There was something about Bucky's demeanor that seemed both very wrong and very familiar.

"Why didn't you tell me before?"

"I didn't tell you last night because you were plastered, and I didn't think we'd be able to have a productive conversation, and I didn't want to have a nonsensical one with a drunk. Then this morning you left before I was awake, then you brought home those people for lunch, then we rushed to pack, and now here we are, and I've told you, so can you stop asking about the *logistics* of my *reporting* to you of this sexual assault committed by your friend against your *wife*?"

"I'm sorry. I'm . . . shocked. I'm horrified,

485

is what I am."

She was on the verge of completely losing it.

"I'm so sorry," he said again, tentatively. Ariel was worried about all this apologizing. Like "thoughts and prayers," it's what people say when what they plan to do is nothing.

"I'm not getting a very supportive vibe from you, Bucky."

"I'm sorry," yet again. "So what do you want to do?"

That's when it hit her, the reason for her déjà vu: her father. *You,* not *we.*

"I think we need to go to the police," Ariel said.

Bucky glanced at her quickly, then said, *"Mmm."*

Ariel could tell that her husband was doing calculations, A to B to C, what Z looks like, for him. Bucky wouldn't find any of those destinations acceptable. He didn't want to say this aloud, but it was written all over his face. All over his silence.

She turned away, disgusted. You can't know how horrible someone is until they're given an opportunity to be horrible. In a privileged life such as Bucky's — or for that matter hers — such an opportunity can take a long while to materialize. Maybe a lifetime. Maybe never.

"I don't know what to think here," he said.

Here was Bucky's opportunity, right now.

Ariel realized this with a sickening thud: She'd married a terrible person, and this was the proof.

"What to *think*?"

Her tears stopped. Her sadness was replaced instantly with fury, which had been lurking just beneath the surface, ready to take over.

"Are you kidding me? Tell me, Bucky — *please* tell me — what it is you think you're debating?"

Ariel stared at him, waiting for an answer.

"I . . ."

Just like that, she made her decision, and in an instant her mind was shifting gears, trying to identify Route 27 landmarks, to figure out where she was in relation to train stations, bus stops, friends' houses. Later Ariel understood how she'd been able to make her decision so fast: because she'd actually made it much earlier. But she'd been hoping to go her whole life pretending she didn't know that Bucky was a terrible person, hoping to never confront the evidence. Even though she was almost certain it was there, somewhere. Here.

The car was crawling at five miles per hour. Up ahead, red taillights were blinking on, headed their way, like a synchronized light show titled Traffic Jam. In a few seconds the standstill would arrive, and Bucky would bring their black Range Rover to a stop.

487

There, that restaurant on the other side of the highway: Ariel knew exactly where they were. She grabbed her wallet from the center console.

"What are you doing?"

She yanked on the door handle, but it was locked.

"Ariel?"

She punched UNLOCK.

"What are —"

She pulled again, and this time the door swung open. The car was still moving, barely. "Stop the car," she said.

"You can't —"

"Stop the car, Bucky, right now." She jumped out, left the door wide open.

"Come on, Ariel. Don't be —" He stopped before he could find an acceptable insult. At that moment, none was acceptable; at least he had the sense to realize it. Bucky may have just proven himself to be horrible, but he wasn't lacking in the self-preservation instinct, and he wasn't stupid.

Ariel yanked open the back door and grabbed her weekend bag. She left that door open too, and walked away from the hulking black car stopped in the middle of a traffic jam on Route 27. There was no way he'd be able to follow her, not on foot, nor in the car.

She never wanted to see Bucky again. Nor of course Charlie Wolfe, especially him, but she did. Painful but necessary, like surgery, with a long, agonizing recovery. A whole lifetime of it.

"Hey," her husband called after her. "Let's —"

"Oh fuck you, Bucky."

Wagstaff stands there admiring the lists spread across his dining table, nodding in appreciation. There are a lot of names.

"Okay," he mutters, "now let's get rid of some of you fellas."

He picks up a red pencil, and starts to run lines through one after another after another: too old, too young, too poor, too gay. It's a lot of names that he crosses off, but there are still a lot left. He switches to blue pencil to run lines through most of the names that remain: men who fifteen years ago were not part of New York society. Congressmen from Texas, CEOs in the Midwest, Silicon Valley venture capitalists. Wagstaff very well may need to walk this back: just because a man didn't live in New York doesn't mean Ariel didn't conceive a child with him. It's just less likely.

Wagstaff is working quickly, making assumptions that may not hold up later, under scrutiny, or sobriety. But his standard is not reasonable doubt; this is not a court of law. All he wants is to quickly identify the most likely possibilities — the low-hanging fruit — and examine those men closely.

He's irrationally confident that this is going to work. Probably because of the cocaine. Which is what makes cocaine so damn constructive: It can keep you up all night, doing something that may not be completely rational.

He does another line. He doesn't kid himself that this one is small.

The CIA's chief of Lisbon station picks up before the first ring is even completed. She's expecting this call.

"Good evening," Nicole Griffiths says. It's the middle of the night in Portugal, but it's just after dinner on the East Coast. Griffiths is already dressed for tomorrow, showered, fresh clothes, passable makeup. She can't imagine any scenario that will allow her to get any real sleep tonight. The most she can hope for is a catnap on her office couch.

"So I've been briefed," Jim Farragut says. "Any new developments in the past two hours?"

"No. The woman and her husband are still at large. By this point they could be anywhere in Portugal, or over the border into Spain. They might be headed to a ferry to Tangier, or a flight from Spain."

"Or hiding somewhere?"

"Maybe. But she has a kid she probably wants to get back to."

"How old?"

"Thirteen."

"Thirteen-year-olds aren't necessarily good company."

"I wouldn't know. But surely even an annoying tween is still a priority."

Griffiths suspects that they're just beating around the bush. Where Pryce and Wright travel, or hide, or how they're interrogated, or when, or by whom: None of this really matters compared to the massive clusterfuck of the fundamental problem.

"Are you *positive* about the identity of the man who supplied the ransom?"

"Not one hundred percent. But have you heard the recording of the call?"

"Yes."

"Well, in addition to the recognizable voice, there's the geolocation of that call, made by the hastily purchased burner in DC to the secure line here in Lisbon, in a conversation that was obviously extortion, under threat of revealing a damaging secret. There's the fact that the burner was purchased by a direct employee of his. That someone provided this Pryce woman with a large amount of cash, on short notice, secretly. That he and Pryce definitely had a personal relationship long ago; that he and the woman's first husband had a business relationship."

"That's a lot of circumstance. But none of that is *proof.*"

"Correct, we have not found a smoking

gun. Not yet. Which doesn't mean that it doesn't exist. Also doesn't mean that no one else has found it. Remember, we've been aware of this situation for only a few hours."

"How many people are in the loop?"

"Here? My circle is small." Griffiths doesn't want to give an exact number. If she tells the director of operations, he might be obliged to tell his boss, who would tell his boss.

"But there's a lot of evidence out there," she continues. "And this evidence is not deeply buried intelligence material. The FBI can find all this too, even the DC cops. Or for that matter the media. In fact maybe they already have. There's at least one journalist on the case, who I believe was leaked some details from one of ours, a half-wit in consular."

"Oh for the love of God."

It doesn't escape Griffiths's notice that the director hasn't asked her for the name of the journalist, nor of the half-wit. These are both good signs. She can hear in the silence that Farragut is weighing his unpalatable options. He's a career intelligence officer, but his boss is a political appointee who has made it clear that his allegiance is not to the CIA that he runs, but to the president who appointed him. If the CIA's intelligence interests and the president's political interests diverge, the DCI is unlikely to side with intelligence.

For the president and the director, this intel

will be very, very unwelcome. The compulsion might arise to shoot the messenger, as well as anyone who happens to be messenger-adjacent. This is definitely a shoot-the-messenger type of administration.

"Can this be shut down?" Farragut asks.

Even before Griffiths placed the call that led to this one, she'd known that this question was coming. She'd already thought this through.

"Ariel Pryce has made a lot of noise here in Lisbon — local police, consular, reporter, plus who knows how many other stray witnesses, hotel employees, taxi drivers. Some of these people can be controlled; obviously we can gag our own employees. And the local police have a finite mandate; we could probably shut them down if they wandered too far. But the reporter."

She doesn't need to say this aloud: The reporter could not be silenced. The CIA could yell "national security!" at reporters all day long, and they'd just yell back "First Amendment!" Even the threat of jail wouldn't be a sufficient deterrent. The solution to the journalist would need to be less public, more drastic, immediate, illegal, and completely unacceptable to Griffiths. Hopefully to Farragut as well. But not necessarily to the people who can give them both orders.

Griffiths pictures Jim Farragut sitting in some wood-paneled Georgetown study, diagramming how the web of revelations might spin outward — consular to journalist to sources to editor to publisher to producer to on-air news reports, social media, NP-fucking-R: everyone on the planet. It could happen fast, beyond anyone's control.

"What do you think is the nightmare scenario, Griffiths?"

"That's a good question," she says. "That depends: for whom?"

"Touché. I guess for the United States."

This answer is absolutely clear to Griffiths. It's why she got on the phone to drag her boss's boss out of a July Fourth dinner party.

"The nightmare scenario is that we pretend we don't know what we just learned, and instead quash this intel, or attempt to. But that doesn't make the underlying facts go away. So instead of this scandal coming out now, before it can do the nation any real harm, we'd instead be opening the door for the Russians or Chinese or North Koreans to exploit the same exact information a few years from now."

She can hear Farragut sigh.

"If you don't mind me saying?"

"Please go ahead."

"I can't actually imagine a *worse* scenario for our national security. Can you?"

"Is it possible that this, now, is already the setup by a hostile?"

This too is something Griffiths has been

494

considering. "Yes, I can definitely see this whole thing being stage-managed by Moscow."

"Do I hear a *but* in there?"

"But even if this whole kidnapping and ransom and phone calls et cetera — even if everything that has happened over the past days *has* been orchestrated by a hostile foreign power, or for that matter by an opposition domestic? Even if that's true? It doesn't change the original sin. It just changes the mechanism of how the punishment is being meted out, and by whom. The original sin, that's still exactly the same."

Farragut continues to mull it over. This is an important decision, ambushing him in the middle of his summer vacation.

"I need to ask," he says, "because I'm definitely going to get this question myself: Can *her* silence be achieved?"

"You mean with money? Paying her off?"

Farragut doesn't answer immediately. Then he says, "No."

Griffiths can see the path, Farragut to DCI, then DCI to the president. For an instant, she considers lying. But that's not a rational option here.

"As far as I know, there are no eyewitnesses. Pryce claims that she has evidence — which we believe is an illicitly recorded private conversation with Wolfe — but we don't know if that's true. If it is, she hasn't indicated that there's anyone else in possession of this evidence, nor that there's any fail-safe that would trigger the release of the evidence in the event of her demise. If either were the case, I think she'd have mentioned it, to guarantee her security. She hasn't."

"And if this evidence did somehow emerge, independent of her?"

"Without her around to authenticate it, it would be pretty easy to discredit. That is, again, if the evidence truly exists, and if it survives her. It's also possible that she's bluffing."

"Has she taken any protective measures?"

"It doesn't look like it."

"So." He pauses. "What would our options be? I'm not advocating. But I need to be able to answer the question."

"Well, *if* we find her?" Griffiths also pauses, allowing this to sink in: Locating Pryce may not be that easy. Especially if the worst-case scenario is true, and this operation has been orchestrated by a foreign entity. At this moment Pryce could already be safe and sound on a private jet en route to Moscow.

"Then we could make her disappear somewhere in Spain. Or she could be found dead in Lisbon. Or she could go home to America, then commit suicide sometime soon. All those scenarios would be plausible given the recent events. But I do have to reiterate: The horse has already left the barn. Where there's one reporter, there will be more."

"Reporters?" Farragut snorts.

Griffiths knows that of course the director is right about this: Reportage doesn't mean what it used to. People already believe what they believe, and these days they go to the media to assure them that they're right, not to learn otherwise.

"But the fact still exists," she says. "And someone else will eventually find it. Getting rid of Pryce doesn't solve that problem."

Farragut takes another long pause before asking, "Doesn't it?"

He's right again. Killing Ariel Pryce might, in fact, solve the problem.

"Are you sure, Griffiths?"

It's just after four A.M. when Wagstaff draws the final blue line through the final list. He has now ruled out ninety-nine percent of these men. On the right side of the table, there are just a dozen names from present-day Washington that aren't crossed out; on the left side, twice as many New York names from a decade and a half ago. This has turned into a satisfyingly small universe of possibilities.

Wagstaff reminds himself that this strategy is still a long shot. He knew it when he started, knew it in the middle, he knows it now that he has come to the end: This is not a reliable method of ID'ing the perpetrator of a crime.

But that doesn't mean it won't work.

Wagstaff reads all the names that haven't been crossed out, then takes a quick second pass. He feels his pulse quicken. It isn't from the cocaine.

There are only four names that appear on both sides of the table. One of them is impossible to ignore.

CHAPTER 42

Day 3. 4:51 a.m.
The sun hasn't yet risen, but the Seville airport is already busy, as airports are in the final predawn hour, with commuters in business suits, and long-distance travelers embarking on first legs, and the bedraggled detritus of last night's missed connections, and the people who simply arrive everywhere way too early, vibrating with misdirected nervous energy.

"Are you sure about this?" Ariel asks.

"Yes," John says. "It's much better this way. Otherwise we'd be two Americans traveling together with no luggage, and me with this beat-up face. Even if the police are *not* searching for us, we'd look suspicious. Why risk it?"

He's right, Ariel thinks. But her brain seems to have stopped functioning properly, after working on overdrive for so long. "I don't know."

"I do. Trust me."

"Okay." Ariel nods. But she's suddenly panicked. "I'll see you at home?" It comes out more of a question than she intended.

John smiles. "Of course."

She turns to walk away, then feels a tug on her arm.

"Hey," he says.

"Yeah?" She half-turns back, meets his eye.

"I love you."

Ariel holds his gaze. Their relationship has been a continuing escalation of trust — that's what relationships are — and this is the apogee, isn't it?

"You know that, right?"

Ariel feels a lump in her throat. She hopes that this fear is completely irrational, caused by nothing except the bizarre circumstance. But she has learned to trust her sudden fears, all of them.

"I do," she says. "I love you too."

There are no direct flights across the Atlantic. Ariel's goal is to get on the earliest flight to the shortest layover to cross the ocean.

The ticket agent's nails clatter across the keyboard, and she glances from screen to passport and back, hits one key and waits, hits another and waits, and why in God's name is this so slow —

The agent rattles off a barrage of Spanish.

"Lo siento," Ariel says, *"no hablo español.* Do you speak English?"

"The first possible connection is in Amsterdam, but that is a very short layover, which you might miss, and then it would be another four hours there. The next possibility is Brussels, which is a longer layover, but much safer. Which do you prefer?"

Ariel feels like she has already made so many hard decisions, has kept her wits through so many individual steps, and she doesn't have any decisiveness left.

"Señora?" The clerk indicates the growing line of impatient customers. *"Por favor?"*

"The safer connection."

"Brussels?"

Is that what the agent had said? Does it even matter? "Yes."

More clicking and clacking and pounding and frowning. "Middle seat is okay?"

After another near-sleepless night, this one at a friend's empty house, Ariel called a taxi early on Monday morning, before she had a chance to change her mind.

"Where to?"

"The police station."

She sat in the back of the cab, considered the answers she'd give to the inevitable questions she didn't want to receive, today or tomorrow or in the future, in depositions and courtrooms, in front of large banks of microphones and cameras.

How many times did you say no? *About ten.*

501

But shouldn't once have been enough? Shouldn't zero times have been enough?

How much alcohol did you consume? *Less than one drink. But I'm curious: What number of drinks makes it okay to rape me?*

How short was your dress? *Short.*

Were you wearing a bra? *No.*

Do you always wear such revealing attire? *This is the type of thing that every woman wears to a summer party on a hot night.*

Were your nipples visible? *Probably.*

How many sexual partners have you had? *You mean consensual? That can't possibly matter. I've been raped by just this one, though a few others have tried.*

"Hey," Jefferson calls out. "I got something: Pryce just bought a ticket in the Seville airport. A flight to New York, connecting in Brussels, departing in just under two hours."

"Seville?" Nicole Griffiths sets a timer on her phone, presses START. She stands. "And the husband?"

"No records yet. Do we have anyone in Seville?"

"I don't think so," Griffiths says as they march down the quiet hall; at this hour they have the embassy to themselves. "No one who can handle this."

Griffiths raps on a door loudly, and waits a couple of seconds before opening the door to see Antonucci rubbing his eyes, but still lying down. His beaten-up face looks even worse after another night of swelling.

"We're going to Spain," Griffiths says.

"Can I have five minutes?"

"You can have one."

"Charlie Wolfe?" The policeman squinted at Ariel. "*The* Charlie Wolfe?"

This was already off to a bad start. "That's right."

"You're saying that Charlie Wolfe, uh, assaulted you? Sexually?" At the time, Charlie wasn't yet famous, not in the *New York Times* sense, the *People* magazine sense. But definitely in the *Hamptons* magazine sense. They were in the Hamptons.

"Yes."

"At his party? On Saturday night?"

"Correct."

"We had someone there . . . I think it was Flintie."

"You mean a police officer was actually at this party where I was assaulted?"

"Well, not *at* the party. But for events such as Mr. Wolfe's, with the celebrities, the bigwigs, we assign someone to hang around. Not like in the *driveway,* which might, y'know, alarm guests. But in a nearby spot, to dissuade troublemakers. Or to intervene in any trouble that isn't, um, dissuaded."

"I see. Well, Saturday night's troublemaker

was the host, and the trouble was rape, and Flintie's presence didn't dissuade it."

Officer Pulaski stared at Ariel, then exhaled long and slow, trying to figure out how to respond. What he came up with was, "Oh boy."

Ariel had asked to see a female cop, but there were apparently none on duty who could've taken her statement.

"Are you sure?"

"Am I sure what? That he raped me?"

"That the sex you had was, um, *nonconsensual.*"

"I'm positive."

"And you're sure that it was Mr. Wolfe?"

"Absolutely."

"You know him?"

"I've known him for years, I've seen him on dozens of occasions. He does business with my husband."

"Oh boy." Pulaski was shaking his head while writing. Then he put his pen down, and took a deep breath, and looked up again at Ariel. "Before we take another step, I need to ask something."

"Yeah?"

"Are you sure you really want to do this?"

She absolutely did not want to do this. Of course she didn't, for many reasons, and here was one of them: She didn't want to confront one man after another, men in authority who'd be skeptical of her claim — skeptical that it was nonconsensual, skeptical that it was sex, skeptical that it was Charlie. She did not want to pollute the pond she swam in, a pond in which Charlie was one of the biggest fish. She did not want to make enemies of Charlie's friends, their wives, people she'd need to see day in and day out, the hush when she'd enter a room, the turned heads, the whispers. She already felt like an outsider, nibbling at the edges of society; her status wouldn't survive this. She'd be ostracized.

So no, she did not want to do this. But was it really an option to do nothing?

Ariel didn't know what she was going to do about her husband, about her whole life, about what type of person she was going to be, and not be. But she did know that if there'd ever be any hope of prosecuting Charlie Wolfe, at any point, she needed to make this report today, and undergo the rape kit to preserve the physical evidence — the evidence of her own body, the evidence of his.

She was no stranger to the statistics. She knew that at the very moment when Charlie Wolfe was assaulting her, the same violent crime was being committed against hundreds or thousands of other women across the United States, to fifteen-year-olds and fifty-year-olds, to white women and Black women and rich women and poor women, to straight women and gay women and women who aren't sure, to drunk women and sober women, to women who'd smoked pot and women who'd been roofied, women at frat parties and house parties and pool parties and birthday parties, women on futons and love seats and the backseats of Honda Accords, all across the country, more than three hundred thousand American women are raped every single year, more than the total number of US soldiers killed since the end of World War II — in Korea, in Vietnam, in Afghanistan, in Iraq, in every armed conflict, combined. A forever war, and these are the casualties. Ariel is one of them.

Somebody needed to do something about this. In fact, everybody needed to do something about this.

"No," Ariel said. "I definitely don't want to do this. But I have to, don't I?"

"This is the dress you were wearing?" the nurse asked Ariel, who'd had the presence of mind to bring along the clothing she'd worn on Saturday night. The dress was rolled up tight in a Ziploc, where it looked tiny, could be a handkerchief in there. Her panties barely anything, not much more than some shoelaces.

"Anything else?"

She shook her head. "It was hot."

"Men don't rape women because of clothes," the nurse said. "You don't need to justify yourself."

Ariel nodded.

"Not to me," the nurse added. Ariel knew exactly what she meant.

"Have you had consensual sex in the past seventy-two hours?"

Seventy-two? This was Monday morning, so seventy-two hours ago was — when? — Friday morning. So Friday night was within that window.

"Yes."

Ariel could see the nurse's pause, her pen hovering over the paper before moving to a slightly different spot. This had not been the right answer.

"Antibiotic, in case of sexually transmitted disease."

The sexual assault forensic examination was finally coming to an end. There had been swabs and dyes, blood test and urine, vaginal exam and rectal, fluids and tissues, this exam had gone on forever, poked and probed, cold hard instruments and cold dispassionate assessments, Ariel's humiliation rising and falling and rising again, reporting and then waiting and then repeating her story, describing her injuries, physical and psychological, her movements, her actions.

She hadn't expected this to be an all-day trauma of one intrusion after another. But then again she hadn't known what to expect;

this type of day is not something you think about until you undergo it, it's not an experience you sit around wondering about.

"And this is a morning-after pill."

"Oh," Ariel said, surprised. She wanted to decline, but she was worried about how that would look. She didn't want to give any more wrong answers. "Oh," she said again, accepting the pill, already planning how she'd throw it away.

Ariel hadn't felt good about any of that — not the cop's questions, nor the nurse's, nor her own answers. Every side has a story — he said, she said — but criminal trials hinge on evidence. Was there evidence to support her story?

She felt a panic attack coming on, and tried to take deep breaths, to control her body. Something you think is entirely yours to control, and you assume that all the choices are up to you, then you learn that you're wrong. The choices are not yours. Neither is the control.

She looks around the airport security area, and can't see John anywhere. He'd waited in line at a different counter, bought a seat on a different flight, maybe went through security at a different checkpoint. He might still be negotiating options with a ticket agent, or he might already be rushing to catch the Amsterdam flight. Ariel doesn't know, and she has

508

no way of contacting him. Radio silence.

John was right: She felt naked in this security line without any luggage, not even a handbag. She isn't looking at her phone because she doesn't have one; no headphones around her neck. Not even a paperback in hand. Not even a newspaper.

Ariel can feel the security guard taking her in, the whole package, all the things that are missing. He waves her ahead, and she leads with her documents, which the officer carefully examines. He inserts the passport into a scanner. Turns over her boarding pass, then looks at her. "No bags?"

Ariel shakes her head. She doesn't trust herself to speak.

"Por qué?"

"They were stolen."

"I am very sorry. Where did this happen?"

"From the cloakroom of our hotel."

"Our hotel?"

Fuck. That was a mistake.

The guard looks past Ariel to the other waiting travelers. "Are you traveling with someone?"

"No." Should she explain about her husband? No, she shouldn't get bogged down in any explanations. "No," she says again.

"Did you report this to the police?"

She shakes her head.

"It is very important to report crimes. For the records."

"Yes, I agree. But I didn't want to waste the time."

Ariel can feel this man's dubious gaze on her, and then he turns away, back to his keyboard, his monitor. Sometimes men are dubious of a woman simply because they're sexist assholes. Sometimes, though, it's because the woman is lying through her teeth.

"I've had a very bad trip," she says. "I just want it to end."

The man looks at her and nods, but doesn't seem to be agreeing, and then suddenly there are two policemen standing beside her, bulletproof vests, tactical rifles strapped across their chests.

"Señora?"

After the hospital, Ariel returned to her friend Jenny's unoccupied house, immediately fell apart, and stayed that way for days on end, barely eating, sleeping all the time but never soundly and never rested, angry at everything, including herself.

Then the weekend loomed. Jenny would be returning with her adoring husband and loud little kids. "You're welcome to stay, there's plenty of room." But Ariel couldn't stand the thought of being with other people. So she locked up the house, returned the key to its hiding spot in the herb bed, and took a taxi to the railroad to the city. She checked herself into a hotel, then promptly emptied their joint checking account before Bucky could consider shutting her out. Who knew how he was going to respond to her flight, her silence, her refusal to even take his calls. She'd have to talk to him sooner or later, but she just couldn't bear it. Not yet.

Ariel knew that this small pile of cash wasn't going to last forever. She'd still need to find a new place to live and furnish it; even if secondhand and yard-sale, this wouldn't be free. Groceries, utilities, she needed to buy a car, fill it with gas, one thing after another, the expenses would add up quickly, over-whelmingly, and Ariel's journey from wealthy housewife to single, unemployed, and penni-less would be very short. And on the near horizon, all sorts of new expenses were loom-ing. And they'd last for decades.

She needed a plan.

To the purely daytime denizens of a town, the late-night ecosystem of restaurants and bars can be unrecognizable, a whole scene of service-industry employees plus the drunks and hustlers and drug dealers and trouble-makers who come out when the respectable citizens go home.

It's eleven at night when Persephone walks into the Sprit, named by the owners for some esoteric part of a boat, hoping to attract the sailing crowd. It worked.

Persephone kisses the hostess on the cheek.

"Hey Lea. How's your dad?"

"He's doing better, thanks for asking."

Persephone nods at Suze, who asks, "The usual?" while pulling a pint for someone else. Nearly all the bar seats are taken. For lunch and dinner, the Sprit is the town's sole fine-dining establishment — local, organic, hand-crafted, small-batch, all the blah-blah-blah that seduces the weekenders, the foodies, the bearded dudes studiously swirling their glasses of biodynamic wines, food bloggers staging their plates for Instagram, oohing and aahing over, what, pea broth.

"Hey," Persephone says, taking the seat saved by Kirsten's knockoff Coach bag, bought on Canal Street. They'd gone to the city together for that shopping expedition.

"Hey yourself."

Dinner service ends at eleven, which is when the other restaurants in town close, the ice cream parlor too, the liquor store, the pizza shop, the clam bar, the seafood shack out on the wharf. For ten miles in every direction, nearly everything closes at the same moment, discharging a whole population — cooks and servers, hostesses and bartenders, busboys and dishwashers — into the world with the night's tips in their pockets and steam to blow off and self-destructive habits to feed. Someone needs to take in all these people; someone needs to take their money.

That's the real source of the Sprit's recent

financial success. It's not the salad of heirloom beets with farmstand chèvre that appears on the cover of the local lifestyle magazine. It's this pint of IPA and shot of whiskey that Suze plunks in front of Persephone, and the hundreds of other drinks that'll be served in the hours between the last boat-shoed retiree's departure and last call, with baskets of fries and cheeseburgers and wings while loose pills and packets of smack and the occasional vial of crack are sold by Greg, who a decade ago was the football team's all-county defensive captain. Kirsten and Persephone had been co-editors of the yearbook, they were ones who put together the full-spread feature about Greg. Now look at him, slinking off to the bathroom. Now look at them.

"So?" Kirsten says. "I'm dying over here."

Persephone holds her whiskey in front of her face, then knocks it back. "Okay. But seriously: no way this can be traced back to me. You have to promise me, K. It's really important."

"I promise."

Persephone reaches into her back pocket while looking around at the other customers. As usual, Jerry the lawyer is staring down into a glass of brown.

"When you freak out, don't do it too loudly." Persephone nods in the lawyer's direction, then hands the folded-over papers to her oldest friend. They played grade-school soccer together, joined the middle-school literary magazine, ran the high-school paper. They both went off to college and grad school to become literary intellectuals; they both slunk home, treading the deep water of semi-adulthood.

"What am I looking at here?"

"That's a police report."

"Yeah I can see that. But who's this? Laurel Turner?"

"That, my friend, is the name of the person who's now known as Ariel Pryce."

Kirsten's mouth falls open. She turns a page, turns back. "This" — her voice lower — "is a fourteen-year-old report of sexual assault?"

Persephone nods.

"And her kid is how old?"

"That's right."

"Oh. My. God."

"But that's not all. In fact, that's not even the bombshell."

Kirsten is turning the pages, shaking her head, not seeing it.

"There," Persephone says, pointing. "That's the name of the alleged perpetrator."

"What the actual fuck? Are you serious?"

"Yes I am."

"Holy. Fucking. Shit."

CHAPTER 43

Day 3. 5:43 a.m.

Ariel can't for the life of her figure out what to say to these Spanish airport police. Her story seems too outlandish to even begin to explain, but she can't seem to come up with any alternative. She's worried that this failure of imagination means that her mind has stopped functioning. Too much stress, too much fear, not enough sleep.

"This is going to sound crazy," she begins, directing herself at the cop who seems to be in charge. Though maybe he's just the one who happens to speak English.

"On Monday morning, while on a business trip in Lisbon, my husband was kidnapped. I reported this to the Lisbon police, and to the American embassy, but there was nothing any of them could do. I was able to get the ransom from an acquaintance in America, and yesterday evening I gave the cash to the kidnappers, and my husband was released. We immediately returned to our hotel to give a statement to the police, but we felt very unsafe in Lisbon, and we didn't especially trust the police, who for all we knew were part of my husband's abduction."

"That is a very grave accusation."

"It's not an accusation. It's a concern. Maybe not a rational concern. But we'd undergone a deeply traumatic experience, and maybe we were not — are not — thinking clearly. We really just wanted to get out of Lisbon, home to America. So late last night, we left the hotel. We didn't take our luggage because we didn't want anyone who might be watching us to know we were leaving."

"Anyone who might be watching you? Such as?"

"Such as whoever kidnapped my husband."

"Why, señora, did you lie about the stolen luggages to the security officer?"

"Because as you just heard, the truth is complicated. I wanted to have a simple interaction."

"Why are you not with your husband?"

"We decided that it was safer to travel separately. To ensure that one of us, at least, would get home safely to my son."

"Where is he now, your husband?"

"I don't know. He was going to purchase a ticket on a different flight to New York."

"Here? In the Sevilla airport? On what airline?"

"I don't know."

"Please write down your husband's name. And his date of birth."

As Ariel does this, the spokesman cop leans over to whisper to the other cop, who nods in agreement, tears off Ariel's piece of paper, and leaves the room. The interrogator seems to be digesting Ariel's story, and doesn't seem to come to a definitive conclusion about its fishiness.

"If we are talking to the Lisbon police? Are they telling us the same story?"

"Definitely. Except they don't know that we don't trust them, of course." Ariel retrieves her wallet, extracts a small pile of business cards, shuffles through. "Here."

She puts Moniz's card on the table, then Santos's.

"These are the detectives investigating the case. They interviewed me and my husband last night. Please call either of them right now so we can clear this up. I have a flight to catch."

A few weeks after she returned to the city, Ariel walked out of the hotel on the Upper East Side where she'd been living, into the stifling humidity of late-afternoon August in New York City, the blacktop shimmering, the car exhaust suffocating, the surprising blasts of cold when shop doors opened, spilling their air-conditioning out onto Madison Avenue along with women carrying shopping bags filled with lingerie or bathing suits, makeup or sunglasses. It never ends, that job.

Ariel arrived early. She wanted to give herself time to collect her wits.

She took a seat at the far end of the long polished bar, votive candles and sprays of tea roses in little vases, barstools of supple chocolate leather, music an unobtrusive tinkle of unobjectionable jazz. Her regular drink here was a delicious *premier cru* Montrachet at twenty-eight dollars per glass, but now she asked for sparkling water, the little bubbles bursting on her tongue and a bit up her nostrils, a tickle from the bitter pith of lemon-peel garnish.

Her senses were heightened, her observations keen. She felt like a scientist, studying her environment. Studying herself.

A decade and a half later, swaths of that period of her life have become vague — whom she saw, how she passed her days, the therapy sessions, the lawyers, her whole life collapsing around her, all a blur. But one thing she remembers clearly is that afternoon. She remembers rehearsing the upcoming interaction dozens of times, preparing herself for a completely different level of negotiation than anything she'd ever before experienced, the irrelevancies of haggling with real-estate agents or job offers or flea markets: all those stakes piddling in comparison.

She chose not to face the front door. She

didn't want to be seen to be waiting for him; she didn't want to be perceived as anxious. Who was she kidding?

From where she sat, Ariel could see the reflection of the entryway through the mirror behind the bar. So she saw him arrive, nod to the hostess, and stride past the maître d' stand as if he owned the joint, wearing the confident smile of a man who had everything, the grown-up version of a boy who'd been promised anything, a person who'd been told again and again, all his life, that he could have whatever he wanted, do whatever he wanted.

Maybe his behavior should not have come as any surprise. Maybe it was foreseeable. Maybe, in fact, it was inevitable.

Charlie didn't know how to greet her. In the past, he would've kissed her on the cheek, holding her arm, or her elbow, or even the small of her back when he thought he could get away with it. He was that kind of handsy. But now he wouldn't dare.

He took the seat next to her, and her body recoiled from his, an involuntary reaction.

The bartender glided over instantly. Charlie Wolfe was a man who rarely waited for anything.

"What can I get for you tonight, Mr. Wolfe?"

Charlie waited an extra second before answering, a micro-pause, a little power play of making someone wait, even if just for a second, as a way of asserting dominance. This was the type of asshole that Charlie Wolfe was. Is.

"A glass of the Barolo, please, Danny. You know the one I like."

Ariel understood that this wine was not on the menu, not available by the glass, not unless you were a man like Charlie, a man who made it a point to ask for things — to demand things — that other people couldn't have, that it wouldn't even occur to them to request. That was the point, wasn't it? Charlie didn't give a damn about any Barolo. He just wanted to demand something expensive, something exclusive, something that proved how important he was.

"My pleasure, Mr. Wolfe."

Ariel still hadn't glanced his way, but she could feel him turn to her, expectant but silent.

"I don't want this to take longer than necessary," she said, staring straight ahead at the array of bottles backed up to the mirror, reflecting the large dining room, all those empty seats, no witnesses.

"Okay." His intonation suggested a lot of things: doubt, hostility, condescension.

"So I'll get right to it." She wanted to see his face when she said the next thing, so she turned to him, and her stomach immediately roiled, she just barely avoided retching. This was the first time Ariel had seen Charlie since he'd raped her, and no matter what she told herself about her control, her advantage, her safety in this public space, her body was telling her different.

She'd expected this confrontation to be difficult in ways that she couldn't expect, and this, apparently, was one of them.

Ariel clenched her jaw, swallowed her nausea, and forged ahead.

"I'm pregnant."

Charlie's mouth did not fall open, his eyebrows did not raise, he did not react in any way. It was impressive, really. She almost admired his self-control. Almost. But what she really felt was revulsion, and loathing, and a horrible type of envy. He could control his own body; he could even control hers. She could not.

She fought another wave of nausea.

The bartender placed a linen doily in front of Charlie, topped by a glass whose bowl was the size of a softball. Danny displayed the label for approval, then slowly poured an inch of the wine, a deep viscous purple, like the blood of some big game that had been hunted and gutted and taxidermied and presented with a flourish and a low groveling bow to the smug hunter. Danny wiped the mouth of the bottle with a towel, and began to retreat, concluding the spectacle of subservience.

"Thanks Danny." Charlie turned back to her. "And you think it's mine?"

"No," Ariel said. "I know it."

Charlie again chose not to respond. Instead he took a sip of wine, replaced the glass carefully to its doily. He looked like he was contemplating the Barolo, whether to judge it a 93 or 94. It was fake, this composure, it had to be. Ariel was positive that this person couldn't be this unflustered about this predicament. No one could.

What would make him more despicable? Real poise in this situation, or fake? Maybe it didn't make a difference. She already hated him to the maximum extent.

"How?" he asked.

"How what?"

"How do you *know*?"

"Do you not understand how human reproduction works?"

"How do you know that I'm the . . . ?" He seemed unable to finish the question. Unwilling.

"No one ever explained this to you?" she asked. "In health class? Or maybe your dad?"

Charlie nodded. Ariel understood this sort of nod, not one of agreement, but a signal of something else, an acceptance of disagreement, of antagonism.

"Okay then," he said, still nodding. "I'll tell you, point-blank: I do not believe you."

"Believe me?" Suddenly she had no more nausea. Now she felt her body rising to rage. "Oh I don't give a damn if you *believe* me.

522

That's the beauty of science, isn't it? It's not a question of belief."

She picked up her own glass, took a sip of water, leaving Charlie to ponder it. There was so much retrievable, identifiable DNA floating around in the world — on wineglasses and toothbrushes, combs and bathroom sinks, in the contents of rape kits, vaginal swabs, semen. She didn't need to explain any of this to him, and they both knew it.

Charlie often bragged about his broad experience negotiating. He studied tactics, he scripted conversations, he practiced in the mirror, he was always prepared to wait it out, to draw it out, to strike first, to do whatever it took, whatever would work, which sometimes was cutting directly to the chase. That's what he decided to do now: "What do you want?"

When you realize that you can't win, don't fight.

"I want you to go to jail."

Charlie took a measured breath through his nostrils, maybe on the verge of losing his meticulously maintained composure. He glanced around, making sure no one could overhear. It was barely five o'clock, too early for a crowd, but this restaurant was in the middle of their neighborhood, and you never knew. It would be easy to be noticed, and the possibility would make him uncomfortable. Which is exactly why Ariel had chosen this spot. Any advantage.

"Then why are you telling me this? What are we doing here?"

"Because I wanted to see the look on your face when you learned that your life was over." She grabbed her purse from the bar. "Sadly, it wasn't worth it. My drink's on you."

She moved her feet off the brass rail to the marble floor, shifted her weight, stood.

That's when he said, "Wait."

Ariel watches the second cop return to the room and exchange a few quick words in Spanish with his colleague, who then says, "Señora, there is no answer at the Lisbon police."

"Well, it's barely six in the morning."

She gets no response.

"Listen, what crime is it that you think I committed?"

"I do not think you committed any crime. But you are an unusual traveler. A person who lied to the police. A person who tells a story that is difficult to believe."

"Exactly: Wouldn't a criminal have a better story?"

This cop smiles indulgently, as if confronting a child who's offering an outrageous excuse for the broken lamp. Ariel can almost see his thought: *No, not if you're stupid.*

"You think I'm stupid, don't you? You think I'm a stupid criminal."

"Please, I do not think you are stupid. I do not think you are a criminal. But surely you can understand why we must verify an unlikely story such as yours?"

Griffiths looks out the helicopter window at dawn breaking over the Iberian Peninsula. "Updated ETA?"

"Touchdown at oh-six-fifty-five," the pilot answers.

"And that's where? How far from the passenger terminal?"

"About a kilometer."

"Do we have someone on the ground with a vehicle?"

"You asking me?" the pilot says.

"No," Jefferson jumps in.

"Then how are we going to get from the landing area to the terminal?"

"Run?"

Antonucci groans. He's not running a kilometer, not on his goddamned feet.

"Fuck," Griffiths says. "And her flight is boarding at seven-ten? We're not going to make it."

She tries to work out the shortest chain of communication from herself in this helicopter to a gate agent at the Seville airport at six-thirty on a weekday morning. It's not that short.

This is becoming a real pain in the ass.

Pete Wagstaff feels like a hypocrite. For years, he'd been so adamant that digitization of archives was an unethical, immoral, and even illegal infringement on his rights as a journalist. He remembers arguing passionately: None of us ever agreed to this, not the reporters nor the photographers nor the columnists, we never acceded that our employment terms granted such an open-ended, permanent exploitation in media that were not even yet contemplated. This argument with management did not do his career any favors.

But now, thanks to the digitized archives he so vehemently opposed, Wagstaff has discovered that in the months preceding the split between Laurel and Bucky Turner, their lives were documented with a half-dozen society-page photographs from three different parties, with captions naming a total of fifteen individuals. That's a lot of potential witnesses to the precipitous demise of a marriage. And what's more, with thanks again to the digital revolution, every single one of those potential witnesses is easily and instantly findable, all of them public figures of varying degrees, or at least the types of figures whose desire to be public makes them easy to contact. Wagstaff already has an email, phone number, or publicly accessible social-media profile for each.

And this photo here? This one is almost too good to be true. It's six people at a summer party, women in little dresses, men in pastel linens, captioned: FROM LEFT TO RIGHT, MR. AND MRS. BUCKINGHAM TURNER, MR. AND MRS. CHARLIE WOLFE, AND MR. AND MRS. SLADE WASSERMAN. Mrs. Wasserman's name is Tory. Her phone number and email address and social handles are all right here, on the contact page for her website: A TORY STORY — EXCLUSIVE STYLE CONSULTANT. Whatever that could mean. These days Wagstaff doesn't understand half the jobs people seem to have.

Charlie glanced around the near-empty restaurant, then back to Ariel. "Your phone, please?"

"What? Why?"

He glowered at her. He didn't want to say it aloud, but she understood why he was asking, and she knew that this was not unreasonable. She placed her Nokia on the bar.

"Unlock it, please."

She did. He examined the screen, then said, "Remove the battery." She did that too, but he wasn't satisfied. Charlie was paranoid about surreptitious recordings long before anyone knew to be worried about that. He was ahead of a lot of curves.

"Danny." He beckoned the bartender.

"We're going to sit at that table for a few minutes. Could I ask you to keep an eye on my friend's bag?"

"Of course," Danny answered without appearing to think twice, though of course he did, you'd have to be an imbecile not to, and imbeciles don't get to tend bar in establishments such as this. But bartenders here did whatever customers like Charlie Wolfe asked, because these were the types who'd get you fired. They'd say so first: "I'm going to get you fired." Men like Charlie loved saying this, even more than they loved actually getting people fired. It was the display of dominance that was so enjoyable. The dominance was irrelevant without the display.

Charlie examined Ariel, maybe wondering if she was wearing a wire, and what he could do about it. He definitely couldn't ask her to accompany him to the bathroom to check.

He strode across the room, slid into a banquette, far from the few other patrons, far from staff, far from her handbag, from any recording devices that might be hidden in there.

"What do you really want?"

"What do I *really* want?" Ariel feigned confusion, but they both knew what she wanted: to hurt him. She wanted him to suffer; she wanted to watch him suffer.

"Don't give me that shit." His voice was quiet but seething. This was something he

528

was good at. "You know what I'm asking."

She knew that she couldn't be so punitive that Charlie wouldn't be able to bear it, that he'd be forced to take his chances in the criminal-justice system. Everyone knows that guilty verdicts are elusive. Ariel's and Charlie's interests were aligned in this respect: neither wanted court.

"What do I want? Hmm, let's see: a minimum of five years. But I'm hoping more like —"

"Oh give me a fucking break."

"I'm sure — I'm *positive* — that once word gets out, once this story hits the newspapers, once people start gossiping — at this bar here, at the Colony Club, at the charcuterie counter at Eli's —"

"Quiet down."

"Once women start recognizing that this particular dam has a crack in it, others will come forward. Plenty of others."

He narrowed his eyes. "How much?"

"The dam will burst, Charlie, and the flood will be catastrophic. You know what happens to men like you in prison, right? You're a man of the world, I'm sure you've heard things."

"How. Much."

Ariel had done research, trying to estimate Charlie's net worth, his possible liquidity levels, to determine the most cash he'd be able to access without selling off long-term assets, the most he'd pay to avoid a highly

529

damaging, highly public spectacle. Ariel's accusation was not of some long-ago youthful "misunderstanding" involving "different recollections." No, this spectacle would be the very recent crime of raping his business associate's wife. His friend's wife. An accusation accompanied by fresh memories, supporting witnesses, physical evidence.

The sum needed to be something that Charlie would be able to access without disrupting his life — without telling his wife — or he might not agree to it. The number that Ariel came up with turned out to be pretty big.

"Five million dollars."

"Fi— ?" He shook his head. "You're out of your mind."

"Am I?" She watched closely as his eyes flickered up and away, then back to counteroffer.

"Two."

"Please." She kept her jaw clenched, maintained eye contact.

One second became two became ten became twenty, and she didn't make another sound. As if hiding in the closet from a murderer.

Finally he said, "Two-five."

She knew that she'd have to make a big concession; a man like Charlie would otherwise never be able to tolerate it, his ego couldn't handle a negotiation that he lost one hundred percent.

"Let's cut to the chase," she said. "Three is my minimum." She'd actually been prepared to accept two-five. But that was before he offered it.

Charlie glowered. It took all her self-control to sit silently, staring at him while he glared, ten seconds, twenty, maybe thirty or forty seconds, she lost track of time, she just kept waiting . . .

Until she won.

"You will obviously sign an NDA," he said.

Yes, obviously: Nondisclosure was the whole point for him, because disclosure was her leverage. At that moment in her life, the long-term ramifications of an NDA seemed irrelevant. Ariel wasn't looking past her immediate needs, the immediate retribution, the private her versus the private him. She didn't foresee a future in which the public would care, in which disclosure itself could become a priority. It never even occurred to her.

This was long before Harvey Weinstein, of course, before grab 'em by the pussy, #MeToo. Expectations of consequences were much dimmer, fourteen years ago; a different era. Hopes for recourse were much slimmer. Ariel had finite goals. This confrontation was just between the two of them, not a political matter, not an issue of national significance.

So she nodded her acceptance, and Charlie

immediately beckoned the bartender while reaching into his breast pocket for his wallet. "Thanks," Charlie said as Danny approached. "I must run. This is for the lady's drink as well."

The lady.

"Of course, Mr. Wolfe. I'll bring your change right over."

"Oh that's all right Danny, you keep it. Thanks."

What a saint.

"Thank *you,* Mr. Wolfe."

Ariel didn't need to look to know that it was a hundred-dollar bill. Charlie made special trips to banks to withdraw hundreds; this was before ATMs dispensed them anywhere except in casinos. Ariel knew this because Bucky did the same thing. The two men were more alike than she wanted to admit. They even looked the same — eyes, hair, shape of the nose. They could be brothers.

She could see a debate crossing Charlie's face. He knew that as soon as you get to yes, you're supposed to walk away, hang up, whatever: Don't risk ruining it. But he must have been fighting an opposite impulse — to insult her, to demean her, to belittle her, to argue with her. The impulse to not allow himself to lose. To not admit that he'd been dominated.

But he swallowed it. He turned and walked

away without another word. And Ariel finally allowed herself to exhale.

Three million dollars.

That was certainly enough for a whole new life. But the money itself wasn't true revenge, because it didn't hurt him. For some problems, money is the entire solution. For others, it's just the start.

Ariel had no expectation of true justice, not ever. Until one day, out of nowhere, she suddenly did.

CHAPTER 44

Day 3. 7:02 a.m.

"I'm begging. *Please.*" Ariel pointedly looks at her watch. "My flight is boarding."

"There will be other flights," the Spanish cop says. "New York City is not an unusual destination."

"But I need to get home to my *child.*"

"I am sure you will. As soon as we are able to talk with the Lisbon police."

The other policeman returns to the room, carrying the slip of paper with John's name and date of birth. He leans over, and the two cops confer in a whisper.

"What is it?" Ariel asks. "Did he speak to Detective Moniz?"

"No, señora. We have been trying to find your husband, but we cannot. He did not purchase a ticket."

Ariel wishes she could marshal some composure here, but she has expended all of it.

"He did not pass through the security

checkpoint."

There's nothing left but panic.

The phone rang long before António Moniz was willing to be awake. He glanced at the number — something from Spain — and hit DECLINE, and tried to go back to sleep, but failed. So he lay in bed and listened to the voicemail. His Spanish was not great, and he needed to repeat the message a couple of times before he was certain he understood: A national policeman at the Sevilla airport had detained an American named Ariel Pryce, who had provided Detective Moniz's name as a reference to verify her story. Could he please return the call as soon as possible?

Well, at least now António knew where the Americans had gone when they'd fled the hotel, eluded the patrolmen, and disappeared into the night.

Moniz trudges to the kitchen, prepares the percolator. While he's waiting for the water to boil, his phone rings again, a call from Santos, who launches right into it without any preamble. "Did you receive a call from a Spanish policeman?"

"A voicemail," he says.

"Me too. I was in the shower. One of us should call back."

"Yes, of course. I will take care of it."

"But what are you going to tell them, António?"

"I don't know. The truth?"

"Which truth?"

Moniz doesn't know what his partner is asking.

"Including our suspicions?"

Moniz doesn't answer.

"Then what?" Santos continues. "Are we going to request that the Spanish arrest John Wright? Extradite the American so we can pursue prosecution for fraudulent kidnapping? How do you think the Spaniards will respond?"

"I think they will be happy to agree."

"Oh yes they will agree, I am sure of that. I am also sure that they will be happy about it."

Moniz turns off the flame under the coffee. He pours a cup for himself, another for Julio.

"But first, António, there will be a few questions. They will ask: Why did you not detain the American yourselves, if you were so sure of his guilt? Why were you not monitoring John Wright? Then we will need to admit that in fact we were watching these Americans, but they eluded us."

Moniz carries one of the cups to the bedroom, and takes a moment to stare at his sleeping husband. Next weekend they will be celebrating their tenth anniversary with a big dinner at his younger sister's house out in Cascais near the beach. Catia married a rich banker, an ass of the very worst sort. But her homes in both the city and the country are spectacular, and Catia has not needed a job in a decade, and their little girl is an angel. Everyone compromises somewhere along the way. At least with Catia the benefits are abundant and obvious.

"Which is to say, António: We will be laughed at. By Spanish *airport security guards.*"

Santos is right. She is almost always right. But not quite as always as she thinks.

"It was very clever of John Wright to run to Spain," she concludes. "Very clever."

Moniz leaves the coffee on Julio's bedside table, and retreats quietly from the bedroom.

"So what do you propose?" he asks, though he is pretty sure he knows where Santos is going with this.

"The crime that seems to have been committed was by one American against his own American wife and another American who provided the ransom. This was, fundamentally, an American crime. No one here in Lisbon was hurt, there were no crimes against property here, no possibility of future law-breaking . . ."

Moniz is not surprised that Santos is choosing to cover her own ass. But he is surprised that she is willing to let an obviously guilty man walk free.

"I think there is not a lot of potential

benefit to the continued involvement of our department. Do you agree, António?"

After Charlie left the restaurant, Ariel took a minute to gather herself before setting off through Manhattan's sweltering streets to the hotel where she'd been living in limbo. That limbo just ended.

"My apologies, Mrs. Turner." This was Mustafah, the hotel's day manager, accosting her in the lobby. "Do you have a moment, please?"

"Of course."

They stepped out of the center of attention. "When we went to settle yesterday's charges, the credit card that we have on file was . . . um, I regret to say, it was declined."

Ariel was not surprised that Bucky had canceled the card; she knew that he had the potential to be a vindictive person. Bucky's ruthless swagger had been one of his appeals, back when she'd held vastly different ideas of what made a man appealing. And when they were first dating, there'd been something that seemed tongue-in-cheek about Bucky's bluster, as if he were self-consciously playing a role, with a little wink for Ariel. She'd loved that playfulness of his, that enthusiasm. Over time, though, his youthful skin of detached irony slowly molted away, until that final transformation in the car on the Montauk Highway, revealing his fully matured adult

538

skin. Impossible to misinterpret, impossible to ignore. Impossible to live with.

Since that aborted drive, Bucky had called her again and again, but she let a week go by before she trusted herself to talk to him. And even then she wanted it to be quick. Rip off the Band-Aid.

"I'm so, so sorry," Bucky began.

"What are you apologizing for? Do you even know?"

Once again he took too long to answer. "For not being more supportive."

Supportive. Listening. Appreciated. Bucky had learned a few catchwords along the way, probably from his friends, sitting in bars, laughing at the stupid shit they needed to tell their wives, to get the women off their backs.

There are many different ways to be a coward, Ariel thought, but Bucky's might be the worst. All of a sudden, she realized that she couldn't stand her husband anymore. It happened just like that, a spigot closed, no more affection.

"Bucky, you let me down in the worst possible way. At the exact moment when I needed you most. Do you understand that?"

"I do," he said, in a tone that meant he didn't. "How can I fix this?" As if maybe he could call a handyman, tip the guy a twenty to repair the marriage that Bucky had carelessly broken.

"I don't think you can, Bucky. And if you're

being honest with yourself: Do you really want to?"

"Of course I do. How can you ask that?"

Ariel had spent the week soul-searching. "I think, Bucky, that maybe you don't love me as much as you'd wanted to. And maybe I feel the same way."

"But —" he began to object, then ran out of steam. Maybe out of ideas.

"I'm sorry," she said, and immediately regretted it. She should not be the one who was apologizing. This was a habit she'd need to break. One of many.

Bucky didn't accept Ariel's reasoning, but there wasn't really anything he could do about her decision. He told her that he'd give her a few days to reconsider, then he'd try her again. He didn't.

That's when Ariel started to call around to the top divorce lawyers — or "matrimonial attorneys" as they kept correcting her, gently — who one after another reported the same thing: They were unable to consider representing her due to previous consultations with her husband. That's when she knew it would just be a matter of time before he cut off the financial support. Bucky could be charming and exciting, fun and friendly. But friendly is not the same thing as nice. Sometimes it's the opposite. Often.

She'd been living in this hotel whose nightly rate was as much as monthly rent on her new

540

apartment, in the new village to which she'd soon decamp, a modest home commensurate with her newly modest situation.

"I understand," Ariel told Mustafah. "I'll depart this evening."

She'd eventually have three million dollars, plus the stipend specified in her prenup with Bucky. But at that moment she had none of that money. She was very nearly broke, and the remaining distance would be closed very quickly. Last night was apparently the final one she'd be spending in New York City.

She handed Mustafah a credit card that predated her marriage, neither black nor platinum nor gold, no unlimited credit line, no access to status or perks, just the usurious interest and draconian penalties that create the type of crippling debt that crushes millions of ordinary struggling Americans, one essential purchase at a time. Ariel was now an ordinary struggling American.

"When's checkout?"

"It was noon, Mrs. Turner. But please, take whatever time you need."

"Thank you," she said. "For everything."

Ariel was a pregnant woman with no money and no assets and no skills and no job, leaving her coward of a husband. It had taken her a couple of weeks to muster the courage to tell her therapist about the assault, and since then it's all they'd worked on, extra sessions, extra emotion. Now that too was finished. Ariel could no longer afford her Park Avenue psychiatrist; she'd no longer even live in this city.

"Of course," Mustafah said. "Would you like us to arrange a car?"

"Hola. Me llamo António Moniz. Hablas portugués?"

"No. Inglés?"

"Yes, good. So: I am returning your call about the American."

"Thank you. We have detained Señora Pryce here at the airport. She came here with no bags, no ticket, and a story about her husband being kidnapped in Lisbon. Did this truly happen?"

"Yes."

"The American John Wright was kidnapped?"

"Correct."

"And his wife paid the ransom and secured his release?"

"Yes."

"And?"

"And, well, what else can I tell you?"

"Perhaps why did they travel all through the night to Sevilla?"

"That I do not know. But I imagine they do not feel completely safe here in Lisboa."

"Why?"

"Well, he was kidnapped here. What does Señor Wright say?"

542

"We have not spoken to him. He was not with his wife when she was detained. Señora Pryce says they agreed it would be safer to travel separately. We have been unable to locate him."

This just became much more interesting. But it is no longer Moniz's concern.

"Detective Moniz, can you think of any reason that we should not let Señora Pryce go freely?"

Moniz regrets that he will probably never know what has gone on. He is suddenly sure that it was not what he had imagined.

"I cannot," he says. "Please give her my goodbye and best wishes."

Her name is being announced over the PA — *"Señora Ah-ree-elle Preece. Ah-ree-elle Preece, por favor"* — and she doesn't need to translate to understand the message: last call, get to your goddamned gate, which is of course at the very end of the terminal, and as she's running she can see that there's no one left in the queue, and the airline agent is at the podium, the doors about to close —

"I'm here! Ariel Pryce!" she calls out her own name, waving her boarding pass, and the agent nods, and then Ariel is gliding through the stuffy gangway, making her way down the center aisle of the plane, plopping down in her middle seat next to an old woman who peers disapprovingly over the

543

rim of her reading glasses, then a flight attendant is announcing, *"Señors y señoras, bienvenidos,"* the cabin door closing, then Ariel finally allows herself to take a deep breath, to let her tense shoulders fall, because she has made it, and this grueling trip is, at last, over —

But what's this?

The cabin door opens for a very Spanish-looking man in a very Spanish-looking preppy-Euro outfit. He speaks closely to the flight attendant, who nods while she listens, then looks down the aisle slowly until she finds Ariel, and meets her eye, while in the same instant another person boards the plane, this is a woman, and Ariel recognizes her, but it takes a split second of denial to admit it.

They have come for her.

"Pete? What the hell?"

"I waited till a reasonable hour."

"In what universe is seven A.M. reasonable?"

Wagstaff has been up all night, his mind blown by his discovery, and he's increasingly positive that he's going to win a Pulitzer. Maybe his editor in London has a point: He doesn't know what reasonable is.

"I know who it is," he says.

"Who who is?"

"The man who provided the ransom, who also fathered her child."

He'd given Judy a few updates over the past day as the parameters of the story had grown. He knows it's never a good idea to ambush your boss.

"Okay then: who?"

"Charlie Wolfe."

Silence.

"Judy? You there?"

"Yeah." Wagstaff can hear her breathing. "How certain are you?"

"Ninety-nine percent."

"Don't fuck with me, Pete. This isn't a game. Are you really that confident?"

"I am."

Wagstaff knows he's going to need more than confidence and circumstantial evidence. He also knows that hard proof is probably going to be elusive for a decades-old affair that resulted in an illegitimate child and a divorce and an NDA. What possible evidence could even exist?

An affair would definitely be very hard to prove. But Wagstaff suspects that it wasn't an affair.

"This woman just extorted the next president of the United States."

■ ■ ■ ■

PART V
THE PAYOFF

■ ■ ■ ■

CHAPTER 45

Day 3. 8:22 a.m.

"Where are we going?" Ariel asks.

"Someplace safe," Griffiths answers. Then no one speaks for five, ten, fifteen minutes. Ariel watches Seville fly by, red-tiled roofs, whitewashed walls, church towers, while the big vehicle turns onto progressively smaller streets, the way you penetrate a European city, from highways down to alleyways. "Get on the floor," Griffiths says.

"What?"

"Lie down." She indicates the backseat floor of the SUV. "On the floor."

"Are you serious?"

Griffiths doesn't even deign to answer.

"Where is my husband?"

"Didn't I already make it clear that I'm not going to answer that question? Antonucci, you heard me, right? I believe I said, I'm not going to answer that question, so stop asking."

Antonucci certainly looks a lot worse for

the pummeling that Ariel gave him on the Lisbon street. She hopes he's not planning on seeking any retribution.

"Yup," Antonucci agrees, "that's exactly what you said."

"I thought so." Griffiths turns back to Ariel. "Now get the fuck on the floor."

John walks through the airport terminal again, taking a more careful look at the clothing boutiques, the gift shops, the duty-free. He already knows which men's rooms are the biggest and busiest, which are smallest and quietest. He knows where the police congregate. He knows where the security checkpoints are. He knows where the exits are.

He also knows that Ariel was dragged off her airplane, then hustled out of the terminal through an emergency-exit door. He watched this happen from behind a tabloid-sized newspaper, hidden in the middle of a large crowd that was waiting to board a commuter flight to Barcelona, which was the cheapest ticket he could find, purchased using a fake passport and a credit card in someone else's name. John never planned on boarding this flight. He just needed to get into the secure area, to see if Ariel boarded hers.

The secure area is also where all the shops are. The first thing he buys is a prepaid cell.

They all climb out of the SUV into a small

courtyard dominated by a lush orange tree laden with fruit, and a small tiled fountain with no water in it.

"This way," says the man Ariel doesn't recognize, who must be a local operative. She assumes that this place is a CIA safe house, up these stone stairs that wind around the courtyard, and down the cool tiled loggia, and behind the battered old wooden door, a homey-looking apartment. There don't seem to be any gates or other security on the windows, and Ariel feels relief at this good news. Her bar has fallen pretty damned low. On the other hand, there's a tripod with a small video camera, which Antonucci now activates.

"Have a seat, please." Griffiths indicates a dining table. The local guy now leaves the apartment, and Antonucci disappears behind a door.

"What do you want from me?" Ariel asks.

"Have. A. Seat. We don't have a lot of time."

Ariel doesn't know what this could mean, but she's afraid to ask.

"How did you meet your husband?"

Ariel expected this line of questioning, but still she's unsure how much to tell this woman, what level of detail the CIA wants, and why. Ariel is prepared to provide as many details as anyone could bear — lines of verbatim dialogue, facial expressions, first-kiss choreography. It wasn't all that long ago, it was important, it was memorable. But that doesn't make it relevant.

"He was a customer in my shop." She begins as simply as possible. If anyone wants embellishment, they can ask. Like Jerry once advised her when preparing for a zoning-board hearing: The answer to the question *Do you know the time?* should be simply *Yes.*

"This is Main Street Books?" Griffiths asks. "Clever name."

The name came with the shop when Ariel bought it, but she doesn't need to explain this.

"Did he purchase any books?"

"Why do you care?"

"I don't really need to say this, do I? That I'm the one asking the questions? Because it feels like a hackneyed line from a cheesy police drama on network television."

"Yes, he bought books."

"Do you remember which?"

"As a matter of fact I do. Both were new bestsellers in hardcover, one a crime novel, the other a presidential history."

"Are those subjects that particularly interest him?"

"I assume so."

"You never asked? Never followed up?"

"No."

"Because to me? To me, those sound like the types of books that a guy would buy if he had no fucking idea what he wanted to read, and was in a bookstore for another reason."

"As I said: I didn't follow up."

"And he asked you out, right there?"

"No."

"So the next time you saw him?"

"I ran into him at a restaurant."

"Did he arrive first, or did you? To this chance encounter?"

"He did."

"And he asked you out then?"

"No. It was few weeks after that, when I ran into him at a grocery store."

"That's a lot of running into one person."

"It's a small town."

"Tell me about the grocery store meeting."

It's now that Ariel registers the large wall mirror. "Such as?"

"Such as what section?"

"Seriously?" Here's another investigator, asking another irrelevant question, to be able to compare Ariel's irrelevant answer to John's.

"Tell me the whole story."

"We were surrounded by big piles of fruit." This woman wants the whole story? She can have it. "He said hi, asked if I remembered him from the bookstore, introduced himself. We chitchatted — he was new to the area, I was not. He asked me if I went to that restaurant often, and I laughed. He said, Sorry, I guess that sounds like a line. I agreed, asked if it really was a line. He said he guessed so. I said, You guess? He blushed,

553

said, No, I don't guess, maybe we could go there together sometime?"

"Aw. That's sweet. You remember that pretty clearly. Pretty specifically."

"It's how I met my husband. Plus it wasn't that long ago."

"And you said yes? When he asked you out, right there in the fruit section?"

"That's right."

"Why'd he choose your town? My understanding is that it's not really where young Manhattan hotshots tend to vacation. Especially with all the chichi Hamptons nearby."

"He didn't want to be with all the chichi people. He doesn't really like New York."

"Then why does he live there?"

"Why does anyone live there?"

"And how did he come to be in *your* town, specifically?"

"Just exploring. Driving around."

"Are there other people like him, driving around, looking to rent houses?"

"What do I know? I'm not in the real-estate business."

"How quickly did your relationship progress?"

Ariel narrows her eyes. "What is it you're asking?"

"Not to put too fine a point on it, but when did you start fucking?"

"Excuse me? That's really none of your business."

"Everything is my business. You've figured that out, haven't you? Was it the first date?"

Ariel sighs. But what does she care? "Second."

"Quick work, huh?"

"No one's getting any younger."

"Did you investigate him at all? Before you started fucking him?"

"Sure, I snooped around the web. I didn't find anything that gave me pause."

"What about his name change?"

"No, I didn't find that on my own. But he told me about that right before we got engaged. We had a — I don't know what to call it — a sort of summit. Here are all the skeletons, take a good look."

"All? So that's when he told you about his arrest for cocaine possession."

Ariel's breath catches.

"No? He failed to mention that, huh? The charges were dropped, eventually. So he doesn't have a criminal record. But still. It was not a small amount of cocaine."

"When was this?"

"Six years ago."

"That's a long time." Ariel is trying to sound dismissive.

"Well, yes," Griffiths says. "But also, no."

"What do you want me to say?" Ariel asks. "I met the guy barely a year ago, and we're both adults. I didn't interrogate him about

555

his youthful indiscretions, because I don't care."

"That's generous of you. So was it at the same summit when he told you about his sister?"

"What about his sister?"

"Her suicide attempt? Or, rather, *attempts* in the plural?"

This hits Ariel like a punch in the gut. She shakes her head.

"Oh no? Why do you think he failed to mention that?"

"I don't know. Maybe because they're not that close."

"Really? You sure?"

Ariel doesn't answer.

"So you'd be surprised to learn that for years they spoke on the phone basically every week?"

Ariel still doesn't respond.

"That is, until three months ago, when the calls stopped completely. Do you know why?"

"No."

"Surely you know what big change happened three months ago. He didn't say anything about this? Why he stopped talking to his sister?"

"No."

"But you've met her?"

"Just at our wedding. She lives in Morocco."

"Yeah, Morocco. I sure wouldn't move to Morocco as a single woman. Not unless I was, well, me. It's a pretty strange choice, don't you think?"

"My understanding is that she's a strange person."

"So you haven't seen her while you've been here in Europe?"

"As I said already, I met her only the one time, and that was three months ago."

"Uh-huh. So, back to this summit."

"Yeah?"

"Is that when you told John that the father of your child is Charlie Wolfe?"

He'd been adamant that the agreement include an abortion. Charlie didn't want any bastard child of his out in the world. Who knew how that would come back and bite him one day, regardless of any NDA.

"That's a deal breaker," Ariel told her lawyer.

"Got it. But just for my clarity on our negotiating position, may I ask why?"

Ariel understood about attorney-client privilege; she understood that it would be an unconscionable — and disbar-able — breach of ethics for a lawyer to ever divulge anything that a client said in a situation like this. But Charlie was a man with immense power who'd likely end up with even more of it. Ariel was a woman with none who'd likely never have any. So she was not comfortable trusting in any norms. Nor trusting anyone,

557

about anything.

"No," Ariel said. "That's all you need to know."

John walks to the very rear of the shop, a table piled with lightweight crewnecks. He stands with his back toward the front, and chooses a navy sweater. On his way to the register, he picks up a red hat with the logo of the local football club; at the counter he plucks a pair of aviator sunglasses out of a carousel. He keeps his haul in a tight bundle in front of him, out of the view of the security camera mounted near the ceiling at the opening to the concourse. When he pushes his bundle across the counter to the clerk, he keeps his body between these goods and the camera.

"Buenos días," he says, in his best Castilian accent, with lisps for the esses, and his biggest smile for the homely clerk.

He pays in cash.

Ariel takes a moment to think this through: Is it remotely possible that this CIA woman *knows* the identity of George's father? For certain?

The answer she comes up with is no. Regardless of where this woman works, what data she can access, this piece of information is simply not knowable. She might suspect it, which is an impressive deduction. But there's no way for her to be certain.

With this realization, Ariel feels a shift in the power dynamic. Griffiths had been confident that she was knocking Ariel off-balance, putting her superior knowledge on display, revealing to Ariel things about her very own husband that she didn't know, his cocaine arrest, his sister's suicide attempts. But then she overplayed her hand with this bluff. Ariel tilts her chin up in defiance, and says nothing.

"And what exactly did John tell you about his time in the CIA?"

Ariel doesn't react to this head-spinner either.

"Oh, did he fail to mention that as well? Yes, after his undergrad in ROTC, and four years in the army, your husband spent a couple of years working for the Central Intelligence Agency."

Ariel shrugs.

"Which is to say that John Wright is a man who spent the better part of a decade learning how to be situationally aware, how to defend himself, how to handle challenging situations. Yet this same man then allowed himself to be abducted in broad daylight in front of a luxury hotel."

This sure is a barrage that's being thrown at Ariel. She doesn't know which way to duck.

"Can you see it now, Ms. Pryce?"

Ariel raises her eyebrows.

"You have been set up. This brand-new husband of yours? He has played you."

The two women stare at each other for a few seconds.

"Please tell me." Ariel is using her most condescending, sure-I'll-humor-you tone. "What's your theory?"

"Not a theory." Griffiths plants her elbows on the table. "This man shows up out of nowhere, in a place where he doesn't belong, and sweeps you off your feet. This good-looking and might I point out much younger man, after just a few months of a part-time relationship, is suddenly so desperate to form a long-distance split household with you — plus your teenaged son and your failing business and your struggling farm — that pretty much out of nowhere he proposes marriage. Is none of this a red flag to you? Are you that confident in your irresistibility?"

Ariel doesn't respond.

"Okay, I get it, maybe he's fucking you silly, you can't tell which end is up. Your, um, faculties have been compromised by multiple-orgasm events."

"That's a terrible thing for one woman to say to another."

"Maybe so. But tell me: Why the rush to wed?"

"We're in love, life is short. Maybe that hasn't sunk in for you, distracted as you are by this busy career of yours, intimidating

560

traumatized American citizens that you abduct off airplanes in foreign airports. But trust me: You have less time than you think."

"Sure." Griffiths smiles. "So this brand-new husband drags you to Lisbon under the demonstrably false pretext that you're somehow necessary for a business trip, during which he's kidnapped, in a city where Americans get kidnapped, on average, zero times per year. To save this husband from this extraordinarily rare peril, you have no choice but to blackmail a man who's in a uniquely inconvenient circumstance to be blackmailed. So you do exactly that, then hand over two million euros to someone in an alley, and lo and behold, your husband is set free with a little cut on his face. Is this what happened?"

"Minus all the sarcasm," Ariel says, but suddenly something new is scratching at her consciousness.

"So why'd you flee Lisbon in the middle of the night? That was a dramatic exit. And, I might say, well planned. Well executed."

Ariel can't figure it out, what's bothering her. "We were uncomfortable in Lisbon," she says. "Is that hard to understand?"

"Sure, but why the overnight drive?"

Now Ariel realizes what's bothering her: Griffiths said two million euros. Even though the ransom was supposed to have been three. Did Ariel ever mention the shortfall to Griffiths? To anyone?

No. Only to the kidnappers. And to John. So how does Griffiths know?

"Ms. Pryce?"

"Sorry, what?"

"Didn't it seem like overkill to drive through the night from Lisbon to Seville?"

"Not to me. Do I need to remind you that my husband had been *kidnapped*?"

"Whose idea was it to get out of Lisbon in such a hasty fashion? Yours or John's?"

"Mine."

"You sure about that? Was it *actually* your idea, or did he make you *think* it was your idea?"

Ariel doesn't answer.

"And whose idea was it to travel separately from Seville?"

"John's."

"That didn't send up any alarm signals?"

Should it? Maybe. But Ariel shakes her head.

"What about Russia? Has your husband spent much time there?"

"Russia?" Ariel feels a tingle run up her spine. "Not that I know of."

"So it would surprise you to learn that last year, he made three separate trips to Moscow?"

Yes, that would definitely surprise Ariel. But "No" is what she says, "though honestly I wouldn't be surprised to learn that he'd been anywhere."

Don't say *honestly,* she reminds herself.

"Traveling to foreign capitals is pretty much his job."

"But *specifically* Moscow: He never mentioned any trips there?"

Did he? Ariel doesn't think so. She shakes her head.

"What about Hamburg? Did he mention traveling there?"

"Yes."

"Antwerp? Belgrade?"

"Yes, I think so."

"What do you think he was doing in Belgrade?"

"The same thing he does on all his business trips."

"Did you know that Belgrade was where he was posted for the CIA? Oh" — snaps her fingers — "that's right: You didn't know about his two years in the Central Intelligence Agency, did you?"

Ariel answers with a sigh.

"So you're saying that of the trips that John made in the year before he met you, he mentioned *all* of them, *except* three visits to Moscow. Do I have that right?"

Ariel shrugs.

"And what about his motorcycle?"

This out-of-left-field question jolts Ariel. "His motorcycle?"

"A few months ago your husband bought a used motorcycle. Why did he pay in cash?"

It takes all her self-control to answer. "Did he? We didn't discuss his payment method."

"Why'd he buy this bike?"

"For fun. He likes riding on country roads."

"Yet when was the last time he'd owned a motorcycle?"

"I don't know."

"He paid twenty-five hundred bucks for this used bike. Are you swimming in money like that?"

"What the hell do you want from me? I don't know anything about this goddamned motorcycle."

"But you've seen it?"

"Of course. It's parked in my barn."

"And you didn't notice the similarity?"

Ariel knows exactly what Griffiths is suggesting. Yet she has no choice but to ask, "What similarity?"

"Between your husband's bike and the one the kidnapper used to deliver a burner to you."

CHAPTER 46

Day 3. 9:09 a.m.

The two women sit in silence. Ariel doesn't know how to respond to this, so she's just going to not respond at all.

"I can't help but wonder," Griffiths finally says, "why in the world would a man in Charlie Wolfe's position give all that money to a woman in your position?"

Ariel knows that this too cannot be a fact in Griffiths's possession. Just as she cannot know that Charlie is George's father. This CIA officer is bluffing again.

"I mean, even if Wolfe were motivated by the purity of the goodness of his heart — which is a big fucking if — this just looks *so bad* for him, doesn't it?"

Ariel doesn't respond.

"Look, we *know* that you blackmailed Charlie Wolfe. That's not even a question. What we need to know is this: How were you able to? And who's behind it?"

Who's behind it? Griffiths jumped to that

conclusion awfully fast. This is another allegation that Ariel simply isn't going to argue about.

"You think you can just sit there and say nothing?"

Ariel folds her arms.

"Okay, sure, maybe you can try. But understand this: You're not leaving here until you give me some fucking answers." Griffiths stands. "I'll give you a few minutes to think about it."

Griffiths can picture it clearly: A smooth, handsome young operator like John Wright meets this older woman, a single mom, lonely, vulnerable, easily seduced. She trusts Wright with the long-buried secret that her child's biological father is a rich, powerful man who has recently achieved national prominence. This seems like a golden opportunity: stage a kidnapping, collect a few million in untraceable cash, disappear in Europe. A simple plot, an easy swindle, especially for a man of Wright's background and skill set. Makes all the sense in the world: a few months' work for a few million dollars.

If it's really this simple, then John Wright is not a matter of national security, not the CIA's concern, not Griffiths's problem. He's just a clever con man who happened to commit his scam in her Lisbon orbit.

On the other hand, it could be much more

complicated, and much more dangerous: John Wright could be working for a hostile foreign government. The cash would not be the point of the exercise; the extortion itself would. The operation's goal would be to turn the next vice president — possibly the next president of the United States — into an enemy asset.

What a great operation that would be. Griffiths would have to admire it.

Even if that's not what's going on — even if no foreign government is involved, even if John Wright himself won't be an ongoing problem — the Charlie Wolfe situation is still a dire national security threat, without doubt. Because it was just proven that Wolfe can be extorted. If it's not by the Russians, if it's not this time, there will always be the possibility of a next time.

John Wright and Ariel Pryce are not the real security risk. The real risk is just days away from being sworn in as the vice president of the United States.

"Russia?" Antonucci asks.

"Worth a shot."

"But Wright never went to Russia, did he?"

"No. But his wife obviously doesn't know that, and now she has to doubt him. Look." They glance at Pryce through the two-way mirror. "She's asking herself: Is it possible that my new husband is a Russian operative?"

"Is that what you believe?"

"Not really. But I wouldn't put it past the Russians to arrange for an operative to marry a woman because she bore Wolfe's illegitimate child, to secure powerful leverage against a man of his position, his access, his prospects for advancement. Hell, I'd do that myself."

"Okay. Say John Wright *is* just that, and his mission was indeed to create the opportunity to blackmail Wolfe. Is Pryce going to know anything about it?"

"No, you're right, that's probably not what we can expect out of her."

"Then what are we going to accomplish here?"

"We're going to scare the shit out of her, then let her go, and see what she does with her fear."

John powers up the minimally charged new phone, and waits for the service to connect. Then he punches in a long string of numbers from memory, and hits CALL.

"Yes?"

"Ten minutes," he says.

"Okay. White Ford Fiesta."

He hangs up. He crosses the concourse into the busiest of all the busy bathrooms in this terminal, where one man after another enters or exits every five seconds. John walks to the very last stall. He yanks the tags off his purchases. Pulls the blue sweater over his black T-shirt, perches the red cap atop his head, slides on the sunglasses. He puts the shopping bag in the trash.

The bank of sinks is crowded with men washing hands, faces, someone is having an electric shave. John checks himself in the mirror, and what he sees is someone who looks like a Spaniard.

It's a short walk through thick crowds from this bustling bathroom to the busy exit that leads to the anarchy of baggage claim, through which he strides without slowing, staring straight ahead, out the doors to the roadway, and into the passenger door of a little white Ford.

"Listen," Ariel says, "you understand what an NDA is, right? You understand what sorts of penalties these agreements include?"

"Sure."

"So you understand that there are no exceptions, right? Just because the CIA is asking, or the FBI, or the police. None of that is any different from a reporter asking, or a sister, or a friend. Nondisclosure is nondisclosure. Even if I were, say, being interrogated by the CIA in an undisclosed location in Europe, without the benefit of legal representation or due process."

"We can protect you."

"Come on," Ariel scoffs. "You don't really believe that. With the people who are involved?"

"I promise."

"Promise? *Pffft.* Get me that promise in the form of a letter signed by the attorney general of the United States."

"You've got to be kidding."

"Absolutely not. You don't agree that this hypothetical situation would rise to the level of the AG? Of course it would. So if you think you have the ability to protect a person like me, that's what you need to do. That's the price here."

Griffiths responds with an exasperated sigh.

"You haven't even told me who you work for," Ariel says, "or what you do. I don't even know your real name, do I? And you want me to trust you? With my *life*? Are you *insane*?" She leans forward. "Listen, we're not enemies, you and me. I don't want to be antagonistic. But I have to ask, with all due respect: What the hell do you want from me?"

"You know what I want: the truth."

"The truth?" Ariel snorts. "The truth has a steep price."

"There!" Kayla Jefferson finally sees it. "Wearing the red cap. Look at the pants, the shoes: That's him."

The Spanish cop nods, and says something to the airport-security technician, who starts loading feeds from other cameras — the concourse, escalator, baggage claim, exit door, sidewalk —

Jefferson is getting ready to call her boss again — "We got him!" — but then gives it a second thought. She asks the cop to call in the license plate, then continues to review the footage with the tech, following the white car to another camera, another, then into the garage.

Then from the first camera within the structure: no little white car.

The second camera: none.

The third and fourth and fifth: no, no, no.

"Where the hell?" Another, another, another. "Can you pull up the past ten minutes from all the garage exits?"

Now the tech is fast-forwarding through this footage, evidence of dozens of cars leaving the structure, maybe a hundred, but none is that little white Ford with the license plate beginning with M.

"What the fuck happened?" This question is rhetorical. Kayla knows that either John Wright is still in the same car hidden somewhere inside the garage, or he has exited a different way. Probably in a different car. "What time was the last visual?"

The tech rechecks the footage, says, "The car entered since twenty-seven minutes."

A lot can be accomplished in twenty-seven minutes.

"Señorita," says the Spanish cop, hanging up the phone, "this vehicle was reported stolen last night."

Damn it.

Kayla leans back, away from the screens. She realizes what has happened: John Wright and the driver abandoned the stolen Ford in the garage, then climbed into a different vehicle, one of the hundred-plus that have exited the building in the past twenty-seven minutes. Exit cameras aren't going to help, because Wright will now be hidden in the backseat, or he and the driver will have switched clothes and switched places, fake beard and a bald cap, she'll have become a nun, whatever.

Yes, it might still be possible to identify whatever car they got into, but it will be a lot harder. And it will take a lot longer, by which point they might have switched vehicles again, or boarded a train, or a plane, or simply disappeared into a crowd . . .

Instead of the triumphant *We got him,* Jefferson makes the opposite call.

"Sorry," she says to her boss, "we lost him."

Griffiths returns to Ariel carrying a single sheet of freshly printed paper, folded in half. She takes a seat again at the small table.

"So where do you think your husband is now?"

"Probably in the airport, waiting for a flight."

Griffiths taps the piece of paper, but doesn't

unfold it, doesn't show it to Ariel.

"He *was* at the airport. Where he seems to have purchased a change of clothes, got into disguise in a bathroom, hustled out of the terminal, and climbed into a waiting car."

Griffiths unfolds the piece of paper, slides it in front of Pryce.

"This waiting car. With this woman at the wheel. Do you recognize her?"

Griffiths sees Ariel's mouth open just the slightest, her head twitch a few degrees. That sure looks like genuine surprise.

The image's quality is awful, taken at a bad angle, through a dirty windshield, of a woman who's wearing large sunglasses and what appears to be a silk scarf tied snugly against her head. It would be hard to identify this person even if she were your best friend. Facial-recognition software can't possibly help. Even on the chance that this woman is in some database somewhere, this image is simply not good enough. Hell, it might not even be a woman.

"No," Pryce says. "I don't recognize her. But based on this, how could I?"

Griffiths takes a few minutes in the other room, gazing through the mirror at Ariel Pryce while picturing the sequence of the next conversations that will happen. First it will be her call to the director of ops, who will have no choice but to inform the DCI, who in turn will be obliged to wake the president, who is not exactly known for making calm, rational decisions in the middle of the night.

She's lying. The president is blindly loyal to all his old cronies, until he isn't. *It's a hoax. Another hoax.*

The CIA director would be reluctant to argue with the president; everyone who has access to the president is reluctant to argue with him, which is how they maintain their access, QED.

This nasty lying woman is in Spain right now?

Yes sir.

She should stay in Spain, the president would say. *In fact she should probably die in Spain.*

And there it would be: a lethal finding by the commander in chief to assassinate an American citizen on foreign soil to keep a secret that would damage his administration.

Would the DCI argue with the president? No. Griffiths has heard rumors that this director is operationally aggressive, aka trigger-happy, as long as it's someone else who's pulling the actual trigger. Which is what amateurs in his position tend to be, thinking that the solution to every problem is a bullet in someone's head.

So the DCI would pass this order down the chain to Farragut, who'd point-blank refuse this illegal directive, and promptly be fired. The director would then give the direct order to Griffiths. She too would refuse, and her career would be summarily terminated. Could Griffiths herself be prosecuted somehow? Yes, of course she could. The president and the director of central intelligence could fabricate anything, on anyone.

And Ariel Pryce would still end up dead.

Griffiths has probably learned all she's going to learn; now it's time to report it all up the chain of command. She places the necessary call.

"Sir, I'm sorry to wake you."

"Oh please. You think I was asleep with this going on?"

"I'm not calling with good news."

"No, I don't imagine you would be."

"The kidnapped man is now in the wind; he took great lengths to evade surveillance and disappear from the airport. He has a female accomplice, and their trail went very cold, very fast."

"Professionally fast?"

"Looks that way. I've just been interviewing the wife in Seville, where we intercepted her after they fled Lisbon in the middle of the night. I'm confident that she doesn't have anything to do with this."

"And him?"

"There's an old drug bust. A name change. Plus the army service and two years with us

575

in the Agency. That employment history doesn't necessarily make him dodgy, but it definitely does make him someone with the tactical training, the skill set, and the disposition to plan and execute a covert active measure."

"Where was his army service?"

"Afghanistan."

They both know that plenty of soldiers came home disillusioned from there.

"And for the Agency?"

"His only posting was in Serbia."

"The Balkans, huh?"

The Balkans have been overrun with Russian operatives since World War II. It's certainly possible that a CIA officer could have been turned by the SVR during a Belgrade posting.

"If this guy is just a solo operator who stumbled into a payday," Griffiths says, "maybe we'd be inclined to simply hand our intel to the Bureau and say you're welcome. But if this is an ongoing active measure by a hostile foreign entity? It's dangerous as hell. It almost doesn't even matter who's responsible, that's just a question of punishment, or retaliation, or whatever. But regardless of who's behind this — even if no one is behind this — we now know that Wolfe can be extorted, because it just happened yesterday. Why won't it happen again two weeks from now when he's vice president? Or two years from now when he's president?"

The deputy director sighs. These conclusions are hard to dispute. "So what do you recommend we do with her?"

Griffiths looks up again at the two-way mirror, at Ariel Pryce slumped in defeat and despair and utter exhaustion. Griffiths very well may be ordered to keep this woman in custody, or to abduct her for extraordinary rendition to an Eastern European black site, or even to kill her, right here, right now. What did Ariel just say? The truth has a steep price.

"I think we should let her go, see what she does. She has a kid to get home to, so she's not going to simply disappear. She herself is not the foreign agent, if that's what's going on; she's an innocent bystander. We'll keep close tabs on her. That is, we'll ask the FBI to."

This conversation might end up in a case study, or congressional testimony, or as evidence in a criminal trial. Griffiths shouldn't admit aloud that the CIA intends to conduct covert surveillance of an American citizen within US borders. That's illegal. Though that's exactly what's going to happen.

"Within a few days," she says, "we'll learn a lot. I'm confident."

"Maybe," Farragut says, sounding unconvinced. "But maybe we can't afford a few days."

No, Griffiths thinks, maybe we can't. But what's the alternative?

Something new is now tickling her consciousness, but Griffiths can't isolate it among the many theories jockeying for position in there, one after another surging to the forefront, only to be pushed aside . . . Something about paying a price for everything. Pryce mentioned this, when was it? A day and a half ago? She was talking about the costs of her old pampered life. Griffiths had been about to ask for specifics, but their conversation was interrupted by the ringing phone.

She looks again at Pryce through the glass, and wonders: What happened to you?

"Everything okay?"

John is gazing at the washed-out Spanish landscape, the olive groves spilling from the highway, the Sierra Nevada in the distance, snowcapped even in the middle of summer.

"Just tired."

The driver lets her right hand fall off the wheel, reaches to take John's, gives him a squeeze.

"Thank you *so* much," she says. "I know you did it for me, and I know it was very hard. I hope you know how much I appreciate it."

John tries to smile. He should feel better. He should feel great, speeding across Europe with someone he loves and two million euros in the trunk. Maybe it's the sheer exhaustion; maybe it's a physiological reaction to all the spent adrenaline; maybe it's the inevitable letdown after momentous events. Or maybe it's because despite everything, he'd actually gone ahead and fallen in love with Ariel Pryce, which wasn't at all part of the plan, and now he'll likely never see her again. How could he not be sad?

"Hey." She still has one hand on the steering wheel, the other atop his. "Look at me."

He does. She's beautiful, always has been. For a long time he thought she was the most beautiful woman in the world.

"I love you," she says.

"I love you too," he answers.

Chapter 47

Day 3. 12:51 p.m.

They are making their way through the crowded departures hall, Ariel clutching a new boarding pass for a new connecting flight, a new arrival time to New York, a new ETA to her house, her kid, her mom whom she just called from a pay phone to give a bare-bones update. Ariel still has seventeen hours of travel in front of her. If all goes well.

"When's the last time you saw your sister-in-law?" Griffiths asks.

"I told you," Ariel says without slowing her pace. "I only ever met Lucy once. At our wedding."

"So you didn't see her in Lisbon?"

The CIA officer is apparently going to make one last run at this. The security checkpoint is just a minute away.

"No."

"And that wasn't her at the wheel of the little white car? Whisking John away?"

"Come on."

"Did you know that Lucy Reitwovski flew into Madrid a couple of weeks ago?"

"The Lisbon police told me that."

"What is she doing in Spain?"

"I have no idea."

"What are *you* doing in Spain? Why did this new husband of yours trick you into coming to Europe? Haven't you asked yourself?"

Ariel's mouth falls open in exasperation; she stops walking. She has no good answer, and no more energy even to say so.

"You don't want to hear this, Ms. Pryce, but your husband is not who you think he is."

Ariel shuts her eyes tight, fighting back the tears. "Even if that's true, what am I supposed to do about that now? Seriously? What is it you want from me?"

Griffiths is extending her hand, and Ariel looks down. A business card.

"I want you to give me a call when you hear from him. *If* you hear from him."

Ariel is not going to call this woman, ever, but there's no harm in taking the card.

"What did you mean when you said that you pay a price for everything?"

Ariel answers with a blank look.

"The other day, when you were talking about your previous marriage. You seemed to be saying that at a certain point, you were no longer willing to pay the required price for that old life of yours. What was that price?"

Ariel feels a nearly overwhelming urge to tell the truth, to let it all come tumbling out in one big gush that will knock over everything in its path, like the tsunami that swept through Lisbon in the eighteenth century, leveling the medieval old city, leaving in its wake the perfect space to build something modern, something intentional, something beautiful.

But she can't.

"You'll see," she says, and walks away.

"Sorry, your name again?"

"Pete Wagstaff."

"And you're asking if I know anything about the end of Laurel and Bucky's marriage?"

"That's right."

"That's *so* weird. I *just* saw her. After, like, forever. I hadn't seen Laurel since she left New York, what, fifteen years ago? Then out of nowhere, boom, I run into her in a bookstore where she apparently *works*. That's. So. Weird."

"Yes it is certainly a coincidence. So her marriage to Mr. Turner?"

"Yeah, well, to begin with, that wasn't exactly a match made in heaven. Laurel was in truth a little superior with him."

"How so?"

"Well, she'd been this *actress,* and then she was doing something in *book* publishing, and she thought she was so *cultured,* but Bucky was so finance-y. Maybe he thought she was a little too artsy, and she thought he was a little too crass. Though she didn't have any trouble spending his crass money."

Maybe she did, Wagstaff thinks. But he's not on the phone to argue with Tory Wasserman.

"Anyway, the last time I saw them together was at this big party in the Hamptons, at Charlie Wolfe's estate. We were seated at the same table. All of a sudden Laurel returns from I don't know where, looking a little green, and she and Bucky get up and leave with another couple."

"Who was the other couple?"

"I don't remember. Then next thing, I'm not seeing her at the gym anymore, she's not doing lunches or dinners, not returning calls. I run into Bucky one night, he says they had a spat, taking some time apart. That time apart turns into forever. Laurel never returns to New York, no one knows what happened to her. And then I run into her just a few days ago. So weird."

Wagstaff can feel himself crashing from the long night of cocaine, followed by the short disco nap, and now a third espresso. He's jittery, quite possibly stupid, and he thinks he may have missed Tory Wasserman's overarching theory. "So what do you think made their marriage fall apart?"

"Well, some people thought that something happened between Laurel and Charlie."

Wagstaff feels his heart start to race, yet again. "Something happened? Like an affair?"

"Um . . . not exactly."

"Then what?"

Silence. "Hello?" He's worried that the call was dropped.

"Yeah, I'm here. But listen, this *has* to be off the record."

"Of course," he says. "This can be on background."

"What does that mean? Like, exactly?"

"That means I can use your words, but not attribute them to you by name. I'd refer to you as a source who knew the couple at the time."

"I don't know about that," she says. "No, I don't think so. No quotes from me at all."

"Okay. Agreed. So?"

"So Charlie used to have a reputation for being a little, uh . . ."

"Forward?" Wagstaff offers.

"No. Forceful."

Holy shit. "A little forceful?"

"No, I guess not a little. Just forceful."

Wagstaff feels like he's going to spontaneously combust. "Are you saying he had a reputation for sexual assault?"

"No, it wasn't a reputation." The objection doesn't sound very strenuous. Or sincere. "Just rumors. It's what some people said."

584

Some people. Wagstaff needs to tread carefully here. He doesn't want to spook this woman; he needs her to lead him to the next step. "Anyone in particular?"

Tory doesn't answer.

"I won't use your name. I promise."

She still doesn't respond.

"This is a man who's about to become vice president, and maybe the next president of the United States."

"So, wait a sec: You already knew, before you called? That Charlie was involved?"

"You're not my only source," Wagstaff says, both honestly and not. "But I need all the corroboration I can find. This sort of accusation, you know, it doesn't stick easily, not to any man, and certainly not to someone like Charlie Wolfe."

Wagstaff can imagine that Tory Wasserman has a lot to lose, getting involved in this. Anyone would. But maybe she has more.

"If this man is a serial rapist," Wagstaff continues, "isn't that something the American people need to know before he becomes the vice president?"

"Off the record?" Tory asks. "You promise?"

"I promise."

"Off the record: Charlie Wolfe is definitely a rapist."

It isn't until her connecting flight is in the air that Ariel feels confident that she's actually

585

going to get home. She still has no phone, no computer, no internet access. She doesn't want any. What she wants is to sleep. She knows that this ordeal isn't over; in fact a large part of it hasn't even begun. This long flight might be her only chance at relaxation for a long while.

Relaxation. Did this count? Would she ever again enjoy the luxury of genuine relaxation?

"My name is Pete Wagstaff. I'm calling about an old incident involving Charlie Wolfe."

"Oh boy." Sigh. "I already told you people: I can't discuss this."

"We've never spoken before, Captain Pulaski. Who do you mean, *you people*?"

"I can't talk about it."

Wagstaff looks down at his notes. Tory Wasserman provided him with the names of a handful of other women, but first Wagstaff wants to check out this lead about the incident that really matters, at least for the first article that he's going to write. He's now certain that it will be a series. This is going to be front-page news for a while.

"I'm calling to confirm that fourteen years ago, Laurel Turner presented herself to your station house to report a sexual assault committed against her by Charlie Wolfe."

Wagstaff doesn't actually know the date of the report, nor its location, nor that any report was ever filed by Laurel Turner or anyone else against Charlie Wolfe. These are all guesses that he's throwing out there for the policeman to confirm or deny or clarify.

But this cop doesn't say anything.

"Hello? Captain Pulaski?"

"I have no comment."

And the line goes dead.

This is certainly not evidence, Wagstaff knows. But at the same time, it is almost certainly proof.

The wheels skid and bounce and skid again, the reverse thrusters roar, the fuselage shudders while everyone ignores all this tremendous violence to reach for their devices, to readjust the settings, stare at the screens, waiting for the connections to be reestablished, impatient to be plugged back into the electronic fabric that binds us together, the giant web that catches everything, and everyone.

Not Ariel. She has now been in a digital blackout for twenty-four hours, the longest she can remember since the advent of smartphones. Since the demise of privacy.

She never thought she'd be so grateful to be trudging through JFK. She stops at a restaurant to pay a dollar for internet access along with five dollars for crappy coffee. The landing page of every news-related website features the same story on an otherwise quiet summer day of a holiday week: Confirmation hearings begin in three days for the nominee for vice president.

Ariel searches the web for herself, and for John, but there's nothing yet, no article anywhere. Disappointing, but at the same time a relief.

For the moment, she's still tomorrow's news.

"It's Nicole Griffiths calling."

"Thanks," Jim Farragut says to his assistant. "I'll take it. Please shut the door."

The deputy director closes the briefing book on his desk, and minimizes the email window on his screen. He wants to pay complete attention to this phone call from Lisbon, of all goddamned places. Certainly not where he expected a national-security crisis to emerge.

"Griffiths?"

"I'm calling with a preliminary report on the history."

"Go ahead."

"After the death of their parents, twelve-year-old John Reitwovski and his fifteen-year-old sister Lucy moved to rural Ohio to live with an uncle, a man who was maybe not cut out for parenting, especially of a nonbiological teenaged daughter. Before long Lucy ran away, and found herself living in a nearby university town. The same year that Charlie Wolfe moved to that same university town to attend law school."

Farragut lets his exhausted head tilt back on his aching neck. *Fuck.*

"Lucy used a fake ID to get a job at a bar called Mulligan's, where she worked as a hostess for a year, then got a waitress job at another bar for a few months, then left town. She and Wolfe overlapped for perhaps eighteen months in a town of about a hundred thousand residents. So far, that's all we know. But we've just begun to investigate this connection."

Farragut knows that this is not going to turn out to be a coincidence. "Anything else?"

"Yes. Please check your email from me. I just sent something."

Farragut opens his window, downloads an attachment. "What am I looking at?"

"That's a Twitter screenshot."

"Yes I know that."

"It's a photo of Ariel Pryce standing in front of the US embassy in Lisbon, taken two days ago, and posted a few hours ago."

The text reads, IS THIS #CHARLIEWOLFEM-ISTRESS A #RUSSIANSPY?

"Good Lord. Has this really been retweeted three hundred times already? How is that possible?"

"Good question: The only way is by bots. At this rate, there will be thousands of retweets within a week. Either someone has spent good money to make sure this reaches

589

everyone on Twitter, or they don't need to spend money to accomplish the same thing, because they already control their own bots."

"The Russians?"

"That's where the smart money would be."

"Is there any way to find out for sure?"

"Probably not. Or, rather, probably not quickly. The post is also trending on Instagram and Facebook in ways that appear to be similarly manipulated. Within two or three days, this rumor will have been put in front of nearly every set of eyeballs in America."

"Jesus Christ. And is there any truth to it?"

"That she's his mistress? No. I'm pretty sure the truth is something different. Something much worse."

"Worse than a mistress?" Farragut has a sinking feeling. "What's that?"

"I think Wolfe raped her."

Throughout the drive from the airport's long-term parking lot, Ariel has been unable to stop glancing in her pickup's rearview. When she notices a state trooper coming up quickly, she double-checks her speedometer: yes, still cruise-controlled at sixty-eight.

The trooper is closing in fast.

There are very few cars on the road. Ariel flips her signal to move from the center lane to the right, ostensibly to get out of the trooper's way, but really just to reassure herself that no, she's not speeding at a meaningful level. You don't get a ticket for sixty-eight on the Long Island Expressway.

The cop turns on his flashing lights.

Her heart is hammering away. She pumps the brakes to release cruise control, preparing to pull over to the shoulder, preparing her arguments, preparing her pleas, preparing to be terrified. If a trooper is pulling her over at sixty-eight, he's doing it for a reason other than speeding. Her taillights are fine, her registration is current, there are no warrants out on her, no good reason for anyone to pull her over.

She cuts her eyes back to the rearview, and suddenly the car isn't even there, and then the strobing colored lights are flying by, in pursuit of someone else, and she lets out a sob of relief.

The sun has set. Traffic has thinned to nothing. The highway is straight, and Ariel can see for a mile in front: not a single set of taillights. Behind her, one car is a half-mile back. That same car has been the same distance behind her for a while.

She takes the exit, pauses at the stop sign at the bottom of the ramp. And yes, here comes the same set of headlights behind her.

Ariel makes a left-hand turn, and accelerates as fast as the old pickup can manage, past the gas station, then she swings around a curve, over the railroad tracks, out into the familiar rural landscape, the fields, the wind turbines, the farm-equipment lot. She turns onto a smaller route, a narrow straightaway with nothing but wide-open farmland on either side, and the last brilliant streaks of summer sunset lingering on the horizon.

Her tail is still with her, albeit farther back, trying to hide, and failing. Or maybe not trying at all. Maybe the CIA wants her to know that they're right there, watching.

She finally turns onto her road in the deep dark of a moonless night. Ariel's house is beyond the next rise, on the gentle slope toward the bluffs a mile away, high above the rocky beach. Her kid, her mom, her dogs, her whole life is just over that ridge.

Everything will be different now. During the many hours of today's travel, Ariel has been trying to picture what her new life will look like, but she's never been able to see it all clearly, only bits and pieces from odd angles that don't add up to a cohesive whole. None of it included pulling into her driveway a quarter-mile in front of a CIA escort.

She can't help but doubt all her choices, yet again. It feels as if that's all she's ever done.

The porch door bangs open, and George comes tumbling out in a jumble of gangly limbs, the tail-wagging dogs on either side, they're all swarming around her.

This, at least, she doesn't have to doubt. Maybe this can be enough.

This, at least, she doesn't have to doubt.
Maybe this can be enough.

CHAPTER 48

Day 4. 5:25 a.m.
Ariel is already at her kitchen table when the sun breaks over the horizon at the far end of her eighty-acre field of corn, reds and golds shot through the green stalks, brilliant, spectacular.

Last night was another of limited sleep ruined by fears and reconsiderations and misgivings, both general and specific. Ariel is again living with that parenting-an-infant level of sleep deprivation, night after night, a mounting tab of exhaustion, more every morning than the day before.

Now it's even harder than it had been thirteen years ago, her body less resilient, less forgiving. She looks, she knows, horrible. That's fine. Horrible is how she should look, for a day like this.

"Still no John?"

Ariel's mom has never met John. If it weren't for George as an eyewitness, she might not even believe that there's any such person. Elaine makes no secret that she thinks her daughter has gone out of her way to make herself unappealing — hard to be attracted to, hard to deal with, hard to love. She probably wonders what sort of man overcame all that. And why he bothered.

"Not yet. He's stuck in Europe."

"Stuck. In Europe. How stupid do you think I am?"

Ariel turns away. The only way to make Elaine understand would be to tell her the whole thing, every bit of it. But Ariel has been down that road before, and her mom had responded poorly. There's no reason to expect a different response the next time. People don't change, not that much. They just become more like themselves.

Plus the truth is that Ariel doesn't actually know where John is. This too is not something she's eager to admit to her mom, nor to anyone else. It's one of many new secrets that Ariel is about to keep, to replace the old ones that are about to be revealed.

Ariel offers her mother a hug instead of an explanation. "Thank you, Mom. For everything."

"Do you know who this is?" Kayla Jefferson extends her tablet.

"For the love of Christ," Griffiths says, "I'm so tired I can barely see. I'm not going to play guessing games with you."

Griffiths has barely slept in two days. She knows that her investigation is a race against time; a bomb is ticking. There's no way she's going to defuse this bomb, but maybe she can figure out who needs to get out of the blast's way, to do the least damage to national security.

That part of this investigation is her job. There's also a part that's something else, beyond her job. Curiosity, definitely. Plus an uncharacteristic sympathy she feels for Ariel Pryce. As well as a strong suspicion that what's going on here is not what it appears.

"This is security-camera footage of Lucy Reitwovski entering a bank branch on the rue du Rhône in Geneva, carrying a bag, which five minutes later she exits without."

"Holy fuck." Griffiths is fully alert again. This case sure is a roller coaster.

"If they drove straight through from Seville, making necessary stops only, they'd have arrived in Geneva two hours ago, which is when this was taken."

Two hours ago. So they could still be in Geneva, though Griffiths suspects not. They could also be somewhere else in Switzerland, or in France or Italy. They could be headed in any direction, and two hours is a big head start.

But there's no harm in trying the most obvious possibilities. "Have some people take a look around Geneva hotels, airport, train station. Was there any sign of Wright himself, or just this woman?"

"Just the woman."

No surprise. Griffiths is pretty sure that they're not going to find John Wright, who's an average-height average-build ex-Army ex-CIA devious motherfucker with two million in cash who has gone to ground in a part of the world where almost everyone looks like him. No one is going to find this guy, at least not until it no longer matters, which will be any day now. Maybe even today.

Griffiths turns back to her research.

"You're going to be hearing some things about me, George, in the coming days."

Ariel and her son are seated side by side in the front of her pickup.

"What sort of things?"

"Some of these things will be true. Some of them, I'm sure, won't be."

Ariel takes a turn slowly onto a street lined by high brush where she often comes across wild turkeys, or a family of deer. Sometimes normal vigilance is not enough; sometimes you need to be extra-careful to avoid inflicting unintentional harm.

"One of the true things is that long ago, before you were born, a man sexually assaulted me. You know what this means?"

"Yeah, I do. I'm sorry, Mom."

Ariel recently learned that the truck is the very best place to have real conversations with her son. A place where neither of them can look the other in the eye; where neither can just get up and leave; where nothing feels like a direct confrontation, even when it is.

The front seat was also where she'd chosen to tell Bucky about the same exact traumatic event.

"This man is now very powerful. In fact this man has been nominated to be vice president."

Out of her peripheral vision Ariel can see the boy turn to face her, then quickly look back out the front windshield. "Are you talking about Charlie Wolfe?"

"Do you know who he is?"

"Of course I do, Mom."

"One of the things you might hear that *isn't* true is that Charlie Wolfe is your father."

"He's not?"

"No."

"Does that mean you actually know who my father is?"

She'd told him differently. "Yes. Your father's name is Bucky Turner. He was my husband for a few years."

The night of the assault, her pregnancy test was positive. She was already pregnant when Charlie raped her. It was a biological certainty that the father was Bucky. So Ariel never submitted to any paternity test, any genetic matching. She didn't want to create any evidence of this truth.

"But you told me that you didn't know my father? That he was an anonymous donor to a sperm bank."

Ariel knows that the boy would never have been able to utter "sperm bank" to his mother in any situation other than while facing this windshield.

"Well, I lied to you. I'm very sorry about that. I lied for a few reasons. One was that I didn't want you to seek out your father, and I was worried that if you knew who he was, then you'd feel like you had to have a relationship with him."

"And what's so horrible about him?"

"Oh Sweetie, I don't know. I guess nothing so horrible."

One of the ways that Ariel has been extra-cautious in her life has been talking to her son about men. She never wanted to sound too negative, too hostile. She doesn't want George to grow up thinking that his mother hates all men; she doesn't want him to hate himself just because he's male. She also doesn't want the boy to grow up dubious of all women because his mother seems to be a noncredible man-hating lunatic. This has been one of the hardest needles to thread while sewing the fabric of this future man's psyche: What will this particular patch look like, the patch where he believes women, or doesn't?

"Bucky is just a man who turned out to be selfish, and something of a coward, and I realized that I didn't want to share my life with him." Ariel feels tears coming on again. Sleep deprivation has always heightened her emotional swings. As has this subject.

"Marrying the wrong person is a mistake that a lot of people make. I'm really grateful that I caught the mistake while I could still do something about it. But I'm also really grateful that I was with Bucky for those years, because that's how I got you."

The boy never responds to anything like this.

"And although Bucky is not horrible, some men are. Charlie Wolfe is one of them."

"Who's definitely not my father?"

"No." Ariel braces herself to admit another very hard thing: "But he believes he is."

George is rightfully confused. "Why does he believe that?"

"He sexually assaulted me, George. You understand how evil that is, right? Well, I didn't think I'd be able to prove it, in court. And I thought that trying might ruin my life."

Ariel was at the time thirty-three years old, unemployed and broke and soon to be divorced, and pregnant, feeling acutely alone in the world. She found herself walking the streets of New York in a daze, plotting the possible narratives, how each would play out, short-term and long-, the investigations, the trial, the TV reports, the witnesses for the defense, the counteraccusations, the character assassinations. There was no way it wouldn't be a horror that would drag on for years, and in the end Charlie would most likely be acquitted.

Pressing charges would probably accomplish nothing other than tossing some pebbles into his smooth path. Afterward, Charlie would be able to move on with his life. But not Ariel. This would be who she'd have become, and who she'd be forever: the woman who accused a powerful man of sexual assault.

Her life didn't yet have a story. She didn't want this to be it.

"Instead I did the only thing I could think of to get justice: I told him that I was pregnant as a result of that assault, and that I could prove it, and that he'd have to pay to keep me quiet."

"So you lied to him too."

Ariel thinks about trying to stifle her tears, or hide them, but this too is something that the boy ought to see; this should be part of his fabric. The lies, the tears, the whole mess.

"Yes, I lied to him too."

Her multimillion-dollar lie. Her first multimillion-dollar lie.

CHAPTER 49

Day 5. 9:19 a.m.

Ariel drives George to camp. She goes to the supermarket, where she dumps items into her cart without thinking. She thanks her mom profusely, dodges more questions from Elaine, says goodbye. She takes the dogs to the beach, doesn't stop throwing the ball until they both give up from exhaustion, then fill the truck with salty sand and the reassuring smell of wet dog. She's trying her best to pretend that life will be normal again. She knows it won't.

Griffiths should let it go, but she can't bring herself to quit, and won't let Jefferson or Antonucci quit either, all of them following the backward trails of John Wright and Lucy Reitwovski, Ariel Pryce and Charlie Wolfe, back fourteen years ago, twenty, twenty-five —

"Yeah, I remember her."

Griffiths catches a strained tone in this woman's voice.

"That was horrible, what happened to that poor girl."

Griffiths sits up straighter. This, finally, is it.

"Can you tell me what you remember?"

"Oh I'll never forget it. There were three of us who closed that night. I was the bartender, so I stayed upstairs to clean the bar, lock up the liquor, count the cash, bring it to the night depository. A bar-back was in the kitchen, washing dishes. Lucy's responsibility was the basement, where there was a small secondary bar to clean, and the pool table and darts to rearrange, lock the fire door, kill the lights."

Griffiths keeps her pen poised over her notepad, but she hasn't written a thing. She's going to remember all this word for word.

"Lucy opened the door to the restroom, and a man yanked her inside, locked the door, and raped her. Afterward, he slunk out the basement door. When I got back from dropping the cash around the corner, I could see that Lucy was shaken, but she wouldn't say anything. Then apparently a week later, she went to the police."

"Why did she wait so long?"

"I don't know. She was underage, working illegally, with a fake ID. Maybe she was worried that she'd lose her job. Or maybe she was worried about all the other things that women — girls — worry about when they report rape."

"Did the police investigate?"

"Yeah, they questioned a guy, I never found out his name. But there was no forensic evidence, no witnesses. She says he raped her; he says it was consensual. The classic. Eventually, she dropped the charges."

"Why?"

"Why do you think?" She laughs, mirthlessly. "His parents paid her off. Ten thousand dollars in exchange for her signature on an NDA."

"His parents. So does that mean that he was a student?"

"Yeah. Our bar was a law-school hangout."

Law school. Bingo.

"Ten thousand dollars. Can you believe it? She was sixteen years old."

The first story that breaks, as is almost always the case these days, does not meet the highest standards of journalistic integrity. This early slapdash feature takes over the landing page of a major aggregator, which happens to be the chief competitor of a news site that's owned by Charlie Wolfe's company; this is probably not a coincidence. This site doesn't have a sterling reputation for credibility, nor does it boast a roster of reputable journalists. That said, Ariel still has the sense that most of their reporting is mostly truthful. They've broken a few stories, all of a similar flavor:

604

celebrities behaving badly, a category of reporting for which Americans have an insatiable appetite. If someone at all famous does something at all bad, ever, Americans will read about it.

Ariel tears through CHARLIE WOLFE'S DIRTY NOT-SO-LITTLE SECRET: a click-bait masterpiece of unsubstantiated allegations of harassment, rumors of assault, no comment from a local police chief, no comment from a DA, no evidence, no quotes from any real source — this reporter never even called Ariel for a comment — but plenty of photos.

There are two names for the byline. One is a hyperactive freelancer who peddles celebrity gossip out of LA; she's obviously the one who was able to get the story placed. The other has no website and very little presence in the world: Kirsten Tabor is a staff writer for a small local newspaper, with no national stories, no prior bylines of celebrity gossip, no experience reporting on politics, no truly relevant experience at all; but she's the one who found the story to begin with.

On social media, Ariel follows just a few dozen people, most of them friends of George; she wants to know what these kids get up to online, even though she understands that she's seeing only what the children are allowing her to see. She doesn't have access to their fake accounts, their aliases, the apps she's never even heard of where they share memes, dirty jokes, who knows what.

One of the few non-tweenagers Ariel follows is Persephone_The_ Book_Goddess. This account is also followed religiously by the local reporter Kirsten Tabor, who likes approximately one hundred percent of Persephone's posts. Especially those photos of the two women together, of which there are plenty, hoisting glasses, showing off new tattoos. Inseparable friends. The type who tell each other every single secret, even those that are not their own.

Wagstaff knows that it's easy to read a tabloid article like this and see nothing but a partisan hit job, the type of sensationalism that's inevitable on the eve of a confirmation hearing, shared and amplified and woven into the national mood. Most consumers of puerile gossip don't give much thought to journalistic ethics. That's what makes it puerile gossip. But just because a story's first coverage is irresponsible doesn't mean there's no real story. And a tiny slice of gossip consumers do care about ethics and facts: serious reporters working for more established outlets, pursuing more serious matters, adhering to more rigorous standards. People like Pete Wagstaff.

Serious reporters also, on occasion, investigate celebrity gossip. Not necessarily the personal-life foibles of overcompensated entertainers. But definitely a violent crime committed by a public official and the measures he's willing to take to cover it up: secretly paying out millions of dollars to kidnappers; making policy decisions to hide personal transgressions; eroding trust in American institutions; compromising national security.

Reporting on this activity is not puerile rumormongering, not exploitative hearsay. This reporting is why the very First Amendment of the US Constitution enshrines freedom of the press. This is something Americans have always known, even if sometimes we neglect it: Nothing is more important to democracy than holding the powerful accountable for their transgressions.

Wagstaff had a big head start. But now that the story has begun to crack open, he won't have much time before other reporters catch up. It's time to make the final call.

Ariel is surprised by the emotion of this moment, reading mediocre prose and slipshod reporting on her smudgy laptop screen, the everyday ordinariness of this act that's about to change everything. After so long as her own private trauma, the story now has a life of its own, out there in the world, out of her control. It's just a matter of time. And then what?

Her phone rings, a number with the 351 country code. "Hello?"

"Hi, this is Pete Wagstaff. Have I reached Ariel Pryce?"

"You have a lot of nerve, calling me."

"First off, I'm really sorry about what you went through. But I'm also really relieved to learn that your husband was released unharmed."

Ariel isn't going to let him off the hook that easy. Or at all. She stays silent.

"And I really don't want to bother you. But it's, you know, my job. So I have to ask: What's your relationship to the Secretary of the Treasury?"

She doesn't answer.

"Evidence suggests that Charlie Wolfe provided you with the cash for the ransom."

"Evidence?" Ariel can't give any information to this reporter, but maybe she can get some. "What evidence?"

"Is it true?"

"I actually respect your job, Pete. But what you did to me was terrible. You know that, don't you?"

"From what I've been able to gather after talking to various witnesses, something happened between you and Charlie Wolfe fourteen years ago, resulting in your pregnancy. You agreed to an out-of-court settlement of cash in exchange for silence. Then when your husband was abducted in Lisbon, you used a threat of exposure to coerce Mr. Wolfe into paying the ransom."

Ariel doesn't respond.

"If a cabinet secretary can be extorted now, in this moment of intense scrutiny into every aspect of his life, is there any reason to think that this vulnerability won't still exist — or even increase — if he becomes vice president?"

Wagstaff again waits for Ariel to jump in, but of course she doesn't.

"Or president?"

Wagstaff must realize that Ariel won't participate in his conjecture. But she supposes he needs to give her the opportunity to comment, to deny, to explain, to protest. Even if he knows she can't, and why. He obviously does.

"Can Americans trust such a person to act in the nation's best interests, instead of his own private ones?"

No, she thinks, we certainly can't.

"Surely you can see, Ms. Pryce, that this is a matter of the utmost national importance; in fact it has global ramifications. The confirmation hearings start tomorrow, which makes this urgent as well as important. And you might be the only person in the world who's in a position to shed definitive light on the situation. So will you? On the record?"

Ariel knows that this call is being recorded, by Wagstaff of course on his end, but also by the CIA, the FBI, both.

"Any comment at all?"

609

This is evidence that's being created right now. The defendant might end up being her. The crimes would be breach of contract and slander, plus whatever else could be trumped up, which would be plenty. Treason is not completely unthinkable.

"Ms. Pryce, is it true that fourteen years ago Charlie Wolfe sexually assaulted you?"

Wow, she thinks: Good job, Pete. That didn't take long.

"I'm sorry," she says, and hangs up.

Then again, it took forever.

CHAPTER 50

Day 5. 1:11 p.m.

Ariel's landline is ringing, a rare event. The only reason she still has this line is because somehow her overall service would be more expensive without it, a state of affairs that makes it clear that someone is getting away with something at her expense. The telecom companies don't even try to hide it anymore.

This call is from an unknown number in area code 201: Washington, DC.

"Hi, Steph Barton here, calling from the office of Senator Alan Brown. Is this Ariel Pryce?"

"Yes."

"Ms. Pryce, do you also go by — or did you once go by — the name Laurel Turner?"

"How can I help you?"

"Well, Ms. Pryce — or is it Turner?"

"Pryce."

"I'm calling about Secretary Wolfe, who as you may know has been nominated to fill the office of vice president, an appointment that's subject to confirmation by Congress, and my boss, Senator Brown, has a senior role in the confirmation process."

"Uh-huh."

"So, Ms. Pryce, I'm calling to ask: Do you know Charlie Wolfe?"

Ariel doesn't respond.

"How long have you known him?"

Ariel still doesn't answer.

"Ms. Pryce? What's your relationship with Secretary Wolfe?"

Relationship. What a word for it.

"When was the last time you saw him? Spoke to him?"

Ariel stares out her window, listening to this woman's conjecture.

"Do you understand that you can be subpoenaed? Compelled to testify before Congress?"

Yes, Ariel thinks, I do understand that. She hangs up.

Ariel sends John an email, just checking. And — why not? — she also calls his cell number. He no longer has the device he brought to Europe. But Ariel bought a new phone that uses the same number; maybe he did too. And even if not, John should still be able to access the voicemailbox.

"Hi," she says. "It's me. I'm getting pretty worried here. Could you please give me a call?"

■ ■ ■

"Can this be silenced?"

Jim Farragut takes a beat before answering; he doesn't want to seem dismissive. He knows that he himself is in a precarious position. He's not worried for his actual physical safety, but his career can certainly end now.

Since the rumors exploded across the internet, Charlie Wolfe has not been doing himself any favors. "No comment" has been his only comment about his possible mistress. Farragut knows that Wolfe can't comment because, like Ariel Pryce, he too is bound by the nondisclosure agreement. But to anyone who doesn't know that — which is to say, to everyone — he looks like a liar. A bad one.

Wolfe's very own NDA has come back to haunt him. Not merely because he needs to remain silent, but because a congressional lawyer has also identified the LLC in the Caymans that made the hush payment to Pryce, turning the very existence of these secret payments into damning evidence. And it has become clear that Pryce was not the only woman to be paid large sums through that same LLC. Which makes it pretty hard for Charlie Wolfe to pretend that there's nothing to see here.

It looks bad for the nominee, and that's not even the worst of it. Ten minutes ago, Far-

613

ragut got off the phone with his Lisbon chief of station, who'd called with news of the smoking gun. A sixteen-year-old girl, for Christ's sake. No way Wolfe can survive this.

That was when Farragut asked for this meeting.

"I'm sorry," Farragut eventually says to his boss. "I'm afraid it's too late for that."

"You're sorry? I doubt that."

Farragut doesn't rise to the director's provocation.

"You never liked this president. That's obvious."

Is it? Farragut doesn't think so. This is just more paranoia, which infects everyone who comes into contact with it. And naturally the director of central intelligence would come down with the most serious case.

"I'm sorry, sir, I don't believe that's true. I'm looking at this professionally and dispassionately, and what I'm seeing is that the secretary's position is untenable. He's simply not going to be the next vice president, and the sooner the president cuts Wolfe loose, the better for the president himself, the whole administration, and the nation. There's really no choice."

"Bullshit, no choice. There's always a choice."

"The facts have migrated into the general atmosphere. The Portuguese police and Portuguese intelligence have it, and they're under no obligation to keep a secret. With the way we've treated the world recently, I wouldn't expect them to go out of their way to do us any favors."

The director glares at him. "Can't this woman be taken into custody?"

Farragut reminds himself to keep his cool, but this is exactly the type of shit he was worried about when he walked into this office: being asked to engage in irrational, unproductive, emotional, and illegal activities.

"Are you saying that you want to arrest the woman Wolfe raped?"

"Allegedly raped."

Farragut nods, trying to appear reasonable in the face of unreasonableness. "I think that having the FBI arrest this woman would be a public-relations debacle of the highest order."

"Yeah, maybe. But I didn't say anything about the FBI."

Farragut raises his eyebrows, wondering what in God's name the DCI thinks he's suggesting.

"I also," the director continues, "didn't say anything about arrest. Nor public."

Ariel picks up George from the final midsummer day of camp. Some of the campers are moving on to other activities for the second half of the season, so today there have been color games, trophies, tearful goodbyes. She looks at George's cohort, the thirteen-year-old girls with their pimples and braces and training bras, a half-foot taller than the boys. And the sixteen-year-old counselors-in-training, their deep summer tans and freckles and saltwater-bleached ponytails. They all seem so young, so naïve, so innocent, so safe. If only.

News of Ariel's existence is spreading like an epidemic — fast-moving, uncontrollable, lethal. She has received an overwhelming number of voicemails and emails and texts, from friends and colleagues and a half-dozen reporters plus two congressional aides and someone who claims to be FBI. Everyone has a few questions, please call back as soon as possible, it's important, it's urgent, it's everything.

Now Ariel understands that this is what happens behind the scenes, all this background before the news is the news, before the vast public knows about it, but plenty of other people do.

Ariel is not going to return any of these calls; people are going to have to try harder than simply leaving messages. She needs this particular bit of security, this shield: to be able to say, truthfully, all I did was answer my phone.

While she's still checking old messages, new ones are arriving; both her phones are under siege. On the landline is another reporter, from another paper, following up on fresh information.

"I've been speaking with a bartender named Dan Shannon who saw you and Mr. Wolfe having a conversation fourteen years ago, at his then-workplace on New York's Upper East Side."

It's impressive how much journalists can unearth, and how quickly, when they care.

"According to Mr. Shannon, you and Mr. Wolfe had tense words with some odd choreography, which made the occasion memorable. What was the topic of that conversation?"

Ariel doesn't answer.

"Then just a few days ago," the reporter continues, "Mr. Wolfe seems to have intervened in the kidnapping of your husband, reportedly providing you with the ransom of five million dollars."

Five million? Where the hell did that number come from? Ariel fights the urge to correct the reporter, that it was two million, and they were euros. But of all the facts in this story, the amount of money is the least important. Of all the responsibilities in Ariel's lap, fact-checking numbers for a professional journalist isn't one of them.

Sometimes it's more important to be silent than to be right.

"Ms. Pryce, I've spoken to multiple sources who have suggested that Charlie Wolfe may have assaulted you fourteen years ago. That following an out-of-court settlement, you declined to press charges. And that all these years later, you used the threat of exposure to coerce Mr. Wolfe into intervening in your husband's kidnapping."

And boom, there it is. Once first blood is drawn, sharks make quick work.

"Ms. Pryce? Can you confirm or deny this sequence of events?"

Ariel has decided that she's not going to respond to anything; she's not even confident that "no comment" is an okay comment. There's no way to know who on the phone might be unscrupulous, lying about bona fides, inventing quotes, misrepresenting conversations. Ariel is in a precarious situation. She can't risk it. And she doesn't need to. For good measure, she's recording all of these calls. Creating her own exculpatory evidence.

The media are going to need to do their reporting without Ariel as a source; law enforcement is going to need to investigate without her testimony. Newspapers, TV shows, Congress, whatever: They'll all need to go through a lawyer she has yet to hire, and the subpoenas and depositions and courtroom testimony will all need to crash against Ariel's unwavering insistence on her inability to comment.

She hangs up again.

■ ■ ■ ■

It's late afternoon when the first picture appears. This is another online story filled with speculation but no certainty, no confirmation. Then the same image is on CNN. Then it's everywhere.

Ariel remembers this photograph. It was taken that very Saturday evening, before sunset; it appeared in the society pages the following weekend. Six people at a party, summer tans and summer clothes, the ocean in the background. She's one of those people. So is Charlie Wolfe.

She knew that a photo was inevitable. But even if you brace yourself, you still feel the punch. You still know that the initial blow will not be the last of the pain.

Ariel is only halfway surprised to find a news van parked in front of her house. She considers ducking back inside, but instead she just locks the door behind her.

"Ms. Pryce, how long have you known Secretary Wolfe?"

She tries to walk calmly to her pickup, not making eye contact with the reporter who's standing on the far side of the split-rail fence that demarcates Ariel's property from the county's.

"When was the last time you spoke to Mr. Wolfe?"

The reporter is holding a microphone; behind him, a cameraman is aiming a big camera; behind the cameraman is the van from a network affiliate, antenna towering into the air.

"Is it true that your husband was kidnapped in Portugal?"

If Ariel says anything now, she'll be on national television within minutes. As easy as that. Like swerving into oncoming traffic.

"Ms. Pryce? Did Secretary Wolfe intervene in your husband's kidnapping?"

She climbs into the truck, slams the door.

"Ms. Pryce?"

Nicole Griffiths is not surprised that the journalists descended upon this story as quickly as they did, as they should. But she does wonder if any of them have put all the pieces together. Maybe none ever will. Maybe you had to be inside from the beginning to be able to step back and appreciate the whole shape of the thing. Maybe if Griffiths hadn't taken the winding journey of discovery, she too wouldn't be able to understand where she'd arrived. Maybe it was investigating the other angle that allowed her to see this one.

She watches the news footage of Ariel Pryce hustling to her pickup, old and rusted, just like she'd claimed. Refusing to comment, just like she needs to. A woman trying to lead a quiet private life, not an activist, not a social-media provocateur, not shouting anything at anyone. Not asking for any credit. Not accepting any.

The genius of it.

Ariel walks into her shop for the first time in more than a week, the longest she's been away from her business since she bought it.

"Hey, Ariel, my God." Persephone gives her a big warm hug. "How are you doing?"

"I'm okay, thanks. How are things here?"

Persephone scrunches up her face. "It's been, um, strange? There are a lot of reporters calling, asking for you by name. Also a few normal citizens who've come here in person. Normal-*ish*. Some of them don't seem super-friendly."

"What have you been telling people?"

"Nothing really. Just that you're not in the shop right now."

Ariel can't help but notice that Persephone hasn't relinquished her cell phone; the device is still in her palm, always there, thumb hovering above screen, cocked, ready to tap and scroll and sweep, to move on. Her generation never had a chance. Their schooling should have included dedicated training on how to put down your phone, exercises on how to focus on talking to real people in person. But no one knew how bad it would become.

"Okay, P., that's good. Keep saying that."

"I should also tell you: We've gotten a few nasty calls."

Ariel nods. So has she. This town has some ugly stripes underneath its pretty summer coat. The hate makes itself known quickly and loudly in the modern world. Backlash can be the loudest.

"I'm keeping a log of numbers, what the callers say. In case we need to involve the police."

"Good idea. Listen, P., I need my paperwork. And the other stuff."

"Oh, of course! I put all that back in the hole in the wall, covered by the poster."

"Good thinking. Thanks."

"Anything else you need?"

"Nope. You're doing a terrific job." Persephone has been running the store for a week without any obvious problems, and it has been a busy time.

"Thanks. Now I understand why that woman called you Laurel Turner last week."

Ariel gives a tight smile, but doesn't say anything. She wants to make it clear that she's not going to discuss this.

After much internal debate, Ariel decided not to confront Persephone about leaking the NDA to her journalist friend Kirsten Tabor. If Ariel even acknowledged what had happened, she'd probably need to fire the young woman; Persephone's behavior was an indefensible breach of trust. Maybe it would even be Ariel's responsibility to call the police, to press charges, to demonstrate her own innocence in the leak.

That would be too much, and it would be unfair. That would be like beating a dog for eating a sausage that you left on a coffee table. Persephone is nosy and indiscreet, that's who she is, consistently and reliably and inevitably. But Ariel was the one who put the sausage on the table.

It's the dogs who notice first, their ears perked up, noses twitching, tails down, a low grumble from the depths of Mallomar's throat. The dogs' behavior is unusual but not unprecedented. Foxes sometimes wander through the yard, raccoons and possums waddle, deer jump fences, moles and voles and rabbits — plenty of natural causes for the dogs to be alarmed.

But Ariel feels it in her gut: This isn't one of those. She turns out the dining room light.

"George," she says, "turn that off."

He's sitting on the living room floor, playing a video game, wearing a headset that makes him look like a helicopter pilot.

"Come on," she says, "now."

"What? Why?"

"Just do it!" Ariel switches off one table lamp, then another. This old house has almost no overhead lights, she's constantly turning lamps on and off.

After the TV light dies, there's nothing else: complete dark.

"Upstairs," she hisses, "come on!"

Both dogs are barking loudly now.

"What's going on?" George is already crying. He doesn't know what this is, but he can tell that it's bad, and Ariel is dialing her phone as they run up the stairs, despite every parent's rule of no running on stairs. In the dark!

"Nine-one-one, what's your emergency?"

The dogs are going nuts. Even non–guard dogs are, at heart, guard dogs.

"My home is being invaded right now! I'm at —"

And that's when all hell breaks loose.

CHAPTER 51

Day 5. 9:09 p.m.

George is sprinting up the staircase in front of her, and he arrives at the top just as the bright lights pierce the windows and the men start yelling and heavy footfalls and dogs barking and the *thump-thump-thump* of joints or limbs or whole bodies falling onto the wooden porch while Ariel keeps racing up the stairs, pushing her child down the hall, into her bedroom, locking the door, crossing to the window that's wide open to admit the breeze, punching out the screen and folding herself through, pulling George after her onto the cedar shakes over the low-pitched roof of the dining room extension that juts away from the original house toward the corn glowing silver in the moonlight, kneeling at the roof's edge and climbing over and hanging for a three-foot drop to the dewy grass, just a few steps to the potting shed filled with sports equipment, into which Ariel closes both of them.

625

"Ms. Pryce! All clear!"

She doesn't know who this man is, yelling at her from the far side of her house, claiming that she's out of danger.

"You're safe now!" Exactly what men say when the truth is the opposite.

She picks up a baseball bat. Beside her, George is shaking.

"Wait here," she whispers.

"Don't leave! Please."

"I need to check. I'm not going far. I promise."

Ariel crosses the small patch of lawn that separates the residential area from the farm out back. She kneels at the boxwood, peers through waxy leaves. She can see a man lying facedown on the porch; a second man clad in black is cinching this guy's wrists behind his back with a plastic tie; a third man, also in black, is surveying the scene. He calls out, "It's just paparazzi!"

Yes, Ariel can see it now, the camera with the telephoto, the lens bag. Yes, she can understand it. She can believe it.

Ariel has been many types of women in her life. Now she has apparently become the type who gets stalked by paparazzi who get taken down by CIA security guards on her front porch.

She didn't see that coming. But it's not, in the end, that big of a surprise. None of this is.

CHAPTER 52

Day 6. 10:08 a.m.

The following morning Ariel is sitting in front of the television, waiting for the hearings to start, when the talking heads are interrupted by a reporter standing in front of the Capitol. Ariel turns up the volume.

"Committee chair Senator Alan Brown has just issued the following statement: Due to unexpected complications, the confirmation hearings for vice president of the United States, due to start this morning at ten a.m., have been suspended until further notice, pending additional investigations."

"Do we know what those unexpected complications are?"

"A wild series of recent events that began earlier this week in Lisbon, where an American woman named Ariel Pryce was traveling with her husband John Wright when he was kidnapped. Ms. Pryce contacted Secretary Wolfe, who is apparently the only person she knows with sufficient liquid resources to pay the ransom, and threatened to reveal a damaging secret unless he helped. Due to the sensitive and complex nature of this situation — an overseas kidnapping of an American citizen, and the involvement of a high-ranking member of the administration who was being extorted — the matter was investigated in real time by US and foreign law enforcement as well as intelligence operatives."

"It was a journalist who exposed this intrigue?"

"That's right. A Lisbon-based newspaper reporter named Pete Wagstaff is the one who put all the pieces together with an article published last night, laying out the case that the long-buried secret is that Mr. Wolfe assaulted Ms. Pryce fourteen years ago. News of this disclosure emboldened two other women to come forward with their own allegations of sexual assault."

"And Ms. Pryce? What does she have to say about all this?"

"She refuses to comment."

"Do we know why this silence?"

"It is almost certainly due to a nondisclosure agreement that she signed as part of an out-of-court settlement with Mr. Wolfe, which included her dropping the charges against him, in exchange for money. Ms. Pryce has been resolute that she cannot and will not comment on any of this."

■ ■ ■ ■

Within hours the press descends en masse, with a dozen vans' antennas piercing the blue sky, towering above the flat fields, plus the rental cars whose floors are littered with sandwich wrappers and coffee cups, disheveled men and women hanging out together on this otherwise quiet rural road, waiting for Ariel to emerge for a picture, waiting for her to comment.

She doesn't.

After lurking around for a day and getting no satisfaction, the reporters start to pack up their toys and move on. But even without any compelling on-scene footage of either the victim or the assailant — Charlie Wolfe has made himself scarce — coverage has been pretty much nonstop on TV, radio, and the internet.

When the story first broke, Ariel realized that she needed to limit her consumption. She couldn't listen to the same thing over and over during all her waking hours, she'd go insane. But now she turns on the radio, hoping to hear something new:

"— bringing the total to four women who have accused the secretary of sexual misconduct, painting a decades-long pattern of criminal behavior that Charlie Wolfe and his family repeatedly squelched using payoffs and

629

nondisclosure agreements to coerce women into lifetimes of silence. Support for the accusers has poured forth on social media and op-ed pages."

"What has been the secretary's response?"

"A spokesperson released a statement that these accusations are categorically without merit."

"And to be clear, these are accusations of what, exactly?"

"Violent sexual assault. Multiple women are accusing Charlie Wolfe of rape."

The next day, the next shoe: "Succumbing to mounting pressure, Charlie Wolfe has resigned his position as Secretary of the Treasury, following yesterday's announcement that the New York district attorney has opened multiple investigations into past accusations. This is a head-spinning change of fortune for a man who just days ago was widely believed to be a shoo-in confirmation to be the next vice president. And there's an increasingly loud chorus calling for an end to punitive nondisclosure agreements in cases of sexual assault, which have long been used by wealthy men to avoid the repercussions of criminal behavior, and to ensure a lifetime of silence from their accusers."

The share price of Charlie Wolfe's publicly traded company plummets, and his net worth falls by a quarter of a billion dollars. His wife leaves him, taking their kids. His life falls apart with dizzying speed, the way it can happen these days — with neither arrest nor indictment nor trial, no appeals, no hope of redemption. Just instant judgment, immediate and complete cancellation.

Ariel parks her beat-up old truck in the lot behind all the shops, then walks around the corner to Main Street, busy on a summer evening, young couples on dates, families getting ice cream. A bachelorette party spills out of the pub, all the young women wearing matching tank tops and radiant smiles, and Ariel quickly identifies the sober one — taking a friend by the arm, looking both ways before crossing the street, turning back to make sure that the group is all together, all safe. Ariel wonders if this is just normal caution, or a more specific vigilance.

Two middle-aged couples are standing in front of the burger joint, blocking the sidewalk, sporting flip-flops and sagging faded tattoos and American flags on shirts and caps. One of the women does a double take when she notices Ariel approaching, says something to her companions.

"Sorry," Ariel says, squeezing between these people and yet another jumbo-sized pickup. It's like these things are driving around swallowing all the other vehicles.

The double-taker mutters something that

Ariel isn't paying attention to, and doesn't quite hear, but she has the distinct impression that it's directed at her. "Excuse me?"

"Fuck you," the woman says, "lying whore."

Ariel is stunned silent, not just by the sentiment — that's life now, isn't it — but by the vitriol, and this person's sense of entitlement to spew it at a stranger. A woman, no less. Ariel walks away.

António Moniz sighs at the woman sitting at his desk. She is obviously a junkie, she is high right now, and has come to the police station with a cockamamie story about getting robbed, she knows exactly who committed the crime, she knows where to find the culprit right now, and yes she does agree that she could probably ID him from a mug shot, but would it not be simpler to just go arrest him? At this moment?

Moniz barely has the energy to take notes.

"And you say that you do not have any relationship with this man?" Carolina Santos asks.

The junkie shakes her head. She does not even trust herself to tell this blatant lie aloud.

There is nothing credible about her story. It is clear that she has come here to get a man arrested, pure and simple. Revenge for something or other, maybe even revenge for robbery, just as this woman is alleging. But not the robbery she is claiming. And the culprit is not a stranger.

Moniz lets his attention wander across the room, where Tomas and Erico are gaping at the television, the spectacular story about how the kidnapping and ransom led to the downfall of the immensely powerful American. And it all began just like this, with a woman marching in here, telling a story that Moniz was reluctant to believe.

"How do you know about the shotgun?" Santos asks.

"He was carrying it with him."

"On the streets? For everyone to see?"

"Under his coat. He carried the gun under his coat."

"Coat?" It is one of the hottest nights of the year.

No, this junkie is not just trying to get a man arrested; she is trying to get him killed. How can she not see how obvious her lies are? How stupid does she think . . . ?

Moniz finds himself standing, walking away —

"António?"

— across the room, to the television, the file footage of the American woman.

"António? What is it?"

Ariel Pryce was prepared to be disbelieved. Of course she was. She knew that her story would sound suspicious, but she also knew that the police would need to look into it, the embassy too, the reporter, they would all

633

need to go through the motions, and they would all end up finding things that Pryce did not intend for them to find . . .

Or did she?

"António?"

He turns to Santos, who has followed him across the room, leaving the junkie to stew in her own lies.

Should Moniz explain it to Santos? Would she believe him? Would anyone believe him? Or would he sound like just another liar, reconstructing history to suit his own preferred narrative?

That is the problem these days. No one believes anyone.

Ariel finds Jerry on exactly the barstool where she expected to, next to the big open window.

"Who *are* all these people?" he asks, gesturing at the Sprit's crowded dining room, the busy street life. People are dressed up in their summer costumes, the super-skinny man in his super-tight PROVINCETOWN T-shirt and handlebar mustache, the Connecticut housewife in horizontal-striped boatneck climbing out of the Mercedes wagon, everyone in character. And Jerry here, playing his part as alcoholic small-town lawyer. Ariel playing hers.

We all look like exactly who we are, unless we're pretending. And it's when we're pretending that we can look even more convincing. If we prepare diligently, practice exhaustively, inhabit the role fully.

This is the most useful skill that Ariel preserved from her training as an actor: how to stay in character even when no one is watching. Even when you're all alone in a hotel room, or worrying your way through a breakfast buffet, or wandering the byzantine streets of a foreign city. Every action, every interaction, every waking moment, and hopefully the sleeping ones too. Not just so you look like the real thing, but also so you're able to tell your story later without needing to invent any lies. All you need to do is tell the truth.

"Thanks for meeting me," Jerry says. "It must be hard right now. Is it?"

"Well, reporters are hounding me, dozens of them. Congressional staffers too. Paparazzi are getting body-slammed onto my porch by the CIA. Oh, and just a minute ago I got cursed out, here on Main Street."

"Oof. I'm sorry," he says. "Unintended consequences, huh?"

Ariel feels a shiver run down her spine. Jerry takes another sip, not quite emptying his glass.

"Suze?" Ariel indicates another round, sets two twenties on the bar. With Jerry, she's always buying.

"How's John holding up?"

"He's fine, thanks for asking."

Ariel has no idea how John is doing. She has sent emails that have gone unanswered, she has tried voice calls that have failed to go through. She tells herself that John will get in touch when he can, when he wants to. If he can.

If he wants to.

"Thanks." Jerry nods at the fresh glass. "This is something, isn't it? This whole circus around your nondisclosure being disclosed."

Ariel's fear is coming on strong now.

"And yet not by you. Everywhere I turn, I find the same thing: Ms. Pryce could not be reached for comment. Ms. Pryce was unavailable. Ms. Pryce refused to say a damn thing."

This sensation in her gut reminds Ariel of when a deer jumps into the road, threatening various types of wrecks, some of them expensive, some of them deadly.

"You're being very diligent about not saying anything, one way or the other."

The same instant churn in her stomach.

"It's my legal obligation."

"Yeah." Jerry takes another sip. "You don't really drink, do you?"

Ariel is only halfway surprised by this abrupt change of subject. Jerry is fond of apparent non sequiturs that always turn out to be not.

"No."

"I've noticed this over the years. Sometimes you allow a second drink to be put in front of you, but then you don't touch more than a sip of it. Were you ever a drinker?"

She shakes her head.

"If you had two drinks, you'd probably be feeling it. Maybe you'd be tipsy. Drunk even?"

Ariel doesn't know exactly where this is going, but Jerry is always on his way to some destination. He'd probably be a great lawyer, if he were a more functional human.

The bartender returns Ariel's change, a small fan of small bills.

"You look at me, and you probably think: That guy is having four, five, *six* drinks in a night. Sometimes more. If you consumed that amount of alcohol, you'd be under the table. So you think, Jerry must be drunk all the time, no way that guy remembers those conversations when he was deep into his cups."

Ariel feels the urge to flee, but knows she can't.

"But I weigh a lot more than you, so the same amount of alcohol affects you and me very differently. Also, the thing about drinking is you build up a tolerance, as with anything. I've sat here with you, what — two dozen times? More?"

Ariel shrugs, forces a feeble smile.

"I know that I have a problem, I know that I shouldn't be operating a motor vehicle

637

many evenings. And I don't, you know that, right?"

"I do."

"But I remember every conversation we've ever had, Ariel. Every single one."

Now Ariel recognizes the destination, just over the next sip —

"After Cyrus died, we discussed the transfer of goat ownership. What's his name?"

Ariel's throat feels tight. She swallows. "Fletcher."

"That's right! Fletcher."

Ariel is pretty sure Jerry recalled the goat's name on his own.

"I remember noticing when something I said seemed to come as a revelation to you. Flipped a switch."

Ariel doesn't need to ask what that was. She looks to her left, and her right, making sure no one can overhear. Another surreptitious conversation, with another man, on another barstool. Another life-defining interaction.

"Ariel, are you familiar with the Latin phrase *cui bono*? It means *who benefits*. This is almost always a guiding principle." Jerry takes another sip, puts his glass down. "But sometimes it's just as important to consider *cui plagalis*. Do you know what that means?"

Ariel can guess, but she won't.

"Who is penalized," Jerry says. "Who is harmed." He stares at her for a few seconds.

"I'm not going to insult your intelligence — nor for that matter mine — by asking you for any specifics. The truth is that for both our sakes, I'm better off not knowing. Much better."

Ariel feels as if looking away would be an admission of something she doesn't want to admit. She forces herself to hold Jerry's gaze.

"Do you understand that you've pissed off not only your, um, intended target, but also the most powerful man in the world?"

Ariel doesn't say anything. In the past couple of days she has grown very accustomed to not responding. Although Jerry has served in the past as her lawyer, Ariel isn't sure how completely she'd be able to trust him if his back were pushed up against the wall. If his livelihood were threatened, or his actual life. She's pretty sure that his back will indeed get pushed up against the wall. Maybe it already is. Maybe that's the point of this conversation. Maybe Jerry's wearing a wire.

The only acceptable level of trust here is one hundred percent, and Ariel has learned that one hundred percent is not realistic. She doesn't say anything.

Jerry plucks one of Ariel's dollar bills off the bar. "May I?"

"Be my guest."

"This is not my area of expertise, Ariel. But who am I kidding, I don't *have* an area of expertise. So you'll definitely want to fire me soon, and hire counsel who know what the hell they're doing. But in the meantime, you just hired me to represent you in this matter." Jerry folds the bill in half, puts it in his pocket. "Here's your one dollar's worth of advice." Jerry turns to face her. "Be very, *very* careful, Ariel. About everything."

This is not news to her, not a warning she needs. Ariel has already been very careful; she has been careful for decades. But careful hasn't sufficed. Careful is defensive.

"Today and tomorrow," Jerry says.

Sometimes, she realized, you need to go on the offensive.

"Forever."

■ ■ ■ ■

EPILOGUE

■ ■ ■ ■

Three Months Later

Ariel awakens, momentarily confused about where she is —

That's right: an airplane. She's wedged into another middle seat in the back of a plane, with her feet cramped by her carry-on. By the time her ticket allowed her to board, there was no more room in the overheads. In the rigid caste system of airlines, Ariel is a person who travels in discomfort.

"I really just need to get away," she explained to her friends, her employees, her mom. "Away from the press, away from home, away from everything."

George is settling in fine to his first year of boarding school, the same institution that Ariel attended three decades ago. When she'd floated the idea of going away to school, she fully expected George to reject it out of hand. But he was receptive, which was both satisfying and devastating to her, a combination that she has come to believe is the definition of

643

parenthood.

The admissions office made an exception for George's midsummer application, after everything that Ariel had gone through, the negative impact it was having on the boy, the excess of attention, the physical danger.

For the past year she'd been confronting the question of what her life will be like when George is gone. The boy's increasingly distant behavior was a constant reminder that this stage of her life was drawing to a close, that soon her kid would be off at college, never home for more than a few days at a time. There was nothing for him in their little town; the nothing was why she'd come. But he probably felt their small town closing in around him, the small class in a small school, small teams, small world.

Maybe this place has served its purpose for Ariel too. When George leaves, she'll be a fifty-year-old woman living alone on a small farm with some small animals, and a struggling small business, and a small group of friends. A small life.

Ariel peers out the window at the European sunrise breaking over the horizon. She'd been expecting to confront that new reality a few years down the line. But here's that future, right now.

Her driver is holding a small whiteboard with her name. The trip takes an hour. She checks into the seaside hotel, changes into a bathing suit, goes for a bracing swim in the Adriatic, mountains looming in the background, shore-line decorated with the stone walls and red roofs of the ancient village, the fortified island, the beach chairs and umbrellas.

She wraps herself in a plush towel, reclines on the squishy chaise, and looks around at all this apparent perfection. It takes a lot of work to keep all these chairs aligned, the lines of tables so straight, the sand so clean, the cleaning crew so polite, her drink refreshed, fresh towels piled high. Ariel suspects there's a lot of misery on the other side of all this perfection.

The resort is nearly empty, the season long over. This makes it easy to recognize all the other guests, just a handful, none even remotely suspicious. Nevertheless, out of an abundance of caution, Ariel requests a room change. "Anything with a terrace that faces the sea?"

"Of course madam. We will move your bags immediately."

The knock startles Ariel, although it's no surprise at all. This knock is why she's here.

She checks herself in the mirror. Smooths her dress. Another self-assessment in another bathroom mirror. Then she opens the door, and there he is, that dazzling smile, that glint in his eyes. But she can also see that there's less of an edge to him. There's less of an edge to her too.

They succeeded, after all. Everything went off exactly as planned.

Everything except the aftermath: She hadn't expected her fame to arrive so swiftly and so oppressively; she hadn't expected the cruelty of the backlash, the persistence of the harassment; she hadn't expected to ship her kid off to boarding school, to accelerate the beginning of the end of that stage of her life. None of those aftershocks were part of the plan, not specifically. But she and John had both known that there would be collateral damage of some sort.

He opens his arms, and Ariel allows herself to be folded in, a tight embrace, a friendly squeeze of the shoulders. But no passionate kiss. They don't really have that type of relationship.

Or at least they didn't, not until that night in Lisbon. But they haven't seen each other since, haven't even spoken, and Ariel doesn't know what type of relationship they have now. It's possible that they have none. It's possible that they have everything.

"My God," she says, "look at you." He's sporting a dark tan, a short beard, long hair. He looks like he belongs here. But what does she know about where he belongs? She barely knows this man.

The only truth to their story was that they did actually meet at the bookstore.

"Just five minutes," he'd said at the counter. "Just let me buy you a coffee."

He'd already called twice, this John Wright. After Ariel hung up on him the second time, she assumed that he'd give up. But a week later there he was, in person, buying her coffee at the café up the street. It seemed like bad manners to allow him to buy her a coffee in her own shop.

"Thanks for your time," he said. "I'll get straight to it. When my sister Lucy was sixteen years old, she was raped by Charlie Wolfe."

Ariel gasped.

"She'd run away from our home, was working in a bar. She was extremely vulnerable. When that predator's parents offered money for her to drop the charges and keep her mouth shut, she didn't really have a choice. She signed the NDA, cashed the ten-thousand-dollar check. Some of which she needed to use for the abortion."

"Oh my God."

"She has never stopped being angry, and from afar she watched him get richer and richer, then more and more famous, and more and more powerful, and then he's named Secretary of the Treasury, and suddenly people are talking about grooming the son of a bitch to be the next president of the United States."

It was true: One day Charlie Wolfe was a minor item in the business pages, and the next he was front-page everywhere, he seemed to be invincible, inevitable.

"This monster" — John could barely contain himself — "*must* be stopped."

Ariel recognized John's fury. She felt exactly the same way. She thought of Charlie in the same exact terms: a monster.

"There's nothing Lucy can do, she lives in Morocco, where I suspect she does something dubious for a living. I don't know what exactly, and frankly I don't want to. She's my sister, and I love her, but there are some things we don't discuss. And I can see clearly that Lucy is not a sufficiently credible accuser, nor a compelling witness. Certainly not in politics, not up against a guy like this, with the type of resources he could throw at her. It's not out of the question that he might even have her killed."

No, Ariel thought, it certainly wasn't.

"A scumbag like this, someone who displayed such callous disregard for a young girl, I think we know that he did not stop his sexual-assault career with just the one. He didn't face any consequences! Why would he stop?"

Ariel felt herself beginning to boil over, even as she knew that she was being swayed by this man's own rage.

"So I started looking around, asking around. I hired a PI, and he came up with a few potential names. Then I hired a second PI to pursue from a different angle, like a science experiment, to see if the conclusions would be the same. I wanted to be extra-sure before I intruded into anyone's life. These two different PIs came up with two slightly different lists of potential victims. But one name was on both lists. In fact one name was at the top of both lists."

Ariel knew exactly where this was going.

Over the years, Ariel's furor had waxed and waned, then had built to a crescendo alongside the arc of Charlie Wolfe's outsize triumphs in every sphere. She was freshly enraged on a daily basis. How could such lavish rewards be bestowed upon this vile man, of all the vile men in the world?

"He raped you. And you too signed an NDA, under duress."

Ariel wouldn't say anything, of course. She couldn't.

"Am I wrong?"

She still didn't answer.

"Ten thousand dollars." He was shaking his head. "That's what my sister's life was worth to him."

Ariel felt no small amount of shame: She'd

extracted three million dollars, money that she'd used to buy the farm, to buy the bookshop, to buy the very best health insurance for herself and her sickly child, to establish a college savings account, to set up a trust for George, to fund her own retirement. But this guy's sixteen-year-old sister?

"We can't just let this predator roam the earth with impunity, can we?"

John looked so pained, so earnest, so desperate. Ariel recognized that desperation, she'd felt it for nearly fifteen years: a willingness to do anything, even as it seemed as if nothing could work.

Ariel almost had to wonder if John's desperation was an act, if she was being set up, entrapped so that the existential threat of her could be removed, once and for all. She had to wonder if she could be jailed merely for admitting the truth to this stranger.

"It's unfair for the burden to rest entirely on the victims' shoulders. It shouldn't be only the accusers who risk everything; it shouldn't be only the aggrieved who grieve. Other people need to take real action. Not just stand in solidarity, not just post on Instagram or hang a banner or donate fifty bucks." John looked Ariel firmly in the eye, and leaned forward. "I'm willing to do *anything*. And there are many things I know how to do."

What was this guy suggesting? An assassination?

"I'm sorry," Ariel said, and she really was. "I wish I could help." She really did.

But instead she left John Wright sitting there with an untouched coffee that he'd driven a hundred miles to not drink. Ariel rushed out onto Main Street, tears streaming down her face, and returned to her quiet little shop, in her quiet little life, totally expecting that she'd never see John Wright again.

"You've been well?" he asks.

They're sitting on a balcony overlooking the Adriatic, where there's no way for anyone to be watching, or aiming directional microphones at their conversation.

"Things have been hard," she says. Ariel switched rooms to guarantee that the new one couldn't be bugged. They're meeting at an off-season resort to ensure manageable crowds, easy for countersurveillance. They're in Montenegro because there's no extradition treaty with the United States, and because that's where John now lives, a combination that's not coincidental.

"I'm sure you saw some of it on the news," she continues. "In a way, the on-air disparagement has been the least of it. I can turn off the TV, ignore social media. You know that I already did that. But the in-person stuff, that's been rough. Hostile people come to the shop, and to my house, and bother George at school, say things to me in the

651

supermarket. There are a lot of crazies in America, and it doesn't take many to make life miserable."

"I'm so sorry."

"How's Lucy doing?" Ariel asks.

"This has definitely brought her consolation. And the money has made a huge difference in her life. And now there's a real chance that Wolfe will go to jail."

Ariel snorts her doubt. Statutes of limitations are shockingly brief in cases of sexual assault; or maybe it isn't so shocking. In her case, Charlie's crime became no longer prosecutable after just five years. No matter what transpired afterward, no matter how many other assaults he committed, no matter what laws were eventually changed. He could never stand trial for raping Ariel.

From her point of view, jail had never been a realistic hope. But John has consistently been the unrealistic one. All along, it was Ariel's role to manage expectations, to concentrate on achieving finite and realistic goals. On making sure, first and foremost, that they didn't get caught.

Ariel was the one who focused on the big picture. She came up with the whole convoluted plan in the first place.

She'd left Jerry sitting at the bar with his fourth or fifth Scotch, and jumped into her truck, rumbling over the rutted roads to her dark farm, new home to Fletcher the orphaned goat as well as her two rescue dogs and an indeterminate number of outdoor cats and her newly surly son, locked in his bedroom doing who knows what.

What was resonating in her brain was Jerry's comment about an NDA: If a nonsignatory discovers the facts completely on his own? There's nothing a nondisclosure agreement can do about that.

By the time she banged through her kitchen door, she'd convinced herself that it was possible. She leafed through her notebook, each page reaching further back in time, weeks and months until she found the name and phone number of the man with whom she'd not drunk coffee.

How are you supposed to plan for life's most important conversations? Do you set them up, construct a stage, establish expectations? Or do you just let the talk happen — push a pebble, start a landslide, gravity, momentum, it'll take care of itself?

In school they teach you trigonometry, fruit-fly reproduction, the periodic table, Shakespeare, all this useless crap. Calculus, for crying out loud. But no one ever teaches you how to do the really important things.

"Hi John, it's Ariel Pryce. Do you remember me?"

"Of course."

"I have an idea."

■ ■ ■ ■

They did get married, which was an easy enough thing to do; it was also too easy to get caught not having done it. They invented their story together — the conversation they'd supposedly had at the grocery store, their awkward unpracticed flirting, their first date, first kiss, first sex, whirlwind romance and thoughtful gifts, their engagement and honeymoon, details large and small and crucial and irrelevant. It's the irrelevant details that make it real. They rehearsed their story again and again and yet again until it was second nature, as real as their real lives. Realer.

John already knew how to ride a motorcycle, but hadn't been on one in years. So he bought a used sport bike from a local mechanic, and practiced for days on end, in all sorts of weather, on the quiet country roads near Ariel's house. He rode the thing into the city and tore along congested city streets, up and down the steep hills in the Bronx, through the tight lanes and sharp turns and thick crowds of Wall Street.

Meanwhile, Lucy did the fieldwork. Her life as a petty criminal in Marrakesh offered her plenty of relevant experience. She spent weeks at a stretch scouting locations in nearby Lisbon, noting the position of security

cameras, the size of the crowds at tourist at-
tractions, the location of funiculars and taxis
and trams, the back doors of restaurants and
bars, the one-way streets and back alleys and
dead ends, the surveillance-free spots in the
Seville airport's parking garage. She purchased the car, she stole old license plates,
she found a secluded abandoned house on
the far side of the Tagus where she and John
could hide for a few days during the supposed kidnapping. She bought herself the full
Halloween-costume hippie getup, one item at
a time, including the wig of blond dreadlocks.

When the time came, Lucy was the one
who showed up at the square at four in the
morning to disable various security cameras;
she drove the kidnapping car; she took the
photo of Ariel at the embassy; she manufactured the social-media blitz. Lucy choreographed every detail: the early-morning
abduction, Ariel's progression from police to
embassy and back again, John's delivery on
motorcycle of the burner, Ariel's evasion
route, and the ransom handoff in the alley
behind a bar. Lucy herself was the woman in
that alley, collecting the cash, then walking
straight through the bar and out again, her
backpack filled with euros, melding seam-
lessly into the crowd out front while uniformed cops rushed by, frantically looking
for her.

That alley was the only time the two women

ever met, other than the wedding and the so-called honeymoon weekend, events that were spent largely on plotting out everything.

Ariel and John did of course exchange a single kiss, in front of the justice of the peace. How could they not? They were getting married. But it was just a peck, mouths closed, lips pursed. Eyes wide open.

The toughest challenge was George. The boy had never known a father; he'd never lived with anyone other than his mom; he'd never even met any of her prior lovers, relationships that had all been conducted at arm's length, with limited expectations, predictable expirations.

"You're going to be seeing more of John for a while. He's going to stay with us sometimes."

George tried momentarily to pretend that he didn't care, but failed. "Is John your boyfriend?"

Ariel didn't know what George's understanding was of boyfriends, girlfriends, sex, marriage. His mind had become impossible to see into, at just the moment when these ideas were taking shape. This was maybe not happenstance.

"No, Sweetie, we don't have that type of relationship."

John had come over a few times, lunch, dinner, an afternoon sitting at the teak table under the old oak, drinking iced tea, talking about the plan. He'd never spent the night. He'd never even been upstairs.

"I don't love John, and he doesn't love me. But we are actually going to get married, temporarily, just for legal reasons."

Ariel needed to tell George the truth, but it didn't need to be all of it. Enough for him to not feel betrayed; for him to accept what she needed him to accept.

"He'll spend a couple of nights per week at our house, in the guest room downstairs. But it's important for people to think that we have a real marriage. Do you understand?"

George continued to stare through the truck's windshield. "Sure. You want me to lie."

"Maybe just a little. And only if people ask. Which they probably won't. Is that okay?"

He shrugged. "But he's not going to become my stepfather?"

"No. Like I said, it's just temporary."

"For legal reasons."

"That's right."

If Ariel had to, she was prepared to tell her son everything. But this was one of those very rare instances when tweenaged taciturnity and anti-parent frostiness were assets.

"Whatever," he said, and turned his attention back to his phone.

Ariel and John told each other the truths

about themselves: tastes in movies, in books, in wines, their favorite TV shows and restaurants and preferred positions of sex. It was impossible to know what sort of interrogation they'd eventually be subjected to, by what authority, in what circumstance, risking what peril. Sure, it was highly unlikely that anyone would ever quiz them separately about their sex life. But if that unlikely interrogation ever did come to pass, the stakes would be high. This was like training to eject from the pilot seat of a fighter jet: If you're going to climb into the cockpit, you need to know how.

Then, finally, it was the eve of the kidnapping. Their supersonic jet was about to take off.

"How are you feeling?" he asked. This was something she'd come to love about the real John: He always wanted to know how she felt. He always asked; he always listened to the answer.

They were walking home from the restaurant where they'd been seen by many witnesses enjoying a romantic dinner, holding hands, sharing dessert with a single spoon, looking a lot like two people who were about to tumble into bed. If you pretend with all your energy and focus, you can forget that you're pretending. The leading man and the leading lady very often end up in a real bed. They sometimes even get married, have children, the whole thing.

"I feel excited," she said. What she felt like was a giant bundle of nerves, practically pulsating with energy, with hormones, with anticipation. What she felt was aroused.

"Me too."

She hadn't planned on consuming any alcohol; she wanted to stay sharp. But when they sat down at the restaurant, they agreed that they needed a drink or they'd explode. So they'd split a bottle of wine, and Ariel felt loosened by it. Not enough to be dangerous, just enough to be free.

They turned a corner onto a beautiful vista, the old buildings, the spires, the river, the moon. They stopped walking to drink it in.

"Oh look at this place," he said. "It's spectacular."

"Yes it is."

Then she felt his eyes turn to her, and she looked over at him.

"So," he said, "are you."

A lot of questions went through her mind in the brief moment before anything else happened: Is he telling the truth? Is this real? Do I want this? What is this?

Maybe it wasn't real. Maybe it was just the wine, just the situation, just the undeniable thrill of the night before a heist that might change the course of world events, all in their hands. So maybe it didn't have anything to do with Ariel and John as real people living real lives. Maybe this was just part of the act.

The last question she asked herself was: Does it matter?

He already knew that she didn't like air-conditioning or oaky chardonnay or anything in the realm of S&M, because she'd told him. He also knew what she did like, what sequence, what positions; she'd told him those things too. The only point of disagreement was the air-conditioning.

Ariel had never really believed in the best-sex-of-your-life superlative. She'd never had that experience. Some sex had been memorable, some not, some of it was downright awful. But sex had never been transcendent. Until that Sunday night in Lisbon.

John takes out a small envelope, and shows her the contents: two brass keys and a business card from a bank branch on the rue du Rhône in Geneva, with a box number stamped on the back.

"No." Ariel shakes her head. "I told you that I don't want any of the money."

For her, the whole thing wasn't about the money. This was a battle in the war; survival was Ariel's first priority, and victory second. But profit would feel like profiteering, getting rich off war. So they'd agreed from the get-go that all the money would be Lucy's.

Ariel was about to come into another

windfall with the sale of the bookshop to the Brooklyn hipster, another woman transplanting out to the country to start a new life with her conceptual-artist husband and seven-year-old son whose hair appears to have never been cut. She'd probably be thrilled to buy the goat as well.

"This is just a little something. In case of an emergency."

"An emergency? One that I find myself in while visiting Switzerland?"

John smiles. "You never know."

The sun has just dropped below the horizon somewhere over Italy. Another spectacular view that they're facing.

"Listen," she says, gathering her strength. "About that night in Lisbon."

This is something she has learned: the importance of being clear, and unequivocal. Not just about what she doesn't want, but also about what she does. That's important too.

"Yes?" John looks at her with that glint in his eyes, that smile across his lips. He knows that this is her choice, and he can tell from her smile what she has chosen.

Anger and rejection had only gotten her so far, saying no to this and no to that, hating this one and that one, lumping all men together in a giant heap of no, along with her discarded hair and tight jeans, until her epiphany, her vision of a different path not only to her own life but also to holding a powerful man to account in a way that can't be achieved by waving around proof of suffering, by telling a story to only those who want to hear it — a story that could always be subject to dismissal, to dispute, to derision for one reason or another, to counteraccusations of bias, of agenda, of politics, of purely personal animus — and instead she saw a clear path to using this man's very wealth and power as weapons against him, to use his own demands to reveal the depths of his depravity, to use her lifetime of being disbelieved as a tool, inducing other people to pursue her story from the outside, to make her story credible precisely because she was not the one shouting it loudly into an echo chamber, but because a fact is a fact, and there's no such thing as an alternative.

ACKNOWLEDGMENTS

As I type this in late 2021, I'm in my thirty-second year of working in publishing. I've been a marketing temp and editorial assistant, copy editor and managing editor, senior editor and executive editor and associate publisher, ghostwriter and, most recently, novelist. During twenty-seven of those thirty-two years, I worked in wildly divergent capacities for the same company. Book publishing is like a small town, and the place that's now called Penguin Random House is where I grew up, filled with people I've known for decades, at Triple Sixes and 201 East 50th Street, at 1540 and 1745, in conference rooms and the cafetorium, dive bars and book parties, Langan's and Ashton's, working on TI sheets and pre-pre-sales and endless revisions of uncountable P&Ls.

Sooner or later, almost everyone leaves the house where they grew up, and for this book I finally decamped PRH and moved to FSG, where I'm grateful to find a few familiar faces, and excited to meet the new ones. That's the trade-off of moving out: sacrificing the security of home for the thrill of adventure.

Daphne Durham was the editor who extended the invitation to come live at this new house, and I couldn't have asked for a better introduction to the family at Farrar, Straus and Giroux. Editing a book, like parenting, is a complex endeavor that encompasses many different, seemingly unrelated activities, and Daphne is good at all of them. Thanks too to Gretchen Achilles for the beautiful interior design, Alex Merto for the sensational cover, Musa Gurnis for the final critical read, Chandra Wohleber for the copyediting, Janet Renard and Elizabeth Schraft for the proofreading, Lydia Zoells for everything every day, and January LaVoy for taking on the challenge of narrating the audiobook.

Also at FSG and Macmillan, thanks to Mitzi Angel, Madeline Day, Daniel Del Valle, Nina Frieman, Jonathan Galassi, Brian Gittis, Jennifer Gonzalez, Debra Helfand, Sean McDonald, Caitlin O'Beirne, Guy Oldfield, Shelia O'Shea, Brianna Panzica, Hillary Tisman, Claire Tobin, Don Weisberg, and Amber Williams.

When I was a kid at Doubleday in the early nineties, the editor in chief of the house seemed like a parent (sort of), and that's still how I've thought of David Gernert for the decade that he's been my agent. David patiently worked through every one of this manuscript's many revisions, humored me through innumerable sessions of overthinking everything, then he went out there to find the book a new home, and held my hand throughout the move.

Tremendous thanks to the other people who read the early drafts of this book: Lily Burnes-Heath, Hannah Griffiths, Katie Lundstrom, Paula McLain, Sarah McNally, Jennifer Wallace, and Anna Worrall, who were extremely generous to provide insightful and invaluable feedback that's reflected on every page. This book would not exist without everything you taught me.

And finally, thanks as ever to my wife, Madeline McIntosh, who has been with me in this same small town for a quarter-century.

I'm immensely grateful to all of you.

ABOUT THE AUTHOR

Chris Pavone is the author of *The Paris Diversion, The Travelers, The Accident,* and *The Expats.* His novels have appeared on the bestseller lists of *The New York Times, USA Today,* and *The Wall Street Journal;* have won both the Edgar and Anthony awards; are in development for film and television; and have been translated into two dozen languages. Chris grew up in Brooklyn, graduated from Cornell, and worked as a book editor for nearly two decades. He lives in New York City and on the North Fork of Long Island with his family.